Frederick Denison Maurice

Medieval Philosophy

A Treatise of Moral and Metaphysical Philosophy

Frederick Denison Maurice

Medieval Philosophy
A Treatise of Moral and Metaphysical Philosophy

ISBN/EAN: 9783742828132

Manufactured in Europe, USA, Canada, Australia, Japa

Cover: Foto ©Andreas Hilbeck / pixelio.de

Manufactured and distributed by brebook publishing software
(www.brebook.com)

Frederick Denison Maurice

Medieval Philosophy

MEDIÆVAL PHILOSOPHY;

OR,

A TREATISE

OF

MORAL AND METAPHYSICAL PHILOSOPHY

FROM

The Fifth to the Fourteenth Century.

BY

FREDERICK DENISON MAURICE

PROFESSOR OF CASUISTRY AND MODERN PHILOSOPHY IN THE UNIVERSITY OF CAMBRIDGE

NEW EDITION.

London:

MACMILLAN AND CO.

1870.

A. J. SCOTT, ESQ.,

MY DEAR SCOTT,

Though this treatise is a manual for the use of students, not a book which can have much interest for scholars, you will perceive that it has cost the compiler of it some time. I hope the time has been honestly bestowed, and that I may help a few young men, who know the names of the great mediæval doctors, to believe that they were not doctors merely—that their thoughts, even when they appear to us most grotesque, had some connection with human life and human history.

A very eminent writer, whose judgment on the art of the Middle Ages is entitled to the highest respect, has lately expressed unbounded contempt for the subjects which are discussed in this volume. I do not think he can speak more bitterly than I have spoken, here and elsewhere, of metaphysical and even of moral questions, when they are left to the schools, still more when they become the gossip of withdrawing rooms. I do not think he can be more tormented than I am by the words "objective" and "subjective," as they are used in our day. I do not think he can be more earnest than I am in protesting against the importation of philosophical formulas from Germany, which may have a sound meaning there, but which will generally conceal the absence of one amongst us. But because I agree with him so far, I consider that he is taking a very unsafe course indeed when he treats the questions which occupied the most earnest minds, at the time when Gothic cathedrals were conceived and raised—when art was, we are told, in its purest form—as if they were of no worth to beings to whom God has given not only eyes, but also thought and speech. As long as men have these gifts they must be moralists and metaphysicians. Those who sneer most at the names, will assume the characters in their discussions upon their own proper topics. If artists do not wholly abandon the human face divine for trees and flowers, they must ask what it speaks of. And then they will be involved in the questions which are considered here. They must ask themselves seriously whether all nature, all art, all individule existence, all human society, has not a moral and metaphysical foundation ; if not, whether they have any foundation at all.

The faith that there is this foundation, and that it should be sought for, and that it may be found, was strong in the mediæval doctors; the little acquaintance with them which this book indicates, makes me certain that it was. The world around them, the words they spoke, all that they had learned from their fathers, all that was weak, all that was firm, in the civil and ecclesiastical order in the midst of which they lived, told them of a ground which must be beneath words, traditions, opinions, social arrangements. The names justice, right, truth, love, *must*, they thought, point to realities; to dwell in them, must be the eternal blessedness of man ; to dwell in that which is contrary to them, his eternal curse. If we could see how these convictions worked in them—how they strove, how they hoped, how they blundered in their efforts to find their way through nature, through words, through opinions, to this divine and permanent ground—we should gain, I think, some lessons, perhaps some encouragement, for ourselves, as well as an increased sympathy with them. Hereafter I hope some person will arise who has both knowledge and insight for the task of illustrating their successes and their failures. This book is merely a hint of what might be done. If it points out an honest method, I have little doubt that it will soon " make itself useless."

Some lectures which you once gave—I only heard one of them—on Anselm, on Bernard, and on the thirteenth century, would, I am sure, if they were worked out, do effectually what I have tried to do. Certain remarks which you made in them respecting Abelard, have helped me to correct a very imperfect and erroneous notion I had formed of his place in history. But I have profited still more by some words you once dropped in conversation, on the subject of Dante. They seemed to me to throw a light upon the relation between the thoughts of our time and of his time—upon the relation between speculation and life, which might guide one through many of the labyrinths into which I have led my readers, and in which many will say I have lost myself.

If you had written a book of this kind, you would have been able to illustrate the physical as well as the moral studies of the Middle Ages. All I can do is to turn my ignorance of much that nearly all my contemporaries are familiar with, to this account: I can enter into the difficulties of those who were stumbling in all their natural inquiries ; I can abstain from any contempt for them which would rebound with tenfold violence upon myself. It is a negative merit, one not likely to excite much envy; therefore I may make the most of it. The Middle Age discussions on words and their connection with things, have also been less offensive to me than they are to many, because I have been forced to go through some of them myself in the effort to escape from the tyranny of words in our own day. Logical trifling is very detestable; but there is another kind of trifling belonging to the age of clubs and newspapers, which I find at least equally dangerous. We are commanded, under the penalty of being called dishonest traffickers with words, palterers with them in a double sense, to take them at exactly their market value, though one is not informed at what *bourse* that value is settled, or which of the varying reports that every sect and school puts forth about it, we are to assume as the authentic one. I hold cheating with words to be in all respects more wicked as well as more mischievous than cheating with cards. The man who does the latter act is playing with a worthless instrument; he probably injures men who are as great rogues as himself, or dupes who may be saved from future ruin by a present loss; he brings into discredit that which one wishes to be discreditable. The other is abusing the holiest and divinest instrument,—he is making the whole commerce of life suspicious—he is leading the most earnest men to despair of attaining the only object which is worth living for. If the one is banished from the fellowship of his own class, ought not the other to be excommunicated by all good men? But to be *accused* of cheating with words is a very different thing, for that we ought all of us to be prepared. And I think the study of these Middle Age controversies about words may both assist us in avoiding the crime, and in enduring the reputation of it.

Pray forgive this long dedication, as well as my presumption in offering you a book about a subject which you understand so much better than the writer of it. I had some scruple in presenting it to you, knowing that from many opinions in it you would entirely dissent; and knowing also, from some painful experience, that I may do injury to the reputation of a friend by associating my name with his. But I could not deny myself the blame of saying how much I owe to your kindness and wisdom, and that I am,

Most affectionately yours,

F. D. MAURICE.

KIRCULLEN, GALWAY,
September 15, 1856.

CONTENTS.

MEDIÆVAL PHILOSOPHY.

INTRODUCTORY CHAPTER.

1. The Latin world, as we have explained already, will occupy us, Some of the History changed almost exclusively, in this division of the history of Moral and Metaphysical Philosophy. The East, henceforth, becomes the background of the picture. On the management of that background, it may greatly depend, whether the more prominent figures are presented distinctly, and in their proper relations, to the eye of the spectator. But he must be made to feel what is the *subject* of the sketch, and what are the subordinate and accessary portions of it.

2. To the end that the reader might fully understand the differ- Only one conspicuous Latin teacher in the former sketch. ence in this respect between the first six centuries after the Christian era and those which follow them, we pursued the history of Greek philosophy till its termination in the reign of Justinian, not suffering ourselves to be diverted from this object by some very celebrated Roman names. One conspicuous exception, indeed, we were obliged to make: Augustin, though a Latin, and though his influence on Latin thought has been so remarkable, could not be passed over. He belonged, emphatically, to the age in which Platonism was the prevailing faith of thoughtful students, whether they sought to satisfy the questions which Plato raised by the help of the New Testament, or through the old mythologies. There was another name, only second, as we hinted, in importance to his, which we expressly reserved for the present volume ; because, though the man who bears it belongs to a period earlier than that from which we commence, he has many of the most remarkable characteristics of the later time, and helped much to determine what those characteristics should be.

3. Anicius Manlius Severinus Boethius was probably born Origin of Boethius in the year 470 or 475. His father was consul in the year

B

487; his grandfather was præfect of the Prætorian guards, and was put to death by order of Valentinian III. He had, therefore, a close hereditary sympathy with the old names and glory of the republic, as well as the strongest and saddest evidence what a miserable and feeble tyranny was permitted to enact its latest crimes in the city of Brutus and Cicero. It cannot be supposed that a young man, bred among these associations, and fully sympathizing in them, can have mourned long and deeply over what *Minister under Theodoric.* we call the extinction of the Western Empire. At all events, he must have hailed, as the termination of anarchy, and the preparation for a better social order, the accession of Theodoric the Goth. He seems to have been an early friend of that monarch, and to have made the best use of his friendship, when he obtained from him the consulship. In that office, he became a faithful administrator of the public revenues. He put the coinage upon a reasonable footing. Finding Italy in a state almost approaching to famine, he took care that the exactions for the support of the army, by which Campania had been almost ruined, should be relaxed. He became the champion of those who had been the victims of false *His public and domestic character.* accusations—a scourge of spies and informers. His domestic life was pure, worthy of a Roman statesman. He was tenderly attached to his wife, Rusticiana. His sons appear to have been worthy; they were created consuls during their boyhood. Such a man would make himself bitter enemies. The profligate courtiers, whose hatred he had deserved, might have many excuses for representing that he was sighing for the older days before the Ostrogothic rule had commenced. Theodoric had reason to suspect that many, especially of his orthodox subjects, would look for *Suspicion of his fidelity.* protection against him to the emperor of the East. He became more suspicious as he grew older. It was a plausible suggestion, readily entertained, that Boethius was intriguing at Constantinople to obtain greater power for the senate. If he had ever cherished so idle a dream, the conduct of the senators to himself must have *His misfortunes.* convinced him of its folly. They abetted his accusers. Theodoric threw him and his father-in-law into prison at Ticinum. Their goods were confiscated. After some years both were put to death, in the sight of their friends. The king is said to have lamented his crime before his own death, which was regarded as the punishment of it. The widow of Boethius, according to Procopius, was forced like Belisarius, in the next age, to beg her bread.

Connection of his thoughts with his life.   4. Those who would understand the life of Boethius the philosopher, must know him first of all as a patriot. That is his truest character. By that, he is at once distinguished from the Athenian schoolmen, whose writings we examined in the last part of this sketch. A tradition, founded upon the misunderstanding of a passage in a letter of Cassiodorus, has given rise to the opinion that he visited the Greek schools, and was a hearer of Proclus. It is probable that he never left Italy. The praise which his correspondent means to bestow upon him is, that he imported Greek wisdom into that country, and made it Roman. To this fame, he is assuredly entitled. And it is by ascertaining what part of Greek wisdom such a Roman as Boethius would desire to naturalize, that we perceive the direction which thought was beginning to take in the West, and which it would take far more determinately, under other influences than his, but yet not without his influence, two or three centuries afterwards.

5. We have observed in many instances, how the reverence for law and order, in which lay the strength of the Roman, disposed him, when he had received the Greek teaching, to seek for that in the world of nature, which he found continually contradicted, in the world of human beings. Even the Epicurism of Lucretius illustrated the assertion. Though he seemed to refer everything to chance, he was really craving for something less irregular, more subject to principle, than the caprices of politicians, and the unrighteous gods of the Pantheon permitted him to behold. The Stoic Seneca fled to nature for the same reason. There only he could discover the quiet undisturbed order, which the philosopher was to reproduce in his own life. Boethius felt neither the disgust for affairs which characterized the earnest mind of the poet, nor the resignation to evil, which the courtier made it his business to cultivate. He had striven to be a righteous man himself, and he had to struggle against unrighteousness not in the closet only, but in the world. But he too wanted to study laws where he could see that they were obeyed. If there was only an approximation to right in the Roman polity, he must contemplate, and encourage his countrymen to contemplate, some other polity where decrees which wisdom and truth had enacted were never infringed. Such a polity, Plato had said must exist. It was morally and spiritually true, though it was nowhere realized. It was implied in the societies of men; though every society of men might be at variance with it. No such vision could present itself to the mind of a man trained in affairs, occupied with outward politics, reminded continually of all their anomalies. To a certain extent Boethius was imaginative, but he distrusted his imagination, and was afraid to believe that there was any truth corresponding to the hopes which it suggested. But in numbers, in lines, in forms, in musical notes, in the motions of the heavenly bodies, there were principles which evidently did not bend to accident or circumstance,—which could not be adjusted, or swayed, at the pleasure of any tyrant. In the investigation of these primary elements, these grounds of the universe, there was rest for a mind which felt that it had no right to shrink from the trivialities of detail, or the vulgarities of

His Roman character.

Wherein he was like and unlike Lucretius and Seneca.

Why he had not sympathy with Plato.

human passions, but which felt also, that it must have something substantial and constant, as a counteraction to them, and a safeguard against them.

The Platonical Idea of Arithmetic and Geometry.

6. It will be perceived by the reader that a man who took up the studies of arithmetic, geometry, music, or astronomy from such motives as these, will have agreed with Plato in his estimate of their importance, but will have differed from him greatly in his judgment of their nature, and of the use to which they should be turned. When Plato commanded that no one should enter his halls who had not been disciplined in geometry, he believed, no doubt, that the student would be led by this preparation to seek for that which is, in every subject which he examined; to endure no shadows or appearances which offered themselves in exchange for it. He would be led by the *method* of geometry to seek in a particular case, for the principle which governs all such cases; not to heap together a multitude of observations and merely deduce a general and probable maxim from them. Boethius expected more certainty in the principles concerning numbers and lines than he could ever apply to human acts and wills; but the evenness and

The Boethian Idea.

harmony to which he became used in one region would reappear in the justness and proportion of his purposes and of his acts, when he was met by disturbing forces which swayed him to the right or to the left. It is not necessary to suppose that he sought no other end and more powerful help against these forces; he must have been aware from experience how little, considerations drawn from the natural world can be brought to bear, in moments of inward conflict and temptation. What we mean to intimate, is, that he wished to produce in himself a certain even habit of mind, rather than to familiarize himself with any lofty idea; and that he looked upon physical studies chiefly as contributing to this object, by the very difference which exists between them and human studies. In other words, he was pursuing the Aristotelian mean. The righteousness he aimed at was that which is so strikingly exhibited in the fourth book of "The Ethics," and which in fact explains the whole of that master work. And his idea of science stood in the closest relation to his idea of the end of life. To know the limitation and boundaries of those things which are the subject of human thought, was according to him to know *them*. This may not have

Science according to Aristotle.

been all that he meant by science; it is not all that Aristotle, or any man at any time, meant by it. But on the whole this is a fair representation of his habitual conviction, and it marks him out as the true successor of Aristotle in the West, as the beginner, classic and Ciceronian though he was, of that which we are wont to call the Barbaric or Gothico-Latin philosophy.

Liber. de Unitate et Uno.

7. The first treatise of Boethius which it behoves us to notice, is the short one "On Unity and the One." The following sentences

are, it seems to us, very important with a view to the understanding of the mind of our author.

"Unity is that in virtue of which anything whatsoever is affirmed to be one. For whether it is simple or compound, spiritual or corporeal, a thing is one by reason of its unity; nor can it be one except by reason of its unity; as a thing cannot be white except from whiteness. But not only is it *one* by reason of its unity, but also it is only so long that which it is, as long as there is unity in it. When it ceases to be one, it ceases to be that which it is; whence comes the maxim, that whatever is, is therefore because it is one. For all being, in things created, belongs to form. But there is no being in form *merely*, but only when form is united to matter. Being, say the philosophers, is the indwelling of Form in Matter. From the conjunction of form with matter, something that is one, is constituted. The destruction of a thing is nothing else than the separation of form from matter." *[Definition of Being.]*

8. The reader will perceive that Boethius is here dealing with our *modes* of thinking and speaking about Being and Unity, not with Being and Unity as the grounds of all thought and speech. It is the more necessary to make this remark, because there is good reason to think, that he was not aware of the distinction himself. It does not appear, that he ever suspected that there was or could be another way of looking at the subject, than that which he followed. He probably read the Platonical philosophers with approbation and sympathy, because he read them according to Aristotle, unconsciously translating them and fitting them into his moulds. The words "*Form and Matter*," which he introduces into this Treatise on Unity, were the common and debateable ground between the two schools. Everything depended on the manner in which they were used. Aristotle perfectly understood that he was not using the word Form in the sense in which his master used it: he is most careful to tell us so in every treatise, ethical, dialectical, metaphysical. Few of his Greek followers perceived as he did, how radical the distinction was; even many of the Platonists, while they followed *their* teacher, did not discern wherein the Stagyrite had diverged from him. For many ages, the Latins were almost wholly unaware that the difference existed, though it was continually perplexing them, and was lying at the root of their most serious controversy. It is interesting and valuable to observe the confusion in a man whose scholarship would have perfectly qualified him to appreciate the diversities of the great teachers, if his habits of mind had not necessarily chained him to one of them. We must always bear in mind that he understands truth and falsehood only in reference to propositions. That which is, is that which can be rightly affirmed concerning any *[Inference from this passage.]* *[Form and Matter.]*

subject. The One is that which we are obliged to consider one by the laws of our understandings.

9. A passage from the opening of the Treatise on Arithmetic is a further and a very consistent illustration of this habit of mind. "We say that those things are, which neither grow by expansion, nor are diminished by contraction, nor are changed by variations; but preserve themselves ever in their own proper force, depending upon nothing which is extraneous to their own nature. Now these are *qualities, quantities, forms, magnitudes, littlenesses, equalities, actions, dispositions, places, times,* and whatsoever is found in some way or other united in bodies. These things are in their own nature incorporeal; they live under the law of an immutable substance; but they are changed by the participation of body, and pass, through contact with variable things, into instability. These things, therefore, seeing as it is said they have by nature an immutable substance and force, are truly and properly said *to be.* Of these things, therefore, that is of those things that properly are, and which deserve the name of essences, true wisdom professes to give us the knowledge. Now of an essence there are two parts. One continuous and united in its different portions, and not distinguished by any boundaries, such as is a tree, a stone, and all bodies of this

universe, which properly are called *Magnitudes.* Others consist of separate and determinate portions, and are brought into one by accumulation, as a flock, a people, a choir. For these the proper

name is *Multitude.* Again, to this head of *multitude* we refer certain things that are in themselves, as *three* or *four,* or any number whatsoever, which require nothing else that they may be. But some do not exist by themselves, but are referred to something else, as *double, half, next but one, next but two,* and so forth. To magnitude, again, belong some things that are stationary, some that are turning

about in perpetual rotation. The first class of multitudes, those which are such in themselves, Arithmetic contemplates. Those which are relative belong to Music. Of immoveable *magnitude,*

Geometry takes cognizance. The knowledge of the moveable the Astronomer promises us. If the inquirer does not recognize these four portions of knowledge, he cannot find truth, and unless he behold truth, no one can be said to have wisdom. For wisdom is the knowledge and entire comprehension of those things which truly are. And I tell any one who despises these different paths of wisdom, that he is no true philosopher. For philosophy is the love of wisdom which, in despising these, he has already despised. I would add further that *multitude* proceeding from a limit, *increases* infinitely. *Magnitude,* on the contrary, beginning from a finite quantity, admits of infinite *division.* This infinity of nature and its indeterminate power, philosophy voluntarily repudiates. For nothing which is infinite can be gathered together in knowledge, or comprehended in the mind. Therefore reason hath made a selection for itself of those things in which she may exercise her skill, as a searcher of truth. For she hath chosen out of the plurality of infinite multitude, a certain term of finite quantity, and rejecting the divisions of interminable magnitude, hath sought out for herself definite spaces for knowledge. It is clear, then, that whosoever has overlooked these, has lost the whole doctrine of philosophy. This, then, is that *quadrivium* in which those must travel whose mind being raised above the senses, is brought to the heights of intelligence. For there are certain steps, by which we must advance and mount, in order that these studies may again illuminate that eye of the mind, sunk and almost blinded in the senses of the body, which, as Plato says, is much more worthy to be opened and made effectual, than many eyes of the body, seeing that by that light only, can truth be sought out or beheld. Which then of these sciences is to be studied first? Must it not be that which has a sort of maternal relation to all the rest? Now this is arithmetic. For this is before all studies, not only because God the founder of this earthly fabric, had it with Him originally as the exemplar of His own design, and framed according to it all things whatsoever, which, His reason comprehending these, found their harmony in the numbers of a determined order. But in this also is arithmetic proved to be before other studies, because the destruction of that which is first in nature involves the destruction of that which is subsequent to it, whereas the converse is not true." We must condense his arguments in support of this proposition, but they cannot be passed over. "If you take away the nature of the animal, you take away man; but the animal may remain though man perishes. In like manner if you take away numbers, what becomes of the triangle and the square in geometry, the very names of which denote the pre-existence of Number; whereas three and four and the names of other numbers will not disappear though the triangle and the square and the whole of geometry were annihilated. So likewise Musical modulation is denoted by the very names of numbers; hence it depends upon number, and must perish with it. Astronomy of course follows the same rule. For both geometry and music, which have been shown to be subordinate to arithmetic, are presumed in astronomy. Circles, the sphere, the centre, the parallels, all belong to geometrical discipline. Moreover all motion is subsequent to rest, and geometry has been defined to be the science of the moveable, astronomy of the immoveable. Every one knows that the stars move according to the laws of harmony. Music therefore must precede the study of the courses of the stars."

10. It would be difficult to select a passage of the same length, as prophetical of the method of study in the Middle Ages as this

Margin notes:
Wisdom and Philosophy.

Philosophy always seeking for definition.

Way to mental vision.

Place of Arithmetic amidst studies.

Reasons for the subordination of Geometry in Arithmetic, and of Astronomy to Music.

A prophetical passage.

one. The rapid arrangément of the Quadrivium, with the reasons
that are assigned for it, the mixture of peremptory dogmatism with
ingenious reasoning, the glimpses of a high intelligence and perception of the destiny of man, with the boldest presumption about
the order of the universe and the scheme of its author, will explain
themselves more and more as we advance in our history.   But

beneath all these Aristotelian tendencies,—hardened, legalized, and
yet dignified by the Roman intellect, which was adopting them,—lies
that deification of Logic which belonged to the original teacher, but
which was to produce far more startling and serious results in his
disciples of the later world.   Qualities, quantities, magnitudes,
multitudes—who does not see that these names were building a
prison for Boethius of which the walls were far higher and more
impenetrable than those of the one to which Theodoric consigned
him ? There was positively no escape above, below, through ceiling,
or pavement, for one confined within this word-fortress; scarcely
an aperture, one would have thought, for air or light to enter in !
And yet we shall find that they did enter through both the material
and the formal ramparts, within which a brave and noble spirit

was enclosed, and that many in after times found not only deliverance out of this confinement, but a certain amount of blessing and
benefit in it.   Indeed it is not possible to read the extract we
have given, without perceiving in it the outlines of an education
which modern Europe was to discover for itself and to pass through;
an education based upon the acknowledgment of an order in the
universe, however that order might be limited by human conceptions; therefore holding out a promise that after a proper period
of pupilage, whatever was forced and unnatural in the system
would be broken through,—whatever there was of true method
latent in it would then or afterwards come forth, and prove itself
a way to knowledge and to freedom.

11. There is much in the two books on Arithmetic which the
student of Middle Age philosophy ought to consider; but we must
pass over these as well as the five on Music. Respecting the two on
Geometry, we must also be silent, only calling the attention of the
reader to an important and characteristic passage near the close of

the treatise, where Boethius sums up the history and the benefits of
this study. In that passage, we discover the link between the
practical moralist and politician, and the scientific doctor. All goodness and all truth he affirms to be fixed, and defined; whereas the
nature of evil and error is infinite and refuses to be reduced under
laws or principles.   The office of the mind is to govern and coerce
the passions which are always seeking to break loose.   That mind
receives strength and stability from culture in the pure sciences. This
hint must not be forgotten.   It will receive illustration, by and
by, from moralists and theologians, with whom Boethius had not

much in common ; its immediate explanation may be found in his own Logical Treatises, to which we must now turn.

12. These consist of commentaries upon the "Categories of Aristotle," upon the "Book of Interpretation," upon both the treatises on "Analytics," on "The Topics" and on the "Confutations of the Sophists." As these books are intended to form a course of instruction for Roman students, Boethius introduces them with two dialogues and three books of commentaries on Porphyry, one of whose treatises he regards as the best vestibule to the Aristotelian temple. Not much pains are taken to make the dialogues dramatic. After a very short opening in the manner of Cicero, our statesman proceeds at once to business, giving Latin equivalents for several familiar Greek technicalities, and then explaining the relation of accident to substance, and the purpose of definition. We have, however, in his introduction some general observations, necessary, he conceives, to the understanding of this subject, which throw great light upon his method of thinking.

Logical Treatises.

In Porphyrian Dialogi a Victorino translati.

13. "It would be desirable," he says, "first of all to consider what philosophy itself is. Philosophy is the love and pursuit of wisdom, and in some sort the fellowship with it. By this wisdom, we must not understand that which has to do with special arts or with some mechanical science, but that which needs nothing besides itself, that which is the quickening mind and the primeval principle of things. This love of wisdom is the illumination of the intelligent mind from the pure wisdom, the drawing back and calling, as it were, that mind to herself. So that it may seem as much the pursuit of divinity as the pursuit of wisdom, the friendship of the pure mind with its object. This wisdom, therefore, imposes the worthiness of its own divinity upon every kind of souls which occupy themselves with it, and brings them to the force and purity of their true nature. Hence arises the truth of speculations and thoughts and the holy chastity of acts. Which consideration enables us to ascertain the proper division of philosophy. Philosophy being the genus, there are two species of it, one theoretic or speculative, the other practical or active. There will be as many species of speculative philosophy as there are subjects for reasonable speculation. There will be as many species and varieties of virtues as there are diversities of acts. Of theoretic philosophy there are three subjects, the intellectible, the intelligible, and the natural." Fabius, one of the persons in the dialogue, is surprised at the newly-coined word *intellectible*. It is explained to mean "that which is one and the same in itself, consisting always in its own divinity; that which is never perceived by the senses, but only by the mind and intellect." It belongs, therefore, to the contemplation of God and to the incorporeal nature of the mind. It is that part of philosophy which is called by the Greeks *Theology*. Things *intelligible*

Dialogue I. Philosophy.

Philosophy theoretic and active.

Three divisions of the theoretic.

have a close connection with the *intellectible*, look up to them, and acquire a higher and purer nature by commerce with them, but by their relation with bodies, under the power of which they may sink, are differenced from them. The third part of speculative philosophy is physiology, and concerns the natures and passions of bodies. Practical philosophy is likewise divided into three parts. The first concerns the growth of the individual soul and its adornment with all virtues. The second has to do with the care of the state. The third with economy or the management of property.

14. We might have expected Boethius to tell us under which of these different heads of philosophy *Logic* is to be reckoned. But such a course would not have been consistent with the tendencies of his mind. He intimates at once that logic is not so much a part of philosophy as that which binds all the parts of it together. He has been obliged to assume it, in making the division which he has just attempted. If he had not started from genus and species, what should we have known about philosophy or that which is speculative and active? All his definitions have involved differences, properties, accidents. Grammar, rhetoric, the whole force of argument, are involved in logic. Our main business, therefore, is to understand what the right order in studying logic is; then we shall understand the very principle of order. He traces rapidly the relation between the different books of Aristotle, shows why the Categories must needs be first, and why something is necessary to prepare the reader for them. The primary distinction, he says, is between substance and accident. The nine conditions of quality, quantity, relation, place, time, position, possession, doing, suffering, are all conditions of accident. Therefore, it was necessary to say something beforehand about substance and accident; in fact we must have a knowledge of the laws of division, before we have a knowledge of these primary divisions. Porphyry, he says, supplies the want. His introduction, about the genuineness of which Boethius affirms there is no doubt, is the proper manual for the beginner. He then proceeds to comment on the book, paragraph by paragraph. In these elements of the study, one might hope to escape any great and dangerous perplexities. But no. The logical Hercules must be assaulted by serpents while he is yet in his cradle. It is just at this very point of the subject, that those monsters which were to acquire in after times the terrible names of Nominalism and Realism lift up their crests and threaten us with destruction. Porphyry, with true Greek dexterity, foreseeing the perils of the battle, avoids it. Our Roman, with the valour of his race and his own personal intrepidity, rushes into it at once, and thus gravely and peremptorily decides a question in which the doctors of Europe for centuries were, one after another, to engage.

15. "What does Porphyry mean," inquires Fabius, "by saying

[margin notes:]

Divisions of practical philosophy

The place of Logic.

Principles of Method.

Difficulties at the outset of the study.

that he merely touches and passes over certain points which elder Commentary on the first paragraph.
philosophers had discussed at great length? He means this;"
answers our author, "he omits the question whether genera and
species have an actual subsistence, or dwell in the intellect and mind
alone; whether they be corporeal or incorporeal; and whether
they are separate or joined to the things which our senses perceive.
On these matters, seeing that the disputation was a deep one, he
promised to be silent. But let us, holding the reins of self-
restraint tightly, touch a little upon each one of them." The
question is stated in this way. "Seeing that the mind of man is Senses and Conceptions.
multiform, it understands things subjected to the *senses*, by the
senses, according to their own quality. *Conceptions*, formed by a
process of contemplation out of these, it uses as a road to the
understanding of incorporeal things. So that when I see individual
men, I both am sure that I have *seen* them, and further I boast
that I have *understood* that they are men. The *intelligence* which Conceptions are of species which are incorporeal.
is thus derived, strengthened as it were by the perception of sensible
things, raises itself to a higher level and now apprehends the very
species of man which exists under the animal, and which contains
the individual men; the mind understands that to be incorporeal,
the corporeal particles of which it had assumed in its sensible perceptions of the individual men. For to say the truth, that Species
Man, which encloses us all within the circle of its name, must not be
spoken of as corporeal, seeing that we conceive it by the mind and
intelligence alone. The mind then resting itself on the first
principles of things, is sublimed by a higher intelligence, with which
the body has nought to do. Hereby it comes to pass that the soul
of man not only becomes capable of understanding incorporeal
things through sensible, but also, of inventing them for itself, and
even of creating falsehood. For instance, out of the form of a Formation of false species.
horse and a man, the intellect framed for itself the false species of
centaurs. These reflections of the mind which rising from the
sensible perception of things to the intelligence, are either perceived
or feigned, the Greeks call Φαντασίαι, and we may call them (visa).
The question then is whether we are to suppose that genera and
species are truly subsisting, that they are essential and fixed, so
that we may believe the species of man has been *truly* and *fairly*
deduced from individual bodies; or whether they are as much
feigned as the animal in the verse of Horace with the human head
and the horse's neck, which neither does exist nor could exist.
The inquiry is a very subtle one, and one of great practical
importance. . *If you weigh the truth of things it is impossible to* Decision in favour of Realism.
doubt that these genera and species are true. For seeing that all
things that are true cannot be without these five, (genus, species,
difference, property, accident,) you cannot doubt that these five
things have been true, and understood. They are embedded,

compacted, conglutinated in all things. Else why should Aristotle
speak about those ten primary names, which signify the genera of
things? Or why should he collect together their differences and
their properties, and treat so specially concerning their accidents,
unless these were wrapt up in the things and intimately joined to
them? If so there is no question that they are true, and that
they are grasped by the certain conclusion of the mind."

The question of the corporeal and Incorporeal.

16. Boethius goes on to maintain that Porphyry, in spite of his
apparent silence, was really of his mind on this subject, otherwise
why should he have discussed the question whether these forms
are corporeal or incorporeal? They must be if they are either one
or the other. To this second question our Roman addresses himself with equal courage. His decision is this. The incorporeal is
the primary nature; the body is something added on to this; so that
you can never deduce the incorporeal from it. Genus, as such, is
neither corporeal nor incorporeal. It includes both as species
within it, and may bring both out of itself. Species may be either
corporeal or incorporeal. If you put man under substance, you
have introduced a corporeal species; if God, an incorporeal. So
with differences. If you compare a quadruped with a biped, the
difference is corporeal; if rational with irrational, the difference is
incorporeal. So of property. If the species is incorporeal, the
property will be incorporeal; if corporeal, corporeal. The same
principle applies to accidents. Hence all of these, though they
may be referred to corporeal or incorporeal subjects, can by no
possibility be themselves considered as under the law of corporeal
or sensible things. He afterwards adds, "If these five, genus, species,
difference, property, or accident, are joined to bodies, they are such
as is that primary incorporality which is outside of limits, and yet
never is severed from body; but if to incorporeal, they are such as
is a mind which is not united to a body." Fabius confesses his inability
to understand this language, and his instructor does not vouchsafe
any further explanation than that the terms or limits of which he
speaks, are the extremities of geometrical figures, and that the
incorporality which has to do with these limits, may be studied in
the first book of the very learned Macrobius Theodosius concerning
the Dream of Scipio. With this information our readers must
also be satisfied.

Porphyry's Aristotelian-ism.

17. We do not intend to follow this treatise into its details. We
are now launched on the ocean of Latinized Aristotelian dialectics.
If we have become somewhat suddenly acquainted with its shoals
and quicksands, we may at least hope that we shall have a better
chance of not being wrecked on them hereafter. Porphyry is, in
many respects, as convenient a guide, for our purpose, as Boethius
considered him, for his countrymen in the fifth century. He
occupied, as we have seen, a middle position between the pure

philosophers of the Neo-Platonic school and the Theurgists—always inclining to the former, but oftentimes driven into unwilling consent with their opponents. The natural issue of such a mind was in Aristotelianism. There he was safe from the necessity of investigating the problems of the spiritual world, of considering how dæmons or gods hold converse with men. Yet, in the forms and conditions of the intellect, he can exercise the abstract talent which his master had cultivated in him; he could feel that he was not dwelling amidst the sensible things which the theoretical man was to eschew. A mind like his, could very well stand on the edge *Difference* of Realism without plunging into it. He had learnt to think of the *between him* spiritual region as a substantial one. He had still the tradition of *and Boethius.* another higher region when he came down into that of names and terms. For a man bred up in actual business as Boethius was, such hesitation was difficult, almost impossible. The forms were to him ridiculous unless he could treat them as he did the things with which he was habitually conversant. Realism was, as his argument shows so clearly, not the result of a process of reasoning, but an assumption from which he started. To have had a doubt on the matter, would have seemed to him monstrous.

18. In the preface to his larger commentaries upon his own *Boethius com-* translation of Porphyry, there are some passages respecting the *mentaries in* rise and use of Logic which the student will do well to compare *& to transla-* with the directly opposite views in the first book of the Novum Orga- *tum.* num. He opens with a triple division of the human mind into the life which it has in common with the vegetables, the sentient life which it shares with other animals, the ratiocinative life which is *Division of* peculiarly and properly human. This last power, he says, is exer- *the human* cised in four ways, in inquiring whether something is, what it is, *faculties.* of what kind it is, lastly, why it is. The mind in virtue of this power, he says, is exercised in the fixed contemplation of things that are present, in the understanding of things that are absent, in the investigation of things unknown. It can conceive of things that do not fall under the senses. It can put names upon things that are absent. What it has perceived intellectually, it can *Quare* express in words. This superiority of the ratiocinative faculty to *hærvate erat* the mere faculty of observation, leads him to condemn Epicurus *abjecta scien-* and the Atomists, because they substituted the exact observation of *tiâ disqu-* nature for processes of reasoning. You cannot, he rightly observes, *rerum naturâ* make them always fit into one another. I tell 100 on my fingers, *Kiel enim* there is an actual 100 corresponding to it. But I may not conclude *sentiam* that whatever our discourse has found out, has its fixed counterpart *venerit, quæ* in nature. We might fancy that this discovery would lead him to *veram* suspect the danger of anticipating inquiries by our reasoning. *tenent dis-* Quite the contrary. It makes him perceive the necessity of a *quæ veritati-* science which shall point out the true and the probable path of dis- *agnoverit*

quæ fida
juvalit cum
quæve sus-
pecta rerum
incorrupta
fides, cû
ratiocina-
tione non po-
test inveniri.
putation. Until we have a science of logic and know how to bring
everything to its rules and tests, he has no hope that we shall arrive
at any safe or satisfactory conclusions respecting the laws of the
world. Here again we perceive the teacher of one important
branch of human knowledge, forging chains which the physical
student would afterwards have the most sore labour to break in
pieces.

Books on the
Categories.
19. The books of Boethius on the writings of Aristotle himself
were more important in his judgment than those which preceded
them, as conducting his pupil into a more advanced stage of the
science. To us they are chiefly valuable, as marking out a track of
thought in which men were intended for a long time to run, as
furnishing a Latin nomenclature for the logician, as carrying out
into detail the principles which we have already shown to be
characteristic of the mind of the writer, as attesting his indefatigable diligence, as proving how much it was the end of that diligence
to supply his countrymen with a regular and systematic course of
instruction. That instruction would have been imperfect, according
Ile treatise
on Rhetoric.
to the notions of either Greeks or Romans, if rhetoric had not
come in as the sister, at all events the handmaid, to logic. The
commentaries on Cicero's Topics were intended to complete the
Boethian circle of studies.

Supposed
treatises
De Trinitate,
and De Per-
sonis et
Naturis
dubæ.
20. We say to complete, because it seems very difficult to resist
the decree of modern criticism which pronounces the theological
treatises of Boethius to be spurious. There are many reasons, we
conceive, besides those which have been derived from the internal
evidence of the treatises themselves, for adopting this opinion,
greatly as it is at variance with an old belief or tradition. First,
the entire absence of anything like a definite recognition of
Christianity in works like those we have commented upon, so far
as they are of a truly formal or scientific character, might be
accounted for. But that, in marking out the different departments
of human thought so carefully as Boethius has done, and in hinting
at theology as one and the highest of these branches, no word should
Reasons for
rejecting
them.
be used to indicate that it was the subject of a revelation or in
whom that revelation had been made to man, must needs seem
almost incredible in one who believed at all, much less who
believed with the kind of earnestness which we must attribute,
in every question that really interested him, to Boethius. Secondly,
it would be painful, and would lower our opinion of the man,
to think that he could have written essays on the Trinity and
on the two natures of Christ, merely as theses or exercises of his
logical faculty. Thirdly, it was almost a matter of course that, if
he left treatises so complete in themselves as those on Geometry,
Arithmetic, Music, Logic, and Astronomy, some doctor of the Middle
Ages would see the necessity of filling up the great blank that was

left, and producing lectures on Divinity as nearly as possible in harmony with those which had been bequeathed by the Roman Senator. Fourthly, the faith in the genuineness of these treatises was inseparable in the Middle Ages from the notion that Boethius died a martyr to Catholicism and Orthodoxy. It is clear that he did die a martyr in a very noble cause, the cause of Roman liberty and justice. But there is nothing whatever in the history of his sufferings which can warrant, or even suggest, the suspicion that the Arianism of Theodoric was the cause of them.

21. On the other hand, we are by no means disposed to adopt the opinion which has been proclaimed by many German scholars, (amongst others by the latest editor of the Consolations,) that Boethius was a heathen. There is not the least evidence, in his writings, of attachment to the forms of the old religion: all external evidence would lead us to conclude that he adopted the established creed. Our readers may fancy, that in this century, there was no middle term between vehement conviction on one side or the other. They will have seen much in our account of the progress of philosophy in Greece to justify such an opinion. But they must beware of applying conclusions which they have rightly drawn respecting the Eastern world, to the West; respecting the Platonical school, to the Aristotelian. Men living at a period when the old imperial traditions were perishing, when the new Gothic world was commencing—surrounded by proofs that Roman law and life which had been so allied to the worship of the old gods had not passed away—with proofs as decisive that the religion which sustained them *had* passed away—may very naturally have endeavoured to hold fast by that which they felt to be an heirloom for all future ages, without attempting to reproduce what had no hold upon the present, and yet without pronouncing whether it was good or evil in the past. A monarch like Theodoric who regarded catholics with jealousy and yet had no affection for paganism, would be likely to encourage men of this class. He would not understand their affection for the old classical world, but their equilibrium of mind and their willingness to treat Arians and Orthodox merely as common citizens of the Republic, would be acceptable to him. They, on their parts, would be confirmed in the position they had taken up, by the apparent uncertainties and the evident disagreements of the Christians. Dogmatism would not have offended Boethius. He was a dogmatist by nature, by principle, by education. But he would certainly be scandalized by any looseness of opinions, by the absence of the logical precision which he demanded of every thinker, by the indefiniteness and infiniteness which he pronounced to be the great enemies of science. These motives, especially the last, had comparatively little influence upon Proclus and the philosophers of

Question about his Christianity.

Possible state of mind in Roman citizens under the Ostrogothic sway.

The Philosophy of Boethius kept him aloof from Theology.

Athens. They were students of the infinite. They believed indeed that very distinct and definite forms discovered themselves to the meditative and abstracted man in the region which lay beyond the measures and rules of the human intellect; but they were much more disposed to complain of the Christian church, for excluding the imagination, than for giving it too wide a scope. They were, as we have so often had occasion to remark, primarily theological. Hence, if they did not accept Christianity, they must come into a direct polemic with it. The Aristotelian laid down his data on Logic, applied these to the physical universe, admitted a metaphysical world beyond that, believed in a certain divine region which the theoretic man might behold and dwell in. But these last were the mere complements of a system which could exist without them, unless some great moral necessity, which neither Aristotle nor Porphyry, nor for a long time Boethius, seems to have felt, should force them first into the thoughts of ordinary men, and thence into the schools.

Why the question is important for our subject.

22. We are afraid we shall seem to our readers to dwell unnecessarily upon these differences between the two countries, two ages, two methods of thought. But the clearness of our future sketch so much depends upon the acknowledgment of them, that we would rather incur the charge of any amount of repetition than pass by the facts upon which the proof of these differences rests. The question concerning the Christianity of Boethius is important, on this ground especially. It is often supposed that the theology of the Middle Ages, such as we have exhibited it, in connection with the name of Gregory the Great, had not only a very close connection with the logic and the philosophy of the Middle Ages, (which it notoriously had, and which we have already said must be confessed by every one who would engage faithfully in the study of either), but that they grew up together, that they were from the first inseparable, that the theology determined the course which the dialectical studies took, imparting to them its own dogmatical and authoritative character. This opinion we believe to be wholly untenable. It has gained strength from the notion that Boethius being the parent of the Latin dialectics and philosophy, was also a theologian, and took pains to give his philosophy a theological and Christian character. The plain statement which we have made of what he actually did, is the refutation of this theory. We have shown, we trust, that there is not a single element in his scientific teaching which is not derived from teachers of the old world, or from teachers who were adverse rather than friendly to Christianity.

The book De Consolatione Philosophiae.

23. Notwithstanding this evidence, we are far from disposed to quarrel with our great Saxon king, or with the teachers whom he followed, for discovering a Christian element in the book which re-

cords the experience of our statesman's prison houses, nay, for pronouncing it a distinctly Christian work. It must be acknowledged at once, that they had no warrant for taking this course from any phrases which occur in the book, that they put an interpretation upon it which the text does not authorize and which Boethius himself would have hesitated to endorse. An argument even might be drawn, and has been drawn, from this treatise, which is more decidedly adverse to the Christianity of Boethius than any of his other works supply. The man who does not directly allude to the Gospel and Him who is the subject of it, when he is speaking of that which supported him in suffering and in the prospect of death, might seem to afford the clearest evidence of his habitual state of mind, one which no other could equal or contradict. Undoubtedly this presumption does not only *look*, but *is* very strong. We can only explain why we do not yield to it, by giving an abstract of the Consolations.

24. The hard Logician with whom we have been conversing hitherto, presents himself to us at the commencement of this book as a poet. The contrast does not seem to us one which warrants a doubt about the genuineness of his earlier or later writings. There is a freshness and vitality in the style of Boethius when he is writing upon formal and scientific subjects, which would justify us in thinking that there was poetry in his nature, and that circumstances might call it out some day into verse. A man who could combine so much of speculation with the habits of practical business, must have had a mind of wonderful spring and elasticity. His life had been poetical and harmonious. When its outward activity was suspended, it was not very strange that he should begin to sing. It is with an elegy about his griefs that he commences. Then he proceeds to tell us in prose, how there came in upon his meditations the vision of a Woman of very reverent countenance, with glowing eyes, penetrating beyond the common power of human eyes, of brilliant complexion, and inexhausted strength, though so full of years, that she could by no means be deemed to belong to that age. Her stature was difficult to describe, for sometimes she appeared to retain it within the common human measure, sometimes she lifted her head so high, that it looked into the very heaven, and was lost to the gaze of the beholder. Her garments were of exquisite workmanship, fashioned, as he afterwards understood, by her own hands. Yet there was a look of antiquity, almost of neglect, about them. On the lower skirt of it he saw inscribed Π; on the upper part of it Θ. There seemed letters between them which rose like the steps of a ladder from one to the other. But the garment had been torn, apparently by violence, and some fragments of it carried away. She had books in her right hand, a sceptre in her left. This majestical lady was greatly

Boethius a poet.

The vision.

c

displeased by the poetical Muses whom she found waiting upon the prisoner's couch. Is it fitting that he, who had studied under the teachers of the Academy and the Porch, should give himself to these Syrens? They must depart at once, that he may submit himself to his true Mistress, who comes, not to soothe him, but to probe and to cure.

The complaint.

25. The visitor, whose name is Philosophy, notwithstanding this harsh commencement, does not disdain herself to speak to him in song; only it is of a grave and inspiring sort, not tender and pathetic. The sufferer craves her compassion, and wonders at her condescension. When he finds that she has come to him, as she did to Anaxagoras and Socrates while they were labouring under false charges and expecting their sentence, he is emboldened to pour out all his griefs into her ear, proclaiming, not untruly but a little boastfully, the good deeds to his country which had deserved another fate, and affirming his innocence of the crimes which spies and sycophants had imputed to him. The thought is oppressive, not for its immediate effects only or chiefly. He has learnt by heart the Pythagorean maxim, "Follow after God;" he has tried to act upon it; and now he is deserted. Has he not a right to suspect that the world is itself given over to chance?

Invocation to the god of nature.

Then in really noble verse, he invokes the Framer of this globe to tell him how it is that sun, and moon, and stars, obey the eternal laws which He has given them; the lesser lights quietly yielding to the greater, the sisterorb increasing or diminishing her horn according to a fixed ordinance, and paling her fires before her brother's brightness; how it is that night and day succeed each other without disturbance and disorder; that the cold of winter yields, at its predestined time, to the fervour of summer; that the leaves which the north wind carries off, the zephyr renews; that, in short, no one thing in all nature breaks loose from its ancient law, or deserts the work that belongs to its proper place; but that He who governs all things with a fixed purpose, leaves the acts of man to the mercy of slippery fortune, which crushes the innocent with the punishment that is due to the guilty; which enthrones perverse manners on high, and enables the wicked to trample on the necks of the just, so that virtue lies hidden in darkness, that lies and perjuries are profitable to those who practise them, that high kings before whom multitudes tremble, own these as their masters. "Look down," he concludes, "on this miserable earth, whosoever thou art that holdest together the bonds of nature. We that are not the worst part of thy great work, are tossed about by every wind and wave of fortune. Mighty Ruler, control these waves, and make the earth firm with that law by which thou rulest the heavens!"

The true cause of lamentation.

26. The divine visitor listens with calmness to this outpouring of grief and indignation, and then begins to compassionate the

Statesman, because he is suffering an exile into which no king or multitude could have driven him, an exile from his own heart's home and resting-place. Seeing that the evil is deeper than she had at first supposed, the gracious physician proceeds to apply such gentle remedies as the weak state of the patient will bear. She brings him to confess that he does not really know what Man is, what he himself is. But he is not to despair. He does recognize at least an order in nature, a Monarch over the world. That is a starting-point of good. From this small spark, true vital heat may be enkindled. Then, in free and lightsome song, she bids him cast away griefs, cast away fears, bid hope and sorrow go together. So will he have a clear eye to see the truth; so will he be able, amidst a multitude of winding paths, to choose the right.

27. The next book introduces an ingenious argument to prove *The government of fortune.* that Boethius has no cause whatever to complain of fortune. If he chooses to accept her as a mistress, he must submit to her ordinary maxims and rules. He knew beforehand what she was. What had she done to him which she had not done to every one of her votaries before? She had been wonderfully liberal in her largesses to him, had given him wealth, friends, education, station. Let him count them up and see whether any man had ever a larger measure of the things which men value most. If they were gone, did not he know the tenure upon which they were granted? All this is acknowledged as very reasonable, but it is complained of as quite ineffectual. After all these calculations, the pain of losing is in proportion to the preciousness of the things possessed. Philosophy reminds him that he is not desolate yet of his best treasures. His wife and children are still his, and dearer than ever. It is something to make him confess that he has no right *The right to complain considered.* to complain of his whole state. How many are there who would feel themselves almost in Heaven, if they had but the relics of his good fortune? How few things taken from the stock of a man used to all indulgences, will make him miserable! How little added to the stock of those who are unused to it, will make them happy! The result is this: is there anything that is more precious to thee than thyself? Then if thou art master of thyself, thou wilt possess that which neither thou wilt wish to lose, nor fortune will be able to take away. The victim of feeble, faltering, outward felicity, either knows that it is mutable, or does not know it. If he does not know it, how can he be happy, seeing that he is shut up in the prison of ignorance? If he does know it, how can he be happy, since he must be continually tormented by fear? Then comes an analysis of the different elements of this external felicity. *Worth of money, dignities, natural beauty.* Is it money? But that you must part with before it is worth anything; you wish to be rid of it, when you prize it most. Is it the beauty of the surrounding world? But this you cannot *have.*

appropriate; you may enjoy it, but it is not yours. Is it the dignities and honours of the world? But these come to the greatest villains; and since contraries cannot exist in harmony, it is impossible that they can have any good in themselves. Music belongs to the musician, rhetoric to the rhetorician; there can be no natural good in these things, seeing they have no natural affinity with the good man. Or is it a great name? Boethius confesses this weakness. He wants space and means for action, that the virtue which is in him may not wear itself out and die in silence. Philosophy admits that this is the last infirmity of noble minds. But yet an Astronomer who has taken any account of the vastness of the universe, should consider within what contemptible limits the widest fame circulates. Cicero was born in the very maturity of Roman glory, yet the fame of the Roman Republic had not then passed the Caucasus. How far then could the name of its noblest citizen have travelled? Perhaps, however, it is the fame of being a philosopher that he covets? His monitress can tell him a good story about that ambition. A man who wanted to pass himself for a sage was told by a severe critic, that he should acknowledge him to be one, if he could bear injuries mildly and patiently. The aspirant exhibited patience under some affront, and then exclaimed, "Do you think that I am a philosopher now?" "I should have thought so," said the keen-sighted judge, "if you had held your tongue." But after all, so Philosophy concludes this portion of her lessons, "I have a good word to say for fortune as well as a bad one. There is a time when she acts as a real benefactress to man. When she smiles sweetly upon him, she is a liar; when she changes her tone and proves her instability, she is always true. In her first shape she is tempting men away from the true good; in her second she is bringing them back to it."

The glory of being a philosopher.

The march for good.

28. It will be remembered that there was another letter besides Π upon the garment of Philosophy. She proceeds in the third book to show what was the meaning of that higher and more mysterious symbol. She is not content with showing that there is no satisfaction in those outward things which fortune presents. There is a meaning, and a very deep meaning, in the longing of men after them, in the variety of their longings, in the evidence which one could produce that that of the other is insufficient. There is a craving for Good, for the highest Good, in the heart, and will, and reason of men; nay, all lower things, all the animals and forms of nature, are in their way, looking up to it and sighing after it. All men, all creatures, want happiness. They say happiness is the *good* they want. How many mists are scattered from their minds when they reverse the proposition, when they look upon the Good as itself their happiness, when they look upon that as drawing up all other ends into itself, power, reverence, glory, joy! when

they see that the Good must be One, and that the One must be The good to
God? That first confession of Boethius which he could not abandon man is the
amidst all his scepticism about the chances of man's life, that there same with Him who
was an order in Nature, and not an order only, but an Orderer, an governs the world.
actual living Ruler,—was not then in vain. That belief was a step
towards the solution of his other and practical difficulty. This
Ruler of nature, in whom is no disorder, no evil, is the Good of
man, that which he is created to seek for and to participate in.
And so this book is wound up with a song respecting Orpheus
and Eurydice, which concludes with these remarkable words:—
" ' We give thee back thy wife,' says the pitiful ruler of the shades,
" ' we give thee her whom thou hast won by thy song. But let
" ' this law control the gift. Till she has left Tartarus, turn not back Orpheus and
" ' thine eyes.' Who can lay down a law for lovers? Love is a Eurydice; the moral of
" greater law of itself. Alas! close to the very limits of night and the tale.
" day, Orpheus looks upon his Eurydice; he loses her; she dies. To
" you this fable refers, whosoever you are, who seek to draw your
" minds towards the upper day. He who being overcome, shall turn
" them towards the cave of Tartarus, loses the bright thing that is
" attracting him, while he gazes upon that which is beneath.'

29. All this is beautiful and divine, our prisoner exclaims, and New doubts.
I was not altogether ignorant of it before. But the old doubt and
misery recur. There is this good Ruler of the universe. But evil
exists, exists unpunished and rewarded. That this should be so,
in the kingdom of a God who knows all things, can do all things,
and who wills only good, one cannot wonder or lament enough.
Philosophy at once grapples with the difficulty, admits that it
would be a thing of infinite horror, beyond all conceivable
monstrosities, if in the beautifully ordered house of such a parent
and economist, vile vessels were honoured, and precious vessels
were lying useless and dusty. Once admit that bad men are
mighty and good men weak, and you must deny a righteous
government altogether. But it is not so, says the celestial teacher.
I will undertake to show you that the good are always mighty,
and the bad always feeble. Once lay hold on this truth and you
will have wings which will lift you on high; you will return under
my guidance, to your proper country and home. Boethius
is astonished at the magnificence of the promise. Philosophy Evil essen-
proceeds, by a Socratic or inductive process, to bring him to a tially weak.
perception of her principle. We will give the result. A man is
weak who fails of obtaining that which he seeks after; he is strong
who reaches it. The appetite for Good has been proved to be in
all men. Every man wants Good, wishes to get it. The bad man
is frustrated of this aim, by misunderstanding what it is, or by
inclinations which draw him aside from it. As we heard just now,
the Orpheus, from looking downwards instead of upwards, loses

his Eurydice. He who seeks Good, gains what he seeks. Can there be a greater test of his power? For what does he seek but Good? Wherein is he good, except as he seeks Good? What reward can be so great as that of finding it? Here, then, is the

Evil always punished, good rewarded.
solution of another difficulty. The evil man is unpunished, the good is unrewarded? No, verily. The evil man has the greatest punishment which it is possible for him to have; he misses Good, he finds Evil. Or, does he find Good? Then that draws him out of his Evil. He has got the thing which, as a man, he was to seek after; but he has got the thing which, as an evil man, he was not seeking after. Any way the evil has been disappointed; that has been punished. The old Platonic principle is true. Only the wise man is able to do that which he wills to do. The bad man does what he has a *liking* for; but his desire is not accomplished; he has not what he wills. Nothing is so mighty, we have agreed, as the highest Good. All that approaches that, and shares in its nature, has a portion of its might; all that recedes from it, is imbecile. In the course of the argument, the great maxim is affirmed; an evil man cannot be said, properly and truly, to be a man. That *is*, which retains its order and preserves its nature. We may call a carcase the remains of a man; we cannot speak of it as if it were one.

Reward and punishment.
30. In these words is implied a view of the nature of punishment as well as of blessedness, which the teacher proceeds to develop. It is in perfect accordance with the principle of Plato's Gorgias. For an evil man to escape punishment, is the most terrible of all punishments; to be brought into punishment, that which he should most desire. The fixedness in evil, a permanent continuance in that, is the horror of all horrors. The threefold calamity of evil men, says the teacher, would be this: to have the will to do it, to have the power to do it, to accomplish it. "Granted, says Boethius. But oh that I could see them quickly deprived of this calamity, the possibility of perpetrating their crime!" "They will be deprived of that possibility, sooner than you, perhaps, may think, or than they themselves may think. There is nothing so distant within the short bounds of life, which an immortal spirit can count it long to wait for. Ofttimes the great hope and high machinery of wickedness is cast down by a sudden and unexpected overthrow, whereby the boundary of the misery (*i.e.* the misery of successful wickedness)

The misery of the wickedness to continue wicked.
is determined for them. For if iniquity makes miserable, the iniquitous man must be more miserable the longer he lasts. I should count him to be most wretched, if there were no ultimate death to terminate his wickedness. For if we have come to a true conclusion respecting the misfortune of depravity, it is clear that that which is an eternal wickedness, is an infinite misery." There is one passage in this inquiry which, though it is not much dwelt upon,

must be quoted by us, for its connection with thoughts which were
to be more developed afterwards. "I pray thee, says Boethius,
dost thou admit no punishment of souls after the death of the
body?" "Great ones indeed, answers Philosophy, some of which I
judge to be exercised with the bitterness of retribution, some with
purgatorial clemency." One sentence more we must quote from
this part of the treatise. "Hence," says Philosophy, "it comes to pass
"that among wise men, no place is left for hatred. For who, but
"the most foolish, would hate the good? To hate the evil is irra- *Folly of*
"tional. For if, as languor is a disease of bodies, so all vice is a *hatred.*
"disease of minds: seeing that we do not consider the sick in body
"worthy of hatred but rather of pity, much more are *they* to be
"pitied, not pursued with hostility, whose minds that more terrible
"disease is tormenting with every kind of feebleness."

31. The remainder of this 4th book is occupied with a discussion *Fate and*
on Fate and Providence. The views of Boethius very closely *providence.*
resemble those of Proclus, of which we have given our readers
some account. The generation of all things, says Philosophy, the
whole progress of natures that are liable to change, derives its
causes, its order, its forms, from the stability of the Divine Mind.
This, fixed in the citadel of its own simplicity, hath devised a
method in the conduct of things, which hath many varieties.
When this method is contemplated in the purity of the Divine
Intelligence, it is named *Providence;* but when it is referred to
those things which it moves and disposes, the Ancients called it
Fate; which two will be easily recognized as diverse, by any one
who has contemplated in his mind the force of both. For
Providence is that divine Reason constituted in the highest Ruler,
which disposeth all things. But Fate is that disposition inherent
in things subject to movement, whereby Providence binds all
things together in their own orders. Providence embraces all *Fate always*
things equally, although diverse, although infinite; but Fate directs *subject to*
individual things, each to its own proper movement, distributing *providence.*
them in forms and times. "So that the unfolding of this temporal
order becomes Providence, when it is harmonized in the perception
of the Divine Mind; and that same harmony, when it is distributed
and unfolded in times, is called Fate. Which things, though they
are diverse, nevertheless, one dependeth on the other." A little
farther on she says: "That which departs farthest from the primary
Mind, is involved in greater and closer bands of Fate; conversely
each thing is free from this Fate in proportion as it approaches nearer
to the hinge and centre of things. Whatsoever clings to the firm-
ness of the higher Mind, being freed from motion, rises also above *How to rise*
the necessity of Fate. Therefore, what reasoning is to the intellect, *above fate.*
what that which is produced is to that which is, what Time is to
Eternity, what the circle is to the centre, that is the moveable

series of Fate to the stable simplicity of Providence." Proceeding from these great maxims, she maintains that however confused and disturbed things may appear to our eyes, nevertheless, there may be a Method which is directing all things to good. "For there is," she says, "a certain order which embraceth all things, so that what hath departed from the course that was marked for it, may, perchance, fall into another order, but still into an order, that nothing in the realm of Providence may be left to chance, or wilfulness." But she adds reverently: "It is not right or possible for a man to comprehend in his mind, and explain in his discourse, all the mechanism of the Divine operations. Be it enough for us to have seen just this, that the same God who has called all natures into existence, disposes all, directing them to good; that He is eager to retain in the likeness of Himself, that which He hath produced; that through that very course of fatal necessity, He is driving all evil out of the boundaries of His republic." She draws this practical inference from all that she has said. "All fortune must be good to those who are possessing and pursuing virtue; all must be bad to those who are remaining in wickedness. It is in your hands to make fortune what you would have her be. For all which seems harsh, unless it either exercises or corrects, punishes."

The ends of the divine will may be known; its means we see but partially.

32. The last book of the Consolations discusses at length the question of free-will and its relation to Prescience. Boethius declares his utter dissatisfaction with the ordinary attempts to reconcile God's foresight with Man's freedom. Once attribute all will and all power to the Foreseer, and it seems to him utterly impossible to suppose that the knowledge of the future does not involve a decree respecting it. We will give a portion of the answer which Philosophy makes, hoping that we may so tempt our readers to study the whole of it:—

Free-will and prescience.

"That God is eternal, is the common judgment of all rational "beings. Let us consider then what eternity is, for this may show us "both what is the divine nature and the divine knowledge. Eternity "then is the whole and perfect possession of interminable life; which "we may apprehend, by comparing temporal things with it. For "whatsoever lives in time, this being present, proceeds from past to "future; and nothing is constituted in time, which can embrace at "once the whole space of its own life. It hath not yet apprehended "to-morrow, it hath lost yesterday; in the life of to-day you live no "longer than in the moveable and transitory moment. Whatever, "therefore, suffers the condition of time, even though it neither ever "began to be, nor ever should cease to be, (as Aristotle supposed "was the case with the world) and though its life should stretch into "an infinity of time, yet it is not such that it deserves to be called "eternal. For it does not comprehend and embrace the whole at

Eternity.

Difference between eternity and infinity.

"once, even though it be that space of infinite life; the future not
"being yet accomplished, *that* it has not." He goes on to vindicate
Plato from the charge of making the world eternal, pointing out
the difference between the *perpetuity* which he supposed might
belong to it, from the *eternity* which he vindicates only for God.
And then he goes on: "Seeing then that every judgment takes in
"the things that are subjected to it, according to the nature of him
"who exercises it; seeing that there is always an eternal and present
"state in God; His knowledge also, transcending all motion of time,
"dwells in the simplicity of its ever present; He embracing all the
"spaces of past and future, contemplates them as if they were now
"carrying on in his own simple cognition. Therefore, if you will
"weigh that present of His, wherein he knoweth all things, you will
"not call it the *pre-science* of the future, but the *science* of that which
"never ceases to be before Him. Therefore we do not call His
"government *previdence* but *providence*." The conclusion, therefore,
is, that supposing we have good reason to speak of anything as
necessary, or anything as free, we cannot be diverted from that
belief by the notion of God's prescience. His knowledge deals
with all things as they are, with those which He has constituted
free, as free; and it is only by introducing a notion of time into
His knowledge, which is inconsistent with his nature, that we fancy
it to be otherwise. And this is the practical lesson from the whole
matter, and the noble termination of a noble book.

Prescience cannot be predicated of an eternal being.

"Wherefore the liberty of will remains to mortals unviolated;
"nor are those laws unrighteous that hold forth rewards and punish-
"ments to Wills that are tied by no necessity. There remains also
"a Spectator from on high of all things, and the present eternity of
"His vision, concurs with the future quality of our acts, dispensing
"to the good, rewards, to the evil, punishments. Nor vainly are
"hopes and prayers laid up in God, which, when they are right,
"cannot be ineffectual. Wherefore, turn away from all vices,
"cultivate virtues, raise your mind to right hopes, send up humble
"prayers on high. Great, if you do not wish to deceive yourself,
"is the need of a clear and honest heart, since you are acting under
"the eyes of a Judge who discerneth all things."

33. Our readers may ask, with some surprise, how it is that the
man whom we have described, on what seems good evidence, as the
sturdiest of Aristotelians, even more in the habit of his mind than
from any sectarian bias, has begun, in his prison hours, to speak
the language of a Platonist, as if it were his native dialect. We
have already opposed the hypothesis which divides the author of
the Consolations from the author of the books on Arithmetic and
on the Categories, and we are not disposed to fall back upon it as
the solution of this difficulty. We can trace, we think, the same
style, the same intellectual peculiarities, the same conscientiousness,

Apparent Platonism of this treatise.

in both classes of writings; sides of the character of the Roman lawgiver and statesman appear in both. If Boethius had again turned his thoughts to numbers or to names, he would have been as much an Aristotelian in his latter days, as he was in his earlier.

But his practical and honest mind is brought into contact with questions, which predicaments and syllogisms do not help him to settle. He finds that, with all his dialectics, he is still a weak man. He had been more sagacious than his contemporaries. But it seems as if his sagacity had profited him little; it not only had not preserved him from the malice of his enemies; it could not teach him to bear that malice. He has done admirable things as a Minister of the Republic. When he recalls them to his mind, they deepen his despondency. He has been an excellent husband and father, therefore he has to suffer the loss of wife and children. We often fancy that the consolation of Philosophy, means the consoling thought that one is a philosopher and not like other people. That consolation which Boethius may have dwelt upon as

much as any one in his sunny hours, utterly deserts him in his dark hours. His discontent and murmurings, his discovery how important external things have been, and are, to him, reduce him into one of the crowd; before he can begin to ascend a step, he must sink lower than it seemed possible he could sink. And so he finds that he needs a hand to raise him out of himself, to set him above himself. He must be catechised, probed, exposed by one who knows him better than he knows himself. He must confess himself, apart from his guide and teacher, as helpless and worthless. He must trust and submit, in order to be exalted. Then, by degrees, he may be able to read the higher letter on the garment, as well as the lower. The teacher, who is with him and knows him, may guide him up to God. Theology cannot be a mere part of a scheme of sciences, something which is wanted for the sublime theoretic man, who has finished his circle of physical and human studies; it is needed for the man himself, for the prisoner, for him who has found that he is not better than his fathers or his neighbours. This is the road by which Boethius arrives at his Platonism, a Roman road cut out of the rock, because it was needed for actual use, for the soldier and the man to pass through. He demands a present Helper, he demands a divine Object, for his hope and trust. Such a One he has acknowledged as presiding over the world; such a One he finds must rule more directly over

his own life, and be the end and good of it. The righteousness which the Senator has tried to practise imperfectly, he finds had its root and ground in One who practises it perfectly. The wisdom which he thought belonged to himself, he finds must uphold him, guide him, correct him. He wants some better ideal than those of Genius, and Species, and Difference, and Property, and Accident.

An ideal he must have, and a substantial ideal. But the ideal must not be his own. It must come to him, and speak to him. He may escape from all Greek dæmonism as unworthy of his manlier race; but he can only do so by confessing a Being whose substance and eternity are not deduced from time, or negations of time. He may not have consciously changed any old conviction on this subject; but every one that he had before, has received a new character, has been translated into a higher meaning by the new knowledge which he has acquired of himself, of his weakness, of his necessities.

84. The conscience of men in the Middle Ages could not but perceive in this history of Boethius, that moral change, that turning of the heart and will from fleeting and temporal things, to the substantial, the living, and the true, of which the Scriptures spoke, and which all faithful preachers longed to be the instruments of producing in those who listened to them. Boethius described the instrument who wrought this alteration in him, who brought him back from his wanderings to his proper country and home, as Philosophy. The expression was manifestly a wrong one, inconsistent with his own previous belief, still more inconsistent with the processes of his own mind, as he records them. In a passage we have already quoted from his commentaries on Porphyry, he speaks of Philosophy as the love and pursuit of Wisdom, and assumes that there is a Wisdom implied in this pursuit, which is distinct from it. However dim that vision may have been to him whilst he was merely a schoolman, it acquired form and substance in his cell. Though he might represent his visitor and his judge in language drawn from the imagination, the use of that language, and the tenor of his discourse, which is anything but fantastical, which is severely true, shows that he felt that he was not merely *personifying*, but that, in the strictest sense, his heart and mind were laid open to the scrutiny of an actual *person*. It was a timidity, an excusable honest timidity, which made him resort to an unscientific phrase, rather than profess more than he felt he had apprehended or could distinctly affirm. But those who were familiar with the language of the book of Proverbs, and of the Prophets, could not but feel that if he had spoken of *Wisdom* as actually coming to him and holding converse with him, he would have more expressed what he meant, he would better have explained what true Philosophy is, and what the reward of it is, than he could do by appearing to clothe a passion or habit of his own mind, with a substance which does not belong to it. Feeling, therefore, that the process which he described was such as He whom they confessed to be the Divine Wisdom and Word, effects in man, Christian teachers did not hesitate to speak of Boethius as a Christian sage, to sit at his feet and to learn from him as one who could explain

Why the Middle Age doctors thought this a Christian book.

Philosophy a false name, but a real person.

to them divine, as well as human, mysteries. When they imputed to him a distinct recognition of Jesus Christ as the Incarnate Word and the Teacher of men, they distorted his phrases to their own wishes. When they confessed that He in whom they hoped and believed, had illuminated the spirit of Boethius, had led him by the path in which it was most accordant to his previous condition of mind that he should walk, into the apprehension of truths which all men need, and which are near to all; they were rising above their own narrow and imperfect notions; they were bearing one of the highest testimonies they could bear to the truth which they professed. And it is a subject for satisfaction, not for regret, that in collections of Doctors and Saints made in our own day, Boethius is still suffered to stand side by side with Popes, some of whom might not have been willing to stand side by side with him on earth, but who may, perhaps, rejoice if the Judge who discerneth all things permits them to stand with him in the world of light.

Return to Gregory.

35. We hope our readers will not complain of us for violating the strict order of events, that we might introduce them to a figure so remarkable in itself as that of Boethius, and occupying so remarkable a position between the eastern world and the western, between the old world and the new. We shall not detain them with any further notices of the time which elapsed between his death and the Popedom of Gregory the Great, but shall take up the history, where we left it at the conclusion of the last part, with the stirring annals of the 7th century.

CHAPTER II.

_____

SEVENTH, EIGHTH, AND NINTH CENTURIES.

1. PHILOSOPHY pointed Boethius to another letter on her vest, *Philosophy the guide to Theology.* different from that which denoted her own name. According to her method, the theologian must rise out of the ethical student; his discoveries are the complement of those which had been made in the Academy or the Porch. The actual order of human training, as the ages which followed Boethius set it forth to us, was the reverse of this. The Π and the Θ were to have the closest affinity *The process reversed.* with each other, to be woven on the same garment. But that which was hidden from the eyes of Boethius was to make itself apparent before the other; to manifest itself by its own light.

2. At the beginning of the 7th century, Constantinople, and its *Constantinople in the age of Heraclius.* monarch Heraclius, were occupied with a question in which the deepest mysteries of Metaphysics were involved with the deepest mysteries of Divinity. The disputes concerning the two natures of Christ, which had agitated former centuries, had given way to the more awful dispute respecting the two wills which were indicated by His conflict and agony. If we looked at this controversy *The Monothelite controversy.* from one side, we might pronounce it one of the most important and serious in which men were ever engaged—the gathering up of all previous disputes respecting freedom and necessity, respecting the relation of the Divine Will to the human, respecting the struggle in the heart of humanity itself. All these arguments *Its ideal importance.* would seem to be raised to their highest power, to be tested by their relation to the highest Person, to have reached the point where profound speculation and daily practice meet and lose themselves in each other. Contemplated from another side, this debate is worthy of all the contempt which indifferent onlookers bestow *What makes it actually insignificant* upon it as upon every other great topic of divinity. For the persons who were engaged in it were utterly frivolous. For them the whole subject involved a theory, and nothing more—a theory in which the most violent passions might be engaged, but which demanded no faith, which led to no moral act; the controversy was the more detestable because such living interests seemed to be concerned in it, while it was in fact but an exercise for the subtlety of an exhausted, emasculated race which had talked and argued itself

Rule to be
followed in
noticing de-
bates of this
kind.
into inanition and death. The historian of human inquiries has
no right to pause long upon this monothelite controversy, merely
because he perceives how much was implied in it. He is to measure debates not by their abstract importance, but by their effects
on the world. He must wait therefore in faith, assured that whatever truth is latent in the minds of mere inquirers will come
forth with power, possibly in some very startling, tremendous form,
to confound all who substitute intellectual conceits for living and
personal realities.

Greece and
Persia.
3. There were proofs in the reign of Heraclius, that the dormant
energies of the Greek people might still be awakened; but that the
awakening must come from the battles of the world, not of the
schools. Two old enemies were again brought face to face with
each other. It was not the dualism of the Magians that struggled
with the dualism of the Christians. The actual armies of Chosroes
threatened Constantinople. For a while it seemed as if the empire of the East might pass into his hands; in an incredible short
time it seemed equally probable that his dominion would be extinguished by the new and miraculous energy which was infused
Mahomet the
Interpreter of
the ideal bat-
tles of Ma-
gians and
Christians.
into the representative of old Roman greatness. Both expectations
were equally disappointed, by the appearance of a Conqueror whom
both despised. But his words and deeds carried out the moral of
the previous history. Mahomet proclaimed an actual God to men
who were disputing concerning His nature and attributes. Mahomet affirmed that there was an actual will before which the will
of men must bow down.

4. It was a tremendous proclamation. Philosophy shrinks and
shrivels before it. All ethical speculations are concluded by the
one maxim, that God's commands are to be obeyed; all metaphysical speculations are silenced by the shout, first of a man, then of
a host; "He is; and we are sent to establish His authority over the
earth." Christian Divinity appears to be still more staggered by
the message. All that was peculiar in it, all that was universal in
Apparently a
destroyer of
the old faith
and philoso-
phy of the
East.
it, and had affected the life of the world, had been connected with
the announcement of a Son of Man, who was also the Son of God.
The new teacher tramples upon that announcement, treats it as
part of the old idolatry. If philosophy and Christian divinity have
not hitherto been able to unite, have they not at least found a
common enemy? Has not that enemy a commission to destroy
them both?

Mahomet a
restorer of
the Greek
faith.
5. Mahomet, as we believe, had a commission to *restore* them
both. Nothing could have raised the Byzantine Christianity out
of the abyss into which it had fallen, but such a voice as that which
came from the Arabian cave. That voice proclaimed the eternal
truth which Greeks were disbelieving. It presented that truth in
the only form in which it could have been practical, in which it

could have told upon people who had talked about the divine and human nature, till they had lost all faith in God or man. What- Revival in the Byzantine Empire after his time. ever Constantinople has done for the world—and it has done much —since the days when Justinian collected the fragments of the old law together; whatever thoughts Constantinople was able to express—and the forms of her architecture show that these were neither few nor insignificant—she owed to the impression which Mahometan life and zeal made upon her, to the positive instruction which they imparted to her, to the reaction in favour of her own convictions, which was provoked by their denials. The glorious defence of the city at the end of the 7th century is the first great sign of the revival of native strength. The Iconoclast battle of the The controversy concerning image worship. 8th century is a still more striking evidence of that twofold influence of the prophet's doctrine to which we have referred. The Isaurian monarchs who determined with so much of the resolution of their prototypes, that Christians should no longer have the stigma of breaking the second commandment, and who enforced the decree with so much of the same tyranny and recklessness; the monks and the people, who rose with such passionate ardour to assert their right to their old symbols, and their belief that the Strong feeling and faith on both sides. human form had been hallowed by its union with the person of the Son of God, were separately and together testifying of the blessing which Mahometanism had conferred upon them. It was nothing like one of the miserable circus-fights of the 6th century. There was intolerance and passion; tyranny and rebellion; but there was faith and earnestness on each side. The conflict, though it bore witness of disease, bore witness also of a stronger health than the Greek empire had known for many centuries.

6. This collision of active principles was equally needed for the Obligations of Philosophy to Mahomet. life of Philosophy as of Theology. But the tendency of the Greek to dissever speculation from practice, made it less likely that *for him* the fruits of the conflict in this direction would be very conspicuous, or at least permanent. Constantinople did more for the Greece enabled to help others more than herself. rest of mankind than for its own subjects in communicating the old lessons of Greek wisdom. The Arabian caught them, mixed them with his ancient lore, and started from a soldier into a scholar. Western Europe, which was much more affected in its political circumstances by the Iconoclastic controversy than the empire in which it arose, also received a decided impression from it and from Mahometanism in the character of its culture, although that culture was destined to be singularly Latin, Gothic, original.

7. Gregory the Great, of whom we have already spoken, may How far the ideas of Gregory the Great resembled that of Mahomet. have been said, in one sense, to have anticipated Mahomet in the proclamation of a Will to which nations must submit, and of which armed men must hold themselves the servants. It was as much the thought of his mind to subdue the rude tribes of the West,

exulting in their strength and in their native traditions, under the
divine order and government, which he believed was exhibited
in the Son of Man, as it was the thought of Mahomet's mind to
make all the established societies and worships of the East stoop to
the one Lord, of whom he proclaimed himself the prophet. In
carrying out that purpose, Gregory would have been willing to
make Rome, in the one division of the earth, what Mecca became
for the other; he would have been glad that its decrees should
be established as firmly as any which Mahomet said that he was
appointed to deliver. Without any scheme of personal ambition,
he would have believed that this was the best and safest condition for Europe and for the world. There was much in the
condition of the West which favoured his purpose, much to thwart

it. It is curious, and worthy of remark, that the helps to it
lay in the character of the Gothic tribes which were afterwards
to be the great antagonists of Latin supremacy. The Gothic
spirit is essentially a kingly one; it rejoices in all exercises of will
and authority; it always prefers government to thought. It was
equally observable, that the hindrances to Roman rule arose in a
great measure from the tendencies which belonged to the Celtic
race. There we might have expected sympathy with sacerdotal

rule, for the mind of the Celt is cast in a sacerdotal mould; he
has far more reverence for the priest than for the king; to priestly
influences, in one form or another, he has owed both his civilization and his ignorance, both his freedom and his slavery. But the
reflective, contemplative character which is seen in the Brahmin of
the East, and the Druid of the West, has little sympathy with laws.
Words of command do not speak directly to his conscience, but
through his affections and his fears. The Celtic culture, though
wanting the freedom and humanity of the Greek, had much of its
speculative uplooking quality. It is always in search of an object
which is hidden; it does not readily submit to a power which has
made itself manifest.

8. These observations receive one of their earliest and most
striking illustrations in our own country. The strength of Gregory's Missionaries lay among our Saxon kings, and in the feelings
of the people, which responded to their government. The influence spread downwards from the royal household. English Christianity, from the beginning, was eminently national. Considering
how little there was of the national spirit in Augustine and his
followers, considering how completely they were the representatives of a man and a Church that would have wished to crush
nationality, the result is remarkable. But it must be observed, at

the same time, that this very circumstance favoured the ecclesiastical assumptions of the Missionaries and of the Pope. The
Saxon wanted such a dominion over the spirit, which he had just

learnt to consider the mightiest part of him, as he already confessed over his outward acts. He desired that his thoughts should be marshalled as his troops were marshalled. He longed for some one to tell the restless powers within him what the centurion told his servant, to go where they should go, to come where they should come. On the other hand, the Celts of Wales and of Ireland, who were already christianized, who, we might have fancied, would have been eager to fraternize with the new comers, who had so few national prejudices, so little of national order to keep them apart from foreigners, whose sympathies would have so much more inclined them to priestly ascendency than to any other, were utterly unable to recognize the demand which was made upon their obedience, could tolerate no Latin yoke, could not the least understand the arguments by which they were urged to part with old traditions for the sake of Christian unity. *A sacerdotal race not equally disposed to be governed.*

9. It is a mistake to suppose that these facts concern only the ecclesiastical or the general historian. The historian of philosophy is especially obliged to take notice of them. There had been, it is evident, a Celtic culture of a curious and interesting kind in the monasteries of Ireland and Wales, long before any Saxon schools were established under the influence of the Roman teachers. Modern French historians have spoken of Pelagius, the Welchman, as a great champion of spiritual freedom. We do not agree with them, if they mean to affirm that the doctrine which has been associated with his name has been favourable to manly strength, or brave resistance to oppression and wrong. With all its fierceness and severity, the Augustinian doctrine seems to us to have been, on the whole, in closer alliance with moral energy, with hope, even with liberty, than its milder opposite. But in so far as Pelagianism is the resistance to the assertion of a dominant will, in so far as it contemplates man as rather climbing up to God than as receiving his state and position from Him, so far it represents very accurately what we take to have been the predominant Celtic tendency, that to which the Saxon and the Latin were for different reasons equally opposed, that which when they understood each other they would conspire in putting down. How far the mere doctrine of Pelagius was diffused among the Celts, how far Celtic influences have conspired to make it the element which it unquestionably became in the after history of Christendom, we may not be able to ascertain. But we may assume that something of the habit of mind which it indicates was prevalent in the schools to which the pre-Gregorian Christianity gave birth. And if so, one can understand very well why that Christianity was not likely to produce any great effect in shaking the old Saxon traditions, however much it might mingle in their faith and leaven their education, after they were converted. *Pelagius. How far a supporter of moral freedom. Inefficiency of the Celtic teachers.*

The new
civilization
of England.

10. It was during the time that the Mahometan armies were
advancing with their resistless might over the kingdoms of the
East and of Egypt, that our island was gradually rising out of its
Paganism, and acquiring its second civilization from Roman hands.
That second civilization resembled the first, in that it was carried
on by a mighty organizing authority, which reduced the different
Barbaric elements it encountered into something like coherency.

How far it
resembled
the earlier
Roman civil-
ization.

It resembled the first in that it would never allow native feelings
and habits to interfere with the subjection to the central government, in that it dealt cautiously and humanely with all those habits
when they accepted that primary condition. But the new civilization, which was conducted by teachers and not legions; which
had to subdue a manly and warlike people, possessing convictions
and purposes of their own, not an effeminate and degraded people
over-ridden by a learned caste; a civilization above all which had
the principle of a divine Humanity for its basis; could not be of
that external superficial character which the first had been. For
the splendid dwellings, and baths and porticos, which had made
the British colony one of the most remarkable evidences of what
such governors as Agricola could effect among a people ignorant
of all the arts and comforts of life, the new Roman cultivators of

Monasteries:
Education.

the Saxon soil substituted monasteries and schools in which men
and boys were treated as spiritual beings connected with an invisible economy; in virtue of that high calling, able to till the earth
out of which they had been taken.

Theology of
the schools

11. The ground of this teaching was unquestionably theological.
It was a kingdom of God, into which the scholar was invited to
enter. God himself was calling him into that kingdom. The
theology was of course essentially Christian; the human studies
received their tone and impress from the belief in a Son of Man.
But Boethius, whose mind had so little of a theological basis, and
was at least three-fourths pagan, supplied the material with which
the Church Doctors worked. That scheme of studies which he

The course
of studies de-
rived from
Boethius.

had wrought out with so much skill and elaboration from Aristotle
and Porphyry, and to which he had imparted his own Roman character and force, reappeared in the schools of Britain. Arithmetic,
geometry, music, astronomy, assumed the places, or very nearly
the places, which he had assigned them. Other arts were contemplated in reference to these; their worth and dependence on
each other were ascertained by the same rules. It would be unwise
to suppose that the monks of the 8th century had any theory about
these studies, or that they understood upon what maxims the
curriculum had been marked out by the Minister of Theodoric.

How it came
to be adopted
by a Saxon
people.

They adopted it no doubt as a Roman tradition; they carried it to
the far West, as they carried other Roman traditions. They found
little in the Saxon mind which it was necessary to propitiate, when

this particular form of instruction was proposed to it. There was, we conceive, a suitableness in it to the time and to the previous condition of the people among whom it came. No other discipline would have reduced their minds into form as rapidly or as effectually. It may even be doubted whether any other would have done as much, for the freedom and the energy of their spirits.

12. This assertion may sound surprising after what was said in the last chapter respecting the tyrannical ascendency which logic assumed in the mind and in the plans of Boethius. But the whole character of *this* tyranny is changed by the introduction of what, some will call, another and more tremendous tyranny. The assertion of a divine Will which orders all things, but which acts directly upon men, which addresses itself, first of all, to the springs of thought in them—this assertion, so long as it is earnestly believed, makes it impossible for a man to feel himself subject to certain forms of the intellect; he may not have the distinct consciousness of anything in himself which surmounts them, but he cannot bow down before them while he practically confesses a higher and living authority. What purpose, then, does the study of these intellectual terms and conditions serve? It protects him from the suspicion, always ready to start up in his mind, that the divine Will which he confesses is a mere arbitrary power, recognizing no laws, bidding him perform certain services, execute certain commands. The Will which the Mahometan warrior and the Christian warrior, so far as he only adopted the Mahometan principle, felt that he must obey by smiting down the Lord's enemies, became an educating Will, which might be obeyed as reverently and as punctually by the student, while he examined into the modes which it had prescribed for his speech and his thought.

Value of Logic in this new civilisation.

How the belief of a Ruling Will conspires with the Logical teaching and tendency.

13. The frequenter of the monastic schools, it must not be forgotten, came to them as God's soldier, who was to learn to fight with words, as other soldiers fought with swords. Everything about him suggested the thought of a battle, and led him to regard his peculiar weapons with a reverence which might easily become excessive and dangerous. Whatever he studied had to do with words; not rhetoric only, but astronomy and geography must be learned through them. No doubt there were counteractions not only in the sensuous worship, but even in these studies themselves. The astronomer could never quite forget that there were actual stars over his head; the still calm evening was felt in the cloister; looked in through the windows of the church. Music spoke of a kind of intercourse for the human spirit to which words might minister, but to which they were not essential, and were always subordinate. Still it can scarcely be said that the lively talking Athenian, in the days when sophistry was most rife—or the grave Roman of the Republic, in the days when the oratory

The moral soldier.

All studies tending to become verbal.

of the Forum was most effective—was more in danger of becoming the victim of words, than the Christian student who saw all around him the trophies which the speaker had won over the helmet and the spear. If he had not been reminded by his studies that words themselves are subject to laws; if logic and grammar had not become the principal and most characteristic parts of his culture; he would have been more liable than he was, to abuse them as mere instruments of his craft. The protection might be very inadequate, the science itself might help at last to foster the tendency which it was designed to check. Then, we may be sure, there would be a rebellion; it would be, perhaps, hurled with dangerous precipitancy from its throne; that which it had kept down would be exalted. But, in the meantime, let us understand what it did for the education of Christendom, and be thankful.

Passage to the 9th century.
14. The remarks we have made refer especially to our own country, for a reason which we have given already. England participated much more obviously and immediately in what we have ventured to describe as the Christian side of the Mahometan revolution, than the other great countries of Europe. M. Guizot, in his History of French Civilization, has pointed out with admirable fairness how much the efforts of British missionaries in Germany prepared the way for the great political revolution in France, and anticipated the victories over the Pagan Saxons by Charlemagne. With equal truth, he has made an assertion which is less agreeable to our national vanity, that the Anglo-Saxon Church was far more directly under the influence of Rome than the Gallican Church; and that no men contributed to establish that influence over Europe
Boniface and the German missionaries preparing the way for Charlemagne.
more than Boniface and the other great English Christianizers of the land from which their fathers sprung. Far from dissembling that fact, we would proclaim it, since without it the distinctive character of our Anglo-Saxon cultivation, and its influence upon the cultivation, especially upon the philosophy, of other countries cannot, we think, be appreciated. We use the words *Anglo-Saxon* strictly, because we shall have presently occasion to show that there was another cultivation, another philosophical influence, of a very different kind, which proceeded from one part of our country. But it was *this* of which we must first speak, seeing that it is very remarkably connected with Christendom generally, and with France particularly, in that great crisis when the monarch of the Franks became the restorer of the Roman Empire in the West.

Influence of the empire of Charles on after times. Guizot, Histoire de la Civilisation de la France, v. ii. Leçon 20.
15. M. Guizot has shown with great skill and power that the dynasty of Charlemagne, which it has been the fashion to represent as so transitory, did in fact produce the most permanent effects upon the condition of Christendom. At the same time he considers there is a justification of the ordinary opinion in the fact that the most glaring and startling part of his policy, that which

makes most impression upon the imagination, was the part which
faded most rapidly away. His victories over German Pagans
and over Saracens, his capitularies, his schools, were to affect
for ever the civilization of the world; the empire itself was
soon dispersed into the elements out of which it was unnaturally
compacted. It is not inconsistent with this observation—it is a
natural deduction from the observations which M. Guizot has made
on Charlemagne as the introducer of the monarchical principle into
a society which was utterly loose and disjointed from the want of it,—
if we observe that the conception of the empire is almost inseparable from those results which are so justly affirmed to have
been a possession for all ages. The fragmentary world which we
see in the West before the commencement of the 9th century,
could present no front to that Eastern world to which the faith of
Mahomet had given organization; no, not even after that world had
divided itself into its various portions, after it had been proved that
the elements of schism existed in the hearts and the breasts of
those who proclaimed the one God and the one prophet. The
Abbassides, the Ommyiades, the Fatamites, had each a cohesion,
and therefore a strength, which was exhibited in no nation of the
opposing faith. The question had to be resolved, whether there
could be a bond in any nation, or in all the nations, which confessed the Son of God, as close as that which held the Islamites
together. Upon the answer to this question, if we have stated the
case rightly, depended not merely the political condition of Western
Europe, but quite as much its internal growth and education: the
belief of an all-ruling Will was as necessary for the formation of
schools as for the subjugation of feudatories. The people would
have been as little taught as they would have been governed, if
the possibility of such a supremacy had not been asserted. The
form which the assertion took, was derived, no doubt, from the
self-will and ambition of a man, and therefore could not abide.
Yet, as his self-will and ambition served to counteract another
which was equally dangerous—as the experiment of an empire at
once explained, upheld and checked the experiment of a Popedom
—it had its worth, and it survived in new and varying forms after
it had been proved to be artificial, and full of danger as well as
weakness. While it lasted, it gave a tone to the mind and thought
of the age, which remained and became stronger and more distinct
in subsequent ages.

16. Charlemagne was in fact carrying out the idea which
Gregory had done so much in his day to substantiate—carrying it out in that new shape which the antagonism of Islam
suggested, carrying it out with the aid of that country which was
the great trophy of Gregory's zeal, and upon which he had impressed so much of his character. We should be suspicious

The Empire
itself neces-
sary to the
organization
of the West.

The Empire
and the
Popedom.

Ateuts the
ally of
Charles in
the work of
organiza-
tion.

of our own patriotic leanings in the emphasis which we put upon this last fact, if the eminent Frenchman, to whom we have just alluded, had not attached even more importance than we should be willing to attach to the influence of Alcuin of York upon the schools of Gaul; and if we were not conscious of rather a disin-

clination to celebrate the praises of that worthy ecclesiastic. A man deficient in originality and depth of thought, who incurred little odium, who seems to have suffered little in his own mind, who knew all that was to be known in his time, who wrote graceful prose and tolerable poetry, who had abundance of civil offices and ecclesiastical patronage, who was the tutor of princes and the favourite of monarchs, who lived very comfortably and died very rich—such a man is not one whom we need go out of our way to eulogize, or whom we are eager to reckon in the roll of the heroes whom England has nourished and sent forth. When we speak of him it is not to claim any merit for him or for ourselves, but simply to

show why the education he had received prepared him to be the minister of a man immensely his superior in genius; why Charlemagne found in a school of Northumbria a teacher not as able as many in his proper dominions, but far fitter than any of them to give that form and character to the schools of the empire which Charlemagne would have desired that they should assume.

17. Charlemagne's work was to bring an anarchy into an order, to show the warring races over which he ruled, that they were under a law which could and would be enforced. The education of a devout monk, bent upon subjecting the minds of men or of children to the rule of his order, would not have conspired with this purpose; *that* rule would have been altogether different in kind from the rule or law of the kingdom; the respect for one would have clashed with the respect for the other. The education of a philosopher, making it his primary and definite object to awaken the energies and faculties of his pupils, might have raised up remarkable men, but would not have constructed a school that would have been the model of a state, and the preparation for it.

Alcuin had been trained in the schools of Britain; under royal, quite as much as monastic influences; in a Roman discipline. He had been taught first of all that moral laws were to be obeyed because they proceeded from the highest Lawgiver; next he had been tutored in the laws of logic and grammar, as derived from the same authority. He was just enough of a questioner to be able to understand for himself what others imparted; not enough of one to be embarrassed with

any serious mental perplexities. He was enough of an Englishman to feel the influence of English government and institutions, and to take an interest in the disputes of the English sovereigns; he was not enough of one to be hindered from receiving a purely Latin culture, or from writing a Latin style, in which are few rugged native idioms: he could dwell happily on a soil remote from that of his birth, and in an empire governed by maxims unlike those under which he had grown up. With nothing irregular or angular in his intellect or character, well-natured, well-nurtured, even and tame, he was the very ideal of a court tutor in the best sense of the word; one who might perhaps have sunk into a mere machine, *in usum Delphini*, in the age of Louis XIV.; but who was quite competent to receive an inspiration from the mind of a Charlemagne, and to fill up the blanks which his sagacity perceived, and his ignorance could not supply.

18. Amidst the mass of Alcuin's writings, in which there is much of grace and little of individuality (even his letters, rather furnishing helps for the study of history than any illustrations of himself), those which relate to the education of the princes and of Charles himself are incomparably the most interesting and the most worthy of study. These exhibit him in his true vocation, not as a respectable theologian or a third-rate *littérateur*, but as an actual doer of work; as training the minds of actual boys, as opening new thoughts to a full-grown man, the most remarkable of his time. When thus brought into collision with life and practice, Alcuin rose to a stature far above his ordinary one; he acquired an insight which no books would have given him; he was able—not certainly to determine but—to point out the course in which his successors for a long time would have to travel. To the children, and to the father alike, he gave lessons in logic. The former may or may not have profited by his instructions. As they took a catechetical form, the dulness of the subject *to them* may have been relieved by the interest of the method. To Charles himself there was probably no dulness in the study which required any such alleviation. It must have been to him like the acquisition of a new sense, or rather like the opening of a new world, to be told what laws he had been unconsciously obeying in his commonest discourse. The wonder to himself would have made him all the more solicitous that such instructions, so invigorating to the faculties and yet so legal, so *capitular*, should be communicated to his subjects. And so the vigorous sense of the warrior quickening the dogmas of the schoolmaster, was the means of giving an intellectual tone to the 9th century, wholly unlike that of the previous one.

19. France, not England, is the country to which we naturally turn in this century, the one especially by which its philosophical character must be judged of. For reasons which we have stated at sufficient length already, the philosophy of that period can in no wise be separated from its theology; less separated even, as we shall have to show presently, than the acutest and ablest commentator upon it has supposed. The great theological subjects that

As a schoolmaster greater than as a theologian or philosopher.

Logic for boys and men.

Character of the 9th century.

Paschasius;
Godeschal-
chus; eccle-
siastical
questions

were debated in it, were that concerning the Eucharist, which was raised by Paschasius Radbertus, and that concerning Predestination, which was raised by Godeschalchus. With these were mixed the ecclesiastical questions concerning the relations of bishops to the inferior clergy, concerning the relations of national bishops to the bishop of Rome, concerning his relation to the Greek Metropolitan, which are associated with the names of Hincmar, Nicholas I., and Photius. The latter we shall avoid as much as possible, though the historian of philosophical inquiries can never forget that they were pending, and that they stand in close relation to those with which he is more properly occupied. On the questions of divinity we shall touch just as far as it is necessary for our purpose, not seeking them or dwelling upon the history of them at any length; but, on the other hand, not shrinking from them under pretext of their mysterious character, or of the fierce strifes which they have occasioned, when we perceive that by overlooking them we should leave a void in the records of human thoughts and struggles which would make later passages in these records incoherent and unintelligible.

The two
Saxons

20. Godeschalchus was a Saxon by birth. Michelet, who is always quick, sometimes over-quick, in detecting the effect of race upon opinions and habits of mind, has been careful to draw the attention of his readers to this fact. They owe him thanks for doing so. But the biographer of Luther ought not to have suggested a parallel between the Saxon of the 9th, and the Saxon of the 16th century, without pointing out—not the differences only but—the glaring contrast of the two men and the two periods. It may be quite true, as Luther affirmed in his controversy with Erasmus, that the doctrine of the natural slavery of man's will, and of its incapacity to emancipate itself, lay at the foundation of all his teaching, of his whole reformation; that without it his doctrine concerning faith would mean nothing, or mean directly the reverse of that which it signified to him. He may, therefore, have justified his Saxon blood and his relationship to Godeschalchus, by asserting the supremacy of the Divine Will, in terms as absolute as those which he used; with the same indifference to the effect of broad statements upon the minds of his hearers; with the same pleasure in defying their feelings and convictions if they interfered, or seemed to interfere, with the object that was directly before him; with the same recklessness of any consequences that he might draw down upon his reputation or upon his person. But here the resemblance ends. The idea of emancipation of man from bondage was that which was present to Luther in all his fiercest words and acts. In the light of that idea they all have their explanation; separated from it they are unintelligible. No such idea seems ever to have dawned on the mind of Godeschalchus; at all events it can never have been the predominant principle of his life. The

Their resem-
blances.

Their great
differences.

very opposite idea to this, that of a crushing, overwhelming sovereignty, which had a right to lift up itself and to trample on all that opposed it, seems to have governed him, and to have given all the direction to his thoughts. There is a dark sublimity in this idea, a profound meaning in it, as the Islamite had proved: one which can prompt to great acts of daring and endurance. But instead of being connected, as it was in the 16th century, with the victory of the living man over rules and circumstances, with an escape of the heart and spirit from the prison-house of logic in which they had been shut up, the doctrine of Godeschalchus was one of the great symptoms that an age was beginning in which the human intellect, for great and wise purposes, would be permitted to pass through a discipline of rules and formalities, and to enclose itself within those bars which in due time it would take all human and all divine aid to smite asunder. *The Logician and the Man.*

21. This difference we have pointed out is in nothing more remarkable, than in the use which the two Saxons made of the illustrious doctor to whom they both appealed. Augustine was to Luther a living man who had under different circumstances fought the battle which he was fighting, who had taken nothing by mere tradition till the necessities of his own being had demanded it. The Confessions, whatever he might think himself, were ten times more to him than all the dogmatical and controversial treatises in which the bishop of Hippo had expounded his maturest conclusions and crushed his opponents. The latter were only intelligible to him through the former. But what had all the Manichean conflicts of Augustine—those in which he had learnt through the mighty pressure of evil in himself, to feel that the Creator and Ruler, whom he was resisting, must be absolutely good—to do with the dogmatists of the 9th century? It was propositions that they wanted, not battles; distinct formulas that could be quoted and pleaded as decisive against all disputants. The anti - Pelagian treatises of Augustine, severed from the context of his life, must be their armoury. If they could fetch from thence phrases—and abundance of such were to be found—which reinvested the Creator with all the attributes of the destroyer, why were such words less useful and available because Augustine might in other days have been led to perceive more profoundly than almost any man, the eternal opposition between them? The older decree of course repealed the earlier. The question whether a man can repeal himself, can repeal the truths in which he lives and moves, was not one which Godeschalchus, or the greater part of his opponents, would be likely to meddle with. It was a war of logic, of formal propositions on this side and on that side. This was the character which the schools of Alcuin and Charlemagne almost inevitably gave to it. But here again, that which seems to make the case other. *What Augustine was to each of them.* *The wrestler for life, and the utterer of dogmas.* *Theology and Logic gaining and suffering from each other.*

worse, is really the redeeming point in the story. The logical wars of the Christian Latins could never become like the wars of Alexandrian or Athenian sophists—they never could be merely word-fights. The deepest moral interests were felt to be involved in them. Theology received from logic a portion of its dryness and formality; logic received from theology its personality and vehemence. But as the theologian gained from his ally the sense of an order which Omnipotent decrees did not set aside, the logician acquired from the higher science—not exactly humanity,—but some of the precious attributes of humanity, zeal, and self-devotion.

The ecclesiastical debate. 22. What we have said of the 9th century is not therefore spoken in the way of complaint. That century had its characteristic infirmities and its characteristic merits. Both were of an intellectual kind, arising out of the great school movement, which was itself a reforming movement, and connected with reforms of another kind. The logical tendency, as such, was opposed to mere sensualism and the coarser kinds of idolatry, though it might, by accident, give them a strength and fixedness which they could not have had without it. This is a distinction which should be always remembered by Protestants, when they pass judgment upon Paschasius and upon the age which brought forth into definite form the dogma of Transubstantiation. We naturally associate with that name a violent outrage upon the intellect; we look upon it as a reduction of that which is in the highest sense spiritual, under the laws of the senses. The Intellect, not the Senses, the origin of their Theory. There is enough in the controversies to which the doctrine of Paschasius immediately gave rise—in the conclusions which his contemporaries not only deduced from it but readily adopted—to justify all that can be said by divines about the degradation of a mystery, or by philosophers of the frightful demands which authority can make upon the reason. But neither can set aside the plain testimony of history, that the dogma was not forced upon the understanding from without, but was demanded by it; that the restless eagerness of a logical age to get theology Not popular, but scholastic. represented in the form of logic, its impatience of any principle which it could not so represent; this, and not any popular craving for a more visible embodiment of that which the eye cannot see, made the opinion which Paschasius put forth—without any especial encouragement from ecclesiastical rulers, very much in obedience to an impulse of his own mind—acceptable either to people or Not invented by ecclesiastical authorities, but imposed upon them. priests. It may be said, without any error or paradox, that the categories governed the doctors, and that the doctors governed the bishops and popes. The people might be ready enough to worship and deify symbols; but of the theory they knew nothing. Those who constructed it, believed that they were hindering the idolatry of that which is seen and tangible, by making it inseparable from that which is divine and eternal.

23. When we say that the understanding of Paschasius and his
supporters rather led than followed the authorities of the church
in his own day, we do not, of course, overlook the fact that they
appealed to the authorities of the great church teachers who had
preceded them. The appeal resembled that of Godeschalchus to the
writings of Augustine, with this important difference. Independently of all opinions on the subject of the Eucharist, contemporary
or ancient, there was the festival itself existing in every church. It
was the acknowledged witness of the relation in which communicants
stood to each other, and to men at the greatest distance from them,
with whom they had never conversed, whom they had never even
seen. By the men of the earlier time this festival could not be
contemplated without reference to the sacrifices which they saw
among the Pagans about them, and to the feasts which accompanied these sacrifices. It signified to their minds that what all
these services were pointing to, had been effected. It commemorated
that deliverance and reconciliation as accomplished for men by God,
which they were seeking to procure by their efforts. The missionaries among the Pagans of Germany might still feel the force
of this comparison; upon an organized Christian society, like that
of France, it was lost almost entirely. The consciousness of deep
and permanent necessities in the heart might, to many a humble
worshipper, be a substitute—far more than a substitute—for the
evidence of them which the inventions of men supplied. But he
would be unable to express what he needed or what he received;
often he would slide back into the very habits which the old services
had embodied, from which the new was to be a deliverance. The
schoolman would feel himself bound to make the wayfarer understand himself and his own acts, would try to show him his dangers. To do so more effectually, he would recur to the reverend
witnesses of other days; he would quote their words confidently
in defence of inferences into which he had been led by processes
of his own mind. They would mean something like—perhaps
something very like—what he meant; nay, he might be sure
that the meaning, the main sense, was identical. But being
entirely unable to put himself into their circumstances, to live
their life, that which was practical in them would translate itself
into a logical conception in him, while he believed that he was
giving the words their natural, their only possible, force. To be
sure he might be puzzled when he found his opponents quoting
from the same teacher, words that seemed to have an opposite
force, that translated themselves into formulas of an opposite
kind; he might, we say, be puzzled; as we descend lower in
the history of thought in the Middle Ages, we shall discover
how much he was puzzled, and to what remarkable and interesting speculations the discovery gave rise. But at present

[margin notes:]
Appeal to the old Doctors.
The difference of their positions.
How words are translated from life into formulas.
Opposing dogmas in the same writer.

the sheer force of conviction, the assurance of the man, that the
sense which he had seen was in the words, and that no other
ought to interfere with it, carried him over all such obstacles, and
made the controversies of the time very earnest and serious, if
they looked also very hopeless. The hopelessness made it necessary that a present authority should interfere. National councils
must decree which of the two conclusions was safe, must anathe-
matize the other. Their decisions being sometimes contradictory,
sometimes reversed, Popes who held the balance, who if they were
judicious decided as rarely as they could, who made the weight of
their decisions felt by suspending them, who were swayed by a
thousand influences themselves to the right and to the left, at last
uttered the word which sometimes destroyed the equilibrium
by affirming one opinion, sometimes preserved it by condemning
both.

24. These different relations between thought and decrees, reasoning and authority, were illustrated again and again in the
ecclesiastical history of the 9th century; in the controversy respecting Predestination, even more than in that respecting the Eucharist.
We introduce the subject here, because there is no one upon which
writers are in the habit of pronouncing so peremptorily, and none
upon which the careful student of the Middle Ages finds it so
hard to make up his mind, and yet so necessary to obtain some
greater clearness than the commonplaces which are current among
us afford him. The notion that, in these ages, authority was everything, and reason nothing, is one which only the most careless
retailer of 18th century dogmas can fall into. But the most
intelligent and painstaking inquirers are puzzled by the union of
restless speculation with servile submission to great names, which
they discover in the most eminent thinkers of this time. Sometimes they are disposed to remove the puzzle by describing the
schoolmen as a set of men who begged their premises, and then
gave themselves unceasing occupation in drawing inferences from
them. There is much excuse for this way of stating the case. A
logical age is an age of deduction. It is not occupied in seeking
the grounds upon which nature or man stands; it is glad to assume
them. But we shall have continual proofs as we proceed, how
much there was in the minds of the students of this time which
thwarted this inclination, how they were driven back upon premises,
how very often they sought the teachers of the past not to furnish
them with maxims for stopping investigation, but to guide them
in conducting it. We are adopting the worst of their habits, forgetting the profitable lessons which they might teach us, if we try
to bind the history by any anticipations of ours, if we do not suffer
it to tell us the actual road which the men of a past time took, when
it seems to us ever so winding, when we can reconcile it ever so little

with the charts of it which we have been used to consult. They often described wearisome circles, rushed vehemently into *culs de sac*, wandered about a labyrinth, vainly demanding an outlet. But we may surely believe that their way was foreseen, that they had a Guide, that there was a method which all these bewilderments were to help them in finding out. Thus much we may perceive, 1st, That they wanted to discover the ground on which they *were* standing, even when they were building towers high and reaching to heaven upon the ground on which they *supposed* they were standing; 2d, That they could not wait for this discovery, before they acknowledged a present Guide who directed their steps, a present Lawgiver who determined that which was right and wrong in their acts. How to reconcile the search for a law with this recognition of a Lawgiver; how to find a Lawgiver in whose decrees they could trust, and who should not merely decree, but should know them and help them to know,—this is a question which God's history, and not men's conjectures, must resolve.

25. These remarks are a necessary preface to the life and works of a very remarkable man, *the* Metaphysician of the 9th century, and we conceive one of the acutest Metaphysicians of any century. We speak of Johannes Scotus, John the Irishman, who was involved in both the great controversies to which we have alluded, who earned honour and disgrace in both, who was recognized by his contemporaries as a strange and notable figure, but who failed to influence them, and has failed to leave any apparent impression of himself upon after times. He has obtained a distinct recognition from some of the most thoughtful men of *our* time, but has scarcely, we think, been rightly appreciated by them, either in the points wherein he was strong, or in those wherein he was feeble. We have called him a great *Metaphysician*, choosing that word in contradistinction from a great *Moralist*, which we think he was not, choosing it in preference to the title *Philosopher*, which he fully deserves, but which has been bestowed upon him in a sense that seems to us erroneous and misleading. We have referred with so much admiration to Guizot's Lectures on French Civilization, and he is in many respects so much safer as well as so much more attractive a guide into the history of Middle Age Philosophy, as well as of Middle Age Politics, than almost any we can avail ourselves of, that it becomes an especial duty to explain when we are obliged to desert his guidance, when we think it tends to confuse us respecting the history of a particular man, or of an age, or of a series of ages. His 29th lesson on the subject of Johannes Scotus is perilous, we think, in all these respects. We shall make no apology for commencing our observations on that author, by a few criticisms upon this lecture, having a strong persuasion that most of our readers will be already acquainted with it, and urging those who

are not to read it along with our observations. Though it must influence them, like all the words of so eminent a writer, we believe that the mistakes of a real student of history are more instructive than the accurate statements of inferior observers.

Histoire de la Civilisation en France, vol. II., p. 364.

26. M. Guizot has selected Hincmar and Johannes Erigena as embodying, one the theological, the other the philosophical, tendencies of the time. In his previous Lecture he had, however, shown very clearly that Hincmar has no claim whatever to the position which he has here, for the convenience of finding a "representative man," assigned him. Hincmar is the acute ecclesiastical politician and ruler of his time; almost any of his contemporaries, Paschasius, Godeschalchus, Rabanus Maurus, we should imagine, would have served better to illustrate that "*élément théologique*" which he is called in to show forth. We might therefore be less surprised to find, notwithstanding M. Guizot's ordinary caution, that the other "representative man"—he who is to exhibit the opposite élément to the theologique—does not exactly sustain *his* part. But we will consider the reasons which have determined the able manager to select him for it.

Hincmar était au fond un théologien; l'esprit de gouvernement, l'habilité pratique dominaient en lui and il n'avait pas fait des pères une étude très attentive. Leçon 22, p. 348.

27. 1st, There is strong evidence that Johannes Erigena was a Greek scholar; was acquainted with the writings of Aristotle, and even Plato, and attached a very high value to them. We certainly are not disposed to gainsay this assertion. But we venture to remark that, to all appearance, Alcuin, who was an orthodox and popular theologian, was better acquainted with Greek, and even with Greek philosophers, than Johannes. The latter was a man of genius, or almost a man of genius, and therefore any remarks he makes upon the ancients are more interesting and suggestive than those of an accomplished pedant; but as far as mere acquaintance with Greek letters goes, there is no question about Alcuin's superiority. We will appeal, therefore, to M. Guizot himself, and the statements in his lectures, whether on this ground any suspicion would have attached to Erigena, whether he might not have quoted Greeks and supported himself by their authority, without being supposed by others, or imagining himself, to be less theological than his neighbours. 2d, The second argument is drawn from an attack made upon Johannes by Florus, priest of the church of Lyons, from a sentence upon him by the council of Valentia in 855, and another of the council of Langres in 859. The passage from Florus, quoted by Guizot, does unquestionably charge our author with opposing the doctrine of Godeschalchus, "*by arguments purely human, or, as he boasts, philosophical.*" This accusation is mixed with others, describing him as a vain coxcomb, who supposed he was saying something new and magnificent, while he was really an object of contempt and ridicule to all faithful readers who were exercised in sacred

Arguments brought to prove that Johannes was a Philosopher and not a Theologian.

His Greek knowledge.

Judgment of his opponents.

learning. What possible inference can be deduced from these commonplaces of controversy which are to be found repeated, with scarcely a variety of expression, by every religious scribe, from the 9th century to the 19th, who has been obliged to eke out a small capital of knowledge with vituperation, or who has found from experience the last to be more available for his purposes than the former? The sentence of the Council which Guizot has produced does not contain any accusation of philosophy, and affects to treat Johannes as really deficient in the secular literature for which his admirers gave him credit. 3dly, A passage is quoted from Johannes Scotus himself, upon which the lecturer grounds this decisive appeal to the judgment of his class. "N'est ce pas là His own statements. evidemment le langage d' un homme, philosophe bien plus que theologien, qui prend dans la philosophie son point de depart et s'efforce de la confondre, de la concilier du moins, avec la Religion, soit parcequ 'en effet il les considère comme une seule et même science soit parcequ' il a besoin du bouclier de la religion contre les attaques dont il est l'objet?" The class having only the extract which M. Guizot furnished them with, could make but one answer to this demand. We shall endeavour presently to give our readers an analysis of the largest and most elaborate work of Johannes, which will enable them to judge for themselves whether he was more a philosopher or a theologian, whether his starting-point was theology or philosophy, whether he used his philosophy to explain away his theology, or to bring out what he conceived to be the fullest meaning of it.

28. M. Guizot is not sufficiently satisfied with the evidence on Another argument. this subject which is supplied by his decisive quotation, to dispense with other proof. The next is drawn from a passage of Johannes Mode of interpreting Scripture. respecting the interpretation of Scripture. It is a very short one. How it bears upon the context of the book, we shall have to explain hereafter; but it supplies an ample ground for another of those rapid conclusions to which the lecturer demands the assent of his pupils:—"Qui ne reconnaît là un effort, bien souvent tenté, pour échapper à la rigueur des textes on des dogmes, et pour introduire dans l'étude de la religion quelque liberté d'esprit sous le voile de l'explication et de l'allegorie?" Now, we happen to disapprove very strongly both of the allegorical method of treating Scripture, into which Origen and others have fallen, and of that method which was adopted by Johannes Scotus, and is indicated in the sentence M. Guizot has quoted from him. But we do not admit, The Allegorical method. 1st, that the allegorical method, much as we dislike it, was devised by Origen or any other person, for the sake of escaping from the rigour of texts and dogmas. It was chosen in hope of arriving at a deeper and more inward sense of texts; from the conviction that they meant more, not less, than the popular expounders had supposed

them to mean. And, 2d, we affirm that the method of Johannes
Scotus is not this, but is one in all respects most unlike it. He de-
fends with great ability, and for really profound reasons, what has
become the most popular, most vulgar, of all schemes of treating the
divine oracles, that which supposes the acts and feelings attributed to

*The accom-
modating
method.*

God in Scripture, to be accommodations to the notions and habits of
men. How he fell into an opinion which seems to us philologically,
morally, theologically unsound, our readers will discover presently.
But we shall have to defend ourselves rather than him from the
charge of abandoning a customary and recognized maxim. If
we could not trace the existing practice by a clear and lineal descent to other ancestors than Johannes, we should be obliged to
retract what we have said about the slight apparent influence which
he has exercised upon the thought of the modern world. Half
the pulpits in England, and probably in France also, would be liable
to the imputation of philosophy if this were one of the signs of it;
we should affix that scandalous imputation upon men who are as
clear of it, as Florus, the priest of Lyons, himself.

*Historical
reason.
Neoplatoni-
cal Chris-
tianity.*

29. Our lecturer proceeds with a statement which will be somewhat astonishing to those of our readers who have acquainted themselves with the history of the Alexandrian school. To understand
the position of Johannes Scotus, he declares that it is necessary to
give a rapid view of the relations between Neoplatonism and
Christianity. "Des le second siècle," he says, "il se fit, entre les
deux doctrines, entre les deux écoles rivales, quelques tentatives de
conciliation ou plutôt d'amalgame. Saint Clément d'Alexandrie
(mort en 220) Origène (de 185 à 254) sont des disciples de la
philosophie Alexandrine, des néoplatoniciens devenus chrétiens, et
qui essaient d'accommoder leurs doctrines philosophiques aux
croyances chrétiennes qui se développent et prennent la consistance
d'un système." We could scarcely wish for a more remarkable
example of the way in which a learned and honest lecturer may
mislead his disciples, and convey a totally false impression of facts,
when he attempts to gather up into a few sentences the history of

*Loose state-
ments re-
specting the
Alexandrian
Teachers.*

as many centuries. To say that Clemens and Origen were Neoplatonists become Christians; when Neoplatonism, as we know it, was
only beginning to form itself in the secret teachings of Ammonius
Saccas; when it had not yet expressed itself in any of the statements
of its real founder Plotinus; when Clemens notoriously derived his
direct instructions from Pantænus, who had been brought up a
Stoic; when there had been for two centuries a school in Alexandria, deriving its origin from Philo the Jew, whose habits of thought
had been adopted by at least one large body of Christians ever
since the gospel was proclaimed; is surely to twist dates, events,
and the faiths of living men, into the support of a baseless
theory.

30. Starting from such a point of view, it was impossible that the history which follows could be very accurate. The statement that there was a great battle between Neoplatonism and Christianity, that the latter remained master of the field, that many philosophers of the falling school, who had become, or were about to become Christians, sought to mix their ancient opinions with their new faith, is of course, as to its bare outline, indisputable. But what an utterly false notion must the well-informed lecturer have conveyed to his less informed pupils, when he speaks of certain writings in the 5th century, as—"écrits dont le dessein est évidemment de faire pénétrer dans la théologie de Saint Athanase, de Saint Jérome, de Saint Augustin, les idées et la forme de la philosophie expirante qui pouvaient s'y accommoder." Leaving Jerome out of the question, who, however, began by being a disciple of Origen before he was converted into his bitterest opponent, we think we gave our readers proofs in the earlier portion of this treatise that the mind of Athanasius was already *penetrated* with the thoughts which these writers of the 5th century so unnecessarily laboured to infuse into him; that they did not hang loosely about him as an appendage to his theology, but entered into the very substance of it. We hope we have made them perceive also that Augustine, more than any man, had his starting-point in philosophy, and that it was his deep and personal interest in philosophical questions which drove him to Christian theology. These writers of the 5th century, whom we believe, with M. Guizot, to have been very numerous, were therefore undertaking a very superfluous task. They might mean to philosophize Christianity, or to Christianize philosophy. They were in fact doing neither; they were mixing together a weak, miserable compound of their own, out of which all the life both of philosophy and Christianity had been extracted. When this was not absolutely the case, they were at best gathering together some of the higher thoughts and speculations of former days, which they were so conscious did not belong to themselves, and had received from them nothing but corrupt additions, that, with a strange mixture of fraud and honesty, they gave the credit of them to some man of former days, who had considerable celebrity, or had fortunately left no writings with which those ascribed to him could be compared.

31. The great sufferer by this treatment was Dionysius the Areopagite, who is mentioned in one sentence of the Acts of the Apostles. As his history is curiously connected with that of the 9th century, and of Johannes Erigena particularly, M. Guizot devotes some space to the illustration of his life. He makes up for the paucity of his materials by quoting from the 17th chapter of the Acts, the whole narrative of St. Paul's visit to Athens, and of his discourse there, as if it were merely a prologue to the last verse,

Side notes:
Alleged attempts to Christianize Neoplatonism in the 5th century.

Athanasius and Augustine more than merely professedly philosophical than the new Philosophizers.

Plagiarisms and Frauds of the Amalgamators.

Dionysius the Areopagite.

E

which announces the conversion of Dionysius. No ordinary student or commentator, we believe, has ever read it under that impression. An unknown woman, named Damaris, is mentioned in the same clause with the Areopagite. St. Luke does not appear to have attached more importance to one than to the other; at all events he never alludes to Dionysius again. Lydia, the seller of purple, who was converted at Philippi, is a more conspicuous person in the Apostolic narrative. That Justin, who spent much of his time in Greece, and that Dionysius of Corinth, should refer to him is natural. But the hints respecting him which can be gathered from the Fathers are very few, nor is there the least reason, except the mere fact of his being an Athenian, for supposing that he was looked upon as specially philosophical; whereas Justin himself, and Athenagoras, notoriously had that character. What is more important, the impostor who took his name in the 5th century, does not appear at all to have considered him in that light. The books which he forged, as their very names indicate, have a certain importance for the theologian, though more on account of the influence which they exerted afterwards than for their own sakes. The historian of philosophy, unless he had very great leisure and space at his command, could never find an excuse for dwelling upon them. They are connected, no doubt, at certain points, with Alexandrian or Neoplatonist philosophy, precisely because *that* in its later stages was so identified with theology and theurgy. The fact, then, that Johannes translated these books and that his mind received a powerful direction from them, instead of being an evidence that he was a pupil of philosophers rather than of theologians, makes all the other way. Possessing the knowledge which he had of Aristotle and Boethius, and regarding them with the greatest admiration, he nevertheless resorted as his special teacher to a third-rate writer on the celestial hierarchy and on mystical theology.

32. The fancy that Dionysius was the Apostle of Gaul and the first Bishop of Paris, which was so much diffused in the 9th century, explains, as M. Guizot himself tells us, the importance which was attached to his name in the French church, apart from his merits either in one character or another. In translating him, Johannes was gratifying his patron, Charles the Bald, and the taste of his contemporaries, quite as much as he was following his own instincts. But there is another person accidentally mentioned in this lecture, (merely as an annotator on Dionysius,) to whom he was not attracted by any such motives. This was Maximus, a Greek divine, whose name occurs very frequently in his great work, and for whose opinions he expresses deference. Now, the work of Maximus which he translated, and which he praises, is a commentary on some difficult passages in the writings of Gregory of Nazi-

The slight notices of him in Scripture, and in the Fathers.

The Pseudo-Dionysius professedly much more theological than philosophical.

Admiration of Johannes for Maximus, and for Gregory of Nazianzum.

anzum. To him there are very frequent allusions in the books De
Divisione Naturæ. But Gregory was καῖ ἰξοχάν, a theologian. No
doubt he had a philosophical education at Athens; but the use he
made of his philosophy was to refute the Arians, and those who,
like his fellow-pupil Julian, deserted Christianity for philosophy.
Of this emperor, as the representative of the Neoplatonists, we have
always considered that Gregory spoke with an asperity and unfairness which are unworthy of his general character.

33. In spite of this fact, M. Guizot proceeds to prove, by two or
three broad statements, that Johannes was really attached to this
defunct party in those points wherein it was opposed to Christianity.
These statements, as they involve the characteristic signs of a
philosophy with which we have been so much occupied in the
previous part of this sketch, as well as the characteristics of the
faith which all the teachers of the Middle Ages regarded as divine,
must needs concern our subject more, even than the conclusion
to which they lead. How important they are, and how entirely
they contradict some of the facts which it has been our duty to
lay before our readers, they will perceive when we quote the
following sentences:—" Le Neoplatonisme est une philosophie, le
Christianisme est une Religion. Le prémier a pour point de depart
la raison humaine; c'est à elle qu'il s'adresse, c'est elle qu'il inter-
roge; c'est en elle qu'il se confis. Le point de depart du second est
au contraire un fait exterieur à la raison humaine; il s'impose à elle
au lieu de l'interroger. De là suit que le libre examen domine dans
le Néoplatonisme, c'est sa methode fondamentale et sa pratique
habituelle; tandis que le Christianisme proclame l'autorité pour son
principe et procède en effet par voie d'autorité." Now, it appears
from the examination which we made of the books in which the genius
of Neoplatonism, in its different periods, is most faithfully represented, 1st, That from the very beginning, its teachers appealed to the
authority of Plato as oracular and decisive. 2d, That the experiment which was made by Porphyry to keep Neoplatonism a philosophy, by appealing to the reason and discarding superstition—an experiment which was most imperfectly carried out by him, which was
not incompatible with the most absolute deference to the *authority*
of Plotinus, which involved the recognition of miracles wrought by
him, and of divine theophanies of which he was the receiver—failed
altogether; and that the Jamblichan school which made theophanies
and the acknowledgment of miraculous powers, the characteristic
features of their system, was, after a short struggle, completely triumphant. 3d, That this school reposed on the traditions of the past,
surrounding itself with all the forms and impressions of the old my-
thology, and denouncing the Christians for their impiety in discarding them. 4th, That the glory, therefore, of being a philosophy and
not a religion, was eagerly disclaimed and spurned by the professors

Guizot's Arguments to prove Johannes a Neoplatonist rather than a Christian.

The supposed difference in the starting-points.

Neoplatonism shows at least as much respect for authority and tradition as Christianity.

of this doctrine; and that all the consequences which M. Guizot supposes to flow from it, were unknown to the philosophers of Julian's
court, to Julian himself, as well as to Proclus, and the members of
the Athenian Succession. 5th, That they felt they had to encounter
Christianity as a power which made a more direct appeal to the
conscience and the inner sense of mankind than they did, and which
had obtained most hearing from this conscience and inner sense,
when it came with the least apparent weight of prescriptive and
external authority. For a parallel investigation into the kind of
influence which this rival had exercised in different periods of *its*
history, brought us to the conclusion, 1st, That though even a
higher pretension was put forward on its behalf than that which is
expressed in the vague word *Religion*, viz., that it was a *Revelation;*
—this very pretension was admitted by those who acknowledged
the justice of it, only because the Gospel appeared to reveal to
them the God their consciences and reasons had been feeling after,
only because it awakened their consciences and reason out of slum-
ber into activity, or, if they had been at work, satisfied cravings
which the existing religions and philosophies had been unable to
satisfy. 2d, That so far from imposing itself upon the conscience
and reason, instead of interrogating them, this Gospel was never
listened to, till it had interrogated them, and had forced them to
give an answer, and till by this process it had emancipated them
from traditions which had imposed themselves for centuries upon
mankind, and had kept the conscience and the reason in chains. 3d,
That free examination into the deepest springs and sources of human
thought and action was therefore excited by the Christian teachers,
whether they desired it or no, whether they appealed to the reasons
of men or appealed to prescription or authority, in a degree to
which it could not be excited by the Neoplatonist, who confined
himself to the schools, and who, even when he spoke most of the
ideal of humanity, looked with scorn upon actual men.

Christianity interrogates the Reason and Conscience more than Neoplatonism.

34. Passing from the starting-point of these rival doctrines, M.
Guizot goes on to test them by entering "dans le fond des idées."
He affirms that the ruling doctrine in the Alexandrian Neoplatonism is Pantheism, the unity of substance and of being; individuality being reduced to the condition of a mere phenomenon, of
a transitory fact. "On the contrary," he continues, "individuality
is the fundamental article of faith in the Christian theology." . .

Argument from the character of the Doctrines. Pantheism.

Loss of Individuality.

. . . . . . "Among various other symptoms, the
diversity of the two doctrines in this respect is clearly manifested
in the idea which they respectively form of the future of man at
the termination of his present existence. What does Neoplatonism
with human beings at the moment of their death? It absorbs
them into the bosom of the great whole, it abolishes all individuality. What, on the other hand, does the Christian doctrine with

them? It perpetuates individuality even into infinity. For the absorption of individual beings it substitutes an eternity of rewards and punishments."

This passage *has* a direct bearing upon the life and writings of Johannes. The contrast which it exhibits has also a far deeper and truer foundation than the one which we have just been considering. We shall find as we proceed, that this philosopher of the 9th century did, in some of his speculations, approach very nearly to the Pantheism which is attributed to the Neoplatonists. It is also true that the professors of that school were distinguished from the most serious and earnest of the Christian teachers; by their indifference to the personality of men, by their belief that absorption into the Divinity is the termination and reward of earthly virtue and philosophical meditation. The Fathers generally—Augustine especially—were driven by a strong sense of an evil which *could not* be contemplated at a distance from the self of each man—which was realized only in that—into a sense of personality, of an enduring imperishable personality, which the Neoplatonist, though an acute speculator about the nature of evil, never reached. But it was by these conflicts that they came to know what is the "fundamental" individuality of the Christian faith. They did not, could not, receive that as an "article of faith" from any external teachings which did not provoke these internal exercises. And the more the Revelation—what the Fathers called the Catholic Faith as such—was received and asserted by them, the more they were led beyond this individuality, the more they showed that they demanded a rest in God, a loss of themselves in Him, which was very different indeed from the absorption of the Brahmin and the Neoplatonist, but which was as real as that, and might often be expressed in terms that bordered very nearly upon theirs; nay which, when the Christian's fights within and without became fewer, were often, even by himself, confounded with them. Although, therefore, they did dwell much on the individual recompenses of a future life, they would have thought, we believe, that they were dropping back into the old heathenism if they separated the idea of reward or punishment from the fruition of God, and the separation from Him. It is, therefore, a bold inference from M. Guizot's data, that the belief of Johannes—if it verged ever so nearly upon Pantheism—was derived from the Neoplatonists; and still bolder, that the character and tendency of his doctrine proves him to have been a philosopher rather than a theologian. On this last point we must make one or two more remarks before we proceed to our proper business.

86. M. Guizot must be aware that his eminent cotemporary, M. Cousin, has refused the Orientals any place among philosophers, treating them as merely theologians. We are convinced that his

The Fathers assert permanent Individuality not as a tenet of Christianity, but as involved in their experience of Evil.

Their Catholic ideas led them beyond Individuality; led them to forget it.

exclusion is not justifiable, that it involves the omission of a great chapter in the history of human thought. But we are not prepared to say that he had *no* plea for the severe rule which he has laid down; we cannot maintain that he has adopted a maxim which is exactly the *reverse* of the true one. M. Guizot must maintain this position if he is consistent with himself. For Pantheism, or the doctrine of absorption into the Divinity, is characteristically and originally oriental. It is worked into the very heart of Brahminism. If, then, Pantheism belongs to Neoplatonism *because* it is a philosophy, if this is the philosophical side of the system, we must not only admit philosophy to be mixed with Brahminism, but we must suppose Brahminism to contain the very essence and type of philosophy. This has certainly not been the common opinion. The very name of *Pantheism* has suggested the thought that theological notions and conceptions were at the root of the doctrine, that from them it derived its character. Everything in the history of Hindoo faith and philosophy supports this *à priori* opinion. If Pantheism has passed as a theory into the philosophy of the Brahmin, it existed first in his practice and worship. The difficulty which the Hindoo felt in distinguishing between the priest and the god, and then between the god and the different forms of nature in which he supposed him to be manifested, gave birth, as the Bhagavad Gita so clearly shows us, to the formal assertion of an identity between them. The history of Neoplatonism, we say confidently, points exactly in the same direction. It was not the philosophy which he learnt from Socrates or Plato that contained the Pantheism of Plotinus. It was the theological system in which he sought for a complement to this philosophy; it was in the desire to escape from the Christian idea of the Word made flesh, it was in the desire to escape from the limitations which the ordinary philosophy imposed upon his ideas of divinity, that his necessity for Pantheism arose. What, then, can be so illogical as to assume that, even if Johannes was altogether like the Neoplatonists on this point, he was flying from theology to philosophy? Would it not be a much more natural supposition (since he certainly held the belief of an Incarnation, since it was worked into the very tissue of his theory) that, like them, he was seeking to rid himself of some fetters which philosophy imposed upon his theology?

36. This we believe to be the true state of the case. Johannes was a Celt, born in Ireland, where, that Celtic cultivation to which we have alluded already had its centre, whence for a long time it diffused a refining, if not a powerful, influence over other lands. He had, if we may judge from the reports of him, many of the specially Irish qualities. The paternity of one very good joke, which is attributed to him at the table of Charles the Bald, may be disputed by the archæologists who devote themselves to this

special subject of inquiry; but he could not have had the reputation of it, if he had not uttered many that were equally clever. We can hardly imagine that a man with so much subtlety of thought, such a quick perception of distinctions, and such a fondness for verbal analogies, as he discovers in his treatise on the Division of Nature, was not a humourist. We can easily imagine that he may have been a very pleasant and genial one, not a stern deliberate Gothic humourist, whose hearty delight in the harmonies of the world is quickened by a painful apprehension of its discords—who is always the Jupiter commanding and directing his own lightnings; but rather a Celt to whom fantastical combinations, grotesque similarities and dissimilarities, are a mere pleasure—whose whole being is phosphoric, throwing off sparks without any intention, not very careful whether one now and then lights upon himself, and singes or even burns him. This feature of the national physiognomy comes out, we think, in all the speculations of Scotus. He is singularly at variance with the spirit of his time, in that the idea of an active energetic working Will is the one which he can least take in, which was most absent from all the habits of his intellect. To this we trace his defects as a moralist; to this his inability to impress his thoughts upon his time on which much less accomplished men could stamp their image. But he was born after the year 800, probably in the early years of the 9th century. Mahomet had wrought his mighty revolution in both worlds, Charlemagne had just effected his in the West. Neither could change the character of individuals or races; that character was compelled, however reluctantly, to receive a direction from both. The age for such a man as Pelagius was past, in one country or another. God must be acknowledged as the root of all things and all thoughts, even by those who shrunk most from contemplating Him as the King and the Lawgiver. John, the Irishman, felt that necessity as strongly as any man could. He did not rise to the theological ground as the Neoplatonist had done, as Pelagius did; that was, whatever any one may say to the contrary, most strikingly his *point de départ*. That ground and substance which has nothing beneath it, was the postulate and preliminary of his mind; all its movements depended upon this. It seemed to him that the logic of his day, the logic which had been brought into all the school teaching, which was implied in all the school divinity, was hemming in this Substance with its accidents and conditions. To proclaim its freedom from such conditions was the work of his life; till he could do this, he had no hope of discovering any safe foundation for human or for physical science.

Without any idea of a Will

But essentially a Divine.

A rebel against the Logic of his day.

37. Hincmar invoked the assistance of Johannes in the battle with Godeschalchus; he seems to have obeyed the call of Charles the Bald when he opposed the dogma of Paschasius. We can easily

Why Johannes engaged in the Predestination Controversy.

admit, with M. Guizot, that Hincmar did not know what an ally he had chosen, and repented of his rashness when he discovered how much scandal the Irishman brought upon his cause. There could not have been one in which Johannes would more readily take up arms, or one in which he was more certain, both by the profundity

Hincmar's mistake.

of his thoughts, and, as we think, by his want of sympathy with the special truth of which Godeschalchus was spokesman, to offend the prejudices as well as the faith of his contemporaries. He would have explained, in terms which would have seemed to them utterly incomprehensible and monstrous, why he discarded their notions of before and after, when he was speaking of the eternal Mind; he would have given them good excuse for saying, that this eternal Mind was not a power which determined them to right or to wrong, or which pronounced judgment upon their acts. Hincmar, with his worldly prudence, may most naturally have resolved that, little as he was of a theologian himself, he could fight the theological battle against the predestinarian with much greater popularity and success than a man who knew a thousand times more of the

Johannes offends his contemporaries more by his treatment of the Controversy than by opposing Paschasius.

Fathers, as well as of the Bible, than he did. Apparently Johannes procured much more odium to himself with doctors and with popes, by the line which he took in this controversy, than by his notions on transubstantiation. Though we have not his treatise on that subject, we may form a tolerable guess as to its character. There will have been the same impatience of dialectical formulæ, the same eagerness to show that the divine substance and the divine communion with man transcended the terms and expressions by which Paschasius was seeking to define it, probably the same indifference to modes of thinking which he found prevalent, the same resolution to follow out his own line of thought without taking the pains to put himself into the position of other men. But it is safer to give our readers positive information respecting a book which we do possess, than to form conjectures respecting one which has perished.

The Five Books De Divisione Naturæ.

38. The leading work of Johannes has a Greek as well as a Latin title, Περὶ Φυσεων Μερισμου, id est De Divisione Naturæ. The subject is discussed in a dialogue between a Master and his Disciple. It is right that we should give the opening passage of the dialogue, though we are far from sure that it will make the purpose of the book intelligible to our readers.

Statement of the Design.

Master. After thinking and inquiring as diligently as my powers permit, I have come to the conclusion that the first and primary division of all things that can be either perceived by the mind, or which transcend its reach, is into those things which are, and into those things which are not. For all these the general word is in Greek Φύσις; in Latin, *Natura.* Are you agreed?

Disciple. Yes. For as often as I aim at any method of reasoning, I find it so to be.

M. As, then, we are agreed about this word, that it is a general one, I wish you would tell me the method of dividing it, by its differences, into species. Or, if you had rather, I will try to make the division, and you shall pass your judgment upon the parts of it.

D. Begin. For I am impatient to learn from you the true The method method of proceeding.

M. It seems to me that the division of Nature is into four species, by means of four differences. The first species is that which creates, and is not created. The second is that which is created and creates. The third is that which is created, and does not create. The fourth is that which is neither created nor creates. Of these the third is opposed to the first, the fourth to the second. But the fourth must be placed among impossibilities; its differentia is that it cannot exist. Do you understand this division?

D. I understand it. Only that fourth species of yours causes me some trouble. About the others I should not dare to hesitate. The first I understand to be the cause of the things that are, and of the things that are not. The second has reference to the primeval causes, or principles of things. The third I perceive must have reference to generations, and times and places, that is, to particulars or individuals.

M. You are right. But in what order we shall proceed, that is to say, what species shall be the subject of our first discussion, I leave you to decide.

D. It seems evident to me that it behoves us to speak first, whatever is permitted us to speak, of the primary species.

39. Then follows a discussion of great importance to the full understanding of our author, and of the later scholastic philosophy, respecting the use and extent of the terms *being* and *not being*, Being and where they can, and where they cannot, be applied. We do not not being. think that we should do justice to the book we are examining if we forced our readers to plunge at once into this metaphysical ocean. After a few coasting voyages we may possibly be more fit to venture upon it. We will give the result so far as it concerns our immediate purpose. God, who creates and is not created, who is the only Being without beginning, who is the cause of all things that were made from Him and by Him, who is the end of all things, whom all things long after, who is beginning, middle, and The Divine end—He must not be spoken of merely as Being. He is super- Nature Being, super-Essence. He must not be called merely Good or dant. Wise, seeing that good and wise admit of contraries, that they imply badness and folly. He must be the super-Wise, the super-Good. All being, all goodness, all wisdom, must be regarded only as arising from a participation and communication or manifestation of His being, and wisdom, and goodness. His nature must never

be deduced or judged of by any that is below it. This we apprehend is the fundamental principle of Johannes which is worked out in reference to the first and highest nature in the first book.

Affirmation
and Negation
included in
this Nature. It is here that he comes into conflict with the habits, even more than with the formal maxims of his time. His object in the use of the words super, or transcendent being, goodness, wisdom, is to take the idea of God out of the region of intellectual forms, to show that it includes the affirmation and negation which in earthly logic are opposed, and that the categories of Essence, Quantity, Quality, Relation, Position, Habit, Place, Time, Action, Suffering, fail altogether in the investigation of the divine nature.

The Categories not applicable to the Divine Nature. 40. Johannes puts forth no claim to originality in making this assertion. He adopts it directly from St. Augustine. Categories or predicaments he had distinctly said belong to the region of sensible and intelligible things; when you ascend to the consideration of Him who transcends sense and intelligence, their virtue is extinguished. They may, our author says, metaphorically, be applied to the Divine Being. Strictly they cannot be; seeing that God is neither genus, nor species, nor accident. The application of the

Essence,
Quality,
Quantity. principle to the categories of Essence, which seems to involve great difficulty, has been made already. *Quantity* is easily disposed of. The doctrine laid down respecting goodness and wisdom has settled the question of *Quality*. But the disciple pauses with anxiety and

Relation. fear when he approaches *Relation*. The master admits that the difficulty demands the most reverent examination. But the law already affirmed is declared to admit of no exception. It would be blasphemous to impute our association with the names of father and son to the divine nature; these names, therefore, denote that which transcends relation; they cannot be brought under it. Johannes perceives that he is on the edge of a precipice; he passes on somewhat hastily to the six following predicaments. The propriety of

Position. a metaphorical use of *Position* in reference to God is at once asserted; seeing that by Him all things hold their position. Its strict or direct application to Him is as strongly denied, seeing the

Habit. Position involves the notion of Place. The predicament of *Habit* gives rise to a rather long discussion. The master remarks that it is involved in all the rest; Quantity, Quality, Relation, Position, &c., each supposes some habit; how comes it, then, to be distinguished from them? The objection anticipates some of those which have been made in more recent times to the arrangement of

The Categories imply each other. Aristotle. It is not, however, introduced here for the purpose of disturbing that arrangement, but rather to show how inevitably any one of these conditions involves the other, and how, nevertheless, each has a sphere and foundation of its own. The effect of the argument is to suggest the thought which Johannes afterwards distinctly enunciates, that the categories exist only in the

mind, and that there is that which underlies them all, and is not
subject to any of them.

41. When our author approaches the predicaments of Place and *Place and Time.*
Time, we find him asserting very vigorously some of the doctrines
which we are wont to connect with more recent philosophies. The
disciple raises all the natural arguments in support of the notion,
that Place has an existence of its own. What do we mean by a
man living in such a place? Do we not speak of water as the
place for fishes, the ether of the celestial sphere of stars?
The answer of the master is very decisive. There is nothing to
be done with people who talk in this way, but to persuade them
if they are open to instruction, and to wish them good morning if
they are contentious. For true reason ridicules those who speak
after this sort. If place is one thing and body another, it follows that place is not body. The air is the fourth part of this
corporal visible world; it is, therefore, not place. We all admit
that this visible world is composed of four elements, as it were, of
four general parts. It is a kind of body compacted of its own parts, *Physical ar-*
out of which general parts, the proper and special bodies of all *gument con-*
animals, trees, herbs, adhering with a wonderful and ineffable mix- *founding Place with*
ture, are composed, and into these they return again at the time of *Body.*
their dissolution. We are bound to show our readers the rashness
and imperfection of our author's physical assumptions, not that
they may transfer the suspicion of a similar ignorance to his intellectual conclusions, but that they may see how much subtlety,
what clear intuitions in one region, are compatible with the most
hasty generalizations in the other. Johannes is in the very act of
clearing away a very serious impediment to natural as well as to *Intellectual*
metaphysical inquiries, of removing a confusion which, as he says *clearness not incom-*
himself, has been the cause of a multitude of other confusions, while *patible with*
he adopts as the basis of his argument one of those superstitions of *ignorance of Physics.*
his age which partly, perhaps through his own assistance, we have
been able to cast off.

42. The disciple is anxious to know how this mode of speech *Explanation*
has come into ordinary use, if it is so contrary to reason. The *of common speech.*
answer leads to some interesting remarks on the metonomies with
which we are all familiar. A family is spoken of as a house. The
eye is confounded with the sight or vision of which it is the organ,
the ear with the power of hearing, and so forth. But the discussion is subordinate to the main argument of the book. Space and
Time are affirmed, each to imply the other. Without them no
generated things can consist or be known. The essence of things
must be conceived of under local and temporal forms. And God,
when he is spoken of or presented to us, must be presented in such
forms, under such conditions. But they must not for a moment *Necessity of*
be supposed to belong to His nature. He is not under them. Hence *Place for our minds.*

the need of the language, however strange and awkward, which was used before to denote Him as transcending even Essence and Being.

43. From these hints our readers may easily gather how Johannes could deal with the categories of Action and Passion, in reference to the awful subject which he is considering. It is at this point that the language of Scripture, of necessity, comes into question. How is that action and passion are so continually there attributed to the Divine Being? In strict consistency with the whole course of his reasoning—not the least with the intention of reducing the authority of Scripture, or of evading the force of its statements— our author affirms that all such modes of speaking are justifiable, are inevitable, but that they are metaphorical; that they are applied to God because we cannot write or speak in intelligible language concerning Him without resorting to them; but that they are the conditions of our speech and intelligence, not of His nature. This is, as we said before, the best and most scientific exposition that can be given of what has now become a commonplace, the easy refuge of the most careless interpreter, of the most thoughtless pulpit rhetorician. We could not venture to dissent from the popular practice, if we did not discover a flaw in the theory upon which it is unconsciously grounded. That flaw we think we can trace through all the statements of Johannes. It does not diminish our respect for the man, or our value for much that he has taught us; yet it is, we believe, the secret of the Pantheism which many have charged him with, not altogether unfairly, but without knowing how easily they might be convicted of the same offence, and from the same evidence.

44. We acknowledge the most perfect sympathy with our author in the object which he has at heart. So far from acknowledging that *object* to be pantheistical, we believe that what he desired was to distinguish the Divine Nature from other natures, to prevent that confusion between God and created or generated things in which Pantheism consists. But it appears to us that there is one way, and but one way, in which this end could be obtained without denying the fact that the Divine nature has been revealed to man, and without confining it within the limits of our created intelligence. These forms of the intellect are inadequate to express that Nature assuredly, but are they adequate to express our human nature, our sympathies and joys and tears? Is the category of relation adequate to express the actual human relations of father and child, of brother and sister? Is the category of action or of passion adequate to express any single action or passion as it has been actually realized in life? Is any one of these categories adequate to express a single living operation of nature, the light or movement of any star, the growth of the meanest flower? Is it

impossible, then, because the nature of the Divine Being cannot be presented under conditions which fail equally with reference to the lower natures, that it may be presented or revealed in them and through them? Is it correct to speak of such a presentation or revelation as metaphorical, or merely an accommodation or adaptation to the narrowness of our intellects? Supposing man to be the image of God, supposing all nature to be an exhibition of His acts and operations, are we not bewildering ourselves when we speak of the mirror as merely presenting to us certain optical delusions? Cannot we suppose it to be purified and prepared for the express purpose of delivering us from such delusions? Cannot we suppose that the delusions which must follow, and which have followed, in such fearful and terrible succession, when men have taken the reflection in the glass for the form which was reflected, when they have constructed an archetype out of the image, may be counteracted if He, who has formed man and the world, shows us how he has used them for His own manifestation? Must not a Bible, if it is to be one, do this for us? Is not what we demand from it this, that it should have precisely that character, that human sensible character, of which Scotus, with the best motives in the world, would deprive it? Have not those who have adopted his rules so slavishly, and without his temptations, shown very clearly that by this very course they make themselves, and make the Divine Nature, subject to that logical tyranny against which he revolted?

The human and sensible language of Scripture, that deliverance from the tyranny of Logic which Johannes required.

45. We are not to blame Johannes, that in an age when the sacredness of human relationships was hidden and kept under, by many of the habits and dogmas of the Church which was to illustrate it—living in a scholastic atmosphere into which the breezes of common human life might sometimes penetrate, but mixed with elements that would often lead him to suspect that they were only carrying disease and contagion—he did not enter into a principle which it has required many centuries to give us even that imperfect apprehension of which we possess. We ought rather to be thankful for the glimpses of this truth which we catch in the midst of apparent contradictions of it, and for the courageous testimony which he was able to bear for (that which it is equally necessary we should acknowledge,) the Absolute and the Eternal. If Johannes showed in his bold endeavour to rescue these from the dominion of logical formulas, how much those formulas had got possession of his own mind, so that he crouches to them while he seeks to break loose from them; if it is equally clear that he could not effect the deliverance which he sought without presenting the absoluteness and perfection of the Divine Nature, sometimes as if it were aloof from all human cognizance and sympathy, sometimes as if it were an abyss in which our knowledge, our sympathy, our

Difficulty of obtaining this deliverance in the 9th century.

Worth of the
s, revelations
of Johannes personality, were at last to be buried; we may surely learn great
lessons for our own guidance from these discoveries; we may gather
from them comfort and satisfaction in considering the devious paths
through which ages and men have been led towards wisdom and
truth, without turning them into an excuse for pronouncing judgment upon a man who would have been most willing to learn
from us and profit by our advantages, and can help us, if we will,
how to recover much that we have lost. The following sentences,
in which he gathers up the result of his first book, seem to us, in
spite of all the strangeness which may appear in them, worthy of
Summary of
the doctrine
of the 1st
book. the most serious meditation. We may not adopt the terminology
of Johannes, we may adhere to one which strikes us as much
simpler and more practical; but in the use of that we may derive
hints and instruction from a man whose faith and charity certainly
rose above all his conceptions or ours.

"God, therefore, in Himself is Love, in Himself is Vision, in
Himself Motion, and, nevertheless, He is neither Motion, nor Vision,
nor Love; but more than Love, more than Vision, more than Motion. And He is in Himself Loving, Seeing, Moving, yet He is
not in Himself Loving, Seeing, Moving, because He is more than
Loving, Seeing, Moving. Further, He is in Himself to be Loved,
to be Seen, to be Moved; and yet He is not in Himself to be
Moved, or Seen, or Loved, because He is more than that. He
can be Seen, or Loved, or Moved. He loves, therefore, Himself, and is loved by Himself in us and in Himself, and yet He
loves not Himself, nor is loved by Himself in us and in Himself, but more than loves, and more than is loved in us and in
Himself, &c."

This method of speaking by affirmations and negations conjointly,
of making each sustain, while it seems to subvert, the other he
His defence
of his doc-
trine as Ca-
tholic and
safe. considers to be the cautious, and salutary, and catholic method.
He establishes his proposition thus :—" What, then, God the Word
made flesh, said to His disciples, 'It is not you who speak, but
the Spirit of your Father which speaketh in you,' true reason
compels us, in other similar things, similarly to believe, to speak,
to understand. It is not you who love, who see, who move, but
the Spirit of your Father, who speaketh in you truth concerning
me and my Father, and Himself. He loves me, and sees me and
my Father and Himself in you, and moves Himself in you, that
you may love me and my Father. If, therefore, the Holy Trinity
loves Itself in us and in Itself, and sees and moves Itself, assuredly
by Itself it is loved, It is seen, It is moved, according to that most
excellent method known to no creature, whereby It loves and sees
and moves Itself, and by Itself, in Itself and in Its creatures, seeing that It is above all things that are spoken concerning it, for
who can speak of the Ineffable? whereof no fitting name or word,

nor any fitting voice is discovered, nor is, nor can be, who only hath immortality, and dwelleth in light inaccessible."

46. We could not omit this passage, since it will show our readers that Johannes is no exception to the remark which we made in the last part of this treatise, that the doctrine of the Trinity was the foundation of all the metaphysical thought and speculation of the ages after Gregory the Great. We shall have an illustration of that fact in the next book of the Division of Nature, which contains what would be called his Anthropology. But we are anxious that our readers should notice it here in connection with a passage of the first book, which, according to M. Guizot, determines the character of our author's mind. "Thou art not ignorant," says the master, "that I think that which is first in nature is of greater dignity than that which is first in time." "This," says the disciple, "is known to almost all." "We have learnt, further," says the master, "that Reason is first in nature, but Authority in time. For although nature was created together with time, Authority did not begin to exist from the beginning of time and nature. But Reason has arisen together with Nature and Time, from the beginning of things." Disciple.—"Reason itself teaches this. For Authority, no doubt, hath proceeded from true Reason, but Reason not by any means from Authority. And all Authority, which is not approved by true Reason, turns out to be weak. But true Reason, seeing that it stands firm and immutable, protected by its own virtues, needs not to be strengthened by any confirmation of Authority. True Authority, indeed, as it seems to me, is nothing else but Truth united by the power of Reason, and transmitted in letters by the holy Fathers for the benefit of posterity. Perhaps, however, you do not agree with me." M.—"Entirely. Therefore, in the subject which is now before us, let us resort, first, to Reason, and then to Authority."

Unquestionably we have here a statement which any modern Rationalist may, if he pleases, make use of in proof that Johannes was one of his progenitors. But he will do well to weigh the words, and give them their full force, or he may find that he is committed unawares to opinions which he would most eagerly repudiate. The *Ratio* which was coeval with Nature, and to which all things in Time must be secondary, is that fixed Purpose, that Eternal Reason and Order which man's Reason is created to investigate and perceive. Authority must not be set before this Reason, precisely because it is the result, as Johannes affirms, of a Reason which is working under temporal conditions, though this Authority may be most helpful in assisting the reason of any individual man in its efforts to break loose from its time boundaries, and to enter into the truth of which it is in search. Whether this view is just or absurd, it is that which any careful reader of Scotus will be quite certain was

Illustration of former remarks respecting the foundation of Middle Age Philosophy.

Nature, Reason, Authority.

Their relation to each other.

What is implied in this statement.

Not incon-
sistent with
the doctrine
of the most
Orthodox
Middle Age
Schoolmen.
his view. That eternal Name which he declares to be at the foundation of all things, and in the image of which he believes man to be
created, will not allow him to glorify the opinions or discoveries of
any man, or any succession of men. The Light which they perceive
is always above that which is in them; it is in God's light only
that they see light. Language, therefore, such as Johannes uses,
however much it may often have offended Popes, and clashed with
many of the Middle Age traditions, is not language which can have
sounded strange to any, even the most popular and orthodox,
doctors of those ages. They will perfectly have understood it.
Nearly all of them, at some time or other, for some purpose or
other, will have resorted to this, or to some equivalent form of
expression. So far from being a rebellion against their ordinary
theology—the effort of a free spirit to shake it off and substitute
for it the conclusions of philosophy—it was just when they were
most theological, just when they were contemplating the name of
God, the Trinity in Unity, as beneath all their thoughts, and implied in all, that they resorted to it most, and that they could least
bear the notion that antiquity, or that any cotemporary dogmatist
was the measure and standard of truth. Again, and again, we shall
see what a protest was borne—now by kings, now by popular
teachers and preachers, now by the most systematic doctors, each
maintaining their own position, each resisting some intrusion upon
their own principle—against the slavery to which they all in turns
submitted.

47. The second book opens with some remarks on the original
quadripartite division of the subject. We are now enlightened
about that last section, of things neither creating nor created, which
caused the disciple so much trouble. It appears that the first and
the fourth divisions both refer to the Divine Nature, the first to it
as the beginning from which all things are derived, the last as the
end at which all things are aiming, and in which they are to terminate. "He is said to be the cause of all things," says our author,
"seeing that from that Cause the whole circle of things which after
it, are created from it, diffuses itself into genera and species, and
numbers and differences, and whatever other distinctions there are
in Nature, with a certain wonderful and divine multiplication. But
seeing that to that same Cause all things which proceed from it,
when they shall come to their end, will return, therefore it is
called the end of all things, and is said neither to create nor to be
created; for after all things have returned into it, nothing further
will proceed from it by generation in place and time, in kinds and
forms, since all will be quiet in it, and will remain an unchanged
and an undivided one." This, which is the most startling announcement of the pantheistical tendency of our author's speculations which we have yet met with, we should not have introduced

till it could receive the elucidations and explanations which are
reserved for the later books, if it did not seem to us very important Double sense of Analysis.
in connection with his views of Man upon which we are about to
enter. In fact, he felt the necessity for this introduction, since a
work on the *Division* of Nature might have seemed not to require
any allusion to this final state of things in which all divisions are
to cease. But Johannes would have us consider that all division
or analysis into parts, involves the idea of a return into the whole
from which those parts have issued. And he would have us look
upon man, as, in one point of view, the cause of all the partitions
and distinctions of the universe; in another, as the reconciliation and
meeting-point of them all.

48. The principle of the Bible, that man is made in the image Man the Image of God.
of God, is the fundamental one of this book. With great force
and ability, Johannes maintains what he believes to be the doctrine of the Scriptures, and of all the great theologians, that the
Divine humanity cannot be adequately contemplated in *men;* that
there must be a Universal Man; that the divine Word could alone
be that Universal Man. It is in the effort to connect this ideal
Humanity with actual human beings and human history, that
Johannes, as it seems to us, stumbles and falls. He quotes the The Univer-sal Man.
New Testament in support of the principle that in the Universal
Man there is neither male nor female. To reconcile that principle
with the distinctions of sex in the actual world, he affirms (in direct
contradiction to the text of the Old Testament) *this* distinction to
be the consequence of the Fall. Of course the abolition of it, and Distinction of Sex attri-buted to the Fall.
with it of all other distinctions of which it is the example and type,
is looked forward to as involved in the final reward and consum-
mation. Let it be well understood, that this doctrine is logically
and consistently carried out in that blank and dreary Unity which
Johannes dreamed of, and thought that he hoped for, and let each
one ask himself how near he has often been—how near the most Whither such an opinion leads.
orthodox members of the Church have often been—to that heresy
which they so reasonably dread. Once admit the thought that
evil is productive and creative, not merely destructive; that it
establishes an order instead of disturbing all order; that it is not
equally the foe of distinction and of Unity, and the inference of
Johannes is irresistible. Our only wonder is that with this opinion
he could unite so very clear and exquisite a sense of perfection and
harmony in the world, the parentage—at least the foster parentage
—of which he regarded as so anti-divine.

49. The doctrine that Humanity in its highest most ideal sense
is the image of the Divinity, is carried out with great consistency
in this book. Brahminical, Buddhist, Platonical, and Neoplato- The Human Trinity.
nical thinkers, had all spoken of a Trinity in Man. The Fathers
had eagerly acknowledged the idea; only they had pointed out

F

the danger of reasoning from that which we discover in ourselves
as our human nature to that which is divine; they had declared
that a revelation of God enables us to see what there is corresponding to it in the Creature. Johannes follows out this principle
to the utmost. He speaks of a threefold motion or rotation of man
about the divine centre. The first or inmost circle is that described
by the Nous, which he renders Intellectus, Animus, or Mens. This
recognizes God as the Principle of its attraction, the source of its
Light, but enters into no thought or conception respecting Him,
confessing Him as the Absolute and the Incomprehensible. The
second is that of the Reason or Virtue (his translation of λόγος
and δύναμις), which acknowledges God as the primary cause of the
things which are, and which takes account of those primordial
causes or ideas which are implied in His creatures and in all his
operations. The third motion is that of the Διάνοια and ἐνέργεια,
which takes notice of all distinct operations, and enters into them.
In translating διάνοια by senses, he feels that he is open to criticism.
He justifies himself by saying that he speaks not of the sense as
existing in penetrative organs, but of an internal perception of the
mind itself. These three elements of humanity form the Triad
of our author, the human Trinity, each of them corresponding to
one of the Ineffable Names.

Christian application of it.

Revolutions about the Divine Centre.

50. Our readers will have perceived that this view of Man, or
Human Nature, is Platonical, not Aristotelian. Man is not a creature who can be contemplated in himself. His habits, energies,
perceptions, intellectual or sensible, cannot be looked upon independently from their centre. From God they have been derived.
About Him they revolve. Into Him they return. Nothing can
be so adverse as such a representation is to the school doctrines of
the time, which were assigning, in true Stagyrite fashion, its own
sphere to each science, and were doing their utmost that each, while
it did homage to theology as the primary architechtonical science,
yet should preserve its due and respectful distance. Johannes does
not discuss theology, anthropology, physiology; but he speaks of
God, of man, of involuntary things, and their relations to each
other. The difference between the two methods is amazing. Each
new period, as it introduces new modifications and applications of
one and the other, only makes the difference more conspicuous.
Nowhere does it appear more remarkably than in the doctrine of
primordial causes, as it is set forth by our author. The disciple is
desirous to know whether these causes are the same with that dark
and formless void of which the sacred historian speaks. Are not,
he demands, the expressions convertible? "For formless matter,
nay, the very want of form, we may in some sort declare to be a
cause of things, seeing that in that they have their beginning,
though it be a formless, that is to say, an imperfect, beginning.

*The Platoni-
cal method
alien from all
the habits of
the 9th cen-
tury.*

*The Primor-
dial Causes
and the
Formless
void.*

And although they are understood to be almost nothing, yet not absolutely nothing, but a kind of inchoation, aiming at form and perfection." The master bids him to fix his attention, that the mists which are clouding his intellect may be scattered. So far **They are** are these primordial causes from being identical with that formless **opposed, not identical.** void which is the nearest conceivable approximation to nothing, that in them we discover the true essence of things, the grounds of all life. "Cause, indeed, if it is truly cause, encloses within itself most perfectly all things of which it is the cause, and perfects in itself its own effects before they appear in anything without. And when they break forth into kinds and visible forms by generation, they lose not their perfection in it, but remain fully and immutably in it, and want no other perfection except the perfection of that one in which they together and for ever subsist." . . . . "The void of things is nothing but a certain **The formless** motion, an escape from not being, a longing and appetency for **an appetency or capacity** being. But primordial causes have been so established in the **of being.** beginning, that is, in the Word of God, that they have no movement or appetency after perfection in anything save in Him in whom they are unchangeably, and in whom they have their perfect form. For always turning towards that one form of all things **The divine** which all things desire, the Word of the Father, they first receive **Word.** their form and never lose it. In them are the causes of places and of times. But those things which are beneath them in the inferior order of things, are in such wise created by them that they attract them to themselves, and aim at the one principle of all things; but they themselves in no wise turn to those things which are beneath them, but ever contemplate that Form of theirs which is above them, so that they never cease to be formed by it. For by themselves they are without form, and in that universal form of theirs they know themselves as perfectly built up. But what **Primordial** reasonable man will dare to affirm concerning that which is with- **causes identical with the** out form, this which may be affirmed concerning the primordial **Substantial** causes, especially when that formless matter cannot be believed to **Ideas.** have proceeded from any other source but from these causes? For if primordial causes are those ideas which are primarily created by the one creative Cause of all things, and create those things which are beneath them, what wonder if we believe, and have the most certain grounds for maintaining, that formless matter itself was created by the primordial causes?"

51. In the final chapter of this book he recurs to the same sub- **Prototype.** ject. "Primordial causes, then, being, as I said before, what the Greeks call Ideas, that is, species and forms, the eternal and unchangeable reasons, according to which, and in which, the visible and the invisible world are formed and governed; and, therefore, by the wise men of the Greeks, were rightly called prototypes, that is,

the primary examples which the Father made in the Son, and by the Holy Spirit divides and multiplies into their own effects. They call them also fore-ordinations, for in them whatever things are coming into existence, or have come into existence, or shall come into existence, are, by the divine Providence, once and at once immutably predestinated. For nothing naturally arises, in the visible or invisible creature, besides that which in them is before all places and times predefined and preordained. Therefore they are further called by philosophers acts or motions of the divine will. Since all things the Lord willed to make, in them He made primordially and causally. The ages which were to be, were created in them before they were. Wherefore they are said to be the principles of all things, seeing that all things whatsoever perceived by sense or intelligence in the visible or invisible creation, subsist by participation in them. And they are themselves participations of the one highest cause of the universe and of the sacred Trinity, and therefore are they said to exist in themselves, because no creature is interposed between them and the one Cause of all things. And while the primordial Causes subsist immutably in it, they become the causes of other causes that follow out to the very extremes of all nature, and are infinitely multiplied; infinitely I mean, not in respect of the Creator, but of the creature; for the end of the multiplication of the creatures is known only to the Creator. The primordial causes, then, which wise men call the principles of all things, are Goodness in itself, Essence in itself, Life in itself, Wisdom in itself, Truth in itself, Intellect in itself, Reason in itself, Virtue in itself, Justice in itself, Health in itself, Magnitude in itself, Omnipotence in itself, Eternity in itself, Peace in itself, and all virtues and reasons which the Father once and at once made in the Son, and according to which is established the order of all things, from the highest to the lowest, that is, from the intellectual creature that is next to God, to the farthest order of things in which bodies are contained."

Movements or energies of the Divine Will.

Derivation and growth of things.

What these causes are.

Difference between the Platonism of Johannes and that of Plato himself, of Plotinus and of the Fathers.

52. Here is the Christian Platonism of the 9th century in its most complete form, exceedingly unlike the Alexandrian Platonism from which it has been supposed to be derived, equally unlike the pure Socratic Platonism of which that was the corruption, different in most important respects from the Augustinian Platonism, or from that of the Greek Fathers with which it stands in much closer affinity. It was impossible for a man with such an idea of the Godhead, and of the divine humanity of the Word, as Johannes had, to be in sympathy with Plotinus, and with those who derived their lore from him. It was as impossible for him, as it was for them, to place himself in the position and point of view of the elder inquirers. It was impossible for one who started with a theory which made man's *actual* condition dependent on the Fall,

even if that theory was in accordance with many of the statements
in the writings of the Fathers, or followed legitimately from them,
to have the same sense which they had of an evil in himself, which
was disturbing all relations with his fellows and with this world.
His Platonism, therefore, stands by itself, unintelligible without
these previous passages in the history of human thought, but not
to be confounded with any of them, interesting as a study for all
times, valuable as a protest in his own time, indispensable as an
illustration of some of the most perplexing problems in the after
scholastical philosophy, but strangely unlike that philosophy in its
foundation, even more than in its superstructure.

53. In the third book we enter upon that species which has ^{The Created}
been described as Created and not Creating. At the opening of ^{and not Creating}
it the disciple raises an important question: "How it is that the ^{species.}
Being who has been so carefully denied to be included under any
of the predicaments, should nevertheless be considered in a treatise
on the division of Nature?" The master answers that he would
by no means speak of God in any of the terms which belong to a
created universe, and which therefore imply limitation; but that ^{How far the}
the universe itself, and nature, so far as it is identical with the ^{Primary Cause may}
universe, must include the Creator as well as the created, and that ^{be included in the Uni-}
without this admission it would be absolutely impossible to treat ^{verse.}
of the created, which is only participant of the goodness, wisdom,
essence, which dwell superlatively and transcendently in Him from
whom they have come. Another question springs out of this. The
different primordial causes were arranged in a certain order in
the last book. Was this order adopted at hazard, or did the writer
mean that Goodness is the first of them, Essence the second, Life
the third? The answer is, that there is a divine order which dwells
only in the mind of God himself, which no creature can dare to
look into. Nevertheless, there is an intuition which is given to ^{The order of}
those who reverently and humbly contemplate the universe, not ^{causes; how far we can}
following their own guesses, but seeking to be led by the higher ^{ascertain it.}
Wisdom, which enables them to see a sequence in principles, and
to trace not perfectly, but with an approximation to certainty, their
evolution. On this ground Johannes ventures to affirm, not without
the authority of Fathers, and especially of Dionysius the Areopagite,
that goodness in itself is the most comprehensive of the divine
donations, and in some sense precedes the others. "For the cause
of all things, that creative goodness which is God, to this end first
of all created that cause which is called goodness in itself, that by
it He might bring all things which are from non-existence into
being. Essence, therefore, must be considered as following Good- ^{Goodness}
ness, not as the ground of it." "And this," he says, "the Scripture ^{before Being.}
openly pronounces, saying, God saw all things, and not, lo they
are, but lo they are very good. What," he adds, "would it

avail only to be, if the well-being were taken away?" "For in
truth all things which are, are in so far forth as they are good;
but to whatever degree they are not good, or rather to whatever
degree they are less good, to that degree they are not. Therefore
if their goodness is altogether taken away, there remains no Being.

For simply to be, or to be essentially, the well-being and the essential well-being being taken away, is an abuse of language, as also
it is to speak of being and eternal being under that condition."
This bold position gives birth to a still bolder. Goodness, he
affirms, may be without Being. "Not only the things which are,
are good, but even those which are not are called good. Yea,
those things are called far better which are not, than those which
are. For in so far forth as through their excellence they transcend Essence, they approach to the super-essential Good, but in
so far as they participate of Essence, they are separated from the

super-essential Good.' Here our subtle Celt enters into one of
those extravagant and monstrous refinements which give us Goths
a right to raise our rough voices against him, and to declare that
into such an impalpable cloud world we, for our parts, have
no wish to ascend. In fact we see here "the Nemesis of logic."
Johannes, the great antagonist of formal distinctions, who has shown
that we cannot be consistent with ourselves that we must use
paradoxical language when we speak of that which is divine, is
driven by the dæmon of logic, by the wildest longing for consistency, into expressions that are almost insane. One must have
great faith in his goodness, and some knowledge of our own temptations, not to suspect him of having lost his earnestness when he
wrote such sentences as these. We do not, however, entertain

any such suspicion. We only read in his rash and wild utterances
the attempt of a courageous and really devout mind to utter that
which it knew to be unutterable, to clothe in the form of conceptions those thoughts which become safe and practical and the beginning of good deeds, when they take the form of adoration. They
show, further, how much the transcendent metaphysics of Johannes
needed to be associated with a sound morality, that they might not
be made the warrant for conclusions which no one would have abhorred more than himself.

54. In the following paragraph, the dependence of Life upon
Essence is in like manner established. A remark which occurs in
the course of the investigation, throws some light upon a distinction
which we have already met with in Aristotle, and which is here

transferred and adapted to Christian ideas. "Wisdom," he says,
"is properly called that virtue whereby the contemplative mind,
whether it be human or angelical, considers eternal and unchangeable things, whether it is occupied about the primary cause of
all things, or about the primordial causes of things which the

Father hath formed in His own Word, which species of study is
called by the wise Theology. But science is the virtue whereby
the theoretical mind, whether human or angelical, treats of the
nature of things proceeding out of the primordial causes by generation, divided into genera and species by differences and properties, whether it is subject to accidents or without them, whether it *Physics.*
is joined to bodies or altogether free from them, whether distributed in places and times, or beyond places and times, united and
inseparable in its own simplicity; which kind of study is called
physics. For physics is the science of all natures that are cognizable by the senses or the intellect."

55. This is in fact the proper subject of our present book.
Hitherto we have been occupied with the causes or first principles
of things; now we are to consider their effects, how they come
forth into forms. We might, therefore, claim a release from our *Forms.*
task, on the plea that Johannes was passing beyond our metaphysical and moral region, into one with which we have no direct
concern. But we are afraid that this excuse will hardly be admitted
by any student of this third book. Our author is never more
metaphysical than when he approaches physics. The question
which occupied all ancient philosophers so much, how the principles of which the world consists can be said to have come into
existence at a certain time, is here discussed at great length, and
with courage as well as humility, by Johannes. He admits, in the
fullest sense, that all visible effects are connected with time, and
have come into existence with time. He does not for a moment
suppose anything to exist independently of God. But since he *The Creation
can attribute no accident to God, he believes that creation itself is* *necessary.*
involved and implied in His Being, or in that which he has told us
is higher than being, His transcendent Goodness; that whatever is
made has in it a divine principle, apart from which it would not be,
and that this principle existed eternally in the Divine Word. So
that it is not incorrect to say that all things are made, and that all
things are eternal, seeing that that which is the very ground and
principle of their being was in Him with whom is no variableness
or shadow of turning, who is the same yesterday, to-day, and for
ever. He quotes the words of St. John, using that punctuation
which is adopted by some of our most modern commentators,—
"What was made in Him was Life," or, as he says Augustine
explains it,—"What was made locally and temporarily, in Him
was life." "For," he goes on, "the same Augustine manifestly
teaches that both places and times, with all things that are made
in them, were made eternally in the Word of God. He understood
the apostle to speak strictly concerning the Word, in whom are
created all things which are in heaven and which are in earth,
visible or invisible. Under the word visible we must include places

and times, and all things which are in them." The conclusion is, that we must not hesitate to say, that all the causes of all things, and all the effects of all causes, are both eternal, and made in the Word.

56. The book concludes with an examination of the 1st chapter of Genesis, which the writer, carefully considering the opposing opinions of different Fathers, and bringing all the philological as well as physical knowledge he had to bear upon the subject, interprets as exhibiting not the production of visible things, but the gradual unfolding of their different orders and species in the divine mind. However much boldness he may show in his treatment of these and other topics which are handled in this book, however unfortunate some of his phrases may seem to us to be, however widely we may dissent from many of his conclusions, we are bound to acknowledge that the habitual temper of his mind is faithfully exhibited in the inference and the petitions which he puts into the mouth of his disciple. "Assuredly the divine clemency suffereth not those who piously and humbly seek the truth to wander in the darkness of ignorance, to fall into the pits of false opinions, and to perish in them. For there is no worse death than the ignorance of truth, no deeper whirlpool than that in which false things are chosen in place of the true, which is the very property of error. For out of these, foul and abominable monsters are wont to shape themselves in human thoughts, while loving and following which, as if they were true, wishing to embrace flying shadows and not able to do it, the carnal soul falls ofttimes into an abyss of misery. Wherefore we ought continually to pray and to say, 'God, our salvation and redemption, who hast given us nature, grant to us also grace. Manifest thy light to us, feeling after Thee, and seeking Thee, in the shades of ignorance. Recall us from our errors. Stretch out thy right hand to us weak ones who cannot, without Thee, come to Thee. Show Thyself to those who seek nothing besides Thee! Break the clouds of vain phantasies which suffer not the eye of the mind to behold Thee in that way in which Thou permittest those that long to behold that face of thine, though it is invisible, which is their rest, the end beyond which they crave for nothing, seeing that there cannot be any good beyond it that is higher than itself!'"

57. The fourth book brings us a great step forward in the inquiry. The master enters upon it with unwonted trembling; all the storms and quicksands they have encountered already are nothing, he says, to those which they must look for in the remainder of their voyage. They start from the words of Genesis in the record of the fifth day's creation, *Let the waters bring forth abundantly the moving creature that hath life; let the earth bring forth the living creature after his kind.* He develops this idea, of which he had

given a hint in the former book, that what is here spoken of is not The Genesis
of things.
the birth of actual things, but the formation of kinds and orders
which had an existence in the Divine Word before they came forth
into visible and material shapes; then he proceeds to the great question of all, how man stands related to the rest of the universe. There
is no flinching or hesitation here. It is laid down as a principle
recognized among the wise, that the whole creation is found in Man the
Microcosm.
man. For he understands and reasons as an angel; he has senses,
and administers a body as an animal. The division of the whole
creation is fivefold. Either it is Corporeal, or Vital, or Sensitive, or
Rational, or Intellectual. And all these are contained in every
man. The extreme of his nature is his body; then comes the The different
kinds of Life
in Man.
Seminal Life governing his body, over which life his sense presides;
then the Reason which contemplates the order and arrangement of
things; then the Intellect, which is occupied with God. This
division, however, is not to be understood as if the Intellect, the
Reason, the Sense, the Seminal Life, were separate entities, to which
a different region is assigned. The word 'parts,' in reference to
man, is ambiguous, though indispensable. Johannes would speak
rather of a variety of movements or administrations. "For when
the reason carefully contemplates the human soul, it finds that
soul to be most simple—a whole in itself—and in no part to
be unlike itself, or to have a higher and lower within itself; in any
of those things, at least, which constitute its essence. The whole
administers the body, nourishes it, causes it to grow. The whole
perceives in the senses; the whole receives the appearances of sensible things; the whole remembers, &c. . . . . Whereby
it is understood how the whole human soul is formed in the
image of God, because the whole intellect is intelligent, the
whole reason discursive, the whole sense sentient, the whole life
vivifying."

58. The body, though administered by these powers, is care- The Body.
fully excluded from the idea of man so made in the image of God;
and the fall of man is again affirmed to be the sole cause of the
division of sexes, and of the multiplication of the species by genera- The Sexes
tion. But the question inevitably suggests itself, Was the body,
then, produced by evil? Was it not contemplated in the original
creation "Let us make man in our image?" The question is re-
solved as one might anticipate. The original body is affirmed to The Body
before and
after the Fall.
have been spiritual and immortal; its corruption to be a super-
venient accident, the consequence of transgression. This opinion,
which, as far as the bare statement of it goes, does not disagree
with the one commonly adopted by divines, is especially necessary
to Johannes, since he could not consistently tolerate the notion of
the created body being subsequent, in time, to the spiritual or intellectual. The form of the body, its primary spiritual constitu-

tion, is declared to remain amidst all the changes which it has undergone from its connection with matter, and from subjection to the accidents of matter. Its outward material vesture will fall off, and be mixed with the elements out of which it is formed. But the true native form, the proper body, will be preserved, and recover its relation to the soul which inhabits it.

59. On this subject, as always, Johannes is careful to support himself with the authority of the Fathers. Gregory of Nyssa is his main prop; but he is honest enough to perceive and acknowledge that there are passages in Augustine which seem to affirm that an animal, earthly, body belonged to man before his fall, and that the plain letter of the Bible is in favour of that opinion. In the effort to reconcile these statements, he encounters the question of all questions, whether the existence of the evil to come was *present* to the mind of the Creator; the phrase whether

He was *præscient* of it, he rejects, as introducing a notion of time into the idea of the Godhead. He disputes the existence of any period of innocence, urging that the Scripture rather compels us to suppose that the Paradisiacal state was lost and the animal condition of man contracted immediately.

60. The discussion on the nature of Paradise which follows, and which is continued to the end of the fourth book, belongs strictly to the province of the interpreter of Scripture. We should gladly pass it over altogether on this plea, were it not necessary for the purpose of our history and for the justification of our objections to M. Guizot that we should show how inseparably the philosophy of Johannes is intertwined with his theology, and how all his considerations respecting man and nature have God for their basis. We are quite aware that we are giving an apparent advantage to the theory respecting our author which we have rejected, when we say that he evidently inclines to the opinion that Paradise is wholly intellectual, and not local; that though he does not positively contradict the opposite doctrine, and admits that there are passages in some of the Fathers in favour of it, he quotes with evident delight and sympathy the numerous sentences from the two Gregories, from Ambrose, and from Augustine, which contain what we call the allegorical sense, and that he looks upon them as governing the interpretation of those which are apparently at variance with them. Considered from our point of view, this evidence would be decisive that he was merely philosophizing away Holy Writ. But

he seemed to *himself* to be vindicating the eternal and invisible, which Holy Writ is making known to us, from a carnal philosophy that explains away whatever it cannot reduce under the forms of sense. He protests vehemently against the letter which killeth, and the Jews who rejected Christ because they could not look beyond that letter, at the same time that he takes great pains by all the aids which he possesses, to arrive at the signification of the letter. Our own opinion has been sufficiently indicated already. We feel not the least disposed to resolve actual men and women into Reason and Sense, actual trees into spiritual principles, actual animals into the lower portions of our own nature. All such reductions and translations savour of the close school-room and cell; they do not belong to the open air, to health and freedom. But just as little do we expect to find health and freedom when men and women and trees and animals are reduced into dry skeletons, from which life and motion and mystery have been exhausted. This is *our* temptation. This is what the interpreters and doctors do, who wrap themselves in their insolent and conceited affectation of being the only sensible men that the world has seen, alike despisers of the past and out of sympathy with the future, incapable of understanding their fathers, heartless and indifferent to all the thoughts that are working in their children. They have ceased even to care for the letter of the books which they esteem divine. They worship nothing but themselves and their own wisdom. We are no disciples of Johannes; but we venture to say that any one page, almost any one sentence, of his book, would suggest more subjects for thought, would awaken more reflection, and, above all, would promote more reverence for the Bible, than folios of their flat and dreary repetitions.

Criticism of them and the Spiritualists.

61. The last book of the treatise, "On the Division of Nature," is, in many respects, the most striking of the five. There are passages in it of very high philosophical eloquence. The tone of it is freer and more exalted. There are fewer refinements—a more evident consciousness of the grandeur and awfulness of the subject. Yet, as might be expected, there is more in it to shock the ordinary reader than in the earlier books, seeing that the principles which are latent in them are here expanded and developed. We are come to the full exposition of the doctrine that all things are to return unto God, that He is to be all in all. We are come, therefore, to the point in which we may expect to find the pantheistical seeds which we have detected in our author coming forth into their full flower. There are passages certainly which justify that expectation; there are many more which will *seem* to justify it to a person who has already passed judgment on Johannes, and is seeking for evidence in support of his foregone conclusion. The sentences in the book which we would especially recommend to such persons are those wherein Johannes speaks, as Buddhists of old and some modern Germans have spoken, of an absolute Nothing, in the contemplation of which, if we interpreted him strictly, the pure and perfected soul at last loses itself. Let no one suppose that we are not aware that he has used such language, or that we are not sensible of its exceeding danger, when we say that on the whole this book mitigates instead of increasing the appre-

The Fifth Book.

The Restoration.

The Absolute Nothing.

Unfair inference from the use of this language.

hensions we had formed of our author's tendencies, and enables us to feel what a deep fountain of inward devotion and spiritual life there was in him to counteract them. If we pronounce condemnation upon him for that word about Nothing, Mde. Guion and Fénélon, and many Protestants whose faith no one would dream of suspecting, must be likewise excommunicated. And when Johannes, who is a much more consistent thinker and reasoner than any of them, develops his idea of the return of all things to their original, he carefully guards against the inference for which some of his phrases in the earlier books gave considerable excuse, that any thing or person must lose his or its distinct substance or personality in order that it may re-ascend to that Fount of Being from which, by transgression, or the effects of transgression, there had been a separation. Whatever the apparent necessities of his theory might demand, his moral instincts and his theological instincts also rebel against the decree that the greatest fulness and perfection of life in any creature can involve the loss and absorption of any of the faculties, energies, affections which had dwelt in it, and therefore of that which has been its

The Individual and the Universal.

characteristic energy and strength and affection. However hard it may be to reconcile the preservation of every type, and of every individual creature with that fulness of the divine perfection, that indwelling of all in God, which the Scriptures taught him to hope for, and to which he found the most illustrious of the Fathers of the Church continually referring, he still felt that there must be

Difference in the practical result between him and the Plotinian Pantheists.

somehow such a reconciliation. His firm and undoubting belief in the Divine Word as Him in whom all things were created, and by whom all things consisted—his equally strong conviction that this Word had been made flesh and dwelt among men, and had redeemed not a part of creation, but the whole of it—offered, as he thought, the solution of the theoretical difficulty, certainly kept him from the practical confusions which it might have engendered. Any one who compares his idea of a return into the divine nature with that of any philosophers or theologians who have never entered into these Christian principles, or have let them go, will feel himself in one case to be ascending through verdant meadows and by sunny slopes, on which cattle are grazing and in which are the habitations of human beings, to the summit of a mountain which may perhaps be covered with snow, which may at times be lost in mist, but from which there is ever and anon, in spite of its own seeming desolation, a glorious prospect of hill, and vale, and river, and from which there is always a descent into the richer and softer regions where breathing is free; that in the other case he is carried at once into a polar region, with scarcely a hope of ever breaking loose from the thick ribbed ice to see once more the face of men, to hear the music of human voices.

62. It must, however, be confessed that Johannes asserts a doc-

trine in this book which we suspect will give far more offence to The
many of his readers in our day than any of the expressions that Termination
savour of Pantheism, and might tempt some readers into that of of Evil
which the author was himself free.   He asserts vehemently that
the extinction of moral evil is implied in the order and in the redemption of the universe, as these are setforth to us in holy Scripture.   The Master says, " Dost thou then consider that evil and
its consequences, death and misery, and the punishments of divers
faults were created by God, and are participant of the divine virtue?   For when it is written, 'death and life are from the Lord,' The Death
I do not think he speaks of that death which humanity dies by that is from
sinning, but of that death to which the Psalmist refers when he Death of Self
says, 'Blessed in the sight of the Lord is the death of His saints,'
that is, precious is the passage of purified souls into the intimate
contemplation of truth, which is the true blessedness and eternity.
'l his is the death which those who live religiously and in chastity of heart seek their God die even while they dwell in this mortal life, seeing what they see in a glass darkly, hereafter to return
to the ancient and original glory of the divine image, the seeing
God face to face.   .   .   .   Where, by face, we are to understand
such an apparition of that divine virtue, which in itself is perceived by no creature, as may be comprehensible to the human
intellect.   Wherefore, if evil, and death, and misery, is repugnant
to the nature that has been so formed, neither is constituted in
Him who is the cause of all things, I wonder on what principle The Extent of
you deliberate and hesitate, thinking that evil and the death of Redemption.
eternal torments can remain for ever in that humanity the whole
of which the Word of God took into Himself and redeemed ;
whereas true reason teacheth that nothing contrary to the divine
goodness, and life, and blessedness, can be co-eternal with them.
For the divine goodness will consume evil, eternal life will absorb
death and misery.   For it is written, ' I will be thy plague,
O death, thy torment, O hell.' "

63. Although Johannes appears in this last passage to reason, it Reason,
will be observed that he appeals to Scripture as the true interpre- Scripture,
ter of the divine reason to men.   Nor does he omit continued re- the Fathers
ference to Ambrose and Augustine (for his partiality for the Greek
Fathers does not make him the least indifferent to the Latin) in
support of the principle which he is defending.   He was aware, of
course, that a number of passages might be produced from them
in direct opposition to the sentiments which he was propounding,
yet he sincerely believed that if they were allowed to explain
themselves, and if their deepest and most deliberate expositions
were taken to control those which furnished the readiest materials for quotations, they would be found to accord with him in
spirit, if not in letter, and to be at hopeless variance with the popu-

lar teachers who relied upon them. It is not likely that these arguments would have much weight with the modern English reader.
He would assume that Johannes was perverting his authorities to
his own use, even when their words seemed to favour him most.
Possibly a sentence or two of his own, which express his most inward thoughts and convictions, may leave a pleasanter impression
on the minds of our readers, and may lead them to part with him,

His practical Truth. as we do, not without some respect and tenderness. "Hence," he
says, "it most clearly follows that nothing else is to be desired except the joy which comes from truth, which is direct, and nothing
else is to be shunned except His absence, which is the one and
sole cause of all eternal sorrow. Take from me Christ, no good
will remain to me, and no torment affrights me. The loss and absence of Christ is the torment of the whole rational creation; nor
do I think there is any other." What else is necessary to be
said, on his behalf, he shall say for himself, in the words with

L'Envoi. which he takes leave of his pupil. "If in this work which I have
now completed, any one shall discover that I have written what
was ignorant and superfluous, let him impute it to my hastiness
and carelessness, and let him, as a humble beholder of man's
poverty, weighed down by his fleshly tabernacle, look upon it with
a pious and pitiful heart. For I deem that there is nothing perfect yet in human studies, nothing without error in this dark life.
Wherefore the Righteous, while they still live in the flesh, are not
called so because they actually are so, but because they wish to be
so, craving for a perfect righteousness which is to be; the affection of their mind wins them their name. . . . But if any one
finds anything in this book that is useful and tends to the building
up of the Catholic faith, let him ascribe it to God alone, who only
brings to light the hidden things of darkness, and brings those who
seek Him to Himself, purged from their errors; and let his Spirit,
joined with us in love, render thanks with us to the universal
Cause of all good things, without whom we can do nothing; not
tempted by the lust of condemning, not kindled by the torch of
envy, which more than all other vices, seeks to break the bond of
charity and brotherhood. And so, in peace with all, whether
they kindly receive that which we have put together, and behold
it with the pure eye of their mind, or whether they unkindly reject it, and judge it before they know what and of what kind it is,
I commit my work first to God, who says 'Ask and it shall be
given you, seek and you shall find,' and next to you, dearest
brother in Christ, my fellow-worker in the pursuit of wisdom, to
be examined and corrected. . . . Hereafter, when these words
shall come into the hands of those who seek wisdom truly, seeing
they will conspire with their previous questionings, they will not
only receive them with a glad mind, but will kiss them as if they

were their own kinsmen come back to them. But if they should fall among those who are quicker in blaming than in sympathizing, I would not contend much with them. Let every one use the sense which he has till that light comes which will make darkness out of the light of those who are philosophizing falsely and unworthily, and will turn the darkness of those who welcome it into light."

Concerning the opinions of the man who could speak thus we may form very different judgments; some of them we shall, most of us, probably, agree in condemning. To the man himself, an earnest and charitable student will be inclined to apply the prayer which was spoken of one in the next century, who honoured Johannes and shared his evil fame:

> Post obitum vivam tecum, tecum requiescam,
> Nec fiat melior sors mea sorte tuâ.

CHAPTER III.

TENTH AND ELEVENTH CENTURIES.

Review of
the Ninth
Century. 1. THE ninth century has detained us longer, than its importance
in the eyes of general readers would appear to justify. But we
cannot apologise for the time we have devoted to it, or to the
eminent, comparatively unknown, man, whom we have taken
as representing some of its deepest thoughts though certainly not
its popular opinions. The controversies of this century are the
proper induction to the school history of the Middle Ages. In
considering how those controversies were involved with the practical life of the period, with its ecclesiastical organization, with the
fears, struggles, hopes of its most remarkable men, we learn not
to treat that School history as the record of barren and by-
gone speculations; it is full of enduring, full of present and personal significance, if we will be at the pains of breaking the rough
and hard shell that we may find what is within. There were deep
fires burning in the hearts, and not seldom breaking forth in the
words of those who, if we judge them from mere reports of their
theories, we should suppose were entirely removed from sympathy
with us their ordinary fellow-creatures.

Barrenness
of the Tenth. 2. The tenth century will afford us no occasion for such explanations. In outward bustle, in the mere number of events,
hard to methodize, but stirring enough, so far as secret and open
crimes can make them so, this age is far more conspicuous than
its predecessor. Nevertheless, the epithet "dark," which has
been bestowed upon it, with very little dissension, by historians,
is justified, especially by those qualities in which it stands distinguished from the time before it and after it. They are often stigma-
tized as "dark" because there was so much thought in them of a
kind which belongs to the cloister rather than the crowd, which is
carried on under ground, and does not, for a long time at least,
make itself felt upon the surface of society. The tenth century is
dark from its broad and manifest abominations, from the utter
absence of principle among Nobles and Churchmen, from the want
of any thinking that can be called earnest by its admirers, or mystical and unpractical by its despisers, from all those indications
which most betray the worldly character and purposes of the

men who, under one mask or another, were playing their different parts.

3. If England presented itself as a kind of intellectual centre in the eighth century, France in the ninth, we may hesitate to what country we should assign that position in the tenth. Italy is, unquestionably, the scene of the most exciting political intrigues of the time; the capital of Western Christendom is the place in which its blackest enormities are gathered up, and from which they diffuse themselves abroad. Italy is the battle-field whereon all the selfish interests of families who claim lands and people for their hereditary possession are engaged. The Popedom becomes the prize for the counts, dukes, and harlots who, by one foul means or another, are enabled to make good their supremacy. But the crimes of Italy call forth an avenger. The tenth century brings the German empire to light. In Germany is the centre of a much more vigorous, and, on the whole, healthy power. The princes and ecclesiastics of Italy are obliged to bow before it, because some of the morality of the north is found in it, and gives it dominion. The world had reason to rejoice when the descendants of Arminius claimed to be the successors of the Cæsars, and to establish or unseat the spiritual fathers at their pleasure. Considering the circumstances of the tenth century, this was a divine boon to the nations. Yet it showed that all but naked despotism was the only possible resource for that wicked time; that the idea of moral and spiritual power was nearly extinct. To call either Italy or Germany, therefore, an intellectual centre of Europe at this time, is an abuse of terms. Possibly we shall be more right if we concede that name to Spain. Humiliating as the confession may be, the sense of a power that was not merely physical or merely artificial, upheld by the strength of the arm or created by man's ingenuity, dwelt with the Saracen. The study of laws of nature, of laws which men could not regulate, but must confess, was pursued more diligently and successfully at Cordova than in any city of Christendom. Thither Christian scholars must resort, if they were not ready to confess that God revealed the secrets of His universe exclusively to the Mussulman, and that those who believed in the Incarnation of His Son were to know nothing but the arts of the basest politicians, or the lies by which the basest churchmen saved them from detection.

4. It was a perilous alternative doubtless. Those who took what seems to us, on the whole, the more honourable course, who thought that it was safer to seek for truth, whatever guides might show them the way to it, than to remain ignorant of it, exposed themselves to great risks, not only in the opinion of their cotemporaries, but even, we should apprehend, in their own inmost convictions. They were suspected of being magicians by those who

G

heard of their exploits in Mathematics and Natural Philosophy. Were they quite sure that the accusation was a false one? Had they not some feeling as if their knowledge might have come to them from an unlawful source? In using it, in exercising it as a power over their fellow-creatures, was there not some temptation to keep up an opinion, even to justify it by acts which increased the dread of their influence, and in that way the influence itself?

Gerbert. See Ritter B. B. c. I. and Gerbert's Letters
5. Modern writers have questioned whether Gerbert, the celebrated Frenchman who became the adviser of the Capets, the ally of the Othos, and finally the spiritual father of Christendom, ever studied at Cordova. They say there is no evidence of his going farther into Spain than Barcelona, or of his mixing with the Saracens. Unquestionably his letters do not convict him of any attachment to the Infidels: on the contrary, the first passionate appeal on behalf of the Sepulchre, and of those who visited it, is to His character. be found in them. He may be looked upon as the ancestor, though not the father, of the crusading movement. There is nothing inconsistent in this enthusiasm with the belief that he may have spoiled the Egyptians of some of their treasures in his youth. Nor would it follow that he had the same dislike for the cultivated Moslems of Spain, as for those who were possessing Jerusalem. At all events, his cotemporaries believed him to have been in commerce with those who could teach him the black arts, and enable him to sway for a time the spirits who would ultimately claim Suspicions of his acts. him as their prize. His success in political negotiations may have given quite as reasonable a colour to the charge, as his acquaintance with the secrets of nature. A person engaged in many important transactions at such a period, and connected more or less closely with two great revolutions, may not have kept his hands as clean as one might wish a Churchman's to be. But that they were cleaner than those of most men of his order in that period, seems to admit of little doubt. His intrigues, if he was engaged in them, were not for sordid, beggarly purposes; they concerned the change His Politics. of dynasties and the consolidation of empires. His more private transactions, as we gather from his letters, related to the removal of disorders and of oppressions which the greater nobles or ecclesiastics were perpetrating in their dioceses, or over the monasteries. It may, therefore, be conjectured that he was aiming at the restoration of the Church to something of the moral and intellectual standing which it had lost, and that he was willing, for this end, to avail himself of the aid of German or French Monarchs, who were probably the honestest and the most purpose-like men he could meet with. And it seems not at all unlikely that, for the His Algebra. same end, he should have studied not only the algebraic symbols of the Spanish doctors, but others which were supposed to have a

more occult signification and virtue. To keep the two apart at such a time was exceedingly difficult. It is clear that they were not absolutely confounded by Christians. William of Malmesbury at least—who, though he belongs to a different period, when the Norman culture had been diffused, must have taken his statements from those who were close to Gerbert's time, and were most prejudiced against him—recognizes very distinctly the value of the lawful sciences in which the Pope was an adept. But to perceive such mysteries of nature as were discovered in lines and numbers, as were guessed at in the relations of the heavenly bodies, and not to dream of other deeper mysteries which might be dived into; to forget altogether that the persons who had the last kind of learning were dangerous men, who could hardly have received it from a holy teacher,—this was nearly impossible for human nature. What more than this is wanted as a legitimate basis for a number of strange stories which have gathered about the name of Gerbert— stories which conspire with other evidence to make us think of him as a remarkable man, which need not prevent us from considering him, on the whole, a useful and a righteous man, though they may show that he was tempted, as all men are, by a false spirit, and that this spirit took a form suitable to the age to which he belonged, and the debasement (moral even more than intellectual) of those among whom he lived?

William of Malmesbury Chronicle, Book II., c. 10.

To what degree Science and Magic were confused then and afterwards.

6. Ritter quotes a passage from a letter of Gerbert's to Pope John, which is undoubtedly of great value in determining his position between the ecclesiastics and the statesmen of the time. He is apologizing for the course which he takes in attaching himself to the latter, especially, no doubt, to the German emperors, and he lays down the maxim that though Divinity takes precedence of Humanity in speculation, Humanity must first be considered in action. No doubt this was the principle upon which many eminent men in his own and in subsequent times acted. It would have been Dante's justification for deserting the Guelphic party in the fourteenth century. These Emperors, Gerbert may have said, keep up the respect for human laws; the ecclesiastics transgress human and divine equally, and lead the people to despise both. Very little stress can be laid on the other member of the sentence (even if its meaning were quite apparent), which declares how Divinity was to make its power felt in speculation. Ritter contends that Gerbert anticipated the movement of the next century in favour of logic, and that this is his characteristic in a history of philosophy. It will be evident to our readers that we cannot adopt this statement. Logic, it seems to us, had already established its ascendency in the ninth century. There is no meaning in the work of Johannes Scotus, unless we assume it to be a struggle on behalf of the elder Platonical theology against a usurping and triumphant rival; no explanation of some

Gerbert's defence of his addiction to Emperors.

His Logic supposed to be a novelty.

of its most remarkable peculiarities, unless we allow him, in spite of himself, to have been overcome by the logical tendencies of his time. If we supposed Johannes to be a legitimate successor of the old Proclus school, and no great Latin movements to have taken place before he flourished, we might say fairly enough that the old philosophy died with him, and that Gerbert, being the only eminent thinker between him and the eleventh century, was the founder, or at least the prophet, of the new. But as Johannes was merely an interloper, and as the theological controversies of the ninth century clearly ascertained its character, we may assume that the papal magician, in his dogmatical treatises, merely travelled in a line which had been already marked out for him, and that any pretensions which he had to originality rested, as the cotemporary authorities would lead us to suppose, upon his physical and demoniacal lore.

7. Gerbert stood on the threshold of the eleventh century. Possibly the horror of his supposed communications both with visible infidels and the invisible powers of darkness, had an effect upon it, in determining what studies should be avoided; still more in promoting the establishment or consolidation of Christian schools, which should be a substitute for the Saracenic, and a counteraction of them. There were other influences working more powerfully to the same result. The first Millennium of Christendom was concluded. "Was it not to terminate," men asked themselves, "in the destruction of the visible world?" The crimes of all classes made such an expectation reasonable; they were greatest and most abominable in the class which existed to testify of righteousness. This belief gave a solemnity to the minds of the better men. It left its impression upon the age. It became an age of movement, of energy, even of reformation; contrasted in all respects with the base and petty one which had preceded it. The intrigues in dukedoms between ambitious proprietors, made way for the conflict between popes and emperors. Great principles are engaged on each side. The common Christendom life is awakening in the West. The life in the schools will, we may be sure, take its form and colour from that which is passing in the world, and will re-act upon it.

8. The doubt which we expressed in reference to the former century has no application to this. We can define exactly the centre of the European movements. For a moment, indeed, the great fame of Hildebrand, and the position which he asserted for the Roman See, might incline us to think of Italy. Unquestionably the relation of the Pope to the rest of Europe *is* the great subject of this century. Apart from the fact that this relation assumed a character it had never assumed before, all the records of the time are unintelligible. But the vicissitudes in the

reign of Hildebrand himself, his unpopularity in Rome, his final *Hildebrand.*
hanishment from it, may show us clearly that it was not to his own
country that he owed the greatness which he vindicated for those
who preceded, and for those who came after him, as much as for
himself. Both of these had to endure the ignominy from which
his own magnanimity scarcely protected him. If Leo IX. was
saved from it, he owed his deliverance to the *Normans*. The *The*
Normans were the real supporters of Gregory's own pretensions. *Normans.*
The Normans enabled Urban to become the head of a crusade, and
so to unite Christendom under his own authority, when the Germans were making its existence doubtful even in his capital.
To Normandy, therefore, we are obliged to turn if we would study
the progress of events. To Normandy we are bound quite as much
to turn if we would understand the movements in philosophy.

9. When we speak of Normandy as an intellectual centre to Europe *Normandy*
in the eleventh century, and when we deny that honour to Italy, *draws the*
we are guilty of an apparent injustice. The most eminent thinkers *Intellect of*
of this time were Italians. The Frenchmen who were distinguished *Europe to*
in the schools did not come from the north. But this is the very *supply the*
point on which we desire to fix our readers' attention. Italians, *intellectual*
with the gifts that fitted them to be scholars and philosophers, *men.*
could not find the kind of culture which they required, the discipline which was fitted to make them great, till they came under the
influence of the Normans. This remarkable people, as they diffused their own energy and arms into all countries of the east and
west, so also attracted into their own land the foreigners whose
qualities and circumstances were the least like their own. They
had no national exclusiveness. The indifference to soil and local *The want of*
attachments which had characterized their first emigration never *nationality*
deserted them. Their position in the north of France was only a *among the*
standing point from which to commence assaults upon the world *Normans*
at large. They belonged to Christendom, not to that place in
which they happened to have obtained a settlement. When they
invaded England, they were quite willing to have Flemings, or men
of any country in Europe, mingling in their hosts. That same
temper fitted them to be the prime movers in the Crusades. And
so they were also able to organize monasteries, in which young
men from all quarters found they could learn the maxims and
practice of obedience and government. There they could welcome Latin with as much affection as the language of their adopted
country—with more, indeed, as being more cosmopolitan.

10. The monastery of Bec is the great illustration of these *The*
remarks. "In the year from the incarnation of our Lord, 1034," *Monastery*
writes the chronicler of this society, "in the fourth year of Henry *of Bec.*
the King of the Franks, Robert, the son of the second Richard,
and brother of the third Richard holding the reins of Normandy,

Chron.
Becomes
appended to
Lanfranc's
works.
Herluinus, at the inspiration of our Lord Jesus Christ, the author of all good things, casting aside the nobility of the earth for which he had been not a little conspicuous, having thrown off the girdle of military service, betook himself with entire devotion to the poverty of Christ, and that he might be free for the service of God alone, through the mere love of God, put upon him with great joy the habit of a monk. This man, who had been a passionate warrior, and who had gotten himself a great name and favour with Robert, and with the lords of different foreign countries, first built a church on a farm of his which was called Burnevilla. But because this place was on a plain, and lacked water, being admonished in a dream by the blessed Mother of God, he retired to a valley close to a river which is called Bec, and there began to build a noble monastery to the honour of the same Saint Mary, which God brought to perfection for the glory of His name, and to be the comfort and salvation of many men. To which Herluinus, God, according to the desire of his heart, gave for his helpers and counsellors Lanfranc, a man every way accomplished in liberal acts; then Anselm, a man approved in all things, a man affable in counsel, pitiful, chaste, sober, in every clerical duty wonderfully instructed—which two men, through God's grace, were afterwards consecrated Archbishops of Canterbury. And to this same Bec, which began in the greatest poverty, so many and such great men, clerical as well as laymen, resorted, that it might fitly be said to the holy abbot—' With the riches of thy name hast thou made thy house drunk, and with the torrent of the wisdom of thy sons hast thou filled the world.' "

Lanfranc
and Anselm.

Lanfranc an
Italian.
Vita
St. Lanfranc.
11. The first of the two men with whom our chronicler has brought us acquainted, was born in Pavia. His parents, says his biographer, were great and honourable citizens of that city. His father is said to be of the order of those who watched over the rights and laws of the state. Lanfranc losing his father in early life, left the lands and dignities which might have fallen to him, and devoted himself to the study of letters. He stayed for some time in Italy, till he became thoroughly imbued with all secular knowledge. Then leaving his country, and passing the Alps, he came to Gaul in the time of William, the glorious Duke of Normandy, who subdued England with his arms. Passing through France, having a number of scholars with him, he came to the city of Avranches, and became a teacher there. Afterwards this learned man, perceiving that to catch the breath of mortals is vanity, and that all things tend to nothing, except Him who made all things and those who follow His will, turned his whole mind to obtaining His love. And because he felt it was needful to be humble that he might be great, he would not go to any place where there were literary men who would hold him in honour and

Comes to
Neustria.

reverence. Late in the evening, as he was going through a wood towards Rouen, he fell among thieves, who took away all he had, bound his hands behind him, bandaged his eyes, and left him in a dark part of the forest. For a while he bewailed his misfortune; then he tried to pay his accustomed praises to God, but could not. Then turning to the Lord, he said, "Lord God, so much time have I spent in learning, and my body and soul have I worn out in the study of letters, and yet have I not learned how I ought to pray to Thee, and to pay to Thee the duties of praise. Deliver me from this tribulation, and with thy help I will so study to correct and establish my life, that I may be able to serve Thee and to know Thee." In the twilight of the morning he heard travellers going their way, and cried to them for help. When they had loosened his bonds, he begged them that they would point out to him the poorest monastery which they knew in that country. They said they knew of none more vile and abject than that which a certain man of God had built hard by. They pointed him to Bec, and departed.

12. Lanfranc found the abbot kindling a fire, and working with his hands. He asked to be made a monk, was shown the rule, promised, with God's help, to observe it, and became a brother of the convent. "Whereupon," continues our author, "the venerable father Herluinus was filled with exceeding joy, because he believed that God had heard his prayers. For, as the necessity of procuring provisions forced him to be often without the cloister, and as there was no one to preside within, and to watch the religion of the household, he had often prayed God for such a one, and now He had granted him the very help which he wanted. You might see, therefore, between them a pious contest. The abbot, lately promoted from an illustrious layman to a clerk, reverenced the dignity of so great a doctor who had become his subject. But he, exhibiting no conceit on the strength of his eminent knowledge, obeyed him humbly in all things, and was wont to say, 'When I wait upon that layman, I know not what to think, except that the Spirit bloweth where it listeth.' The abbot showed to him the veneration which was his due; he paid the abbot the profoundest submission. Each presented to the flock a specimen of a different kind of life, the one active, the other contemplative."

13. For a while Lanfranc devoted himself in the strictest sense to the contemplative and solitary life. "But soon his fame," says the chronicler, "spread throughout the world, and brought dukes, sons of dukes, the most conspicuous masters of the Latin schools, and noblemen in multitudes to the convent." The doctor was not exalted. His biographer relates with much satisfaction how he took care of some land which had been left to the church of Bec, and how he brought a cat under his gown to repress the fury of

some rats and mice that had invaded it. He tells another story of his humility, which is considerably more to the purpose, and illustrates the man and the time. While he was reading aloud one day at the table, the presiding monk, who was probably a Norman, and like Herlwin, knew more of swords than of the quantities of words, corrected him for saying docére. The learned Italian instantly shortened the middle syllable, "knowing," his biographer says, "that he owed more obedience to Christ than to Donatus; that it was not a capital crime to violate prosody, but that not to obey one who commanded him in the name of God, was a serious error."

Docêre, or Docére?

Obedience.

His life in the Monastery.

14. After a while, Lanfranc grew thoroughly tired of the indolence, irregularity, and immorality of his brethren, and feigned a disorder of the stomach, that he might eat only radishes, and so fit himself to escape from the monastery, and live in the desert, which design was defeated by a vision to the abbot, who brought Lanfranc to confession and submission, constituted him prior, and enabled him to effect a reform in the monastery. Except in this instance, the mispronunciation of *docere* may be taken as a key to our scholar's life. Not but that he was capable of an inconvenient as well as of a successful joke when the temptation offered. When

His introduction to William.

a chaplain of Duke William came to Bec in great pomp to attend the dialectical exercises, which had become famous, Lanfranc having discovered that he was profoundly ignorant, and somewhat presumptuous, requested him, with Italian politeness, to clear up a passage in a logical treatise. The Norman resented the affront, and brought Lanfranc into disgrace with Duke William. He was ordered hastily to quit Normandy, but meeting William on his road, he respectfully requested the Duke, as he had appointed him to take so long a journey, to furnish him with a better horse. He evidently understood the man. He very soon rose into high favour. William revoked a command for laying waste certain lands belonging to Bec, and bestowed fresh lands upon it. Lanfranc was soon able to return the service. Neustria had been laid under an interdict, because the Duke had married the daughter of the Count of Flanders, who was within the prohibited degrees of relationship. Lanfranc went to Rome, and succeeded in persuading Nicholas the Second that it would be much wiser to grant William a dispensation, seeing that he was not the least likely to part with his wife, and that he might easily be induced to build two monasteries if he were permitted to retain her. Caen received the benefit of this arrangement, and Lanfranc proved that Bec was as good a school for diplomacy as for logic and theology.

Doing William's work at Rome.

15. Lanfranc's mission to the pope had not only reference to his patron's marriage, he had himself been accused of a heavy offence. He was the friend and correspondent of Berengarius of

Tours. This is a name with which most of our readers are familiar. They associate with it certain notions of independence of thought not to be looked for in the 11th century, and of a feebleness of purpose which may be condemned in all centuries. They probably suppose Berengarius to have been something of a philosopher, who had not courage to stand against the theologians of his time; they suppose those theologians to have been merely defending a coarse and carnal hypothesis by the force of traditions and papal decrees. None of these opinions are exactly in accordance with the facts, though all of them touch so nearly upon the truth as to satisfy the careless students of various parties and communions. The subject is most important to the history of Philosophy, otherwise we should not have meddled with it. The disputes of the next century, which had a formally philosophical character, grew out of the great theological dispute of this. We cannot understand the minds of any of the remarkable thinkers of the age without considering it. All that we have said of the Norman and Italian temper, as they came together in the Monastery of Bec, is illustrated by it. But we should commit a great mistake if we assumed Berengarius to be a philosopher, or those who contended with him to have any horror of philosophy. He was, so far as we can make out from the testimonies of his cotemporaries, and from what is preserved of his own writings, a hard-working, earnest, simple-minded priest, who, instead of cultivating subtleties, had a horror of them. It may seem at variance with this statement that he professed a respect for so subtle a philosopher as Johannes Scotus, and was scandalized at being told that he was a heretic. But he evidently clung to the conclusion of Johannes Scotus without caring very much for his arguments. That conclusion, he said, he found expressed as clearly in the writings of Augustine and Ambrose as of the Irishman. He was probably bewildered by the distinctions and formulas of the Italians, as much as by their diplomacy. A Frenchman, but no Norman, he shrunk from submitting to mere decrees when his conscience went the other way. Yet he had so little confidence in his own judgment, there was in him so little of the desire to be singular, that he accepted again and again formulas which he did not understand or approve. That he was a coward in doing so, no one acknowledged so readily as himself. He did not even avail himself of the half-justification which we have put forward for him; he simply accuses himself of recanting through fear of death. When that terror was removed, and he had time for reflection, he was convinced that it was a solemn duty to retract the retractation, however much opening such a course would give to the ridicule as well as to the grave revilings of his adversaries. Lessing has contended with admirable clearness and force that the charge of

Margin notes: Berenger of Tours. Common notions about him. The Eucharistic controversy. Berengarius not primarily a philosopher. His mind and country. His alleged cowardice.

Lessing's
Werke, vol.
15. (pp. 19-
72.)
intentionally concealing his opinion, which Mosheim brought
against him, is absolutely untenable. He might not have courage
always to maintain his conviction; he certainly never wished to
disguise it.

Gregory VII.
and Beren-
garius.
16. Such a man as this Pope Hildebrand could appreciate.
He did not in his heart dislike any one for fighting against authority; great part of his own life was spent in doing so. He vindicated his right to set his feet on the necks of kings. The ambition
of setting his feet upon the necks of poor parish priests, because
they objected to certain forms of expression, was altogether too
mean a one for him. It is evident that he would have sheltered
Berengarius if he could; that when he opposed him it was done
reluctantly; in spite of the condemnation of former popes, and of
the contumacy of Berengarius, he loved him to the last. With
Lanfranc it was otherwise. He and the heretic had been friends
Why Lan-
franc was so
much less
tolerant.
in youth; he had suffered in reputation at Rome from the intimacy.
Not, we believe, from meanness, not because he shrunk from an imputation which he really deserved, but because he never could have
had much inward sympathy with a man of a character so unlike
his own, because his conscience was of an altogether different quality from that of Berengarius, because it was a conscience which
looked upon disobedience as the great sin, and would have parted
with the strongest perception and conviction of its own rather than
be guilty of it, he at once disproved the calumny against himself
by becoming the most vehement champion of the Paschasian dogma
against its impugner.

Lanfranci
Opera
(Dacherius),
p. 231.
De
Eucharisti
Sacramento
contra
Berengarium
Liber.

See
Berengarius
Turonensis.
Lessing's
Werke,
vol. 15, pp.
1-158.
17. His book against Berengarius was for a long time, with the
exception of a few letters, the only document from which a knowledge of the doctrines of the offender could be obtained. Lanfranc
quotes passages from him at the head of each of his chapters; to
which he replies. The supporters of transubstantiation referred to
his treatise as triumphant; they even ventured to conjecture that
it silenced, humbled, converted Berengarius. An unfortunate
discovery made by the keen eye of Lessing in the library of
Wolfenbüttel, dispelled these dreams. Berengarius was found to
have answered Lanfranc in an elaborate discourse. By the care
of Lessing, and of subsequent editors, we now possess it almost
entire. A comparison of the two documents does not, however,
entitle us to set the intellectual qualities of Berengarius above
those of the Prior of Bec. Lanfranc's book is haughty and scorn-
ful; that of Berengarius is earnest and vehement. The one writes
with all the consciousness of maintaining the maxim which a
Council and a Pope had pronounced in favour of; the other
writes with a strong assurance that majorities and the existing
authorities of the Church may be utterly wrong, that it is impossible to read the Old and New Testament with open eyes and not

think so. But if it is a great privilege that we may retain an
affection for the oppressed and earnest man,—not shaken in that
sympathy by the fact that Luther denounced him as much as any
Romanist, and looked upon the denunciation of Pope Nicholas as
one of the decrees of the papal synod which might be justified and
admired,—it is also a duty to confess the ability of Lanfranc, the
skill and neatness with which he arranges his points and constructs
his arguments, the advantage which he has often over his fervid
antagonist, his avoidance of all that is most coarse and material in
the view of Paschasius, the facility and gracefulness of his style,
and the comparative moderation with which he asserts the claims
of the Roman See, when Berengarius could call it nothing less than
antichristian. Those who like to see a true man trampled upon,
may enjoy the satisfaction as well in Lanfranc's treatise as in any
that we know of. He is very imperious, but far less vulgar and
brutal than the majority of polemics. And one feels that he was
not merely holding a brief for the papal court, that his heart sym-
pathized with what he was doing, and that having given up the
right quantity of a Latin infinitive to preserve his own obedience,
having cultivated to the utmost all moral submission and humiliation, he felt he had a right to demand the same of all other divines.
He was maintaining not only what seemed to him, but what really
was, the great secret of the power which the Norman scholar, as
well as the Norman warrior, was exercising in that day. All his
victories were owing to his caring more for the commands of the
superior than for any judgment of his own. If there had been
none to assert that a man has a conscience to which God speaks
directly, and which must hear His voice, however other voices may
clash with it, the after condition of the world would have been
very sad; but one may surely acknowledge that there were to be
men who had the opposite habit of mind; that with all their faults
the world could not have spared them; that each class had its own
humility as well as its own pride; and that even success and cotemporary approbation, though they may diminish our interest in
those who possessed them, by making us think of the words,
"*they have their reward*," ought not to blind us to their positive
worth.

18. We must not suppose that more of dialectical science, either in
the larger or the narrower sense, found its way into this controversy
in the 11th century than in the 9th. The opposite assertion would
be far nearer the truth. The schools were in the first fervour of
their qualities and quantities in the age of Charlemagne. This
they imported into their theological discussions. With these, old
Platonists like Johannes had to do battle, endeavouring as far
as they could to supplant the Aristotelian dialectic with a more
spiritual one. The first stage of that struggle was over. Beren-

Marginal notes:

D. Martin Luther's Bekenntniss vom Abendmahl Christi. an. 1678. Luther's Werke, Walch, p. 1291. "Wollte Gott, alie Päbste hätten so Christlich in allen Stücken gehandelt als dieser Pabst mit dem Berenger in solcher Bekenntniss gehandelt hat."

Character of Lanfranc's book.

How he asserts the principle.

Use of the opposing Teachers.

How far Logic entered into the question.

garius introduced some logical formulas into his first treatise;
Lanfranc ridicules him for his pedantry, and insinuates that he
was showing off his learning for the sake of throwing dust in the
eyes of simple people. The charge was an unfair one. Berengarius assuredly desired to present the things which he had heard
and seen more directly to the consciences of his people than he
thought the Paschasian dogma suffered him to do. If he ever
resorted to logic unnecessarily, it was through the weakness into
which practical men often fall in trying to fight their opponents
with their own weapons. Lanfranc takes the school logic for
granted. But subjection to *that* was not what he cared to establish. Political order, subjection to the rule of the monastery, the
kingdom, the whole church, was the end to be attained. Though
he had many of the qualities to fit him for a schoolman, at least
for a theological doctor, these were by no means his most conspicuous or characteristic qualities. His genius was that of a statesman, as it was clearly shown to be when he became attached to
William of Normandy and accompanied him to England. There
all the skill which had been ripened in Bec displayed itself in a
larger sphere. His idea of the position of an Archbishop of Canterbury was not at all that he should be setting up the church
against the crown, or pushing the maxims of Hildebrand. Obedience, the watchword of his life, was to be manifested in that
relation as in every other,—to the near authority first, then, so far
as they might be reconciled, to the more distant one. Partly the
wisdom and the circumstances of William, partly the sagacity and
peculiar temperament of his prime bishop and prime minister,
partly the judicious confidence of the pope in the one, and his
judicious fear of the other, made this reconciliation in the days of
our first Norman sovereign, however difficult, not impossible.
Lanfranc could pervert a quantity, or defend a formula, or swallow
a mere ecclesiastical scruple, with the same facility, and for the
same end. Certainly a very sagacious man! with a wonderful
faculty for managing the things of earth, but with little, if any, of
the finer sensibility, or of the stern love of truth, which we are
taught to look for in one who seeks the Kingdom of Heaven.

19. In these respects, as well as in all the circumstances of their
English lives, he stands out in curious contrast to the other ornament of the Monastery of Bec, to the other Archbishop of Canterbury—his friend Anselm. Of him we have a much better right
to speak in this treatise than of Lanfranc. For he was a philosopher, *the* philosopher of the 11th century. To understand what
position he occupies in philosophical history, we must, however,
view him in connection with one whose mind was cast in an altogether different mould from his. Their relation to each other
explains the relation in which each stood to his time. We begin

Lanfranc far
less a Logi-
cian than a
statesman.

Lanfranc
finding his
true position.

Consistency
of his
character.

Anselm.

Difference
from Lan-
franc in
character.

to apprehend how Anselm, who is represented in our ordinary English histories as the arrogant and rebellious churchman, is connected with the Anselm, who, to judge from the statements of the man who knew him best, and from the evidence of his own writings, must have been one of the meekest, least assuming, least worldly of men. We discover what were the characteristics of the thinking man of that age, wherein he was strong, wherein he was feeble, how far he was an asserter of liberty for his own times and for the times to come, how far he was bringing in a new bondage upon either. The opposite reports of him.

20. Anselm was born in Aoste. His father and mother both belonged to Lombardy. The former was generous to prodigality; greatly devoted to the world during the best part of his life; a monk at the close of it. The latter was a prudent housekeeper, of a thoughtful and earnest character. The boy was bred among the mountains; he fancied that the palace of God must be on the summit of one of them. At fifteen he longed to be a monk. The abbot to whom he applied refused him; his health grew weak, which increased his desire for the convent. When he recovered he plunged for awhile into the pleasures of the world, and lost even his taste for letters to which he had been much devoted. His mother's influence restrained him for awhile. On her death he fell under the displeasure of his father. His home became intolerable; he fled from it, went into Gaul, spent three years in France and Burgundy, finally came to Normandy. The fame of Lanfranc drew him to Bec. In a short time his character and work filled him with admiration. He became a student again; he aspired once more to be a monk. For awhile he was haunted by the ambitious feeling that he should be entirely eclipsed at Bec by Lanfranc, and that it would be better to go elsewhere. That temptation being overcome, and his patrimony having fallen in by the death of his father, he laid the question before his spiritual counsellor, whether he should be a monk of Bec, a hermit in the woods, or a landlord distributing his goods to the poor. If Lanfranc, says his biographer, had bid him go into a wood and never come out of it again, he would have done it at once. But it was decided that his early passion marked his vocation, and at the age of 27 he entered the convent of which Lanfranc was prior. Lanfranc was removed to Caen; Anselm became prior of Bec. His loving friend, Eadmer, describes his life in this office as severe to himself, gentle to all around him, as acting with particular force and success upon children, as overcoming those who hated him by laborious kindness. Government, however, was oppressive to him; he was with difficulty prevented from throwing off his authority and reducing himself again to a simple monk. But he did resist this evil thought also, and was able to find time for correcting

Vita S. Anselmi auctore Eadmero Cantuarensi Monacho & Anselmi discipulo et comite individuo. Youth of Anselm, c. 1, sec. 3-6.

His ambition crushed, c. 1, sec. 7.

c. 1. sec 7.

Prior at Bec. c. 2. His life.

manuscripts and writing books in the midst of his incessant tasks
as a counsellor and administrator. It was at this time that he
wrote "On Truth," on "The Liberty of the Will," on "The
Grammarian," and a book entitled "Monologium," to which he
added afterwards "The Proslogium." As we propose to give
some account of most of these books hereafter, we would only remark here that they were all suggested by the circumstances of
the monastery, and that their form as well as their substance were
determined by the questions and doubts of the brethren at Bec.

21. Of Anselm's visions and miracles, of the far more interesting
stories which are related respecting his management of the children in the convent, of his reluctant appointment to be abbot on
the death of Herluin, of his hospitality in that character, we shall
say nothing. But we must make room for a conversation which
took place between him and Lanfranc when he went to visit his
old superior at Canterbury—the business of the convent, which
had many possessions in England, having called him thither. Once
upon a time, says Eadmer, Lanfranc said to him, "These Angles
among whom we are living have fixed upon certain persons whom
they shall reverence as saints. I have been considering their
claims to sanctity, and I am in great perplexity. For instance,
there is one who rests in that sacred place over which we preside,
Alphege by name, a good man assuredly, and an archbishop in
his time. Him they reckon not only among saints, but even
among martyrs; and this though they do not deny that he did not
die for the confession of the Name of Christ, but because he would
not redeem himself with money. For when, to use the words of
these Angles, the Pagans, the enemies of God, had taken him
prisoner, they were willing, through reverence for his character, to
set him free on the payment of a large ransom. That ransom
would have robbed his own citizens of their money, would perhaps
have reduced some to beggary; therefore he chose rather to lose
his life than to keep it on such terms. What say you, my
brother, to this claim of sanctity?" Anselm suggested first, with
great deference to Lanfranc, that one who would give up his life
to save his brethren from ruin, would certainly have given it up
rather than have denied Christ; and then he went on, "There
must have been a wonderful righteousness in the heart of that
man, seeing that he preferred giving up his life to scandalizing his
neighbours by want of charity towards them. Surely he, who for
such righteousness willingly sustains death, is truly reckoned
among martyrs. The blessed John the Baptist is venerated as a
martyr by the whole church, not because he was put to death for
refusing to deny Christ, but for refusing to conceal the truth.
And what is the difference between dying for righteousness and
dying for truth? Christ, says the Scripture, is righteousness and

*Sec. 20; his
works.*

*Eadmer, lib.
1, c. 4 and 5.*

*Lanfranc and
Anselm in
England.*

*In quantum
numera et
multorum
fert opinio,
non erat illo
tempore ullus
qui ant
Lanfranco in
auctoritate
vel multiplici
rerum
scientia
aut Anselmo
praestaret in
sanctitate
vel Dei
sapientia,
c. 5, sec. 42.*

*Claims to
saintship.*

*Alphege the
English
patriot.*

*Anselm's
decision.*

truth. He who dies for righteousness and truth dies for Christ; The true martyr.
therefore he is a martyr." Lanfranc was convinced. "Taught by
thy wisdom," he said, "I will henceforth, God's grace assisting
me, reverence Alphege as a great and glorious martyr of Christ."

22. Eadmer had a right to consider this dialogue as a proof Erat præterea Lanfrancus adhuc quasi rudis Angliæ, sec. 42.
that, with all his political sagacity, Lanfranc was still young in his
knowledge of his adopted country, and that Anselm, through his
moral instinct, had arrived at a clearer apprehension of our habits
and institutions, and of the way in which the church could most
effectually act upon them. On the other hand, there can be no
question, that when Anselm actually took the place which Lanfranc's death left vacant, he was far less adapted to it, far less able
to reconcile the obligations of a servant of the King of kings with
those of the subject of an earthly sovereign. The difference did
not arise wholly from the characters of the two ecclesiastics.
William the Conqueror was dead, as well as his minister. All the
cleverness of the latter might not have enabled him to keep terms
with William Rufus. In him we see the worst elements of the Nor- William Rufus.
man character, with only here and there a trace of that which gave
it its mighty influence over Europe. He thought of the subject His theory of the world.
race as of little more than a race of slaves, whom he might now
and then turn to account in the quarrels into which he was continually liable to fall with his own barons. The strong hand of
law which belonged to his father was changed for the mere strong
hand of power. Letters, of which the Conqueror saw the worth,
were mere hieroglyphical tricks to his successor, the miserable
amusements of those who had not sense and courage enough for
the chase. He had met with prelates as unscrupulous as himself; Eadmer, lib. 2, c. 2.
it was an easy inference that every priest was a hypocrite, bent
upon advancing his own interests or those of his order, a dangerous though a contemptible rival of the military—for Rufus had no
notion of the civil—ruler. Anselm had a reasonable dread of
coming into contact with such a monarch. He had also a cordial
affection for Bec, and an honest dislike of the grandeur and secu-
larity of the archiepiscopal office. But William had suffered it to
be long vacant, and had appropriated the revenues of it. When
a temporary sickness had made him penitent, and the accident of
a visit of Anselm to the Count of Chester had led him to think
that the most eminent man of the day might be the fittest for Can-
terbury, there was a general call that Anselm, for the sake of the Acclamatur ab universis et dictum regis laudat clerus et populus omnis, c. 2. Portatur magis quem ducimus, lib.
whole church, should not suffer a moment to pass which might
never return, and timidly shrink from a work which was divinely
imposed upon him. Most reluctantly he suffered the crosier to be
thrust into his hand, foreseeing too well, not only that he was
parting with a life which had been as dear to him as it had probably been unsuitable to Lanfranc, but that he was entering upon

one in which he should have only the use of his left hand, and would perhaps often have to doubt whether he was using that rightly.

His political life.

23. The remainder of the story belongs partly to ordinary English history, partly to the private biography of Anselm. We have no right here to enter upon the questions which arose between him and Rufus, upon their connection with the general dispute concerning investiture which agitated Europe, upon Anselm's journey to Rome and his adventures by the way, upon his experiences of popes and councils, upon the tears which he shed when he received the news of the death of his great enemy, upon his return to England, and his misunderstandings with the wiser monarch who had at first sought his friendship, or upon the peaceful

Reason for alluding to it.

death which wound up a life of struggles. It would scarcely have become us even to take notice of these facts, if it was not necessary to remove a certain prepossession on the subject of this eminent man, which is likely to interfere with any fair judgment of his

Hume, vol 1. 8vo. p. 303, says that the "noted historian of Anselm, who was also his companion and secretary, celebrates highly the effect of his zeal and piety in decrying long hair and curled locks." He refers to Eadmer, p. 23, not mentioning whether he quotes from the Life or from the Historia Novorum.

philosophical writings. If he had been the turbulent asserter of ecclesiastical rights which Hume and others have supposed him to be, still more if his main crusade had been, as our Scotch historian would have us believe, against long shoes, the portion of his work in the world with which we have to do, would stand strangely apart from the rest of it; since in that, at all events, he is very little occupied with controversies about the respective authority of the ecclesiastic and the civilian, since it is hard to detect in them any lurking signs of prelatical ambition, since he is always earnestly occupied with the serious and moral aspects of the very serious questions which he discusses. The truth is, that Anselm was not too much, but too little of a politician. He could not neglect any of the pastoral duties of his see, any more than he neglected the brethren and children of the convent for the sake of indulging his meditative tastes. But the diplomacy which was attached to it he knew nothing of. He could meet the greatest offender as a brother, and help him in any troubles of conscience. But William had no such troubles. He simply opposed what must have seemed to

The king and priest.

Anselm a dead weight of ignorance and brutality against everything that was spiritual and humanizing. Under these circumstances the asserter of spiritual rights and powers, even if he did at times infringe upon rights which it behoved the national monarch, if he *had been* a national monarch, to assert, was, to a very great extent, the vindicator of science, of liberty, of the crushed serf. The form which the conflict took was determined by the events and controversies of the time. It happened, unfortunately for Anselm, that he could not maintain his cause except by connecting it with that general cause of the papacy, which was mixed with so much that all kings and all nations, the best as well as the worst had a right to complain of as essentially oppressive, essentially secular. But there were few men pledged to that cause, fewer still perhaps who were pledged to the opposite cause, that had less of these evil dispositions in their own hearts, or more earnestly desired the extirpation of them, than Anselm. *Anselm's nobleness.*

24. It is an agreeable characteristic of Anselm's works that a very small portion of them indeed belong to controversy. There is one treatise, written at the instigation of the pope on the Greek doctrine of the procession of the Holy Ghost, and one against Roscellinus on the Incarnation. With these exceptions, meditations, prayers, letters and books written for the solution of difficulties which had actually occurred to some person who had consulted him, generally to some brother at Bec, form his contribution to Middle Age literature. Not more for the honour of Anselm himself than for the comprehension of his books, this last characteristic should be recollected. They were not hard dogmatical treatises written in cold blood, to build up a system or to vanquish opponents. They were actual guides to the doubter; attempts, often made with much reluctant modesty, to untie knots which worthy men found to be interfering with their peace and with their practice. *His writings.*

25. The characteristic of Anselm as a man was, we think, a love of righteousness for its own sake. That noble habit of mind is illustrated in his conversation respecting Alphege, scarcely less in a sentence of his, reported by Eadmer, which has given rise to some very uncharitable Protestant commentaries, that "he would rather be in Hell if he were pure of sin, than possess the Kingdom of Heaven under the pollution of sin." This too is the spirit of his writings. It is from this that they derive their substantial and permanent worth. Right there must be—that is the postulate of his mind. Then, partly for the sake of entering more deeply into the apprehension and possession of that which he inwardly acknowledged, partly for the sake of removing confusions from the minds of his brethren, he undertakes to establish his assumption by proof. Oftentimes we are compelled to doubt the success of these demonstrations. We have an uncomfortable feeling, that the principle which we are to arrive at by an elaborate process of reasoning has been taken for granted at the commencement of it; some of the arguments seem scarcely worthy of their object, some of them seem to interfere with it, by tempting us to accept one mode of contemplating it instead of the object itself. Theology has cause to complain of Anselm for having suggested theories and argumentations in connection with Articles of the Creed, which through their plausibility and through the excellency of the writer have gained currency in the Church, till they have been adopted as essential parts of that of which they were at best only defences and explanations. But viewing him, as we are privileged to do, *Anselm's greatness.* *His arguments.* *See the Cur Deus Homo.*

H

simply as philosophical students,—caring less about the results to
which his treatises have led dogmatists, than about his principles
and about his method of thought,—he offers us a very interesting
subject of examination. In Johannes Scotus the metaphysical ele-
Emphatically ment was evidently predominant over the ethical; in Anselm the
a moralist. moral absorbs everything into itself. Moral ends are first in his
mind; scientific truth he learns to love, because he is too honest a
man not to feel that Goodness is a contradiction if it has not Truth
for its support. But the difference in the starting-point of these
two writers affects all their intellectual habits. Anselm is much
more of a *formal* reasoner than Johannes; amongst ordinary
school-readers he would pass for a much more *accurate* reasoner.
His differ- He supplies many more producible arguments; he meets the per-
ence from
Johannes plexities which the use of words occasions more promptly; though
Scotus. far enough from a superficial thinker, he keeps much more the
high road of the intellect, and is not tempted to explore caverns.
For such a person, Logic becomes an invaluable auxiliary; he has
not the dread of its limiting the infinite which the other had; he
secures his moral truth from all verbal invasions; then he can let
verbal refinements have their full swing in the discussing of objections and in the effort to remove them.

His Mono- 26. Anselm's "Monologue on the Essence of the Divinity"
logue. was undertaken, he tells us, at the instance of many of his brethren of the Monastery, he himself shrinking from the task at
first, oftentimes feeling disgust at what he had written, but after
careful examination finding nothing in it at variance with Scripture or the Fathers, though the nature of his task required that
he should not refer to them as authorities, but should consider the
Object of it. question as one who was reasoning it out in his own mind. A
passage from the first chapter will show us the course which the
Monologue will take. "A person may speak thus with himself in
silence. Seeing that there are innumerable good things, the great
diversity of which we experience with the senses of our body and
discern with the reasoning of our mind, are we to believe that
there is some *one* thing, in virtue of which one all good things are
good, or are they good, some for this cause, some for that?" To
answer this question is the business of the book. We may speak
of a good horse, meaning that it is a strong horse or a swift horse;
but we may also speak of a strong thief or a swift thief, though we
admit the thief to be bad. How is this? For a moment, Anselm
would appear to rest in the utilitarian solution of this difference.
The strength and swiftness of the horse are beneficial, the strength
Process from and swiftness of the thief are mischievous. But he speedily dis-
the finite to covers that there is an ultimate end implied in utility, a Good
the Infinite. which is presumed in all particular Good. *That* Good is identical
with the Divine.

27. A mind which has been led into this acknowledgment will, of necessity, proceed to confess that this Good must *be*, that it must be *perfect*, that it must be *one*. The steps by which these thoughts unfold themselves in the thinker, are full of solemn interest. We should be most thankful for a guide so conscientious as Anselm, in tracing them, if ever and anon, instead of faithfully exhibiting the workings of his spirit, he did not withdraw us into an outer circle where we bear such a disputation as might have obtained laurels for an opponent and respondent in the dialectical exercises of Bec, not such a one as is carried on in the soul's secret chambers. Thus, for example, in the sixth chapter, where the subject is the self-subsistence of the Supreme Nature, we are instructed that "whatever exists by something else, exists either in virtue of an Efficient (cause), or of Matter, or of some Instrument." No doubt these are convenient distinctions for certain purposes. They are legitimate helps in arranging our thoughts; they may be forms of our understanding itself; but if there is a Nature which passes our understanding, which is implied in its operations, but which is not subject to them, surely we cannot hope to climb by any of these ladders to the apprehension of it. What they can bring us to, is but a Negative; that which is *without* matter, *without* instrument, *without* cause. And accordingly Anselm does find himself at once encountered, as so many had been encountered before him, by this frightful spectre of *Nothing*. Like a brave man, as he is, he faces it; he is sure he has no business with it. He treats the possibility of such a difficulty occurring as one of those which, for the comfort of weak brethren, he must not pass over, since he is bound to remove every obstacle, however slight, which may hinder the contemplation of the object that is so habitually present to himself, and that he would lead his readers to behold. Dear devout Teacher and Friend! Is that *a very small* obstacle? For a man who is sure that Good is, whose soul rests on that rock, a very pebble doubtless—a little snow-drift, which the eye hardly discerns, which one may sweep away or pass by. But for the mere logician?—for him who has been working night and day among Efficients, and Instruments, and Materials?—for him who has conceived all the Universe under these heads? Is the abyss of nothingness which lies beyond their clear definite circles not an appalling void to him? Can he find any footing in it? Will you tempt him to try? Had you not better say to him, "After all, brethren! are we not MEN; *must* not we have something to stand upon, that we may live and not die, even though our efficients and coefficients, and all this matter—yes, all that we have thought, and conceived, and imagined, should break to pieces under us!" That Anselm *meant* this, none can believe more firmly than we do; but we should be violating the fidelity of our narrative and

[marginal notes:]
Consequences.
Logical divisions.
They end in a Negation.
Et si forte rei quod specdior persuadere voluero, omni, vel modico, remoto obstaculo quilibet tardus intellectus ad audita facile possit accredere, &c.
Anselm's arguments failing of their purpose.

confusing the course of it, if we pretended that he always *said* this; that he did not say much which may have led disciples—may have helped to lead a whole generation—along a wilderness in which there was often no water, and sometimes no manna. Yet believing, as we do, that the way to a better land lay through that wilderness, and that freedom could not have been attained without its hunger and drouth, we can never think except with reverence of one of those who was a temporary guide in it, though perhaps not into it, certainly not through it.

The Trinity the ground of Anselm's mind.

28. Upon the technically theological part of this Monologue (*strictly* theological, of course, it is throughout) we shall not enter further than to remark, that it abundantly confirms the observations which we made in reference to the Middle Age period generally, that the Name into which Christians are baptized is the underground of the whole thought and speculation of its eminent

Dogmas and Foundations.

men, in fact, of the whole scholastic philosophy. Dogmatism had, no doubt, especially since the 9th century, encroached upon that which, according to Plato's nomenclature, is the direct opposite to it, the acknowledgment of *substance*, of that which is. Men were beginning to think of the Divine Name as a doctrine which they held, not as a reality which upheld them. There were some tendencies in the 11th century which favoured this habit of mind; there were some which counteracted it. Anselm as an arguer and a prover conspired with it. But Anselm as a deep student of himself, and as a practical worker, was resisting it. In this treatise, one discovers both aspects of his character; the higher and more beautiful part comes out more strongly towards the conclu-

Anselm in heart a Platonist, in understanding an Aristotelian.

sion of it. We will give our readers the titles of a few of the chapters, from which they may gather how much of what would be called in our days (and not wrongly called) the Platonical temper, mixed with the drier Aristotelianism of our Author's mind. The 66th chapter teaches us, that by the rational mind we ascend to the knowledge of the highest Essence. The 67th, that the mind is its mirror and its image. The 68th, that the rational creature is created to love this Essence. The 69th, that the soul which loves it will some time or other be truly and perfectly

Anselm's Transcendental doctrines.

blessed. The 70th, that this Essence gives itself back to that which loves it that it may be eternally blessed. The 74th, that despising it the soul is eternally miserable. The 76th, that every human soul is immortal, and that it must be either always miserable or some time or other truly blessed. And this is the conclusion. "Very difficult, yea, nearly impossible, it seems for any mortal by reasoning to be able to ascertain what souls may be at once judged to have so loved that which they have been made to love, that they may some time or other enjoy it; which have so despised it that they may deserve for ever to be without it; or

according to what measure, or by what rule, those who seem as if Anselm's practical faith.
they might be said neither to love it nor to despise it, may be
assigned to eternal blessedness or misery. But this are we to hold
most certainly, that by a supremely just and supremely good
Creator nothing will be unjustly deprived of that good for which The reward of Love.
it was made, and that for this good every man should strive with
his whole heart, and whole soul, and whole mind, by loving it and
longing for it. The human soul, however, can in no wise exercise The duty of Hope.
itself in this effort and intention, if it despairs of being able to come
at that at which it aims. Wherefore, just so far as the practice of
this effort is useful to the soul, just so far is the *hope* of arriving at
the end necessary to the soul. But it is not possible to love and
hope for that which one does not *believe*. It is fitting, therefore, The necessity of Faith.
for the same human soul to believe this supreme Essence and those
things without which it cannot be loved, that by believing it may
stretch towards it."

29. The Proslogion differs considerably from the Monologue, The Proslogion.
and differs, we think, advantageously; though its merits make it
less suitable for our work. Anselm describes the one as a *Soli-
loquy*, the other as an *Alloquy*, the one as the man's discourse with
himself concerning God, the other as a supplication to God to be
his teacher concerning Himself. It resembles, therefore, the petitions which constitute so substantial a part of St. Augustine's
Confessions. In the old time it would have been most truly con- Is it devotional or Philosophical?
sidered a philosophical work, the man seeking for wisdom, crying
for it as for a hid treasure; in our days it would be described as
a devotional treatise, and therefore as having no place in a Philosophical History. But if we may not deal with it directly, certain
consequences followed from it, of which it behoves us to speak, as
they throw a curious light upon processes of mind that characterized the 11th century, especially its monasteries. Anselm, in
his 2d chapter, had used these words,—" O Lord, we believe Thee The answer to the Atheist.
to be something than which no greater thing can be conceived of.
Is there then not a Nature of this kind, as the fool affirms, when
he says in his heart 'There is no God'? But assuredly this same
fool when he hears this very thing which I say, hears of something
than which nothing greater can be conceived of. He understands
what he hears, and what he understands is in his intellect, even
though he does not understand that it is. For it is not the same
that a thing should be in the intellect, and that we should understand the thing to be. For when a painter thinks beforehand of
that which he is about to make, he has it indeed in his intellect,
but he doth not yet understand what he hath not yet made. But Argument from the mind to that which is in itself.
when he hath painted it, he both has it in the intellect and under-
stands what he has now made. Therefore the fool also is convinced
that there is even in his intellect something than which nothing

greater can be conceived of, because when he hears this he understands it, and whatever is understood is in the intellect. But
assuredly that, than which nothing greater can be conceived of,
cannot be in the intellect *alone*; for if it is in the intellect alone,
it may be conceived of as being also in reality. If therefore that,
than which nothing greater can be conceived of, is in the intellect
alone, that very thing than which nothing greater can be conceived
of, is where something greater can be conceived of. But this is
impossible. There exists, therefore, beyond doubt, something than
which nothing greater can be conceived of, both in the intellect
and in the reality." He goes on in the next chapter to argue
that God cannot be thought not to be, and that the very saying in
the heart is thinking, and that the thinking presupposes Him.

Why such an argument, even if sound, ought not to be resorted to in this day. In the present day, when the arguments for the Divine existence
from the constitution of the visible world have displaced all others
in the minds of theological advocates, and when these are in their
turn exposed to the severest criticism from philosophers, such a
subtlety as this of Anselm's would be dismissed by both parties
with indifference or scorn. Without participating in either
feeling, or prejudging the question whether the argument is ten-
able in itself, we may express our opinion, that in a time of clubs
and newspapers it would be a serious moral offence to introduce into
a discussion, upon a subject of the greatest interest to all men, that
which must appear to nine out of ten a play upon words, or conjuror's trick. That objection does not apply in the least to the
writer of a MS. in a learned language, to be read only by students, whose own minds were habitually turned inwards, and who
felt the force of appeals to their consciousness, far more than of any
to the scheme of the world and the marks of design in it. We
must not, however, suppose that because this was the case, an
argument endorsed by the high authority of Anselm, and used to
maintain the most sacred conclusions, would pass in the 11th century without examination, or might not find stout and able opponents. Gaunilon's objection. Gaunilon, a monk, boldly wrote "a book on behalf of the
Fool." He admitted the Proslogion to be full of unction and in
general to be soundly reasoned. But he demurred to the statements we have quoted, as detracting from its general truth.
Anselm, in an elaborate answer, treats his opponent with courtesy,
denies his right to the name which he had claimed, and pronounces him a good Catholic, in spite of his unwillingness to use
a particular weapon against Atheism. He maintains, however,
that the weapon is a good one; he is not the least prepared to
abandon his method of thought; it is evidently very dear and
sacred in his eyes. Not from a wish to entertain our readers with
a passage of arms between two accomplished doctors of this age,
but because we do think that principles, the importance of which

would be better appreciated by their successors, were asserted on each side, we shall give a short account of this discussion.

30. Gaunilon's first objection will suggest itself to most readers. *1st objection —Possibility of understanding what is not true.* "Do I then never hear *false* words, *false* statements? Do I not understand them? If you draw a distinction in kind between 'understand them' and 'having them in my intellect,' so that you should say, 'I understand what you mean, but as there is nothing answering to it in fact, I cannot entertain it in my mind'—how does the analogy of the picture apply?" For there the having in the intellect, and the understanding, were the same process at different stages or points of time; one before the picture had actually existed, the other when it was produced.

31. He has another and still stronger complaint against this analogy. The very life of the picture is in the art, that is to say, in the intellect of the painter; the work is the mere expression or embodying of this life. How does this relation resemble that which exists between the word that is heard, or the thought that is understood by my mind, and the reality to which that word or thought corresponds? In one case the mental operation is clearly the first; in the other it presumes a foregone conclusion. *The analogy of the picture faulty.*

32. The third objection has reference to the nature of that which the fool is accused of not acknowledging. There is an *à fortiori* reason against the application of Anselm's argument to the existence of God. If I am told of a certain man, quite unknown to me, I have the general notion of a man in my understanding; so that if my informant has lied and there is not *such* a man as the one he spoke of, still the thought suggested by his words has something corresponding to it. But, by the hypothesis, *this* word is spoken to me concerning GOD, or concerning that which is greater than all things; concerning a Being, that is to say, who can be referred to no species previously known to me; who is not like anything else. Supposing then, and no other supposition will serve to meet the case, the man has not derived his knowledge in some other way previously, what will the announcement that there is such a Nature be to him but a succession of sounds, true no doubt as such, true as making certain vibrations on the ear, but not awakening any thought within to which the reality without can answer? *No species to which the name of God can be referred.*

33. The inference follows, that the method of reasoning from the intellectual apprehension to that which is apprehended, is a false one; that I must take the reverse method; establishing the existence of my apprehension by its correspondence with that which is previously ascertained; otherwise, Gaunilon asks, why, if I am told of the lost island, which surpasses in its treasures and beauty all that I have ever seen and dreamed of, is not the possibility of understanding the announcement, which no one will dispute, to *Why not believe in an Atlantis?*

be taken as conclusive evidence that such an island exists? Surely, continues the critic, the man who endeavours to persuade me to believe him on such a ground, must either be joking with me, or must be very simple himself, or must give me credit for being simpler than he is.

34. With one more argument—a very suggestive one, he concludes. Possibly when you say that the non-existence of this supreme nature cannot be even thought of, you mean that it cannot be understood, because, strictly speaking, that which is false is not, as such, capable of being understood. But if that is your meaning, how is the argument *specially* applicable to the supreme Nature? I cannot *understand* that I myself do not exist, though I can understand the possibility of any one's non-existence, and though I can think of my own non-existence. Is it otherwise in the case of *the* Being?

35. The commencement of Anselm's reply to this skilful reasoner will appear to most readers to involve an awkward *petitio principii*. His opponent and he being agreed in their conclusion, he can ask him triumphantly, whether the denial that the thought in the mind of a supreme nature does not involve a reality corresponding to it, is not at variance with his convictions and conscience, and whether, therefore, he must not suspect a flaw in the process by which he has arrived at it? We have explained already that, in our judgment, this is an apparent rather than a real unfairness. If it is fatal to the probative force of Anselm's arguments upon an impartial judge, that is to say, upon a person who tries to divest himself of his humanity that he may be a logician merely, it is extremely interesting and illustrative of Anselm's character, that he is obviously unable to do this, even when he endeavours it most, and when the logical fever is most strong upon him. And, to do him justice, though he takes this ground at starting, he does not consciously allow it to interfere with his subsequent reasonings. Of these, when they do not bear directly on Gaunilon's, we will give only one specimen. "That, than which nothing greater can be thought or conceived of, must

be thought of as without a beginning. But whatever can be thought or conceived of, and is not, can be thought of as having a beginning " (*the thought is the beginning.*) "Therefore such a nature cannot be thought of and not be: therefore if it be thought of, it must be."

36. Anselm insists that every one of Gaunilon's objections turns upon a forgetfulness of the terms of the original proposition. What is the use of talking about a lost island? Is that something, than

which nothing greater can be conceived? If it is, unquestionably such an island must be. It exists, and can never be lost again. Is it not? How does it affect the point in dispute? Here, of course, the *definiteness* which is presumed in the very name and nature of an island gives the respondent an obvious advantage. Pressing this advantage, he proceeds to dispose of Gaunilon's assertion, that there is nothing in the argument which applies to the denial of the supreme nature more than to the denial of anything else which exists, *e.g.* ourselves. If for the words, "thought or conceived of," Gaunilon was at liberty to substitute "understood," as he proposes, doubtless it might be said that nothing false, strictly speaking, could be understood. But it is, he contends, the peculiarity of this higher nature, that it could not be "thought or conceived of," if it did not exist. "For all those things, and those alone, can be thought not to be, which have beginning, or end, or conjunction of parts, and generally, whatsoever at some time or in some place is not a whole; and that alone cannot be thought or conceived not to be, in which the thought finds neither end, nor beginning, nor conjunction of parts, and which always and everywhere it finds only as a whole,"—a great and pregnant assertion, upon which every earnest man will meditate deeply, but which he must not hope to be made much clearer or more satisfactory to him by the syllogisms of Anselm or any one else.

Why the argument affects the Supreme Nature differently from any other subject.

37. Anselm complains of Gaunilon for substituting the phrase, "that which is greater than all things," for his, "that than which nothing greater can be conceived of or thought of," and of drawing inferences from the one which are quite inapplicable to the other. The distinction is undoubtedly of great importance, and one which throws a valuable light on the subject. The way to the absolutely greatest is through the thought. To spring by a leap to it, is to overlook that very relationship for which our doctor is contending. Another distinction is also asserted. Gaunilon says that we can understand the words which express a false proposition;—undoubtedly; but is that the same thing as understanding or taking into the intellect the assertion that a thing actually exists? Anselm says that the fool does this, even when he says there is no God. He understands or receives into his intellect, of necessity, the assertion that there is that which is greater than he can think of. This is not merely to understand the words of the proposition. It is to confess that which is implied in them, the very sense of them. Not indeed—for this is a point carefully to be noticed—that the argument assumes GOD, as such, to be known by the fool; but only this, that there is such a highest nature, as he seeks to deny, such a highest nature as he should wish, in whatever way that is possible, to be acquainted with.

Anselm's process misunderstood by his opponent.

Why the fool though he denies God, may acknowledge an inconceivable nature.

38. By far the most satisfactory, and as it seems to us, the most practically useful, part of Anselm's answer is that in which he disposes of the objection which is drawn from the absence of any

species to which the Divine Being can be referred, of any likeness
with which he can be compared. Every lower good, implies a
higher one. There is a continual ascent in the thought, from the
which it feels to be partial and to have flaws, to that which is full
and immaculate. All reasonable people acknowledge it to be so;
the Scriptures clearly affirm that the invisible things from the
creation of the world are seen through those which we understand;
to wit, the eternal power and Godhead. Hence he proceeds to
the remark, that to assume that which is greater than our thought
as being the subject of our thought, is no greater contradiction
than to speak of the ineffable. It is a contradiction implied
in the very nature of speech and thought; they lose themselves in that which is deeper than themselves. In concluding
the argument, he declares that he looks upon man's thought
as necessarily predicating of the Divine essence whatever quality
it confesses to be better than the negation of that quality. Eternity
is better than non-eternity; goodness than non-goodness; goodness in its very self than that which is not goodness in itself.

89. There are two dialogues of Anselm's—one concerning
Truth, one concerning Free-will—of which it behoves us to give
our readers some account. The person who represents the scholar
in the first dialogue opens with this question, " Seeing that we
believe God to be Truth, and seeing that we affirm Truth to be
in many other things, I should be glad to know whether, whenever Truth is spoken of, we ought to confess it to be God." A
passage in the Monologue, in which Truth is said to be without
beginning or end, raises this doubt. The master does not remember to have met with any definition of Truth, but he thinks that
by examining the different subjects of which it is predicated, there
may be a hope of discovering what it is. He begins with Truth
in *Enunciation.*   When do we say that Enunciation is true?
The inquiry is pursued with minute, and what we should most of us
call unnecessary, elaboration. It results in the conclusion, that
Truth in enunciation or speech is identical with rectitude. The
speech does what it ought to do, imperfectly when it is merely self-
consistent, perfectly when besides being self-consistent, it answers
to the fact. Next they consider the truth of *Opinion.* The decision
here is the same as in the former case. Truth of opinion is identical with rectitude of opinion. The *thought* corresponds to the
fact, as the *word* in the other case did. Thence we ascend to the
truth of *Will.* The devil stood not in the truth, he did not will
what he ought. Rectitude is the truth of Will. Fourthly,
how stands it with *Actions?* These are twofold: the actions of
voluntary and those of involuntary, creatures. Can we say that
the fire acts truth when it warms? It is determined that we
can. It does what it ought. But when it is said, " He that

Ascent from
the imperfect
to the
perfect.

Final
inference.

Dialogue
De
Veritate.

The
Question.

Truth in
Enunciation.

Truth in
Opinion.

Truth of
Will.

Truth in
Acts.

doeth the Truth cometh to the light," is the principle different? *The necessary and voluntary act-* Only in this, that the action of coming to the light is not necessary. It is an act of will, but it is an act of will doing what it ought, fulfilling its proper function just as the fire does. In this way we may explain a paradox which was spoken of under the first head, that speech may be true even though the proposition which it *Speech may be true when it utters a lie.* enunciates is false. The speech fulfils its own natural function, it says what the speaker means to say, but the meaning is falsified by the will. A fifth question follows about the truth of *Truth in the Senses.* the *Senses.* Do they not deceive us? The answer is "No," the deception is not in the sense but in opinion. The boy fears the picture of a dragon with an open mouth. It is not that his out- *The outer and inner sense.* ward sense makes a different report of the picture from that which the outward sense of an old man makes; it is that his inner boyish sense has not yet been able to distinguish a picture from a reality, as that of the other does. All supposed cases, it is contended, of optical deception, or of deception through any sense, may be resolved in the same manner.

40. We now approach the point which has given rise to these *Relation of Truth to God.* separate investigations. Nothing is true which does not derive its truth from the highest Truth. *Essentially,* everything is true because it derives its essence from that in which there is no falsehood. Truth and rectitude are identical in the highest subject, as they have been shown to be in every subordinate subject. But *Whatever is, is right; how then comes wrong?* the grand affirmation, that everything is what it ought to be, of course at once suggests the question, "Are there not then many evil works which it is certain ought not to be?" "Is that wonderful," asks the Master, "if the same thing ought to be and ought not to be?" "How is that possible?" asks the disciple. To the proof of this paradox his companion addresses himself. The gene- *The general proposition.* ral inclusive proposition is, that God permits some to do evil because they will to do evil; that the permission is good and ought to be; that the evil, by the very force of the term, ought not to be. But there are various particular illustrations to show that the principle cannot be gainsayed even by those who refuse to recognize that which is the deepest ground of it. An act may be right in itself; it ought to be; and yet the doer of it ought not to *Ought; the power that lies in the word.* be the doer. There cannot be a blow given which is not received; yet the "ought" may be altogether different in relation to the receiver and the giver. The nail may do its own appointed work upon human flesh; the flesh may do its appointed work in receiving the impression from it; each of these instruments does what it ought to do; but he who drives the nail may be doing that which ought not to be done. Nay, there is a use of "ought" which suggests the very opposite of what it actually means. "I ought to be loved by you," would seem to imply that I owe something to you,

whereas it does imply, that you owe something to me. The
Master remarks by the way, that there is a similar ambiguity in
the use of the words, "might," "could," "was able." Hector was
able to be conquered by Achilles, Achilles could not be conquered
by Hector. You would suppose the power was in Hector, whereas
in truth the weakness was in him.

41. The Master proceeds in the next chapter to show, that Truth
is at least as reasonably affirmed to reside in acts as in words; and
that a true act is nearer to the nature and essence of truth, than
even a true word. All this, of course, bears upon the great object of the Dialogue, the identification of *Truth* with *Rectitude*.
This identification is traced at last to the *Highest Truth;* there
you have a Rectitude not involving obligation but the ground of
obligation; the primary Eternal Rectitude which is the cause of
all Rectitudes. And so the doctrine of the Monologue, that a
truth without a beginning or an end is involved in speech, though
it may predicate of this thing that it has been, or of that thing
that it is to be, is justified. These very pasts and futures, and
the language which denotes them, presume that Supreme Truth
which comprehends them in its own eternity.

42. The way is now open for the definition we sought for.
Truth and Rectitude have appeared to be one in all cases. A
single difficulty remains. When we speak of a straight twig or
stick, do we not ascribe rectitude to it? Must we not, therefore,
distinguish between the truth that is cognizable by the eye and by
the mind? Or shall we not rather say, that even *this* rectitude is
cognizable by the mind, seeing that we should have no reason for
calling a particular twig or stick, straight, if we had not in our
mind a standard of straightness to which we referred it? May we
not then affirm truth to be rectitude perceptible only by the mind?
In this sense is *Rectitude* identical with *Justice?* Not surely if we
attribute rectitude (as we have done) to natural things, as fire,
when they fulfil their functions. Justice must be *voluntary* rectitude.—Is that an adequate definition? May not a man do right
acts willingly, without being a just man? Yes! The *Will* must
have a *Reason* with which it is in accordance. That only is justice,
the Master concludes, which is "Rectitude of Will sustained for
its own sake." May this definition be applied to the Highest
Being, to the Essential Righteousness? There can be no subject
to which it is equally applicable. Rectitude of will in the created,
though preserved for the sake of rectitude, yet looks up to a
higher Will which is THE Right, which stands in itself and upholds
all others. Thus we are drawn on to the final inference that the
truth of each subject is distinct, in so far as it is limited by
the nature of that subject, but that the very distinctions
imply that that Truth is one and the same in all things, and

that there is a self-subsisting Truth which is not included in any thing.

43. We need scarcely point out to our readers how remarkably this treatise illustrates what we have described as the characteristic feature of Anselm's mind. The resolute predominance of the moral over the intellectual in his apprehension of truth, gives all the interest and variety to this investigation. The short book on the Will (Voluntas), which is less theological than the Dialogue (De Libero Arbitrio), brings us by a different road to the same point. He begins by giving a double explanation of the Will. " It is an instrument, as the eye is the instrument of seeing; it is an affection of that same instrument, *e.g.* the mother's love to her child, which is always latent in the will, whether it comes forth into thought or not. The will, then, is the natural instrument of the soul; when the soul thinks, the instrument works. Its affections are two, the affection of willing advantage, and of willing justice. The one is inseparable from the instrument. The other may be entirely absent, or may be present at times and absent at other times. It is only when the will to advantage is absorbed into the will to justice that the man attains his appointed end, and therefore is blessed." This is the substance of his doctrine. But he touches in passing upon the question of the permission of evil, and of God's hardening a man's heart, which belongs more properly to the Dialogue.

The Will an Instrument, and an exercise of the Instru- ment.

44. The principle asserted in this dialogue cannot be new to any thoughtful student of the subject; it is worked out with the logical minuteness which belongs to the time and to the writer. Starting from the maxim that free choice is the same in all beings to whom it appertains, in God and holy angels as in men; he goes on to argue that this freedom is not identical with the power of sinning. Assuredly that power could not have been exercised by any being in whom free choice did not reside; but inasmuch as Sin is the recognition of a foreign, unnatural dominion, inasmuch as it involves slavery, it is a contradiction in terms to speak of it as the proof and token of Freedom. On the contrary, the deliverance from such a power, and from all desire to use it, is the very condition of freedom. The difficulty, that the man retains freedom of choice after he has sinned, is met by a reference to the doctrine of the former treatise. The Will (Voluntas), in the sense of an instrument created to desire Justice and Right, has the freedom of choice (*liberum arbitrium*) conferred on it that it may pursue this end. Forsaking this end, the freedom of choice, the power of embracing and also of recovering the Right, deserts it. But the instrument remains under its original law and definition, just as the power of seeing remains, though the object to be seen may be hidden, or though there may be some obstruction inter-

Dialogue De Libero Arbitrio.

Free Choice in the Perfect Being.

Why the power of doing evil cannot be identified with freedom of choice.

In what sense choice remains after slavery has begun.

posed between it and the eye. From these premises, the conclusions are deduced in the subsequent chapters, that no temptation
forces any one to sin against his will; that our will, though it
seems impotent, has a power against temptations; that the will is
stronger than the temptation, even when overcome by it; that
God himself cannot take away the rectitude of the will, (since if
He did, His will would not be a will to right); that nothing is
freer than a right will; that it is a greater miracle when God
restores rectitude to a will that has abandoned it, than when He
restores life to the dead; that the power of pursuing rectitude for
its own sake is the complete definition of free choice.

45. The Discussion on the reconciliation of Præscience and
Predestination with Free will, follows naturally upon these two.
We shall not enter into it, as we have already given our readers
specimens enough to guide them in appreciating the purpose and
the method of Anselm. The idea which is so ably worked out by
Boethius, that a Being who sees all natures truly, and as they are,
must recognize in all his acts of seeing and foreseeing that distinction between voluntary and necessary existences which He has
established, and that to speak of his præscience as superseding and
abolishing that distinction is a contradiction in terms—this idea
is adopted and enforced in his own way by the doctor of the 11th
century. He dwells too, as strongly as Boethius, on the difference
between the same things considered under the law of Time and
under the law of Eternity, "in which there is no past or future,
but only present;" "in which all things are contained."

46. It may seem like a farce after a very solemn tragedy, to
pass from debates such as these to the Dialogue on the Grammarian, the genuineness of which has never, we believe, been
questioned. But our reader must be content to look at times and
at men from all sides if he would understand them. The discussion opens with the appalling doubt whether a Grammarian is a
Substance or a Quality. We are in hopes for a moment that this
perplexity, in which so many venerable persons are interested,
may be set at rest by the timid suggestion of the disciple, that the
Grammarian is a man, and that therefore he may share the privilege of a man in not being reduced into a Quality. But we were
too hasty. He discovers that this proposition, "A Grammarian is
a man," so far from being irrefragable, is scarcely defensible. For
a grammarian without grammar is inconceivable, but surely a man
may go comfortably through the world without any such addition.
How are we to untie this knot? By no means let it be cut; we
must proceed very gradually. By perceiving that rationality is
predicated of man as man, though man is an animal, and though
rationality is not predicated of the animal as an animal, we begin
to perceive that the grammarian may require grammar to make him

Inferences
from these
premises.

Dialogus
De Concordia
Prescientia
Dei cum
libero
arbitrio.

Time and
Eternity.

Dialogus
De
Grammatico.

Is a Gram-
marian a
Substance?

Is the
Grammarian
a Man?

a grammarian, and yet may be a man, though grammar is not involved in the existence of a man. Hence we can go on to the other argument. It is not necessary to rob our unhappy grammarian of substance, because a certain quality is necessary to make him that which he is; because, apart from that quality, he could not be a grammarian.

47. All this will, no doubt, appear to the critic of the 19th century purely ridiculous. But it is not ridiculous; not even irrelevant as a treatise on Grammar. In a particular instance, the teacher brings to light a set of verbal confusions into which the men of that time often fell from an excess of subtilty, we perhaps scarcely less often from indolence and contempt of distinctions. The relation between Grammar and Logic is illustrated. The syllogism is vindicated, for its use in detecting confusions of thought as well as of expression. Let it be frankly admitted, that through the meshes of this dialectic, the paltriest trivialities, the most mischievous sophisms may break in; but we must maintain as firmly, that it was the purpose of all righteous men, such as Anselm was, to keep them out, and that if they spent their time in such dialogues as these, it was because they did not see any other way so effectual of accomplishing that purpose. Wisdom is justified of all her children, with whatever weapons they fight; whether the scene of their battle is laid among the cleverest and busiest of all people in the open haunts of Athens during the Peloponnesian war, or among students in the cloisters of Bec in the age of William of Normandy. And Folly is justified of her children, by the contempt she casts upon one as much as the other; these children in each age being incapable of looking beyond its modes and conventions, or of seeing that which time and circumstance cannot alter.

CHAPTER IV.

TWELFTH CENTURY.

The beginning and end of the 11th century. 1. THE century, which opened with gloomy visions of coming destruction to Christendom and to the world, closed grandly with the conquest of Jerusalem, and the establishment of European chivalry in the East. From these incidents the 12th century takes its commencement; in a certain sense, they give it its character. The crusading impulse was not felt more by the warriors who went forth with Godfrey, than by the inmates of the most solitary convent. It penetrated the heart of society, it bound together him who wore the helmet with him who wore the cowl. Their char-The two orders.acters, their very functions, were scarcely distinguishable. The member of the military order had surely a calling as sacred as that of the priest; they were blended together in the minds of the people. The templar is the brother of a society bound by solemn vows, dedicated to Christ. The cloistered man must be a soldier. Do not talk of his occupations as peaceful. He is sent into the world with a sword; his whole life is to be a fight.

False inference from the spread of Monasteries. 2. This fact must be always kept in mind when we are contemplating this period under any of its aspects. From the amazing power which the monastic life and discipline exercised over the hearts of men, and over the affairs of the world, at all events during the first half of the 12th century, we might easily draw the inference, that we had fallen upon a torpid age, which succumbed easily to those who had spiritual terrors at command, because all other energies were suspended. But read any of the books which exhibit this monkish influence and enable us to judge of the ways in which it exerted itself, and you are struck at once with the various kinds of forces, physical and intellectual, which were acting and reacting upon each other throughout the whole of western Europe. Influence of the Cloister upon the world. The acknowledgment of the spiritual ascendency certainly does not come from men who are too weak to resist it, or who do not actually resist it, even while they pay it homage. Counts, kings, bishops, in the fulness of their wealth and barbaric splendour, may be bowing before a monk, who writes them letters from a cell in which he is living upon vegetables and water; it is not that they set no value upon their possessions, or that they are merely influenced by the dread of exchanging them for sufferings hereafter; it is that there is a power in a man who speaks as if there were a righteous order in the world, and as if they were bound by it, which they cannot gainsay, which rises above all their turbulence and selfishness. If the name and pretensions of the pope, with all the outward grandeur which supported them, had been the sole or the main object of reverence at this time, one might have explained it by superstition, or by an ecclesiastical theory. But that power was often mocked and set at nought, not only by the emperors of Germany, but by the citizens of Rome. Popes themselves were forced to ask the aid of those who had no splendour, no material appliances, no claims to traditional homage. Bernard of Clairvaux had an influence over the councils of Europe which they could not exercise. He could awaken the hearts of men to a crusade, could heal differences, could regulate the transactions of the world, in which he took no personal interest, while bishops of Rome had to beg that he would decide which of two claimants to their dignity ought to be esteemed the vicar of Christ, and the father of the faithful. *{The Popes bowing to the Monks.}* *{Bernard of Clairvaux.}*

3. But if an influence such as this was compatible with the kind of might which dwelt in swords and spears, was it equally compatible with the kind of energy which the thinking man puts forth? Was not the spiritual assumption of the monk certain to keep down *this* energy—certain, at all events, to trample it out, if it should anywhere give signs of its existence? These questions must be answered carefully. A hasty resolution of them is sure to be a false one. In truth, they are most different questions, to which history gives most different answers. The facts show clearly enough, that neither the material forces of this time, nor the spiritual, could restrain the exercises of thought in the minds of those who devoted themselves to study, nor could prevent the infection of these thoughts from spreading where one would have supposed there was the least susceptibility of them. The evidence which we shall have presently to produce upon this point is irresistible. If the 12th century was an age of martial prowess, of monastical domination, it was quite as much, quite as characteristically, an age of intellectual vigour and restlessness—an age when intellectual pursuits established themselves as part of the business of the world, and became, in some directions, more strictly popular than they have ever been since. But to determine how these intellectual studies were related to the spiritual thoughts and affections of the religious monk on the one side, and to the impulses and purposes of the statesman and warrior on the other, whether on the whole they were coincident or hostile forces,—how they became one or the other,—what alliances, temporary or permanent, there may have been between either of the two against the third, this is far *{Intellectual power in this age.}* *{How related to the other influences at work in it.}*

1

more difficult. To do this effectually would be to write—what has never yet been written—a complete theological, philosophical, and political history of the period.

Cousin's view of this age.

4. Of course we do not aspire to supply this want, but merely to offer a few hints, which may assist the moral and metaphysical student in finding a clue to a labyrinth in which he is very likely indeed to lose his way. If he takes up M. Cousin's preface to the works of Abelard, and surrenders himself to the guidance of a teacher whom he cannot fail to admire for his eloquence, for his learning, and for his sympathy with the subject on which he is writing, he will certainly arrive at the conclusion, that Abelard was the first man, or nearly the first, in modern Europe, who had the courage to think, who believed the intellect was to be exercised

Inconsistent with facts already stated.

upon moral or theological questions, who did not merely shape himself upon the decisions of popes or councils. We have given, in this sketch, some specimens of the writings of the most eminent and the most orthodox Doctor of the 11th century; and we venture to ask, whether these extracts, which we have at all events endeavoured to make faithfully, and which may be compared with the books whence they are taken, bear out M. Cousin's statement? Anselm may have applied his intellect rightly or wrongly to the discovery and enforcement of truth, or to the defence of

Reference to Anselm.

sophisms,—that is not the point. Clearly he *did* employ it, and that with a very deliberate purpose,—foregoing all advantages which ecclesiastical decrees or the authority of Scripture might give him, appealing to principles of the human mind for his premises, and addressing himself to the conscience and the intellect in his inferences. The intellect, in the ordinary sense of the word, was as much called into play in the discussions of Gaunilon with Anselm, as in any to which the 12th century gave birth. Theology, in its strictest sense, furnished the motive and occasion for this intellectual gladiatorship. Nor can it be said that the gravest objections to a theological statement were not put forth on one side, and tolerated on the other.

Character-istics of the two periods.

5. But though this is not the distinction between the two periods, there is a very marked distinction between them,—a distinction sufficient to explain M. Cousin's opinion, though not sufficient to justify

Bernard no enemy of worldly business; but a great enemy of school Logic.

it. One can with difficulty conceive of Bernard, forced, as Anselm was, into an archbishopric. He would have felt the humiliation even more keenly than his predecessor. Probably he might have been involved in fewer conflicts, or in more successful conflicts, with princes; his skill in the management of worldly affairs might have been greater. But one *cannot* conceive of Bernard as writing a logical treatise, even to remove the greatest perplexities from a brother's mind. Such a book as that on Truth, or that on the Will, to say nothing of the Grammarian, would have been abhorrent from the mind which found nothing inconsistent with its habits or tendencies in preaching a religious war. On the other hand, the temper of Anselm's mind, which is expressed in his Proslogium, the temper which found its most suitable utterance in meditations and prayers, has evidently very little which corresponds to it in the writings of Abelard. These men furnish accurate texts and *Anselm and Abelard.* illustrations of their period. The spiritual and intellectual tendency which had been combined in different measures and degrees during the former time—which had not been formally separated in Berengarius any more than in Lanfranc or Anselm—which had been comprehended in the impartial hatred of William Rufus—were now breaking loose from each other. The Monastery was beginning to be regarded more as exclusively the place for cultivating the divine affections, for seeking inward converse with God, for humbling the flesh. Thoughts, learning, study, though not banished from it, were absorbed, in the stricter societies—in those which gave most the tone to the age—into devotion. The warrior or statesman, exhausted with the outward world, did not want this kind of occupation. The enthusiastic youth who found in the Monastery an employment for his energies, not altogether unlike that which his parent or his brother sought in the field with the Saracen, did not care to mix his direct faith with questions about predicaments and middle terms. Even where the rule was less stringent, where the copying and illuminating of manuscripts, and the studying of classical authors, preserved their reputation, letters rather took the place of logic—the religious man became more of a *scholar*, in the modern sense of the word, than of a *student*. *The Monastery more strictly a place of Devotion.*

6. What, then, were those to do in whom the *student* impulse, which had been awakened in the Monasteries of the last century, was still vigorously at work? It was impossible that there should not be a number of such. Anselm, and many very inferior to him, but still men of note and reputation, had helped to call such a class into existence. Long before their time, theology and logic had been regarded as sisters, if not twins. *A priori*, we might fancy that the rage for dialectics would be extinguished by the rage for Eastern conquest. But experience does not justify such anticipations. When there is fervour in one direction, there is commonly fervour in all. The distinctions of talents and vocations are not lost, but whatever a man sets before him, his pursuit of it becomes a passion. If the religious man disowned the logician, and fraternized with the man of action rather than with him, he would assuredly have his revenge. His mistress might be called by those who did not know her, cold, phlegmatic, repulsive; he would prove that she possessed life, grace, every possible charm. There might be as much of fighting, and earnest fighting, in these lists as in any. What is more, spectators might be as glad to witness such contests, *The Student of this time.* *Dialectical fervour compatible with military fervour.*

and might take as lively an interest in the falls and prizes of the
The word-fighters. combatants. For what if they are called word-fights? Are they
less human for that? Is not every man in possession of words,
even if other possessions are not very abundant with him? May
he not be glad to know the use of them, and the feats that may be
done with them? If Monks fancy themselves above such knowledge, may not the people be glad of any teacher who will bring
it within their reach? These are the movements in the world and
in men's minds, which help to explain how divinity and dialectics
acquired that new position in respect to each other which M.
Cousin speaks of; to explain why the 12th century became the age
in which the Universities of Europe started into life. And all these
movements are gathered up and illustrated in the striking and
tragical history of Peter Abelard.

Life of Peter Abelard. 7. There are very few histories of which we possess so much
accurate information as this. That it has been disguised by French
and English sentimentalists—scarcely less, perhaps, by Churchmen,
who have denounced Abelard as a heretic,—by philosophers, who
have exalted him into a hero,—by critics, incapable of looking beyond the habits of their own age, who have questioned the traditions
respecting the power of his intellect—is quite true. But it is our
own fault if we are misled by any of these partial guides, when we
have the autobiography of the person whose position we are studying,—the letters between him and his wife, written with the most
perfect freedom, and in the maturity of the character, intellect,
The materials for judging of him. misfortunes of both,—the writings, both theological and dialectical,
of Abelard, of which quite enough are preserved to guide our
judgments about his opinions and his powers,—finally, the letters
of his most eminent opponents, with the records and decrees of
the councils who were called to pass sentence upon him. Those
who suspect all lives which men write of themselves,—that is to
say, those who always fancy that they must be cheated by the
vanity and partial representations of a fellow-creature, even though
they begin with arming themselves at all points against the danger,
by divesting themselves of any sympathy with him,—these cautious
and sagacious persons may take it for granted that Abelard's Book
The Liber Calamitatum a trustworthy book. of Calamities, even with all the aids which we have to qualify its
statements, must mislead them. To us it seems a book of trans-
parent fidelity, exposing, both consciously and unconsciously, all that
was weakest and worst in the writer; imputing not more injustice
to his adversaries than evidence internal and external would lead
us to suppose they may have committed, without being worse
people than we ourselves are; justifying itself to our judgments
and consciences by the very terrible revelations which it makes of
dangers to which we are all prone, however the circumstances of
different periods may alter their form.

8. Abelard was born in the year 1079, at Paluis, near Nantes. ^{The Breton} "I sprung from a country," he says, "of which the soil is light, ^{The Breton choosing his} and the temper of the inhabitants is light; and I had a wonderful ^{profession.} facility for acquiring knowledge. My father had some taste for letters before he became a soldier. He wished all his boys to be scholars before they gave themselves to arms. Me, his eldest-born, he was especially careful to educate. But I soon abandoned the privileges of my primogeniture to my brothers, leaving them to follow Mars, and casting myself into the lap of Minerva. And ^{The young Disputant.} since I preferred dialectical reasoning to all the other documents of philosophy, I changed other weapons for these, and abandoned the trophies of wars for the conflicts of arguments. So, travelling through different provinces, wherever I heard that the study of this art of disputation was flourishing, exercising it also myself as I went, I became a rival of the Peripatetics."

9. With this ambition our young recruit comes to Paris. He ^{Paris in the 11th century} has heard of the fame of William of Champeaux, who is established there, and at once becomes his pupil in dialectics. William discovers that he has received a most dangerous member into his class. Instead of meekly listening to his lessons, Abelard begins at once to practise them by answering his Master. The elder students are scandalized at the impertinence of the new comer. "Hence," ^{The scholar turning Master.} says Abelard, "my calamities began. Presuming on my talents I aspired, youth as I was, to the government of schools. I fixed upon Melun, the seat of a royal palace, as the place in which I would exhibit my powers." William of Champeaux, and the rival students, threw all difficulties in the way. But the Doctor also had his enemies among the powerful of the earth; these became Abelard's patrons. It was only necessary that they should find him ^{Preparations for war.} a field; he could work it for himself. Soon his dialectical fame began to spread everywhere. The name of William himself quailed before that of Abelard. Bodily sickness, brought on by intense application, drove him back to Brittany. All who were smitten with the dialectical passion, craved for his return. After a few years he was again confronting his old preceptor, now become Archdeacon of Paris, and aspiring to a Bishopric. Though it might have been more seemly for the venerable disputant, now that he had such objects before him, to have abandoned his old pursuits, he could not resist the temptation of descending into the field, even at the manifest risk of being defeated by a disciple, who now added something of experience to his youthful valour.

10. It must have been a terrible engagement. William of ^{Doctrine of William of Champeaux.} Champeaux had been used to maintain in his school, that the same whole thing dwells essentially in every one of the individual things which are comprehended under it. We shall hereafter

endeavour to make our readers understand what we suppose he
meant; now we will only observe, that we enter into the heart of that
controversy respecting universals, which was to affect the thought of
many centuries consciously, and of many more unconsciously; the
controversy which was foretold in the commentary of old Boethius
upon his Greek teacher Porphyry. "By most patent arguments,"
boasts Abelard, "I compelled William of Champeaux to change
his opinion; yea, to abandon it." The routed Archdeacon thought
to save his reputation by substituting the word *indifferently* for
essentially, in his original proposition. The change, we shall find,
was not an "indifferent" but an "essential" one; nevertheless, such
a concession could never save a man who had an opponent so
active as Peter at his heels. He affirmed, and Paris seems to
have assented, that this is the great question of all in dialectics—
in the judgment of Porphyry, the very crux upon which the
whole science turns. The lectures, which had been once so
popular, were utterly neglected; William was scarcely admitted
to read upon dialectics at all. "Those who had most adhered
to our Master, and most denounced my doctrine," says our
author, "fled to my school. Even his successor offered me his
place, and handed himself over with the rest to my teaching
where before his master and ours had flourished." Unutterable seems to have been the grief and envy of the discomfited
William. Abelard could not be directly attacked, but cruel slan-
ders were raised against the colleague who had been his opponent,
and a rival put in his place. Then follows a series of manœuvres,
which Abelard describes in the military language, that seemed
to him most suitable to the subject. He retreats for a while to
Melun, where his influence increases with the enmity of William.
The latter hearing that suspicions are circulated about the sincerity of his religious vows and clerical professions, withdraws to a
convent of brothers not far from the city. Straightway Abelard
descends from Melun to Paris, "thinking that I should now have
peace with him." "But," he says, "as my younger rival still
held the school at Paris, I placed my camp on the Mount
of St. Genoveva, outside the city, with the purpose of besieging
him who had taken possession of my place. On hearing which,
our Master imprudently returns to the city, bringing his school and
his convent of brothers into the old Monastery, designing to relieve
his soldier, whom he had deserted, from our blockade." The
succour is most unfortunate. William's patronage destroys the
school of his friend. "He had had some pupils," Abelard says,
"for he was supposed to be a good teacher of Priscian; but now
he lost them all, till, despairing of earthly glory, he also betook
himself to the monastic life." Then the strife was renewed between
the old combatants. "What conflicts," says Abelard, "our scholars

had after the return of the Master to the city, as well with him as
with his disciples, and what results fortune granted to our party in
these wars, yea, to me myself in them, facts have sufficiently informed thee. I might boldly, and yet with moderation, use the
words of Ajax, 'If you inquire the fortune of this fight, I was not
vanquished by him.'"

11. Abelard was recalled from these trials to Brittany by his
mother, who was about to enter upon a religious life, as his father
had done before her. When he returned into France, it was not *Abelard
to resume his battles with William of Champeaux, who had now studying
attained the object of his life by becoming a Bishop, but to study
Divinity. The popular teacher of the day in theology was Anselm
of Laon, a very different person in all respects from the Anselm of
Bec, who occupied us so much in the last century. We must make *Sketch of a
room for Abelard's characteristic description of him. "If any one *Theologian.*
came to him," he says, "in uncertainty of mind to urge him upon
any question, he returned more uncertain. He was a wonderful
man in the eyes of those who listened to him, but he was nought
in the sight of those who asked him questions. He had a wonderful practice of words, but it was a practice that was contemptible
in sense and empty of reason. When he kindled a fire, he filled
his house with smoke. That great tree of his attracted you by its
leaves when you saw it afar off; when you came near and looked
carefully at it, you found it bore no fruit. I perceived, when I
sought fruit upon it, that it was the fig-tree which our Lord had
cursed, or that old oak to which Lucan compares Pompey. Having
made this discovery, I did not lie for many days idle under its
shadow." Our readers will easily anticipate that the old story is *Abelard
coming over again, but with a more dangerous subject for a con- *Theological
test of wits. It is seen that Peter has no respect for his Master. *Teacher.*
His brother scholars set them at war. But they do Abelard a
greater injury. One day while they are joking together, he expresses his wonder at the barrenness of theologians, who were
always merely repeating each other, and following in the track of
old commentators; who could never venture to grapple with the
text of Scripture, or of the Fathers themselves. He is asked *The Exposi-
whether he would dare to become an expositor of some book *ture.*
which was not much read, and in which he had not much prepared himself. He undertakes the task. The prophecy of Ezekiel,
as being particularly obscure, is chosen for the trial. He is advised that he ought to devote himself to some preparatory studies.
He answers with contempt, that it is not his custom to trust to
experience, but to intuition; and insists that they shall not evade
the trial upon which he is willing to enter. Few came to the
first lecture. Those who were present extolled it so highly that
numbers appeared at the second and third. He is solicited to

transcribe his commentary. Anselm, at the instigation of two of his fellow-students, interferes to prevent it, pretending that his own character might be compromised. In proportion to the opposition which he encounters is his fame. He returns to Paris to the schools from which he had been formerly expelled, finishes the commentary which he had begun at Laon, becomes more popular as a theologian even than he had been as a dialectician. Money, as well as fame, he says, poured in upon him.

12. "But seeing," says Abelard, "that prosperity always puffs up fools, and that the world's tranquillity enervates the vigour of the mind, and loosens it by the temptations of the flesh, as I fancied I was now the one philosopher that was left in the world, and dreaded no longer molestations from any one, I that had hitherto lived as it behoves a philosopher and divine to live, now began to give the reins to my appetite." Not that it was possible for him to sink into the utter grossness into which so many ecclesiastics and monks of the time were plunged. It was through his intellect that his degradation came. It was through the worship of the intellect that shame and sorrow were prepared for his victim. "There was," he says, "in the city of Paris, a young maiden named Heloisa, the niece of a certain canon, named Fulbert, who, as he loved her very dearly, took great pains that she might have all facilities in the study of letters. In face she was not insignificant; in her abundance of learning she was unparalleled. And because this gift is rare in women, so much the more did it make this girl illustrious through the whole kingdom." The clergyman and philosopher tells his story plainly. He attempts to make out no good case for himself. He singled out this girl from the number whom his fame and beauty attracted. He profited by her passion for knowledge, as well as by the covetousness and ambition of Fulbert. He established himself in his house, was intrusted with the entire guardianship of Heloisa, wondered at the simplicity of a man who could trust a lamb to a wolf, and accomplished the ruin which he had purposed. There was no surprise on his part, no sudden gust of passion. He describes it as a deliberate plot; he knew perfectly what he was doing. The story is very frightful, and it has the clearest tokens of veracity. The self-glorifying intellect, the man who had exhausted all dialectical reasonings, and understood all the maxims of theology, could sin in no way but this. The diabolical contrivance must have predominated over passion and appetite, and converted them both into its instruments. It is a proof of the sincerity of Abelard's repentance, that he puts no gloss upon the story, covers it with no veil of sentiment. The effect upon his studies was what might be imagined. "It was horribly tedious to me to go into the schools, and to stay in them." Just what he had scorned his contemporaries for being, he became

himself. There was no more wit and invention; he was a mere repeater of other men's discoveries and doctrines. He could produce songs now and then, as he had done of old; but they were amatory, not philosophical. They obtained currency, however, and were often sung by those whose practice and discipline had been in the court of love.

13. The scholars mourned the degeneracy of the sage. All knew the cause of it before it was suspected by Fulbert. Heloisa escaped from his house. A child was born, which was called Astrolabius. The uncle dissembled his fury for a while that he might enforce a marriage. Abelard consented. Heloisa alone, with the most vehement arguments, besought him to leave her in her disgrace, and not to sacrifice his position and his future influence by entering into bonds which must be fatal to him. It is wonderful to read these arguments, to see how entirely absorbed she was in affection for him, how perfectly indifferent to her own character and reputation,—still more wonderful to see how little she had lost her faith in him as a philosopher or a divine, how impossible it was for her to impute the evil to him from which she had suffered so intolerably. In spite of her remonstrances the marriage took place. Fulbert proclaimed it; the bride denied it, betook herself to a convent near Paris, where she had been educated, and clothed herself in the garments of a novice. A frightful vengeance followed. Heloisa, at the command of her husband, took the veil, declaring that she did it merely in obedience to him and from no other motive, lamenting his misery and not her own. Abelard himself in shame, as he declares, and not in devotion, entered the Abbey of St. Dionysius.

The catastrophe.

Heloisa opposing a marriage.

14. The broken and crushed man had not nearly sounded the depths of the suffering into which he was to fall, though, in a moral sense, every step of his history from this time is upwards. He had not been long in the Abbey, before a number of clerks implored both him and the Abbot of his convent that he would not hide the great talents that had been committed to him in a napkin, but would do now for the honour of God what hitherto he had done for the sake of money or of fame, would consider himself set apart by the most tremendous discipline to be the philosopher not of the world, but of God. These arguments had all the more effect upon Abelard, because the convent to which he had come was one of the vilest of the time,—the Abbot an example of all corruption to his house. The brothers were rejoiced to be freed from Abelard's presence. He was not less pleased to escape from them, by becoming the lecturer to the multitudes who flocked from all quarters to a cell where he established himself. The crowds there, he tells us, that flowed to hear him, could find neither food sufficient to nourish them, nor places to dwell in. To them he lectured mainly on divine topics, using his human knowledge " only

Abelard after his fall.

His popularity returning.

as a hook," he says, "whereby they might be drawn to the study of the true philosophy."

15. A remark which we have already repeated to weariness, respecting the relation in which the belief in the Trinity stands to all the Middle Age philosophy, must be recollected in the 11th century, or Abelard's life and its connection with his time will be unintelligible. It was during his residence in the Monastery of St. Dionysius, that he composed a book on the Trinity in Unity, which had a most serious influence upon his after fortunes. His account of the matter is this. The scholars begged him to write a treatise on this subject, in which human and philosophical reasons might be adduced, "because," they said, "it seemed to them an idle thing to bring forth a multitude of words which the intelligence did not go along with, and that nothing could be believed unless it was understood, and that it was ridiculous for any one to preach to others what neither he nor they whom he taught could receive with their intellects; the Lord himself saying, that such were blind leaders of the blind." There was a general delight, he says, at the treatise when it came forth, those who had been exercised with questions on the subject finding the solution which they wanted. Thereupon two of his old enemies, pupils respectively of William and Anselm, both of whom were now dead, accused him to their Archbishop, and by his means induced the Bishop, who was then acting as the papal Legate in Gaul, to summon a Council at Soissons. When he came there he found the people much incensed against him, almost ready to stone him, because they heard he believed in three Gods. He presented himself and his book to the Legate, declared that if he had written anything which departed from the Catholic faith, he was ready to retract it and to make satisfaction, then defended his principles so successfully, that the popular feeling and the feeling of the council were inclining in his favour. One of his opponents accused him of denying that God had begotten Himself, which he must hold if he supposed that the Only-begotten Son was God, bidding him at the same time support himself, if he could, not by arguments but by authority. He instantly produced a passage from Augustine which expressly rejected that phrase as unorthodox and monstrous. The opponent replied, that this passage was to be understood in a certain sense. "By all means," said Abelard. "I thought you wanted the *words*. If you wish me to consider the *sense*, I shall be prepared to discuss the question at any moment." The double answer, he says, incensed his rival so much, that he swore neither his reasons nor his authority should be of any avail to him. The threat was fulfilled. The Bishop of Chartres in vain counselled moderation and fairness. The Legate wavered, but was at last overcome. Finally, the book was burnt before his eyes. All his previous disgraces and suffer-

His book on the Trinity.

Arguments by which he is induced to undertake it.

Abelard before a Council.

The book burnt.

ings, he frankly confesses, seemed to him less than this one. For
a time he appears to have been utterly crushed by it; though
afterwards he could acknowledge the mercy of God in humbling
his intellectual pride, as He had before punished his animal self-
indulgence.

16. In his own monastery, Abelard had to sustain persecutions His offence
for a very different reason. The question, so sacred in the minds against
of Frenchmen, whether their Dionysius was really Dionysius the traditions.
Areopagite, was rashly mooted by him while he was lecturing on
the Acts of the Apostles. No moral crime or theological heresy
could have been so atrocious as this doubt. A solemn meeting of
the Brethren was called. It was resolved to deliver up the philosopher to the king of France as a traitor against his crown and
dignity. Abelard, almost desperate, fled to the protection of Count
Theobald. In his dominions one of the curious vicissitudes of his
life occurred. He dwelt like one of the old hermits in a desert.
But crowds from all the cities around came to hear him. "We have
gained nothing," said his opponents, as he reports, "by persecuting
him. His fame is only spreading the wider." His scholars brought
him the means of livelihood in return for his spiritual food. He
felt that there was consolation in the midst of his troubles. He
built an Oratory, and dedicated it to the Paraclete. This act was His Oratory.
turned against him. It was not usual, they said, to dedicate temples
to the Holy Spirit; it indicated heresy, if it was not heretical.

17. It is scarcely possible that such an act as this could have His relation
seemed very shocking to the great teacher of the age, Bernard of with Ber-
Clairvaux. It is doubtful whether, of his own accord, he would nard.
have meddled with Abelard for any of his offences. He had
listened, it would seem, to some of the lectures of the great dialectician when he was in the height of his popularity at Paris, and
had not discovered the danger which was lurking in them. Yet
the danger could scarcely have been less at that period, when
Abelard was revelling in pride and self-exaltation, when he was
on the edge of the greatest moral debasement. Possibly Bernard
regarded him at that time merely as the most astute of logicians.
He may have felt that his own province was entirely different, that
he was looking on all subjects from an opposite point of view, that Bernard of
it would not be wise to attempt an estimate of disagreements with- himself dis-
out discovering first what they had in common. Many have wished Abelard
for Bernard's sake, as well as Abelard's, that he had maintained alone.
the same neutrality to the end; that, content with his own high
position and mighty influence, he had left it to a better Wisdom
to decide what there was of wheat, what of tares, in the doctrine
which his contemporary was sowing. It could not be so, however,
at that time, nor perhaps in any time. A man occupying the
place which Bernard occupied, is seldom allowed to judge for him-

self whom he shall interfere with or let alone. Some admiring
friend, some zealous pupil, is sure to suggest flattering thoughts of
his power and the responsibility which it involves, and to rebuke
him bitterly for his indolence in suffering dangerous opinions to
spread, which a few words from his lips might silence. William,
Abbot of Thierry, fulfilled this office on the present occasion. He
was one of those who caught so much of the style and expression
of the great divine, that certain treatises of his have been mistaken
for Bernard's, and included in editions of his works. His letter
to the Abbot of Clairvaux, and to Godfrey, Bishop of Chartres, is
exactly what one might have expected from so sedulous an imitator, he being also a zealous, somewhat officious, man. It is a
fac-simile of hundreds which have been sent forth in different
periods. He has lately become acquainted with some of Abelard's
views on the Trinity; he collects a series of heretical propositions
which he has deduced from his books; he has heard of two others,
one called "Sic et non;" he has not read them, but the titles are
enough, and he has no doubt the contents correspond to them.
He is utterly shocked that the great leaders of the Church, the
lights of the age, should allow such heresies to spread and take no
notice of them. He alludes to his own insignificance, &c. It is
evident from Bernard's answer that he is not much obliged to his
correspondent for imposing a new task upon him; he has more
than enough on his hands. Still he must not be silent. He has
glanced at the offensive book, and thinks that it deserves the censure of the Abbot of Thierry. He will look more at it after Easter.

18. There could be no doubt as to the result. The last infirmity of Bernard's very noble mind was, that he must meddle in
all kinds of business, whether it was such as suited his character
and his peculiar powers or not. He was evidently very much at the
mercy of such men as William of Thierry. Strokes by their rods
called forth some of the better springs in his mind, and some of those
also which were less pure. He would, we think, have shown more
faith in God if he had not believed that he was obliged to write
letters to Pope Innocent, or to the Council of Sens, or to different
bishops, against Peter Abelard. But it was quite inevitable that if
he did once come into contact with the books or with the man, he
should be revolted by them. When we assign the reason, we shall
surprise some of our readers,—perhaps we shall seem to be uttering
a very impertinent paradox. Bernard did not dislike Abelard
mainly as a rebel against authority, but as outraging what he conceived to be the divine Charity or Love. Righteousness was not
as much the foundation of his mind as it was of Anselm's. He
was not nearly so just a man. But no writer of any age has dwelt
more upon Love as constituting the very being and nature of God;
and as the perfection of man, because he is made in the image of

The remon-
strance of
the Abbot of
Thierry.

His letter,
No. 826, in
the letters of
St. Bernard.

Epistola 327.
S. B.

Bernard
obeys.

Why Bernard
must dislike
Abelard.

God. This is the characteristical feature of his mind; in it, we believe, lay the secret of his power. The idea of the Trinity was in him the idea of the absolute, all-embracing Love. Any other basis of Divinity he abhorred. The intellectual conceptions of Abelard were indifferent to him when they were applied to any other subject, were utterly offensive when they were applied to Theology. The explanations which were welcomed with so much enthusiasm by Abelard's youthful hearers, were to him the dry hard substitutes for a living truth. That which appeared to quicken and inspire them, smelt in his nostrils of the grave and the charnel-house. Was he right or wrong? If we ventured to pronounce on such a subject, which we have no right to do, it must be in the words which gave such offence to poor William of Thierry, *Sic et non*. That Abelard was in the state of mind to enter upon the deepest of all subjects, we do not believe. There never had been, there was not then, the moral basis in his character, apart from which all thoughts and speculations about the Godhead must be unreal and unsatisfactory. And this consideration applies directly to the charge of Tritheism, which was brought against him. Bernard might have a good right to say, that without a foundation of Love there could be no unity, Logic could give only separation. But, on the other hand, we are not prepared to affirm that Abelard was not doing a positive good to all ages in showing how far logic could go and could not go. We are not prepared to say, that he was not meeting a necessity of *that* age when he led the youths, who hung upon his lips, to believe that Divinity was not a mere collection of terms, that God opens a more inward eye in the mind of those who desire to behold Him, but does not put out the eye which He has given them already. Under Bernard's faith and Bernard's love, a set of dry dogmatists who believed nothing and loved nothing, were hiding their own dislike of all thought, their own dread lest God and the universe should prove to be nothing. Could he be right in affording countenance and protection to these?

19. Whatever we or others may think of Bernard's conduct to Abelard, there was one whose judgment upon it was very decisive. The Theologian had not quite forgotten the woman whom he had so greatly wronged. The mode in which their intercourse was renewed was, perhaps, the best possible. Heloisa and her Nuns were driven from their convent; the husband had left the valley in which he had built the offensive chapel; he gave it up with the buildings adjoining it to their use. But they did not begin a correspondence till the book of calamities had fallen into the hands of Heloise. When she had read it, she could forbear no longer. She poured forth her feelings of indignation against her husband's enemies, of reverence for his gifts, of inextinguishable love for himself, of complaint that he had never written to her, though besides her

[margin: Bernard's idea of Charity. Read as a specimen of his doctrine and character the 11th Epistle.]

[margin: His charity makes him intolerant of Abelard's formal distinctions.]

[margin: But leads him to protect some who were more thoroughly formalists.]

[margin: Heloise and her Nuns.]

[margin: Style of her Letters.]

own claims upon him, he was bound to act as spiritual adviser to the sisters for whom he had provided a home. With severe but most affectionate faithfulness she expresses her fears that what others have said of him may be true, that his love for her may have been wholly sensual and earthly, and may have perished when the outward indulgence of it was no longer possible. The letter is written with marvellous frankness and carelessness of conventual proprieties, like a person who was by no means sure that she did not love a man better than God, and yet wished Him to read her whole heart. She is entirely free from the affectation which Pope attributes to her. There is no nonsense about writing the name by accident and blotting it out with her tears. She writes it boldly and deliberately, joins with it all the tenderest epithets which any wife could use in addressing her husband, and declares at the same time she had never sought that title, and that he knows she would not have exchanged her former relation to him to be Empress of Germany. The answer of Abelard to this epistle has often been censured as cold, formal, and heartless. Compared with what called it forth, it may merit such epithets. But it does not strike us as on the whole dishonourable to his character. He writes with the constraint of a man who knew inwardly that the heavy charge which Heloise brought against him was true, who under the weight of that consciousness found himself treated as a Confessor and a Divine, who was the author of all that was wrong in the feelings that were laid bare before him, who was obliged to look up with reverence and shame to the revelation of a higher and better mind in her who, nevertheless, accepted him with unfeigned humility as her guide in the right way. A position so strange and anomalous may surely excuse much that may seem to the reader dry and cold. It is evident, we think, that he had more real affection, because more real reverence, for Heloise than he had ever had before. These feelings were in fact just beginning to awaken in his mind. The absence of reverence both towards his fellow-creatures and towards God had been *the* defect in a soul which possessed many rare gifts. If there is an awkwardness and timidity in the expression of this newly-formed habit, we certainly see no cause for wonder, but rather for thankfulness that by any instrument or through any discipline such a treasure should be granted to a man who had reached Abelard's age and fallen into his transgressions.

20. But we must not dwell longer upon these letters, much as they illustrate the tendencies of the period and the relations of the schoolman and the man. What remains of Abelard's present history shall be told in the words of a divine who, in a history of the Church or of Literature, would deserve much more than the transient notice we can bestow upon him. Peter of Clugni, always

Margin notes:
Abelard's answer.

Strangeness of his position.

Abelard's latest friend.

Peter of Clugni.

the friend and admirer of Bernard, was not seldom his antagonist, because their views of the cloister life were so widely different. The Abbot of Clugni would have wished the Monk to be rather an example to men of the world of what they might become, than the type of a kind of life which was in opposition to theirs. He feared that a grievously stringent rule would lead ultimately to a terrible laxity. He wished Letters always to be the handmaids of devotion. Though such an idea was not one which naturally belonged to this age of sharp and definite contrasts—though it could not effect what was effected either by the champion of Devotion or of Dialectics, Peter of Clugni did not live in vain. His kindly and Christian spirit could do something to reconcile their opposing claims—at all events to make the grave a bond of peace between those who in life had been bitterly opposed.

21. Our first extract is from a letter "to the Supreme Pontiff *Letters from Clugny.* and our especial Father Pope Innocent." "Master Peter," he says, "well known as I think to your Wisdom, lately coming from France, passed through Clugny. I asked him whither he was going. He said that being weighed down by the vexations of certain who laid on him the name of Heretic, which was very hateful to him, he was approaching to the Apostolical Majesty, and wished to take refuge with it. I praised his intention, and advised him to flee to that common refuge, and assured him that the apostolical justice, which was never wanting to any stranger, would not be *Reconcili- ation.* wanting to him. I promised him that its compassion, if there was need of it, would be open to him. Meantime came the Abbot of Citeaux to treat about peace between Peter and the Abbot of Clairvaux. I did what I could for that reconciliation, and urged him to go to Bernard. I added this to my admonition, that if he had written or spoken anything that offended Catholic ears, he should at the solicitation of him (Bernard) and of other good and wise men, remove it from his words and erase it from his books. So it came to pass. He went, he returned, and announced to us that through *Abelard's* the mediation of the Abbot of Citeaux he had had a peaceful meet- *desire for* ing with the Abbot of Clairvaux, all past grudges being set at rest. *rest.* Meantime, admonished by us, but rather, as I think, inspired by God, he has dismissed the tumults of schools and studies, and chosen for himself a dwelling in your Clugny. Which desire of his, thinking that it accorded with his age, his weakness, his religion, and believing that his knowledge, which is not unknown to you, might be of the greatest benefit to a multitude of our brethren, I have readily assented to; and if it shall be pleasing to your goodness it will be a delight to all of us, who are, as you know, your care, that he should stay with us. Be pleased then to grant that he may spend the rest of his days, which perchance are not many, in your Clugny, and that he may not be driven by the eagerness

of any from that roof to which as a sparrow he has fled, from that
nest which as a dove he rejoices to have found."

22. A much longer epistle is addressed to Heloise. It opens
with expressions of the admiration and affection with which the
old Monk recollects the lady of whom he had heard in his youth
as devoting herself to letters, "wherein she surpassed not only all
women, but nearly all men; and who in her later years had given
herself to still nobler pursuits, who being now a wholly sacrificed
and truly philosophical woman, had chosen the Gospel in preference
to Logic, the Apostle to Physics, Christ to Plato, the Cloister to
the Academy." Then follows a good deal about Penthesilea and
Deborah, which belongs to the time, and which we may pass over;
then a wish expressed with much chivalry and brotherly love, that
she and her sisters could have taken up their abode in his Clugny.

"But," he adds, coming to the business of his letter, "this is denied
us by that providence of God which disposes of all things, as far as
you are concerned; albeit, one great favour has been granted to
us. That same divine disposition has sent to us in the last years
of his life him who was thine, that ever-to-be honoured servant
and true philosopher of Christ, Master Peter. I consider that in
him God enriched our Clugny with a treasure above gold or precious stones. How humble, holy, and devoted his conversation
among us was, a short letter could not declare. I do not recollect
ever to have seen one that equalled him in every indication of humility. . . . . Oftentimes I have wondered,

I have been almost confounded, that a man of so great and so
widely spread fame should so despise himself and make light
of himself. . . . . He was constant in reading,
frequent in prayer, given to silence. . . . . By his
mind, by his tongue, by his work, he was ever teaching, manifesting, confessing that which was divine, that which was philosophical, that which tended to edification. As this simple, honest,
God-fearing, evil-shunning man was much oppressed by pains of
body, I looked out for him a place which excels every other in our
part of Burgundy for the amenity of its soil and climate. There,
as far as his sickness permitted, recalling his old studies, he was
ever devoted to books, so that what was said of the great Gregory
may be said of him, that he allowed no moment to pass by him in
which he was not either praying or reading or writing, or dictating.
In such exercises the coming of the divine Visitor found him, not
sleeping but waking, and called him not as a foolish but as a wise
virgin to the eternal nuptials, for he had with him a lamp full of
oil, that is to say, a conscience which testified of a holy life. How
holily, how devotedly, in what a Catholic spirit he first made con-

fession of his faith, then of his sins; with what an affection of heart
he received the food for his journey, the pledge of eternal life, the

Body of the Redeemer; how faithfully he commended his body and soul to Him; our brothers are witness, and the whole society of that Monastery. Thus Master Peter finished his days, and he who was known throughout the world for an unparalleled master of science, persevering in the learning of Him who said 'learn of Me for I am meek and lowly of heart,' passed, as we have a right to believe, into His presence."

23. The Book of Calamities and the correspondence with Heloise were for a long time without any commentary except what was furnished by certain theological writings of Abelard. These were manifestly insufficient to explain the passages in the biography which have reference to his dialectical exploits. They were not even sufficient to illustrate those passages which directly refer to him as a theologian, the other character being, as we have seen, that which was evidently predominant in him. The world is therefore under very great obligations to M. Cousin for the discovery which, either in his own person or through some of his fellow-labourers, he made in the King's library at Paris, of a whole treatise on logic, of various commentaries on Boethius and Porphyry, and above all, of an Essay on Genera and Species, which are probably genuine works of Abelard. The learned exposition and historical sketch with which the Editor has accompanied them, add immensely to their value, and may well secure our forgiveness for any extravagant language in which he has indulged respecting Abelard as the first champion of free inquiry; that praise itself being considerably modified by the remarks which M. Cousin has made respecting Roscellinus and William of Champeaux, when he has descended from the panegyrist into the philosophical historian. No student of Middle Age philosophy ought to overlook this introduction, though no one, we think, should hastily take its statements or its method for granted. The former will sometimes suggest important corrections of the latter. We are not quite sure whether M. Cousin's ingenious and plausible arguments establish the fact that Abelard was the pupil of Roscellinus at a very early age in Brittany, and overthrow the strong negative argument which has been drawn from the omission of his name in the Book of Calamities. But, supposing that point to be proved, it will lead us to conclusions respecting the history of this period which appear to us very sound, but which are not the same with those of M. Cousin. Our first knowledge of Roscellinus is derived from a treatise of Anselm, to which we merely alluded in our sketch of that philosopher, his treatise on the Trinity, and the Incarnation of the Word. It is this treatise, as M. Cousin well points out, which exhibits in an earlier form the conflict respecting Universals, to which Abelard introduces us in his remarks on William of Champeaux. Strict history therefore requires us to consider the controversy as

New lights, or Abelard's position and intellect.

See the Introduction to Œuvres Inédites d'Abelard pour servir à l'histoire de la Philosophie Scolastique en France Publiées par M. Victor Cousin. Paris, 1836.

Great value of M. Cousin's historical Elucidations.

Roscellinus: his conversation with Anselm of Bec.

K

starting from this point. Abelard may have first separated the dialectics from the theological principles with which they were involved, then in his later days have recombined them; but they had an earlier association, the subject of Universals first became important through its connection with the doctrine about which Anselm and Roscellinus dissented.

In what the heresy of Roscellinus was alleged to consist. 24. It was not any form of Arianism, far less of Sabellianism, which Anselm imputed to his opponent. It was that opinion which is the direct opposite of Sabellianism, which Sabellianism is a contrivance to avoid. Roscellinus could conceive of three distinct persons; their unity he could not conceive of. Was there anything inconsistent with orthodoxy in his saying so? In one sense he was asserting the very maxim of the creed to which Anselm yielded the most hearty assent. The teacher of Bec undoubtedly believed this unity to be *inconceivable*, quite as much as the Breton did. But we have seen how much Anselm built upon the argument, that our power of acknowledging that which is Relation of this argument to that contained in the Proslogion. beyond our conception proves it to exist. We have already expressed our opinion that in his discussions upon this point he was on the edge of a precipice, balancing himself no doubt with great skill, walking steadily because his eyes were upwards and not towards his feet, but still marking out a track in which many would try and scarcely any would be able to follow him, without great stumbling. He was appealing to the mind against itself; he was bringing into the strangest juxtaposition the conceiving power with that which is beyond it, and sustaining the last upon the first. The consequence was inevitable. He had no wish to do Roscellinus injustice. But he saw on the one hand that all theology was subverted—he believed that all unity among men would be subverted—if Tritheism came in under the protection of Logic. On the other hand he could not admit the impossibility which Roscellinus proclaimed, though it might be so well justified by principles which he confessed, without injuring the validity of that mode of reasoning which had become almost a part of himself and was blended The consequence to Anselm's reasoning. with his most sacred convictions. He therefore refutes the implicit Tritheism, by a course of reasoning which, as M. Cousin has well remarked, combines the most inconsistent propositions. He treats the question as if it was only between the senses and the spiritual perception. Of course, we only see things in their separate indi- The reality of colours asserted as strongly as the reality of Mankind vidualities. But are we not obliged to *conceive* of something beyond that—of humanity, for instance, and not merely of a man: of colours, for instance, and not merely of that which is coloured? Plato (in his Republic) had with infinite pains vindicated the doctrine of a substantial political unity underlying the acts and thoughts of individual men. But he had as carefully endeavoured in his Theœtetus to prove that colour has no such reality, that it is simply

a product of the eye and the object.   Here we have Platonism
and anti-Platonism in the strangest fellowship; and inevitably. For
there is a *conception* of colour as well as a *conception* of humanity;
if the reality depends upon the conception, the first is as substantial as the second; nay, it *appears* to be more substantial, because
sense lends its aid to the very mental act that is set in opposition
to it; the colour *is* seen, though it is never seen in that separate
condition under which the mind takes account of it.

25. M. Cousin has justified by his high authority the remark ^(Boethius, the Latin Realist.)
which we have so often made in this sketch, that Boethius first
dropped that seed in the Latin mind which germinated in the controversies between the Realists and Nominalists.   He has vindicated also by his theory respecting the spiritual pedigree of Abelard,
what we said respecting the inadequacy of the logic of Boethius
to produce such grave consequences, if it had not been combined
with more transcendent ideas, of which, in his formal treatises at
all events, the Roman statesman appeared to take little account.
But M. Cousin has not, we think, perceived how much the after ^(Union of Logic and)
history of this great struggle depends upon the blending of these ^(Theology in)
apparently incongruous elements; how little we can understand ^(this strife.)
what was at issue between the two parties in the schools if we
violently separate their controversy from the practical one with
which it was mingled and reduce it to the terms in which
Porphyry and Boethius would have stated it.   Abelard, perhaps
warned by the dangers to which Roscellinus had been exposed—
perhaps merely influenced by a just opinion that his own genius
fitted him far better for dialectical than theological exercises—undoubtedly made the experiment.   But we have seen from his own ^(Illustrations)
statement that he did not, that he could not, persevere in it.   An ^(from Abe-)
impulse which he could not resist drew him into the vortex, from ^(lard's life.)
which he appeared to have escaped; whatever might be the wis-
dom of severing his doctrine of Universals from questions directly
concerning the faith of the Church, he could not do it justice, or
satisfy his own peculiar impulses, without putting forth the statements which exposed him to the indignation of Bernard and the
decrees of the Council of Soissons.

26. In truth, the twofold name which this controversy bears is ^(The two)
only intelligible when we are content to trace its origin historically. ^(names which the Contro-)
Modern philosophers dwell too exclusively on the words *Realism* ^(versy bears.)
and *Nominalism*, as if they were adequate to describe its subject and
its issues.   Abelard has told us how much more, in his judgment,
it deserved to be called a battle concerning Universals.   Before he
became the pupil of Anselm of Laon,—while he was still the restless hearer or the bold defier of William of Champeaux—the question that was uppermost in his mind concerned the presence of the
whole in each individual thing.   How did this question arise?

What gave it, even when it exhibited itself in its driest and most technical form, such a personal and human interest? Allow anything you please for the passions of disputants which any big-or-little endian theory may arouse to madness—still the zeal of the bystanders—*their* conviction that heaven and earth were earnest spectators of the combat—demands explanation. If there was a thought — ever so imperfectly realized—that the very nature of the Being whom men worshipped, into whose name they were baptized, was involved in this logical argumentation—if the reasoners, however they might shrink from the reflection or hide it under terms of the understanding, yet ever and anon were tormented with the doubt whether what they were contending for might not contain the assertion or the denial that there was a whole, a unity, at the basis of their idea of God—that he was the All in All—does it require much experience to know that what was strongest in their minds would claim the benefit of the imputation, or would repel it; that what was pettiest would be justified and, in a certain sense, glorified?

Why it became so solemn.

Use of the words Realism and Nominalism. Why perplexing.

27. Is the Universal—that whole, that Unity, which we must attribute to a family, a nation, a race, merely *attributed?* is it not there? thus did the controversy respecting Universals become the controversy respecting the Real and the Nominal. But the word Real, though inevitable, was decidedly unfortunate. The argument takes gradually this shape. Is the Universal, the whole, the one, *res* a thing, or is it *nomen* a name? How often must the combatants, when this was the issue, have exchanged their rapiers and each have been wounded by his own! In divinity you must speak of a Name as that with which we are sealed; that which is to be hallowed and which is to make all else holy. This is the language of the Baptismal formula and of the Lord's Prayer. On the other hand, thing (from 'think,' as 'res' from 'reor')— (the subject of thought) is opposed in all the highest morality to the Person, the Thinker, the Speaker, the Actor. Yet the necessity of the argument drove him who was vindicating the divine Essence as the foundation of all things to treat it as if it possessed the nature of those things. A consideration of this enormous practical difficulty—for such it was, however much it was a verbal difficulty —may well make us tolerant and kindly to both parties. But it cannot make us think lightly—far less, contemptuously—of that which occupied their whole souls. They were often lost in the smoke which they raised; in the darkness they often struck right and left at friend and foe. But it was absolutely needful that the fight should be fought out; if the dread of killing each other for trifles had led them to conclude a hasty and unsatisfactory peace, all generations would have been the worse for it.

Greatness of the Name in divinity.

Comparative Insignificance of the Thing.

28. The fragment of Abelard on Genera and Species, the most

vuluable of all the documents which the diligence of M. Cousin has rescued for us, was written apparently in his later days, when he had leisure to review the whole subject, and when he had learned to do justice to some of the opponents of whom in his Book of Calamities he had spoken hastily. Theology, which he had avoided through preference for Dialectics in early days, into which he had plunged from logical necessity and from ambition in his middle age, might now be regarded more in its moral aspects. He had probably made his peace with the Doctors and the Pope; subdued and humbled he could have had no wish to awaken questions which had caused him so much sorrow. The treatise therefore is purely what it professes to be. But it asserts the doctrines which Abelard had always maintained on the subject of Universals. The habit of his intellect was not changed, however much his temper might be.

Fragmentum Sangerma nense de Generibus et Speciebus. (Œuvres, pp. 507–550.

29. We may speak of a house, he says, either as a disintegrated whole or as a continuous whole. Supposing we speak of it as a continuous whole, some reason thus:—If there is a house there is a wall, and if there is a wall there is a half wall, and if there is the half wall there is the half of the half, and so on to the last stone. Therefore if there is the house, there is this last little stone, and if there is not that little stone, there is no house. State this conclusion in general terms and there is nothing startling in it. Apply it to a particular house and you become sensible of a contradiction. How then are we to get rid of a conclusion that seems inevitable? William of Champeaux, according to Abelard, escaped from it by referring to the definition of a point that has no parts. Supposing, then, you take a line consisting of two points, you may say that the part follows its whole in the first case. But when you have got so far you can proceed no farther. Therefore, generally, you cannot assume that, because a part follows its own whole, the same may be affirmed of a part of that part; in other words, there must be a limit. Without objecting to this solution, Abelard suggests another. The part of every continuous whole is either principal or secondary. The principal part is either principal in quantity or principal in essence. I may destroy more than half of Socrates and he will remain; I destroy his heart or brain, and he is destroyed. Apply this to the case of the house, considered as a continuous whole, and you may go on with your divisions of quantity as much as you please: so long as that which is essential to the house or the wall or the half wall remains, so long the house or the wall or the half wall remains. Contemplate the house again as a disintegrated whole, and then every tile or separate particle being destroyed, destroys the house. Thus, supposing I assume a flock to consist of a hundred sheep, the absence of one of these sheep destroys that flock so contemplated. But here

Disgregatum totum vel continuum.

Necessity of the part to the whole; how far it extends.

William's Solution.

The Essential and the Non-essential

Disintegration.

again the former law will apply in the case of any particular sheep ;
to ascertain whether he is wanting to the flock, I must ascertain
what is essential to him, what makes him that sheep.

De Socratis
destructione.

80. Our readers might have wished that we should have passed
over this beginning as well as a subsequent chapter, which is headed
"Concerning the Destruction of Socrates," the questions raised in
which may seem to them rather fantastic and the solutions unnecessary, and have proceeded at once to the remarks of Abelard on
Genera and Species. But we apprehend that the preface is necessary to the right apprehension of the book. The satisfaction of
this doubt about the relation of the whole to the part was not so
easy in that age, is not so easy in ours, as we may conjecture when
it is presented to us in the old formulæ and with the old illustra-

Need of a
living exam-
ple.

tions. And it is not an insignificant fact in illustration of Abelard's
character or of his philosophy, that he mixes so much of the actual
house and wall with the terms which represent it, or that he carries us from a wall to a man in order to get some probable and
reasonable way of solving the difficulty or even of stating it. It is
not a little matter that the accomplished logician is driven so near
the outset of his undertaking to talk of that which forms the
essence of a building, and thence to proceed to the heart and brain
as the essence of the human creature. Let us be thankful for
such witnesses that words when they seem most trying to de-
nude themselves of all associations, "do still savour of the
realty." That recollection may help us better to understand
some of the difficulties of the Middle Ages, when the question
at issue was how much or how little of that savour they must
retain.

The three
opinions.

31. This treatise of Abelard explains the point of his differences
with his old Master, to which he had alluded in his Book of Calamities as well as the general aspect of the Nominal and Real controversy in the 11th century. He discusses three opinions, against
each of which he produces arguments of more or less ingenuity

Fingunt
Essentias
quædam uni-
versales in
singulis indi-
viduis totas
essentialiter
esse, p. 513.

and weight; then he announces his own. The first opinion is,
that there are some universal essences which exist in their totality
in each individual. He states this opinion, which was the original
one of William of Champeaux, thus : "There is a certain species,
Man, one thing essentially. To this are superadded certain forms
which make the man Socrates. Other supervenient forms, infer-
encing that same thing essentially in the same manner, produce

Universal
form, super-
venient form.

Plato and other individuals. Nor is there anything in Socrates
besides those forms which inform that matter which makes Socrates,
which does not at the same time dwell in Plato informed with the
forms of Plato." Abelard's objections are of the most plausible
and obvious kind. If it is so, why may not Socrates be at
the same time in Rome and at Athens? for where Socrates is,

there the universal man is informed to the extent of his whole quantity with Socraticity. For whatsoever the universal thing receives, it receives in its whole quantity. Wheresoever the Socraticity is in a man, there is Socrates, for Socrates is nothing but the Socratic man. The next argument is, that since health and sickness belong to the animal, if the whole animal existing in Socrates is sick, it must also be sick in Plato. He disposes triumphantly of the evasion that the universal animal may be sick, but not in so far forth as it is universal, for the singular and the universal according to this scheme become identical. The third objection is, that as the difference added to the genus makes up the species, to the genus animal you may add the difference rationality and the difference irrationality, and these will coexist in the same universal. The fourth argument takes us to a more awful ground, and shows with what tremendous questions these logical subtleties became blended and how easy it was for the disputants on either side to involve their opponents in the charges of blasphemy or of atheism. Abelard distinctly maintains that this theory of Universals involves the co-eternity of form as well as matter with God; nay, that it makes the individual man consist of two co-eternal Gods.

[margin: Humanity and Socraticity.]

[margin: Grave principles involved in the controversy.]

[margin: Nam æque ut materia ita et forma universalis est et ita Deo coæterna; quod quantum a vero deviet palam est.]

32. The second opinion which he controverts is that which William of Champeaux adopted after Abelard had driven him from his earlier faith respecting the presence of the universal essence in each individual thing. The new doctrine is that which is described in the Book of Calamities as the presence of the Universal not *essentially* but *indifferently* in each thing. Abelard represents it thus: "There is nothing at all except the individual; but this drawn out or expanded in different degrees becomes species and genus and that which is most general. Socrates in that nature in which he is subject to sensible observation is individual, because there is that belonging to him the whole of which is never found in another. But the intellect may forget that which is denoted by the word Socrates, and think only of that which is denoted by the word Man, that is a rational mortal animal; in this sense he is species. If again the intellect overlooks the rationality and mortality and only contemplates what the word animal denotes; in this state it is genus. But if, leaving all forms, we consider only Socrates in that which denotes substance; here is the highest generality; Socrates, therefore, as an *individual*, has nothing which is not proper to himself; but as *species*, he has that which belongs to him indifferently with all men—as genus, he has that which belongs to him indifferently with all animals. Abelard says that this position is alike inconsistent with authority and with reason. His authorities are Porphyry and Boethius. Porphyry says the species is the collection of many into one nature, and genus of still more.

[margin: The second opinion. p. 514. Nunc itaque illam quæ de indifferentia est sententiam persequamur.]

[margin: How the individual becomes Species and Genus.]

[margin: Arguments against the Doctrine of Indifference.]

But how can it be said that Socrates is the gathering up of many
into one nature? Neither the man Socrates nor the animal
Socrates is in anything out of Socrates. They affirm that Socrates,
as man, collects Plato and all men into himself; hence, since the
essence exists indifferently in the man, Socrates is Plato and he
himself and Plato and a multitude of others go to form himself the
species and himself the genus." The argument from reason is
stated thus: "Every individual man, in so far as he is man, is
affirmed by this doctrine to be a species; whence, it may be truly
affirmed of Socrates. This man Socrates is species. If Socrates is
species, Socrates is universal; if he is universal he is not singular,
whence it follows he is not Socrates." This consequence, he says,
they deny, for they affirm that every universal is singular and
every singular is universal. In the ashes of Abelard there still
lived the wonted fires. This attempt to confound all sacred distinctions awakens the temper which had been so much softened by
his residence at Clugny. "What impudence," he exclaims, when
he finds that his opponents are escaping from a precept which
Boethius had declared to concern all logical divisions by the lying
assertion that he only meant it in certain cases. He appears to be
still more provoked when he finds them trusting in their formula
"in so far forth," as if that could change facts and laws. And
though we cannot work ourselves into his passionate feelings
against this doctrine of Indifference, we do confess to some
sympathy with him in his indignation against this very helpful
resource for eluding an opponent and concealing the absence of a
meaning.

p. 521.
Vide quanta
impudentia
sint!

Abelard—is
he a Nomin-
alist?
33. Abelard proceeds to his third doctrine, which would be
commonly represented as the doctrine of pure Nominalism. It is
so usual to describe him as the very representative of Nominalism
that we must hear what he has to say against the opinion which
affirms that Genera and Species are mere universal and particular
names and not things. He quotes the passages from Boethius to
which we referred at the beginning of this sketch, and then declares that seeing the Nominalists are not able rationally to resist
these authorities which make so manifestly against them, they
either say that the authorities are false, or labouring to explain them
put a skin upon them because they cannot find any way of stripping
them of their proper skin. But Abelard, though he may appeal
to authorities, seldom rests in them; he must have his own refutation. It is this: "Just as a statue consists of brass, which is its
matter, of figure which is its form, so species consists of genus
which is its matter, of differentia which is its form." But to reduce
these into words is impossible. Animal is the genus of man. But
how can the word animal be the matter of the word man, seeing
that it neither comes from it nor is in it? They answer, he says,

p. 522.
Nunc illam
sententiam
quæ vocce
solas genera
et species
universales
et particula-
les prædicias
et subjectas
asserit et non
res, perquira-
mus.

The argu-
ment against
reducing
things into
names.

that this whole mode of speech is figurative; genus is the material of species, that is to say, that which is signified by genus is the matter of that which is signified by species. But how, he asks, will this work? They admit nothing besides individuals, and these are denoted as well by universal as by singular words. You might just as well therefore say, that which is signified by the species is the matter of that which is signified by the genus. But if this is admitted, the whole principle of logical division, as it is laid down by all eminent authors, is subverted.

34. Having disposed of these theories, he goes on to declare his own. "Every individual is composed of matter and of forms. Socrates is in matter a man, in form Socrates. And as the Socraticity which formally constitutes Socrates is nowhere out of Socrates, so the human essence which sustains the Socraticity in Socrates is nowhere except in Socrates. I say then that species is not that essence of man only which is in Socrates or which is in any other individual, but is the whole united collection of all the distinct elements of this nature. This whole collection, although it is essentially plural, is nevertheless called by the authorities one species, one universal, one nature; as a people, although it is formed of many persons, is called one. So also the essence of this collection, which is called humanity, consists of matter and form—to wit, of the animal as its matter, but of form which is not one but plural, of rationality and mortality and bipedality, and if there are any other substantial qualities requisite thereto. And what is said of man—to wit, that that in man which sustains Socraticity does not essentially sustain Platonicity; this also is true of the animal. For that animal which sustains the form of that humanity which is in me, this is essentially not elsewhere, but dwells indifferently in the particular matter of each individual animal. This multitude then of essences of the animal, which sustains the forms of each species of animal, I would call genus, which herein is diverse from that multitude which forms species; for that is gathered from those essences alone which receive the substantial differences of diverse species. Furthermore, if we ascend upwards to the very first principle, we may assume that every essence of that multitude which is called the genus, animal, consists of some matter that is essential to body and of substantial forms, animation and sensibility, which, as has been said concerning the animal, are nowhere else essentially present; but indifferently sustain the forms of all species of body. These primary essences constitute the matter, which is the genus, as the form corporeity, when added thereto, constitutes the species. These indifferent essences also are the sustaining matter which, united with the form incorporeity, constitute the incorporeal species. And the multitude of such essences is that substance

n. 524.
Quid velit
potius tenen-
dum videatur
de his Deo
annuente
modo osten-
demus.

Matter and
Form.

Essential
Forms.

The most
General Prin-
ciple of all.

which is the most general thing of all, which is not, however, simple, but consists of mere essence as its matter and of the susceptibility of contraries as its form." He promises to explain afterwards why this substance is not to be called genus.

Sic et Non.
Œuvres, pp.
2-170.
35. As our readers are probably well tired of these quiddities, we shall not trouble them with the authorities or reasons by which Abelard supports his own propositions; but shall endeavour presently to gather up as well as we can the thread of these thoughts, and to show how they bear on the philosophy as well as the life of the period. But we shall be better able to estimate the position of this remarkable man if we give a very brief account of one of his theological treatises, the title of which has already occurred in the course of our sketch. That title, *Sic et Non*, Yes and No, in fact contains the meaning of the book. It contains little of the author himself, and yet, perhaps, it throws more light upon his mind than any of his most elaborate and original works could have done. He states in the prologue that many words of holy men seem not only diverse but contradictory; that, nevertheless, we are not to judge them, seeing that the world is to be judged by them; that we are not to accuse them of being false or despise them as erroneous, seeing that the Lord hath said, " he who heareth you, heareth me, and he that despiseth you, despiseth me." They have the Spirit, he says, we have not. Their words are often unfamiliar to us and puzzling; they were often taught to vary them, that the repetition might not produce satiety. He proceeds to state many other causes of perplexity, which are well worth the reader's consideration, but which do not directly concern us, and then concludes. " These things premised, we have thought it good to collect the divers sayings of the Holy Fathers, as they have occurred to our memory, containing some question which they appear to raise by their dissonance, so that the reader may be excited to the greater energy in inquiring for truth, and may be made more acute in the pursuit of it. For this is the first key to wisdom, assiduous and frequent interrogation." He supports himself by the authority of Aristotle, then proceeds. " By doubting we come to inquiry; by inquiry we perceive the truth, as He who is the Truth said, 'seek and ye shall find, knock and it shall be opened to you.' Which lesson he also confirmed by his own example, at twelve years old sitting in the midst of the doctors asking them questions, rather assuming the form of a disciple by questioning than of a Master by preaching, albeit there was in Him the full and perfect wisdom of God."

Preface.
Reasons of
the Treatise.

Doubt and
Search.

Subjects of
Sic et Non.
36. We shall simply enumerate the heads of some of the chapters of this book, which are not only curious in themselves, but which will prepare us for the form into which some of the most orthodox writings of the following century were cast. The first

chapter contains a series of testimonies from the Fathers and Doctors of the Church, apparently favouring the position that Faith is to be sustained by human reason and apparently contradicting it. The second contains a similar balance of opinions on the question whether faith is wholly conversant with things that do not appear. The third proposes statements *pro* and *contra* the maxim that our faith is to be in God only. The fourth is on the point whether knowledge as well as faith, or only faith, has reference to things that do not appear. The articles from the fifth to the twenty-fifth contain different, apparently adverse, propositions concerning the Trinity, the points which drew so much obloquy on Abelard being dwelt upon, but not with any seemingly controversial design. The twenty-sixth gives conflicting judgments on the question whether the old philosophers believed in a Trinity and a Divine Word. Propositions concerning prescience and predestination occupy the chapters from the twenty-sixth to the thirtieth; the origin and nature of sin and its relation to God, the two following; the possibility or impossibility of resisting God's will, the relation of His will to His power and His acts and His knowledge, several more.

37. If Bernard's friend and counsellor had possessed even the slight knowledge of this book which our readers may obtain from these specimens of its topics and its design, his judgment would probably have been at least as severe as the one which he arrived at from merely hearing its name. Nevertheless we must not conceal our opinion that the intentions of the writer were strictly honest; that he had no secret purpose of undermining the reputation of the Church teachers by making a display of their seeming contradictions; that he did believe they were not at variance with themselves, and that the truth which they desired to enforce would be more thoroughly and practically embraced, if a student would give himself the trouble of considering how two clashing assertions can have dwelt together in the mind of the same man, than if he hastily rejected either and took the one which was most convenient for some temporary service. That there was a characteristic rashness in this course we do not deny; if Abelard had pretended that he himself had found out the receipt for solving all puzzles, we must have used a harsher word and spoken of a self-conceit which also may be called, at least in one stage of his life, characteristic. But we are not sure that his rashness did not on the whole conduce to safety and prevent, instead of foster, the tendency to incredulity which the disputatious temper of the times was encouraging. And we are not sure that such a collection may not serve much better to keep an earnest seeker humble, self-distrustful, eager for divine help, than a collection of phrases from high authorities, adduced to sustain some conclusion which

Object of Abelard in this Treatise.

Boldness of the plan.

the student boasts of as his, and in which he may trust much more than in God Himself.

Abelard's disclaimer of Spiritual Illumination. 88. The greatest blot in this treatise is, it seems to us, to be found in that passage of it which the Author regarded, and many of his readers probably will regard, as the most modest which he ever wrote. When he declares that the Fathers of old had the Spirit of God, and that he and his contemporaries were bound to pay them reverence because *they* had not, we believe he made a disclaimer which no Christian man has a right to make—one which involves at the same time an abject slavery to the past, and an incapacity of appreciating the treasures of the past. If the Fathers wrote whatever was good and universal in their works, whatever was not the result of the crudities of their minds or of their age, under the guidance of a higher Spirit than their own, Abelard could only divine their meaning, could only enter into sympathy with them, in so far as he was illuminated by that same Spirit. Without this aid, he could only listen to the sounds which came from their lips, read the letters which were shaped by their pens, not understand the men who uttered the sounds, and wielded the pens. False Modesty the cause of Arrogance. In this fatal mock humility lay, we conceive, the secret of much of his arrogance. He was conscious of a discernment which was far beyond that of the majority of the men around him, a discernment of the sense that was in books, of the laws of the intellect by which books are composed, and to which they address themselves. It would have been a lie to pretend that he had not this discernment. He had not the courage to attribute it to a higher Wisdom than his own; he, therefore, gave himself credit for it. And so, as we have seen, he came, sometimes deservedly, sometimes undeservedly, under the censure of men like Bernard, who, whatever their theory on the subject might be, whatever their deference to the Doctors of other times, acted on the conviction that they had a Divine Spirit with them, and attributed all the true operations of their minds to His agency. Because they had that faith, there was a unity in their deeds and lives which Abelard was seeking for, but can scarcely be said to have found. He had a subtlety in distinction which did not belong to them; but he did not find how distinctions are reconciled, what truth lies beneath them and justifies them.

Abelard's knowledge of Aristotle. 39. Abelard's skill in distinguishing, great as it was, suffered seriously from this want. We have allowed him to explain for himself the doctrine by which he hoped to escape from the errors of several classes of Realists as well as from those of the Nominalists. If our readers should be able to recall the passages which we quoted from the Metaphysics of Aristotle respecting Matter and Form, they may fancy that they have detected the teacher from whom the Breton derived his solution. But they must beware how they hasten to that conclusion. It is exceedingly doubtful whether Abelard possessed even an indifferent translation of the Metaphysics, whether he knew the great master at all, except through Boethius and Porphyry. Perhaps a more careful comparison of their opinions on this subject may greatly strengthen that doubt. At all events, if Abelard read Aristotle, he must either have misunderstood him or have deliberately departed from his instructions. For it cannot escape any thoughtful reader, that the Greek and the Latin are directly opposed to each other as to the relation between the two constituents which they assume in every subject which we contemplate. *Form* is with Aristotle the ground of the house, the tree, the man—that which makes it what it is; *Matter* is that which is necessary to make it actual, to bring it into the circle of other existences. With Abelard Matter is the essential, Form is superinduced upon it. A more striking illustration can hardly be found of the contrast between the greatest logician of the Greek and the greatest we have yet met with in the Latin world. The one, though the opposer of ideas in the Platonical sense, yet must have the invisible incorporeal Eidos at the root of all his conceptions; the other when he is most aiming at intellectual subtlety must still base his thoughts upon that which he can see and handle. *A priori*, one would have expected that the Christian divine, in whatever other respects he was inferior to the Pagan philosopher, would have more easily and immediately acknowledged a spiritual substance, a spiritual foundation. It is not so. And we think Abelard's confession in the preface to the *Sic et non*, has shown us why it is not so. The Greek could see that there was implied in the very existence of everything visible, an invisible; without which it would *appear* only and not *be*. The Christian, not acknowledging a spiritual bond between the Divine Creator and himself, is driven by his very belief in a Maker of the world to regard Him first of all as the Maker of what is visible and tangible; so this becomes unawares the first in his own conception. Though he feels that his own thoughts are higher than the things that they deal with, he cannot persuade himself that these things have not an older and a more substantial being than those thoughts or than whatever is homogeneous with them.

40. In these remarks we have said all that it is needful to say here respecting Abelard's mode of cutting the knot which his different contemporaries had not been able to untie. The experiment was of real worth. The man who made it, showed that he had a far keener intellect than had been granted to his opponents or to any of his fellow-workers. His solution was one which affected all the after history of scholastical philosophy, which was adopted consciously or unconsciously by many who regarded him as a heretic, which is recognized in the speculations and in the practice of

many in later times who despise him as a mere word-fighter. But
it entirely failed to terminate the controversy; it could not satisfy
the minds of those who accepted it. There were truths and principles involved in the strife upon which all the skill of a series of
dialecticians would be exercised, and which dialecticians would at
last be found utterly unable to vindicate or to overthrow.

Ritter Ge-
schichte der
Philosophie
v. 7, p. 452,
note 2.
NOTE.—[It ought not to be concealed from the reader that Ritter attributes the
treatise, "De Generibus et Speciebus," which Cousin claims for Abelard, to Joscelin,
Bishop of Soissons, or to one of his disciples. The grounds for this positive conclusion appear to us very weak. They rest upon a passage in John of Salisbury
to this effect :—" There are some, moreover, who, with Gauslenus, the Bishop of
Soissons, attribute universality to things collected into one, and take it away from
individual things." This Ritter maintains to be the doctrine of the treatise, and
thereupon refers it to a person or a school, otherwise very little known to us. His
arguments against M. Cousin's conclusions have more weight, though he has not
stated his opponent's case fairly. It is admitted that there is no name of an
author on the manuscript. The assignment of it must therefore depend upon
little points of evidence chiefly internal. Cousin rests too much perhaps upon the
allusions which are made in it to William of Champeaux, and takes too much for
granted a very ingenious emendation of his own of *Indifferenter* for *Individualiter*,
in the passage in the Book of Calamities which describes the controversy between
Abelard and his old master. But that correction, to say the least, is exceedingly
plausible, and if it is admitted, the statement of William of Champeaux's views in
the treatise on Genera and Species, throws wonderful light upon what was before
an obscure and scarcely intelligible statement. To say, as Ritter does, that
Cousin has no better plea for his opinion than the notion that there are but three
possible doctrines—Nominalism, Realism, and Conceptualism—and that since
Abelard did not embrace either of the two former, he must have embraced the last,
which is the one defended in this treatise, is to caricature the love of system, which
is no doubt the infirmity of all clever Frenchmen, but which does not display itself
with any peculiar extravagance in this instance. For Cousin distinctly affirms,
on the plain evidence of the treatise itself, that there were several different modes
under which Realism could be contemplated, and merely maintains, what Ritter
himself is obliged to confess, that Abelard was not, as is vulgarly supposed, a
Nominalist. The evidence which the German critic deduces from a comparison
of the style in which Abelard ordinarily wrote with that of the treatise, will have
little effect upon an English reader who has been sated with that kind of argument in the case of Junius and a hundred other authors. When scales are nearly
balanced, a feather may make one of them sink; but suggestions about style are
lighter than feathers. An author changes his style with the changes of his subject, of his temper, of his digestion. Each reader changes his opinion about the
resemblance of the style in one book and another, as he is inclined to establish the
identity or the diversity of the authors. In fact, style must have reference to
some accidents without or some principles within. And in this and in all cases,
we shall judge about it correctly or incorrectly as we judge correctly or incorrectly
of the spirit of the person who uses it. We do not hesitate to say, that we think
Cousin has entered more into the spirit of Abelard than Ritter has done,—that
he knows the man better, partly because he loves him better. Though we have
presumed to differ from him in several points, and though we accept his authority
with some hesitation on this, we are inclined to think and hope that he may
have divined rightly the source from which the book on Genera and Species proceeded. If not, we trust our readers will judge us tolerantly for having fallen into
this error, rather than into the more wilful one of ascribing the book to the Bishop
of Soissons].

41. Abelard has been always supposed to present one phase of *Why Bernard cannot strictly be compared with Abelard.* this period, Bernard the opposite phase. This is, on the whole, a true statement. Yet Bernard, if we take in his relations with Dukes, Kings, Popes, Crusaders, is too busy a man to be exactly compared with a student, however much that student may have influenced his time, and however much his personal life may be mixed with his philosophical. The most direct opposite of Abelard *Hugo de St. Victore.* is perhaps Hugo de St. Victore. It is common to speak of him as a mystic, and the head of a mystical school. These words will not perhaps convey any very distinct impression to our readers, as they do not to us. They are the cold formal generalizations of a later period, commenting on men with whom it has no sympathy. They scarcely help us more than the distinctions which are some- *Mystics.* times drawn by philosophical historians between the Platonists and Aristotelians of this and the contiguous centuries. Our readers will have seen that the same man was oftentimes by turns an Aris- *Aristotelians and Platonists.* totelian and a Platonist, that it was inevitable that he should be so, because his logical impulses were drawing him in one direction, his Christian theology in another. To which side any inclined most, depended much upon the conditions of their practical life; Boethius was one man in his study, another in his prison. And even when they were very strongly determined either way, the habits of the Latin mind were so unlike those of the Greek, that we are liable to continual blunders in our efforts to bring them together. These very habits, as we have endeavoured to show, unconsciously influenced the middle-ages doctor to fall into the harder, more formal line of thought in which the Stagyrite had been, and always will be, the great guide; but, at the same time, as the book on Genera and Species has taught us, they led to the obscuration and even the reversal of some of Aristotle's most precious and vital maxims. If, therefore, we are compelled to use these modes of defining particular teachers, they should be applied *The historian must break through classifications.* with the greatest caution; the historian and biographer should be less afraid of appearing to contradict himself than of consistently adhering to a formula which at some point or other is sure to break down. With even more caution, if it is possible, he should resort to the words mystic and anti-mystic. They do point to certain undoubted tendencies in the minds of thoughtful men, tendencies which have never been wanting in any age, which are not more characteristic of the eleventh century than of the nineteenth. But we are in continual danger of confounding the manifestations of those tendencies in one state of society with those in another, and of making our own experiences the rule for the periods that are gone by. We are in equal danger of not perceiving what was in a man because we have begun by putting a label upon him, which, if there was anything in him worthy to be remembered, must be

utterly inadequate to describe him. The student, therefore, who wishes to apply Bacon's maxims respecting Nature to the history of man and his thoughts, will do well to distrust these convenient modes of arranging phenomena before they have been investigated, just as vigorously and conscientiously as he does parallel modes of anticipating and circumscribing the discoveries and laws of the external world.

Hugo's coun- try.

42. The opposition between Hugo and Peter Abelard is, however, remarkable and worthy to be considered, though we shall not arrive at the true nature of it by calling one a master among logicians, and the other a master among mystics. Their countries were different, a circumstance which we have already discovered to be of great importance. Abelard has described to us the tendencies of his Breton race, which he exhibited in such perfection. Hugo was a German, apparently connected with some of the noble families of Germany. Nevertheless, he, as much as the Frenchman, came to that which was then, as since, the chief intellectual

At Paris.

mart of Europe; not, indeed, to hold disputations with William of Champeaux, or to establish a reputation in the University of Paris, but to dwell in a cloister of St. Victor, whose name he assumed. Little is known of him further as a man, but his influence in that and subsequent ages appears to have been deep and extensive. The book which unquestionably produced this effect, and which we may fairly take to be the most characteristic of himself, is that on *Sacraments*, though there is another, the *Didascalon*, which

His book De Sacramentis.

perhaps more strictly belongs to our subject. Perhaps we shall put our readers in the best position for understanding Hugo's place in a history of philosophy, and the relation in which his thoughts stood to those of questions respecting things and names with which we have recently been conversant, if we extract a passage from the eleventh part of his first book on Sacraments, a chapter which bears the title, "Concerning the Sacrament and virtue of Faith." If it should seem at first that we have merely chosen a striking theological statement—for striking most will allow it to be—we think we shall be able to show hereafter that it touches upon the very heart of all the moral and metaphysical speculations of that time, if not of later times.

Images in a Mirror.

43. "First let us consider in what wise, Faith itself is called a Sacrament, and of what thing it is understood to be a Sacrament. The Apostle says, 'We see now through a glass in an enigma, then face to face.' That is to say, now while we are seeing by faith, we see through a glass in an enigma; but then when we shall see by contemplation, we shall see face to face. To see in a glass is to see an image; to see face to face is to see the thing. Suppose some one to be behind you or above you, you are turned from him, you do not see him face to face. And if he looks at you it does not

therefore follow that you can look at *him*. Bring out the glass, place
it before you, straightway you will see the image of him who is at
your back or is over your head; you will say, 'I see thee.' What
is it you see? You see something doubtless, but an image only, *The Image*
you see him but in his image. Not yet in his own face. You do *and the Archetype.*
not yet know as you are known, you do not see as you are seen,
you are seen in yourself, you see in an image. He looks at you,
you are turned from him. Turn yourself to him, oppose face to
face, now you will see not an image, but the very thing. You saw
him before, but you saw him in his image only, now in his face. . . .
That which is seen in an image is a sacrament, that which is seen *Application*
in the thing (in reality) is the thing (the reality) of the sacrament. *of the illustration.*
What therefore we now see through a glass in an enigma, is the
sacrament to that which we shall see face to face in open contemplation. But what is the enigma in which the image is seen until
the thing itself may be seen? The enigma is the Sacred Scripture.
Why? Because it has an obscure signification. And the glass is
your heart, if so be it be pure, and cleansed, and clarified. The
image in the glass is the faith in your heart, for faith itself is an
image and a sacrament; but the contemplation that is to be, is the
thing, and the virtue of the sacrament. Those who have not faith *That which*
see nothing; those who have faith are beginning to see something, *is and is to be.*
but the image only. For if the faithful saw nothing, there would
be no illumination for faith, nor would the faithful be said to be
illuminated. But if they saw the very thing, and did not expect
anything more that is to be seen, they would not see through a
glass in an enigma, but face to face. If then the highest good for
a man is the contemplation of his Creator, that faith by which he
begins in some way to see Him who is absent, is rightly spoken of
as the initial good, the beginning of his restoration. This restoration grows as faith itself grows, he is more and more illuminated
by knowledge that he may know more fully, and is influenced by
love that he may love more ardently. If then the righteous man, *The renova-*
as long as he is in this body, is away from his Lord, here he has *tion of Man by Faith.*
the life of faith. But so soon as he is brought out of this prison-
house and brought into the joy of his Lord, he will have the life of
contemplation. . . . . . . In the Sacraments, as has been
said, arms are supplied to this man whereby he may protect himself in good works, as well as weapons wherewith he may overthrow his enemy, so that charity and hope being joined to faith,
he may have an ever renewed and renewing strength, and life."

44. It will be obvious to the reader of this passage that in it *Things* *Things and*
are not opposed to *Names* but to *Signs*. He will perceive too that *Signs.*
things here stand for invisible substances, the objects of spiritual
apprehension, and that the visible universe is regarded chiefly as
furnishing instruments whereby the man is educated for this con-

L

templation. Nothing can be further from Hugo's disposition than that kind of Mysticism which glorifies sudden apprehensions or intuitions of individual men respecting the invisible world. His book is an orderly exhibition of the different Sacraments which the Creator has used in different stages and dispensations of history; it assumes the knowledge of the invisible to be the proper and legitimate condition of the human creature, the one from which it is his full and evil to have departed, and to which the grace of the Creator would restore him. Assuredly there is nothing novel in these opinions. They were the commonplaces of the old theology; no divines in any age have wholly lost sight of them. But it makes all the difference whether they are the governing thoughts in a man's mind or only the subordinate; whether they determine his view of life and studies or only qualify it. In the case of Abelard and the Logicians, they were clearly not the governing thoughts. Even in their theology the idea of sacraments was not a cardinal but an accessory one; their dialectics and even their ethics were quite independent of it. The Didascalon of Hugo shows that with him the case was altogether otherwise. His conception of all other subjects is moulded by his theology, and that theology is throughout sacramental.

45. Our readers will have put a very wrong construction upon our last words, if they suppose that Hugo was either indifferent to human learning, or that he supposed Theology was to contract its sphere and fix limits to its progress. He lays it down in the commencement of his first book, that "of all things to be desired, Wisdom is the first, wherein the form of the perfect Good consists. Wisdom illuminates the man, that he may know himself." He is full of admiration of Pythagoras for calling the searchers for truth not wise men but lovers of wisdom. He would have the mind burn with the love of it, exercise itself to the search of it, and feel how difficult it is to embrace it in its own very nature. He recognizes the threefold division of the soul into the crescent or vegetative, the sentient and the rational. The last belongs specially and characteristically to man. It occupies itself with inquiring concerning any subject, whether it is, what it is, of what kind or class it is, finally, why it is. He affirms that it is not inconsistent with the etymology of philosophy, to which he has already attached so much value, to define it as the discipline which investigates fully the reasons or principles of all things human and divine. He vindicates this definition from the charge to which its comprehensiveness would naturally expose it, by saying that certain acts belong to philosophy in respect of their principle, and must be excluded from it in respect of their administration. Agriculture, in so far as it is occupied with laws of nature, falls within the province of philosophy—so far as concerns its operation, within the province

[margin notes]
The Education of Man by His Creator.

Characteristic difference between Abelard and Hugo.

Hugo's idea of human learning. Didascalon, lib. 1 c. 2 & 3.

Division of the Soul, c. 4.

Definition of Philosophy. c. 3.

of the labourer. He explains how the necessity for pathology as Curative Processes, c. 6 well as for physiology arises. "There are two things in man," he says, " good and evil, nature and vice. Our business is to repair nature and to banish, as far as in us lies, that which has corrupted it. The integrity of human life," he says, " requires for its fulfilment science and virtue, wherein consists our only resemblance to the superior and divine substances. For," he goes on, " man, —seeing he is not a simple nature,—in one aspect of his being, which is the better, and that I may speak more openly what I ought to speak, his very self, is immortal; but on the other side, which is weak and fallen, and which alone is known to those who have no faith except in sensible things, he is obnoxious to mortality and mutability." He divides all things into those that have neither The Temporal, the Perpetual, and the Eternal, c. 7. beginning nor end, and which are called eternal, those which have beginning but no end, which are called perpetual, those which have both beginning and end, which are called temporal. "Two things there are," he says, " which repair the divine likeness in man, the beholding of truth and the exercise of virtue. God being *the* Just and *the* Wise immutably, Man being just and wise mutably." He distinguishes three kinds of works, the work of God, The work of the Creator, the Artificer, and of Nature, c. 10. the work of Nature, the work of the artificer imitating nature. The work of God is indicated in the words, "In the beginning He created heaven and earth;" the work of Nature in the words, "Let the earth bring forth the green herb;" "the business of the artificer," he says, " is to unite things which are separate and to distinguish things that are joined." He then discusses the faculties of man as exercised in different acts of production and imitation. The statue, he says, comes from the contemplation of a man, the house from the contemplation of a mountain which is a protection against the tempest, the invention of clothes from the observation of the bark of trees and the feathers of birds and the scales of fishes. He inquires into the true definition of Nature, acknow- What Nature is, c. 11. ledges the difficulty of the question, and proceeds to show the different senses that have been given to it, that they may not be confounded. First, it has been taken for the archetypal example of all things in the divine mind; then it is defined as that which assigns to each thing its own; secondly, Nature has been called the property of each thing or that which informs each thing with its proper differentia; in this sense we speak of all things by nature tending to the earth, of its being the nature of fire to burn, &c. A third definition is that Nature is the internal fire which penetrates all sensible things and causes them to bring forth. The last sub- Logic, c. 12. ject in his first book is the origin and purpose of Logic. He places this study last, he says, because it was discovered last; other things had been found out, then it was necessary that logic also should be found out, because no one could properly speak of things unless be first recognized the method of speaking rightly. In treating this subject he does little more than quote certain passages from Boethius, which we have already brought under the notice of our readers. Hugo is chiefly useful for the pains which he takes in pointing out the truth, obvious enough but likely to be forgotten in that age, that the practice of all arts, of speaking and reasoning especially, must have preceded the discovery of the maxims and principles which regulate them.

Hugo's place in Philosophical History. 46. We think our readers will agree with us that we have here an interesting specimen of a 12th century student and religious philosopher. If Hugo was, as is alleged, a Mystic, it can hardly be denied that a Mystic is capable of exhibiting practical sense and considerable erudition. Indeed, after all that has been said about Abelard's spirit of investigation—and we certainly have shown no wish to disparage Abelard—it might fairly be contended that there is more of the spirit of progress in Hugo than in his contemporary, that though he might dispute less ably, he would also be less likely to limit knowledge by the rules and terms of dialectics. The theology of Hugo compels him to be a continual searcher, the ever expanding knowledge of the infinite and eternal God is the only ultimate end he can think of, as it is the only reward after which he aspires. A man with such aims and with so much diligence and courage in carrying them out, must have given a powerful impetus to the minds of his cotemporaries. His name has been less remembered in later times than it deserves, because it has been overshadowed by those of other men who met some of the tastes of the age more successfully, though their actual power was not greater than his, perhaps not equal to his.

Arnold of Brescia. 47. Peter Abelard had an eminent pupil, of whose projects, whose failure, and whose death it is the business of the political not of the philosophical historian to speak. But we have so often broken through the limits which it becomes us, according to precedent, to observe, that we shall make no excuse for at least mentioning the name of Arnold of Brescia. How the speculations on dialectics, or even on theology, in which Abelard indulged, can have borne fruit in a scheme for restoring a Senate and Tribunes to Rome, for making the ecclesiastical world give place to the classical, it is not easy at once to conceive. And any theories about the links between the two sets of thoughts are nearly sure to be hasty and unsatisfactory in proportion to their ingenuity. Much might be said of the way in which a spirit of inquiry when it has commenced in one direction, spreads into another. But though Abelard was a vigorous and even a restless inquirer, one does not perceive how his investigations should have led any one to disturb the peace of cities, far less to organize a society by restoring older forms than those which were displaced. It is only in

How Abelard influenced him is not obvious.

connection with the general movements of the time that one can understand how Abelard drew such audiences to his lectures on Universals at Paris, and it is only by attention to the same movements that one can understand how the acts of an enthusiast like Arnold should have become serious in the eyes of Popes and Emperors, and should have reacted on the philosophy of the schools.

48. Arnold sought the assistance of Frederick Barbarossa in support of his popular movement against the Pope, or rather offered to fraternize with him. Though his proposals were received with little respect, they proved that there was a new element at work in the world, and that henceforth the conflict would not be merely between the civil and ecclesiastical heads of the Roman empire. The memorable struggles between the Italian cities which brought the Popedom into the new and curious position of a champion of freedom against the German despotism, revealed still more clearly the existence of this third power, and showed that it would have an increasing influence on the destinies of Europe. It is evident that the question of Unity, what it means, how it was to be preserved under its present conditions, or under what new conditions it was possible, had been debated elsewhere than in the University of Paris, between other combatants than William of Champeaux and Abelard or even Bernard. The failure of the second crusade, which had been so powerfully advocated by the Abbot of Clairvaux, showed that the unity of Christendom, even when it was represented by powerful kings, was still an imperfect one, scarcely able to match itself against the unity of Islamism. Evidently its spiritual centre was not firm. Italy felt its weakness even more than the rest of Europe. But all felt it, Churchmen as well as Statesmen, Becket as much as Henry II. How was Unity to be maintained? Who were to discover the secret of it? Might not the Doctors do what the Popes were failing to do? Might not they lay bare the very principle which could keep the minds of men as well as societies together? They believed that they could. The secret of all strifes and discoveries lay, as it seemed to them, within. Heresies and evil opinions were the radical causes of them. To extirpate these was the great work of which the world was in need.

49. Such became the leading characteristical thought of the latter part of the 12th century. Was it not also the thought of that earlier half which Bernard represented? Not precisely in the same sense. Bernard had a horror of heresies as foes to practical life, as disturbers of the devotion of Monasteries, as hinderers of the common action of the Christian nations against the Infidels. But he was, as we have seen, a Saint and not a Doctor; with little skill in tracing the rise and growth of an opinion, however he might

[margin notes:] The Pope, the Emperor, and the Cities. / Question of Unity in the Schools and in the World. / The war with Heresies. / The Saint and the Doctor.

wish to drive it away; much more capable of pouring forth earnest exhortations than of giving learned solutions of difficulties. Another kind of man was needed when dialectical skill had established itself in the Universities as part of the profession of those who taught in them, and when political rebellion had gone so far in shaking the prestige of Papal dominion.

50. Peter the Lombard, though of Italian birth, got his learning where almost every one else got it at this time, in Paris. He had profited by the teaching both of St. Bernard and of Hugo de St. Victore. In 1159 he became Bishop of Paris. He died, according to some authorities, in 1160, according to others, in 1164. Perhaps it was fitting that the Master of Sentences should have a scanty personal biography, that he should be known to us almost entirely through a book. That book has an oracular form and character which does not belong to any earlier composition of the

Middle Ages. Oracles were what people who had been wearied of Abelard's continual questioning were longing for. But such oracles would have been less satisfactory to the spirit of this age, perhaps would have been rejected by it, if they had proceeded from an authoritative tribunal like that of Rome. A Bishop had less chance of being listened to than a simple Doctor. The Master of Sentences did not create his fame or increase it by his mitre. His decrees came forth in the shape of 'Distinctions;' he paid reverence to the intellect even while he was uttering decrees to which it bowed.

51. This remark must be remembered by every reader of the Sentences. Though they were the foundation of a number of anathemas against Heretics which issued from Paris and are commonly appended to Peter's four books, they themselves were not received at first without suspicion. They contain a careful examination of opinions and a statement, generally an honest statement, of the perplexities of the student's mind out of which they have arisen. The teacher does not forbid but encourages the diligent weighing of words, the following out acts and thoughts to their principle. He complains of those whom he calls Heretics rather for precipitation in their decisions than for too much hesitation. He believes that there is certainty at the root of all things; but he allows for the thorns and thistles which oppose themselves to him who is digging down to it.

52. The first distinction of Peter the Lombard is between *things* and *signs.* His inclination to make this contrast the ground of his whole treatise may be traced probably to the influence of Hugo. Things, are with him, as with the writer on Sacra-

ments, eternal realities: Signs, the tokens by which they make themselves known in the outward world. But the mind of Peter is far less historical than that of Hugo. He does not trace the use

of these signs in different periods, but he advances at once to the heart
of the mystery which was occupying the whole thought of the Middle
Ages from whatever point that thought might start, in whatever
direction it might seem to be moving. The first book of the Sentences is professedly on the mystery of the Trinity. The other three
books are derived from this; implicitly their subject is the same.

53. He begins with Things. Of these some are to be enjoyed, *Use and En-*
joyment.
some are to be used; there are some which both enjoy and use. *lib. 1, dist. 1,*
Those things which are to be enjoyed make us blessed. By *c. (6—14.)*
those which are to be used, we are assisted in tending to blessedness, so that we may come to the truly good things and dwell
in them. *We* are the things that both enjoy and use; placed
between the two, as the saints and angels are also. To *enjoy* is to
dwell in the love of anything for its own sake; to *use* is to turn
to account that which is presented to us for this end. All other
use is named abuse. The things, then, which we are to enjoy are
the Father, the Son, and the Holy Spirit. The Trinity is that
supreme thing, common to all who enjoy it, if, indeed, it may
be called a thing, and not rather the cause of all things, nay,
if the word *cause* itself is not too mean. The things we are to
use are the world and the creatures in it. The invisible things
of God are to be understood through the things that are made,
the use of the world is, that out of temporal things eternal things
may be taken in.

54. The last of these sentences is taken from Augustine, who is *The Fathers;*
what use
the great authority for both the distinctions which we have touched *Peter Lom-*
upon; indeed, for the whole treatise. Peter Lombard avowedly *bard made of*
them.
builds his book upon the Fathers. He wishes rather to be considered a collector of their judgments than an utterer of his own.
Still he is not a copyist or a plagiarist. The Fathers have cultivated in him the power of original thinking and of methodizing his
thoughts. When he quotes them, it is not as a slavish repeater of
their words, but as a student and interpreter of their sense. It is
otherwise, we think, when he appeals to the Scriptures. There
he often does catch at mere sounds; the historical spirit of the
Scriptures puzzles him; he cannot deduce formulas and maxims
from them so quickly as from Augustine, therefore they are introduced rather to sustain a conclusion he has already formed than to
suggest one. When they are troublesome, and do not bear out his
conclusion, he treats them much as other commentators do. For *His use of*
the Bible.
instance, St. Paul's sentence, "God will have all men to believe *Distinction,*
46 c. (He
and come to the knowledge of the truth," strikes him as perilously *treats the*
comprehensive; he therefore proposes the very simple expedient *words in*
John, c. i. v.
of inverting it; it means only that "all come to the knowledge of *9, upon the*
same prin-
the truth whom God wills to do so." *ciple.)*

55. It is not for the pleasure of pointing out a weakness in our

eminent schoolman that we have alluded to this monstrous interpretation. It illustrates a contradiction which was not confined to him, which he inherited in part from his master, Augustine, and which has descended upon some who have known little either of the master or the pupil. Contemplated as an object of trust and delight to the purified spirit, the Divine nature always presents itself to him as essential Charity. Each Person exhibits some aspect of that love, which he regards as only another name for the holy and undivided Trinity. But when the Being whom he has spoken of in this rapturous language, presents himself as an originating Will, another thought intrudes itself—Omnipotence takes the place of Charity. If the two seem to come into collision, the second must be sacrificed to the first. It is supposed to be an act of reverence to confess absolute power; merely an act of self-indulgence to believe in an absolute love. And this, through the very condition of a heavenly spirit, is declared to be that it should enter into this absolute love, and should refer all powers to it. Or else our finite faculties are called in to justify our attempting to grasp the one kind of infinity instead of acknowledging the other. The philosophy, as much as the theology of Peter Lombard is affected by this inconsistency; we could not, therefore, pass it over. But we must do justice to the strength of his philosophy as well as of his theology. No student of divinity can read his first book, we should conceive, without acquiring a deeper and clearer conception of principles in which he has implicitly believed, without cultivating the precious habit of distinction. And we doubt whether any student of philosophy can read large portions of that book and of the three following, without acquiring a new sense of the dignity and responsibility of the name which he has taken upon him; without confessing that the dogmatist has taught him to be more of an inquirer than he was before.

56. It will be evident from the hints which we have given already that Augustine not only influenced very powerfully the mind of Peter Lombard, as he did the whole mind of the Middle Ages, but that he imparted to his pupil that habit of thought respecting the will of God and His determinations, as to the well-doing and well-being of His creatures, which we ordinarily associate with the Bishop of Hippo. Perhaps the 38th Distinction of the first book, which relates to this subject, may be as helpful as any we could select, in enabling the reader to understand the tendencies and the method of our author.

"It has been said above that the prescience of God is only of future things, but of *all* future things as well good as evil. Knowledge or wisdom, on the other hand, has respect not only to future things, but also to present; not only to temporal things, but also to eternal, seeing that God knows himself. Hence arises a question which cannot be evaded—whether divine knowledge or prescience is the cause of the things, or the things are the causes of the knowledge or prescience. For it would seem as if the prescience of God were the cause of those things which fall under it, seeing that they would not have come to pass unless God had foreseen them, and it was impossible for them not to happen, seeing that God did foresee them. . . . . . . The same also must be affirmed of knowledge, to wit, that because God hath known certain things, therefore they are. Which sentiment Augustine seems to support, saying, God knew not these things from a certain time, but all temporal things that were to be, and among these what and when we should beg from Him, and when and concerning what things He would hear or not hear; this he foresaw without beginning. For He did not know all creatures because they are, but they are because He knew them." . . . . And again, in the 6th book of his Ecclesiastes—" When times depart and succeed, nothing departs or succeeds in the knowledge of God wherein He knew all things which He made by it." Peter Lombard then goes on to point out the inconveniences which would follow if this doctrine were admitted. "If the knowledge or the prescience of God is the cause of all things, it is the cause of all evils; therefore God would be the author of evils, which is altogether false. But again, there is equal inconvenience in assuming that the things which are to be, are the cause of the knowledge or prescience of God. Were this so, then something would exist as the cause of that which is eternal, something alien and diverse from it; the knowledge of the Creator would depend upon the creatures; the created would be the cause of the uncreated. How is this contradiction to be cleared up? Identify knowledge with acquaintance (Scientia with Notitia), and we may say boldly, the Science or Prescience of God is *not* the cause of things that come to pass in any other sense than that without it they do not come to pass. But if under the name of knowledge, you include good pleasure and disposition, then it may be rightly called the cause of those things which God creates. In this way perhaps we may understand Augustine, ' they are because He knew them;' that is, because knowing, He was satisfied, and because He disposed them according to His knowledge. This sense is the more probable, because Augustine is there speaking only of things that are good, of the creatures which God makes, all which He knows, not simply, but with a knowledge which includes satisfaction and disposition. But evil things God knows and foresees before they come to pass, by simple acquaintance or external understanding. God foresees and predicts that which He will not produce, as He foresaw and predicted the infidelity of the Jews, but did not produce it. He did not force them

Marginal notes:
Whether the necessity of acts is involved in the divine prescience or knowledge of them

The consequences of each alternative.

Solution. Notitia et Scientia.

Beneplacitum et Dispositio.

into the sin of infidelity because He foresaw it, nor would He have
foreseen or predicted their evils unless those evils were to be actually in them. Augustine says, He did not therefore force any
one to sin because He foreknew what would be the sins of men,
for He foresaw *their* sins, not His own. Therefore, if those things
which He foresaw were not theirs, He foresaw what was not true.
But seeing His prescience cannot be deceived, beyond a doubt it
was not another sinned, but *they* sinned—this God foreknew. And
therefore, if they had wished not to do evil but good, it would have
been foreseen that they would not do evil by Him who knew what
each one would do." There is still a difficulty which our author
thinks it his duty to state, "Either, it is said, things happen
otherwise than God foresaw them, or not otherwise. If not otherwise, then all things happen by necessity; if otherwise, the prescience of God may be deceived or may be changed. But they may
happen otherwise, because they may happen otherwise than they
do happen; but they do happen as has been foreseen, therefore they may happen otherwise than was foreseen. The answer
is: All such phrases as these, *it is impossible that that should not be*
which God has foreseen, it is impossible that all things should not be
foreseen that come to pass, may be taken conjunctively or dis-
junctively. For if you understand it thus, 'It cannot be otherwise
than God hath foreseen,' that is to say, it cannot be that God has
foreseen it one way and it comes to pass in another way, you understand what is true. But if you say 'This cannot happen otherwise
than it does happen, and in another way than that in which God
foresaw it would happen,' that is false. It might have happened
otherwise than it did, and God saw it would happen as it did.
The same distinction applies to the other saying, that it is impossible that that should not happen which God has foreseen, or when
God has foreseen it. To say that it is impossible that all which
comes to pass should not be foreseen, that is to say, that it should
come to pass and not be foreseen, is true. To say that it was impossible for God not to foresee everything which comes to pass, is
false. For He might cause that it should not come to pass, and so
that it should not be foreseen."

57. Every reader will perceive how easily the habit of word-
splitting, in its worst form, might be cultivated by such teaching
as this. And when word-splitting went along with stringent dogmatism, when men were condemned for not apprehending the
accurate terms which the doctor had used to guard against errors
on the right or the left, there would be great danger lest the
student, having first become the slave of words, should afterwards
make them the excuse for establishing a tyranny over his brethren.
We have some sense of the greatness of these perils, and we are
sure that they were greater in reality than they can be in our

Marginal notes:
Dis. 39 c. The Dilemma.
The Solution.
Dangers in the Sen- tences.

apprehension. Yet we must maintain that such writers as Peter The Compen-
Lombard were doing something to counteract this danger, if by sation.
accident they may have promoted it. The cure for the extreme
lust of distinction certainly is not found in overlooking distinctions
or denying their importance. It is not found by shrinking from
the severe examination of words and of their shades of meaning.
The more carefully that examination is pursued, the more we are
led to feel the significance and sacredness of words, the less are we
likely to play dishonest tricks with them. That words are things,
mighty and terrible things, was the special lesson which the middle
ages had to learn, and which they had to impart. Many superstitions they indulged unquestionably concerning these words, many
magical arts were practised by means of them. But when they
descended into the subterranean world and discovered in what
vulcanian fires their weapons were fashioned, they were more on
their guard against those above ground who gave them an unnatural sharpness or used earthly herbs and medicaments to make
them poisonous. If there was mischief in connecting them with
the deepest principles of theology, there was also the benefit of
making the use of them more cautious and earnest. He who
speculated or traded with them might win unusual profits by his
venture; but the risks were also terrific

58. Those who have gone with us so far, will not need to be Words and
Facts.
told what we suppose these schoolmen needed, to make their distinctions effectual for their own age and for other ages, even when
they worked them out most honestly and most diligently. The
old Socratic commerce with facts and nature, was required by the
craftsmen in the University of Paris, as it had been by those in the
School of Alexandria, to prevent refined investigations into the force
of words from becoming embarrassing to the intellects which they
might have helped to make clearer. This evil was greater in the
twelfth century than it had been in the eleventh. When scholar- The Univer-
ship belonged to the monasteries, there was a homely life of dig- sities less in
commerce
ging, draining, building, managing accounts, punishing the refrac- with life than
tory, teaching the children, which helped to make study practical, the Monas-
teries.
or to remind students that *they* ought to be so. The Universities
were more exclusively word-laboratories. There was a likeness of
the family in the first, if family ties in their ordinary sense were
renounced. In the other, the tie was almost exclusively that between teacher and disciple; often, it may be, a very cordial and
affectionate one, but in its nature temporary, liable to be determined by changes of place and changes of opinion; if prolonged
beyond a certain time, often prolonged to the injury of the pupil's
growth; wanting therefore the stability of the other more general
relations. It was advantageous, we conceive, to Hugo and to Peter
Lombard, that their University experience was in a considerable

degree founded upon and blended with their Monastic, so that
they did not set up the latter against the former, as Bernard did,
or merely resort to it in hours of sorrow and exhaustion, as Abelard did.   Still both of them belong, Peter Lombard especially, to
what we may call the University age, an age which had not begun
in the days of Anselm, and which underwent great changes, if it
may not be said to have passed into another, before the days of
Aquinas.   It was a very critical moment in the history of European
culture, not altogether unlike the one in individual life when the boy
leaves the school forms for a more elaborate and systematic course of
instruction.   In both there is the danger that what was vital and
energetic, however immature, in the first stage, should be exchanged
for formality in the second; the equal danger that there should be a
reaction against this formality, and that a stormy life should take
the place of a calm one.

59. Europe in the twelfth century had no exemption from this
last hazard more than from the other.   We have spoken of the
Distinctions and the protests against heresy in Peter the Lombard,
as indicating what confused elements there were in the world
around, and how little the schools could preserve themselves
from the turmoil.   It must not be forgotten that the time in which he
wrote was not merely the time of the struggles of the Italian Republics
with each other and with Germany, but also of those battles of our
Henry II. and his Archbishop, which form so memorable a chapter in English history.   It is a countryman of our own who, better
perhaps than any one else, makes us feel the relation between the
outward and inward life of the time.   John of Salisbury, the
friend of Becket, before the end of his life the Bishop of Chartres,
was not perhaps a philosopher in the strict sense of the word.   Like
most of his countrymen he was, by nature, less of a metaphysician
than of a politician.   It was in the business of the world that he
learnt what inner lore is needful to direct it.   For that very
reason he was more competent than those who were immersed in
school pursuits, to make observations upon their influence and their
connection with other very different influences.   A few of the hints
which his *Polycraticus* supplies on this subject may afford much help
to the student of middle age philosophy in understanding the kind
of atmosphere by which the schoolmen were surrounded, and which
even in their cloisters and closets they were forced to breathe.

60. We should especially recommend our readers to look at the
18th Chapter of the Second Book, wherein the author treats of
" the foundation of Mathematics, and the exercise of the senses and
the energies of the soul, and the profit of reason, and the efficacy of
liberal arts."   The main object of the chapter which bears this
comprehensive title, is to distinguish between the Mathēsis and
Mathĕsis, the first being, as he says, " founded in nature, proved

The Univer-
sity age.

John of
Salisbury.

Mathesis
with the
short and the
long penul-
tima.

by reason, confirmed by experience; the other, its pernicious and
reprobate counterfeit." Starting with this design, he touches upon [—] Investigation of Nature.
the investigation of nature, which he distinguishes into the inquiry
that is conducted by the dissection of things into their parts, and
that which refers the whole to its two elements of Form and Matter.
" Here," he says, " the heaviness of the senses makes itself manifest, seeing they can only deal with the nature of corporeal things,
and with this nature divided into portions, the eye only reporting of
colour, quantities, figures—the ear of sounds," &c. Touch, he looks [—] The Senses
upon as a kind of connecting link between body and soul. Thence
he passes to the power of Imagination in presenting absent forms; The Imagi-
thence to the Reason or Intellect, " which can deal with the incor- nation.
poreal, which now looks upon things as they are, now otherwise
than as they are; which now unites things distinct, now severs and
disjoins things united." He regards the " power of Abstraction Abstraction.
in the intellect, that which conceives Form apart from Matter, and
Matter apart from Form (though they do not actually exist apart),
as the very instrument of philosophy, the workshop of all liberal
arts, without which nothing could be rightly held or rightly
taught." He traces clearly and gracefully the process of abstraction; how it excludes whiteness and blackness, and the other accidents of particular men from the general notion of a man; " the
reason defining what the intellect conceives, and treating all particular cases as comprehended under the general title, mortal—
rational—animal. Whilst, therefore, the intellect collects likenesses and unlikenesses, while it carefully scrutinizes the agreement
of things that differ and the differences of things that agree, while it
diligently investigates what each thing has in common with many
things, what with fewer, while it penetrates into that which is necessary to each thing, it discovers many conditions,—some universal,
some individual. Which conditions, defining and dividing in various The anti-
ways at its pleasure, the glance of the mind is sent into the very Baconian
secret of nature itself, so that nothing natural may be hidden method.
from it." Our excellent critic, who had a great dread of presumption, and was very anxious to cultivate humility, was quite
unaware of the arrogance of this statement, and would have
been startled if he had been told how much of nature was hidden,
and must for ever remain hidden, from those who were using this
method of divining its secrets, who were permitting the intellect
to prescribe and teach, when its business was to obey and learn.
Still nothing can be better and more felicitous than John of Salisbury's account of the order and derivation of sciences as they then
existed. " How magnitude and multitude circumscribe the whole The Quad-
world; how by the abstracting intellect the soul ascends through rivium.
different degrees of honourable arts to the throne of perfect philosophy: how arithmetic, music, geometry and astronomy, constitute

the true Mathēsis ; how by them the height of earthly wisdom is
attained," he describes in words which he had partly learnt from
Boethius, but which he had understood and made his own. Thence
the transition is natural to the false Mathēsis, or the doctrine of the
astrologers, which is not so much ridiculed for its folly as denounced for its impiety. Unquestionably there was ground for
both charges. The astrologers were substituting audacious guesses
for science ; they were practically setting up the government of
the stars in place of the government of God. Nevertheless, we
may believe that they too had a work for mankind which they
were performing, however rashly and ignorantly, and which in due
time they would leave to worthier hands. While the rigid forms
of logic were controlling the free dynamics of nature, they were
bearing witness that there must be some way of entering into
dynamical secrets, that there must be a knowledge of laws by which
man is governed and which he does not create out of the forms of
his own mind. The explorers of planetary influence, though in
one respect the most unscientific of all men, were in *this* sense the
harbingers of a truer and more living kind of science than any
which it was possible for the schools to engage in or to recognize.

61. The Seventh Book, however, is that which most concerns us.
About this part of our learned countryman's writings we can
scarcely be expected to speak without some jealousy, seeing he
assumes our office, and becomes the historian of Metaphysical and
Moral Philosophy. We hope we are not betraying our bad motives if we say, that the opinions of John of Salisbury respecting
Epicureans, Stoics, and Academicians, respecting Socrates, Plato,
and Aristotle, and respecting the whole course of later studies in
the east or west, are more valuable as illustrations of the mind of
the 12th century, represented in one of its most accomplished men,
than for any special light which they throw on the times before
him. Most of his remarks are judicious and practical, and marked
by some of the characteristics of an English mind. He dislikes the
dogmatists, he dislikes the extreme of scepticism. He values Socrates, because he looks upon him chiefly as a moralist. He has
the respect for Plato which might be expected from an admirer of
Augustine, without any very accurate conception of what he
thought or did. Practically obeying Aristotle in the whole habit
of thought and study which he had inherited from him through
Porphyry and Boethius, he yet entertains us with extremely uncertain legends about the man, and had probably a very second-hand
acquaintance with his books. He makes, as Ritter has remarked,
the most curious mistakes in the names of the philosophers whose
opinions he describes.

   62. John of Salisbury becomes very valuable when he tells us
what was passing around him. His words are not indeed to be

taken for Gospel on this subject more than upon the history of the past. His tendency is to be over-critical; and since he sets up philosophy as the proper refuge from the trifles of the Court, he is apt to be particularly impatient when he supposes that it is beginning to trifle itself. Nevertheless he is always lively, and generally fixes his mark on things and persons which really deserve ridicule or reprobation. The following observations refer to all times, but have a special bearing on his own. "They err impudently who think that philosophy consists only in words. . . . . Those creatures who live in words had rather seem wise than be wise. They go about the streets; they besiege the thresholds of men more learned than themselves; they stir up little questions; they make words into nets that they may catch the sense of other men and their own; they are always more ready to raise a wind of arguments than to winnow a question if any difficulty hath arisen. These boasters of wisdom, not lovers of it, are afraid to betray their want of knowledge; through base shame they had rather be ignorant of that which they are ignorant of, than seek it out and learn it, especially if others are present who have the information. They talk hastily upon every subject, they judge all, they blame some, they glorify themselves; they boast that they have found out fresh what has been well rubbed by the ancients and has been handed down for many ages by the testimony of books to our times. They succeed in making themselves not understood rather from the weight and multitude of their words than from any difficulty in the things, and when they have accomplished this high object, they think they deserve to be reckoned philosophers above all others. . . . . Sometimes they wind and wind and reproduce the same things, drawing wonder to themselves from the very labours and tortures to which they are reduced by the ignorance which prevents them from turning in any new direction. Yet the would-be sage has no one profession or art. Like the hungry Greek in Juvenal, he is everything,—grammarian, rhetorician, geometrician, painter, athlete, augur, rope-dancer, physician, astrologer; his knowledge is universal. And like that same Greek, if you bid him, he will go off to Heaven, and wiser than Dedalus will bear you whithersoever you wish, safe through the empty air. If you crave modestly that you may be taught what authors have meant in their writings, which you hope to discover by penetrating through the letter of them, he will tell you that you are duller than an Arcadian ass. Who but a fool would trouble himself about the letter which kills? who but a serpent would go upon his belly and eat dust all the days of his life? Play with words, tell stories with words, dispute with words, that is the business of the learned man. So long as he can speak, it is no matter where he gets his thoughts, or what they are, or about what."

His notices of contemporary philosophy.

Lib. vii. c. 12.

The Sophists of the 11th century.

Ashamed to seek knowledge by owning ignorance.

Passing off old words for new.

Wilfully unintelligible.

Quack arts.

Contempt of the Letter.

63. Our author proceeds for some pages in this strain, describing the rhetorician and sophist of the Middle Ages, whose features, as we hinted in the first part of this treatise, may be compared but must by no means be confounded with those of the rhetoricians and sophists who called forth the wit and wisdom of Socrates, seeing that these latter had always a practical field for the exercise of their powers, could influence multitudes and govern commonwealths; while those whom John of Salisbury described dealt in words for the words' sake, and could hope to do little more than raise up a set of pupils who should enlarge or refine the quibbles which they were to inherit. The dialectics of this time, therefore, unless when they became involved with theological controversies, were always liable to be regarded as exercises of skill apart from any result. Logic *threatened* to occupy the whole field of science, and those who resisted its incursions were not unfrequently driven to ineffectual complaints or to ridicule, because they could not tell themselves where they should fix the limits which the usurper might not transgress. To this subject John of Salisbury addresses himself, and in the course of his criticisms gives us some valuable hints respecting the condition of Nominalist and Realist controversies in his time. "Many," he says, "dress themselves in some few fragments or rags of the garments of philosophy and boast among the unlearned as if the whole of it was within their jurisdiction. . . . . They bring forth, perhaps, some new opinion about genera and species, which had escaped Boethius, of which Plato knew nothing, but which they by wonderful luck have extracted from the mines of Aristotle. They are prepared to solve the old question, in working at which the world has grown old, in which more time has been consumed than the Cæsars consumed in acquiring and governing the universe, more money spent than Crœsus ever possessed. Long has this question exercised numbers through their whole life; this one discovery has been the object of their search; they have at last arrived at no result at all. The reason I suppose was that their curiosity was never satisfied with that which alone could be discovered. For as in the shadow of any body the substance of solidity is vainly sought for, so in those things which belong to the intellect and which can be only conceived as universals but cannot exist as universals, the substance of a more solid existence is nowise traceable. To wear out a life in things of this kind is to work, teach, and do nothing. For these are the clouds of things which are always in flight, and which vanish the more quickly the more eagerly you pursue them. Authors solve this question in many ways and in various discourses; and since they have used words which are capable of different senses, they have left to men of a litigious temper plentiful material for contention. Thence it comes to pass that, when

[marginal notes:]

The Sophist of Christendom unlike the Sophist of the age of Pericles.

In what respect the study of Words signified more to the one than to the other.

Sneers at the Nominalist controversy.

Realism practically denied.

things that are objects of the senses and other individual things have been apprehended, seeing that these only are said truly to exist, the intellect transfers them into different conditions, in respect of which the individuals become specifical and general. There are those who after the manner of mathematicians abstract forms and refer to these whatever is said concerning universals. Others analyze our intellects themselves, and would have them invested with the names which denote universals. (They would refer universality to the intellect itself.) There have been those who said that Genera and Species were the very names which represent them. But their opinion is now exploded and has disappeared with their author. There are, however, those who may be caught treading in their footsteps, though they blush to confess either their leader or his doctrine, teachers who, adhering only to the names, ascribe to the nature of language that which they would withdraw from the things and the intellects. Each appeals to the authority of some great judge, sustaining the doctrine or their error by the opinions of authors who have indifferently used names for things or things for names. Hence spring up great seminaries of disputants, and each one collects the sentiments whereby he can establish his own heresy. There is no getting away from Genera and Species. From whatever point the discourse begins, thither you will find it turning. . . . . . Whatever Rufus is doing, there is nothing but Nevia for Rufus. If he is glad, if he weeps, if he is silent, he speaks only of her. Does he sup, does he drink, does he ask, does he refuse, does he nod assent, it is only Nevia. If there is no Nevia, he is dumb." John of Salisbury is fond of poetical quotations, and often applies them wittily. This perhaps is one of his happiest, and illustrates well the absorbing passion of the Middle Age doctor; with the insanity to which he was liable both in the presence and absence of its object.

64. Such were the opinions of a man of letters, who had been also a man of the world and was a man of the Church, about the great philosophical argument of his day. His division of the combatants into the champions of substantial forms, of the abstracting intellect and, under some modification or other, of pure Nominalism, is one which the latest historians have followed. That he himself inclined to the second class appears tolerably clear from his language; though he is evidently not a dogmatical sectarian, and felt that there was something in each of the opinions to which he did not subscribe, which ought to be confessed and accounted for. His statement respecting the *indifferent* use of the names Words and Things by the greater writers, who felt that each did involve the other, and that an absolute separation between them was impossible, while the sects or heresies which bore their name were founded on that separation, is of high practical worth and of wide

M

Marginal notes:
The believers in Universal Forms.
The Conceptualists. Alii discurrunt intellectum et eos universalium nominibus censeri confirmant.
Ultra Nominalista.
Quod rebus et intellectibus subtrahunt nominibus ascribunt.
The Lesson to be drawn from this criticism.

application. The reader must not, however, suppose that this equitable solution of the difficulty relieves him of any further concern with the question out of which it arises, so that he may henceforth part company with Genera and Species, and devote himself to some more agreeable topic. The thirteenth century will present us with another phase of this Realist struggle. It will tell us whether the science of words was able to come to any understanding and reconciliation with those which concern the life of nature, the doings of man, the being of God.

CHAPTER V.

THIRTEENTH CENTURY.

1. IF the 11th century has deserved to be called the age of Hilde- Innocent III.
brand, it is difficult for the student of the first sixteen years of the
13th century not to name it the age of Innocent III. Those years
certainly passed quickly away. The popes who succeeded occupied a very different position from that which the grand politician
filled, and were men of far inferior ability. Yet the temper and
spirit of Innocent survived in their battles with Frederick II. and
the Swabian family. Their triumph was indeed preparing the
way for calamities, not for Italy only but, for the popedom. The
wicked policy which brought Charles of Anjou into Italy as a
counterweight to the Imperialists, was avenged when Philip le
Bel hurled Boniface from his throne. But even in the midst of
Innocent's tyranny, there were indications that the national kings
—that the French kings especially,—might one day break the
ecclesiastical yoke from their necks. The events which introduced
the 14th century, were not in themselves proofs that the 13th century may not be claimed for the man of many devices, who combined
so remarkably the power which belongs to this period with that
which characterized Italians in the more refined time of Machiavelli.

2. But this title, however plausible, cannot be supported by the ^{The 13th cen-}
analogy which suggests it. Mere skill in managing the wires of a ^{tury not the}
machine, however consummate, indicates nothing but the talent of ^{cent III.}
an individual. The age may be affected by it in its inward life,
as well as in its outward condition; but it cannot represent the
thought which is at work in an age. Hildebrand's conception
of the popedom indicated that striving after unity which could
be traced equally in the union of the west against the east, in
the efforts after spiritual concentration by the Norman divines, in
the effort after civil concentration by our Norman conqueror. The
heart of the 13th century must be sought for elsewhere than in a
heartless man and in a heartless scheme of policy. These might
produce whirlwinds, and fires, and earthquakes, but the Lord was
not in them. The still small voice which really rules the conflicting elements of thought in any period, must be listened for
somewhere else than in the Vatican.

3. The rise of the Mendicant Orders will be regarded by every
sound thinker as immeasurably more important to Europe than
the negotiations, legations, and bulls of Innocent. These orders
arrived apparently at the same result which he was compassing by
his stratagems. To bring all men in all nations into one, to make
them feel that they had a centre of unity, this was the design
equally of Francis, the lover of the poor,—and of Dominic the
underminer of heresy. Each sought the aid of the papal court to
legitimate his scheme. When that aid had been reluctantly granted,
each returned the service by doing more for the papacy than it had
ever been able to do for itself. But the means which conduce to an
end, prove not seldom greater than the end itself; sometimes they
counteract it in one way, as they contribute to it in another. Jesus
Christ, as the friend of the poor, was the watchword in the early
preaching of Francis. His human sympathy and human sorrow
were to be the lodestone of all hearts. The exclusive exaltation
of His Humanity, led to the exaltation of the female qualities
of Humanity. The idolatry of the Virgin became extravagant.
That idolatry passed into the idolatry of the leader himself; in
whom so much of actual compassion and self-sacrifice had been
manifested. In each of these tendencies, there was something that
clashed with the respect for the papal throne, which, nevertheless,
it was the business of the Order to exalt. Where there was no
knowledge of its actual nature, where it was merely the shadow
of a name, it might stand as the representative of Apostolical poverty, in opposition to the splendour of the kings who ruled in the
different lands. That vision was always liable to be scattered by
the news which sometimes reached even peasants through some returning pilgrim or crusader, that money-getting by all means fair
or foul was the especial characteristic of the Holy See. The exaltation of poverty and the poor man, while it was honest, was
most mighty; but it threatened dangers to those whom for the
present it upheld. The corruptions, divisions, heresies in the
Franciscan Order, if they weakened itself, may have been the
means of saving Rome from the terrors of its patronage.

4. The Dominican Order may have seemed less likely to produce these results, seeing that from the first it contemplated the
extinction of heresy as its ultimate end, fellowship with the poor
and abandonment of wealth as means to that end. But Dominic,
even more than Francis, proclaimed the wealth of the clergy to be
the great stumbling-block to the spread of Catholic doctrine, and
the society which called itself by his name became formidable to
the papacy by drawing to itself the functions and the power of the
papacy. To explain how it did so is to explain one of the curious
phenomena of this century. The Mendicant Orders seemed as if
they were appealing to the conscience and the sympathies of the

unlearned, as if they existed to draw those who could understand *ing. how far consistent* nothing but sensible representations and popular legends into the *with its original inten-* church's net.   The Mendicant Orders actually became the guides *tion.* of European thought, the directors of school speculations.   If we studied merely the life of St. Francis, such a change in the direction of their duties and powers would appear simply miraculous.   But the starting point of the Dominicans was intellectual ; the intellectual doubts and controversies in the south of France called them into being.   That they should become connected with the Universities was but the fulfilment of their original design.   Had they confined themselves to popular appeals, that design could never have been accomplished.   They may have risen by levelling themselves to the position, to the habits, even to the apprehensions of common people ; they could only maintain their ground by showing themselves ready to encounter the most cultivated, by using the leisure and the power which their indifference to money and sensual gratifications gave them, in acquiring all the knowledge which it was possible for any of their day to possess.   That men having *Their success* so definite an object, and being so clear about the way in which it *certain.* might be attained, should have triumphed over all obstacles, and should, at last, have stamped their own image upon the intellect of those times, is no cause for wonder ; or at least that wonder must be renewed in each successive age because success is in every age the reward of the like devotion.

5. It is not our business to relate the steps of the conflict by *Change in* which the Mendicant Orders acquired dominion in the Universities, *the Univer- sities* which, in the last century, as we have seen were the centres of much independent thinking ; which even might be called antimonastic ; which had nourished a Peter Abelard, and only with reluctance—never, perhaps, completely—yielded to the sentences of Peter Lombard.   The history would be very interesting, but we should have to trace it through details which would withdraw us unreasonably from the main business of this treatise.   It should always be remembered that Paris was the grand battle-field on which the old and the new powers tried their strength, and that many local and national questions, as well as ecclesiastical, were involved in the struggle and the decision.   It should also be understood that when once the Dominicans had asserted an authority over what appeared in some sense *their* destined province, the Franciscans were under a kind of necessity to labour in the same sphere.   It was a clear sign of a divine Providence that they did. The habits of the two orders, great as were their outward resemblances, were essentially and radically different.   To organize and *Action and* systematize was the taste and business of the one.   To bring out the *reaction of the Orders* human, sentimental, individual aspects of theology and of humanity *upon each* was the characteristic effort of the other.   The Dominican was *other.*

always verging upon the hardest intellectualism; but he was exempt from much of the superstition to which the Franciscan yielded. *He* was liable to all the diseases which assault men of spiritual aspirations, to much of the sensualism into which they fall, through a desire of finding outward images by which they may represent their deeper intuitions; but he could not be withheld by mere maxims and formulas from tracing the windings of a thought, or from following nature into her hiding places. Both were dangerous, each would have been terrible without the other. Together they served to show forth the counteracting tendencies of a very memorable period. If each held down some truth, each brought some side of truth into light which its rival would have crushed. If they left many pernicious influences to after ages, they awakened a spiritual and intellectual energy, without which those ages would have been very barren.

Rebellion of Common Sense against School trifling. 6. The passages which we extracted from John of Salisbury at the close of the last chapter will have shown that intelligent men were beginning to be impatient of the disputes in the schools on another ground than their tendency to produce heretical speculations. The practical sense of those who had seen something of the world, the moral sense of those who had felt the grand issues to which Philosophy should lead, was scandalized by these disputes. What link was there between them and human action? Must they not end at last in mere conjuring tricks? So great a movement as that which gave birth to the Mendicant Orders indicated that this feeling was awake, and added enormous The poor prove the revivers of learning, and saviours of the upper classes. strength to it. In every age the impulse to bring forth the under strata of society, to address the hearts and understandings of those whom the rich suppose only to have hands for raising the fruits of the earth, and stomachs for receiving a small portion of them, arises from a disgust at the trifles of the court and of the schools, from a belief that the upper classes and the learned classes must die of innnition if they do not receive a quickening impulse from the clods. "God is able out of these stones to raise up children:" this has been the trumpet note of reformers in all ages. With this they have shaken the self-conceit of the rulers of nations, and the rulers of sects, of the religious Pharisee and the intellectual Sadducee. And there never has been a movement of this kind which has not done more to save the upper classes, and to save learning, than all the feeble experiments of statesmen and scholars who mistake the upholding of privileges for the preservation of power, or who think that there can be progress where there is no great and common goal on which the eyes of all runners may be fixed. A dreary, hopeless period had succeeded to the living energies which were at work in the commencement of the 12th century. Thought was awake, but it was restless thought revolving continually about itself. There was enterprise; but instead of being connected with any great Christendom object, it was turned like the Venetian crusade to commercial aggrandizement, or at best to the extension of Latin dominion. There was the most skilful diplomacy, but its highest end was to outwit monarchs, traffic with the life of nations, identify the Churchman with the man of cunning. To give thought an object beyond itself, to make the plots of kings and states contemptible beside the great interests of humanity, to show that spiritual power is mightier than all material power, and can cause dry bones to awake and arise,—this was the effect of the new inspiration of the 13th century. It is for these reasons that the names of Dominic and of Francis, in spite of their own errors, and of the sins of their followers, must be always venerable and precious to mankind.

7. Peter the Lombard, as we have seen, had done much to reduce dialectics into a minister of theology. What more, it may be asked, did the doctors of the 13th century accomplish than this? We do not wish to anticipate the answers to this question, which ought to be gained from the writers themselves, and which we hope will come out with sufficient clearness in the extracts which we shall make from them. But as a notion has gone forth that Aquinas and his fellow-workers achieved this victory, and established the perpetual dominion of divine lore over every other in the schools, we wish to explain in what sense we assent to this statement, and how we believe it has led the writers on the Middle Age philosophy astray. It is unquestionable that a much vaster domain of thought is embraced by the eminent teachers of this age, than by the one who uttered his sentences in the last. It is equally unquestionable that over the whole of this domain, theology became at last the absolute ruler. She does not merely assert a reserved dominion, she does not merely hold a court to which a few of the initiated are admitted, while her distant provinces are managed by satraps and pachas. She comes forth into open day, legislates, not indeed without consulting the other estates of the realm, but still in an altogether princely manner. She takes the highest judgment-seat, decides personally in all greater causes, regulates the principles upon which every minor controversy is to be determined. So far the claim which has been urged on behalf of this age or the crime which has been imputed to it, must be fully acknowledged, and the consequences of the acknowledgment are manifold and important. But it should be also recollected that theology is not in this age what it was before the appearance of the Mendicant Orders. That which claimed dominion over humanity, had first stooped to humanity. To the Franciscan, most conspicuously, but practically also to the Dominican, doctrines had presented themselves as precious for the sake of the life of the wayfarer. The

[marginal notes:] Theology and the other sciences

The Victory of Theology

Theology far more human than heretofore.

Dominican could even boast that his zeal against heresy was prompted by the interest which he felt that all should share that which was intended for all, that the poor should not be stripped of his inheritance by the tricks and subtleties of disputants. This was evidently a new state of things. Other sciences might less reluctantly consent to receive the yoke of one which could assert a closer relation to the student than all others and could vindicate for the student the higher glory of being a man.

The Arabian learning.

8. Other circumstances with which this change in the bearing and temper of the theologian had greatly to do, were powerfully affecting the general thought and the technical philosophy of this period. In a former chapter we hinted at the influence of the Saracenic teaching, especially in the schools of Spain, upon the mind of Christendom, or if that is too strong an expression, upon some minds in Christendom. In the 10th century this influence was discernible chiefly in the vague impressions which prevailed respecting the sorcery of Pope Gerbert. Such impressions were due partly to his superior acquaintance with physical science, partly to his imperial tendencies; there is no-proof that he or his contemporaries had been affected by any metaphysical doctrines which prevailed in the Arabian schools. Metaphysics, however, had even then a great hold on the Arabian schools; they were touching the heart of Moslem orthodoxy,—they often mingled in curious combination with the political strifes which led to the great changes in Moslem history. We have deliberately determined that

Reasons for not entering on the specific doctrines of the Arabian schools.

we will not attempt to furnish our readers with any account of the philosophical sects which arose in the centres of Islamite cultivation, because we could at best only give them second-hand reports, and because those from whom we should derive our information appear to be uncertain whether they have understood the authors, whom they quote, correctly. To follow the mere Arabic scholar, who has no knowledge of philosophy, is unsafe, for he may overlook shades of meaning, and put a popular sense upon technical words which would often lead us into gross misunderstandings and misrepresentations. To follow the modern interpreter, who comes armed with all the philosophical apparatus of the last hundred years, is more unsafe still, for he reads himself into the old times, and finds Kant or Schelling in El-Farabi or Ibn Sina. Nevertheless the subject is evidently of great importance for the history of Christian Europe, and especially for the history of the 13th century. And without entering into any particulars respecting the Mahometan sects, we think that it is not difficult to discover what the subject of all their inquiries was, what principal aids they resorted to in pursuing them, how both the end they were setting before them, and their methods became interesting to the students of a different faith.

9. God, in His own naked majesty and power, separated from **Ground of Islamite thought.** all the creatures He had made, but ruling them, communicating His mind through angels, prophets, and kings, at last, through *the* Prophet, the ruler of kingdoms, the destroyer of idols; this was the ground of all Moslem action and obedience. Whenever Moslem action and obedience should be mixed with or should give way to Moslem speculation, this must be its starting point. The invisible Being was there—the object and the foundation of belief. The world was there which He had made, revealing its outward surface to the eye, discovering some of its secret powers to the intellect. How the different portions of it were related to each other, what kind of dynasty the heaven and the luminous forms that appeared in it exercised over the earth, had been the question of questions for the Magian of Persia. They who succeeded to his dominions inherited also his curiosity. Astrology could never be **Astrology.** indifferent to any oriental, whether Zoroaster or Mahomet was the teacher from whom he received his first lore. If he trembled lest he should fall back into the worship of the Sabean whilst he was busy with his observations, so much the more was he disposed to seek for the laws that govern the motions of the bodies which others had made into gods. But, in pursuing these inquiries, what had become of *the* God, the one God in whose Name the hosts of the faithful had triumphed? How was He related to this earth, those stars, the laws which governed either or both? He had created them, of course. Moses said so; Mahomet had adopted the words. They were enough for the simple warrior. How did **Creation.** they satisfy the reflecting sage? What *was* creation? What was that word which had called all these creatures into existence? How were they preserved in existence? What meant the secret life that was in them? What meant the renewal of that life from age to age? What had the life of each particular thing to do with the great whole to which it belonged? How did each thing sustain its own distinctness in the midst of that whole? Whence had that whole come? Were there elements of matter out of which it had been generated? Had it some mysterious relation to its Author? Could it in any sense have flowed forth from Him?

10. Such seem to have been, so far as reports may be relied **The puzzles of the Islamite.** upon—such, we might almost say, *must* have been—the questions that forced themselves upon the Islamite so soon as he began to be a thinker. Thus would he become involved in those perplexities which the Hindoo, starting from the very opposite point to his, had for so many ages been involved in. The conquest of Hindostan may have brought to light a world of thoughts and speculations. But the commencement of the Mahometan movement towards philosophy seems to have preceded that event, and

may at first have been retarded rather than accelerated by it. The
disciples of the Prophet must have felt the strength of arms, of
action, of Monotheism, and may have renewed their old contempt
for dreamers and idolators. Nevertheless the same world surrounded them as the races which they had subjected, and the very
Koran compelled them to ask questions as well as to smite down
infidels. Presently they learnt that Pagans had discovered, many
centuries before, the puzzles which were tormenting them. With
the Brahminical Theists or Atheists, world worshippers or priest
worshippers, they might have little sympathy even if they ever

*Their ac-
quaintance
with Greek
teachers.*

learnt what had been passing in their minds. But the stately
calmness and exquisite clearness of the Greek writers awed and
fascinated them. Plato's love of geometry was attractive; there
were thoughts which he awakened that could not be put by.

Aristotle.

But Aristotle soon became their favourite guide; for he had dealt
with every portion of that universe which the Koran had not dealt
with, while there was nothing to shock them as students of the
Koran in his thoughts respecting the Divine nature. If he was a
pagan, his paganism was most unobtrusive. Fables and traditions
did not interfere with his careful observations of nature; interfered
as little with his ethics, his politics, and his metaphysics. Here
seemed to be a man who might be safely trusted to fill up the
gaps in their knowledge. Here was a sage of the most comprehensive character and intellect who could meet them at all points,
who seemed to have anticipated all questions, and yet who never
claimed that sort of inspiration which would have jarred with
their reverence for *the* prophet or for the elder prophets whose
mission he acknowledged.

*The Koran
and Aris-
totle.*

11. Once embarked on this sea, the Islamite student was involved in perils which he had not looked for. It was easy to settle
that the visible world should be given to Aristotle, the revelation
of the unknown to Mahomet; but as the relation between the
two had been the original cause of their perplexity, as the desire
of investigating this relation had driven them to seek for Greek
aid, it was not possible to prevent a continual intermingling of
the provinces in fact, however accurately the charts might assign
their limits. The Arabian teachers of philosophy exposed themselves to the continual suspicion of slighting the words of the
Koran, of departing from its principles. Sects arose which attempted to bring the maxims they had learnt from Aristotle into
accordance with the popular faith,—sects which strained the popular faith to meet the Aristotelian logic and physics. Theology
and nature, as one might expect, were the two grand subjects of
Arabian contemplation; they were not, however, the only subjects.

*The Arabian
sages. Physi-
cians.*

Many, perhaps the greater part, of the Islamite doctors were
physicians in the double sense of the word—healers of the human

body as well as investigators of nature. They were commonly, And states-
also, mixed up in civil affairs, often, it would appear, accomplished men.
statesmen. There were the widest differences between them in
moral practice; Avicenna, if reports may be trusted, was extrava-
gantly dissolute; Averroes was a strict observer of the law, and
had no notion that men could attain to any philosophical insight
without obedience and self-control.

12. The last mentioned name is the one most familiar to western Averroes:
ears. The comments of Averroes upon Aristotle exerted a great the Christian School-
influence upon the Christian schoolmen of the 13th century. The men.
time had evidently come when these schoolmen must make up
their minds about their own position in reference to the great
teachers of antiquity. The names of Plato and Aristotle, as we
have seen, had been mighty names for the Latin world. They
had been referred to with honour by orthodox divines as well as
by heretics. It was impossible to set aside the claims of a man
whom the Bishop of Hippo revered. It was impossible not to
suppose that there was some transcendent wisdom in a man to
whom Boethius traced the greater part of his wisdom. But was
not the Tritheism of Abelard in some sense connected with lessons
which he had learnt from one of these teachers—it was not always Church sus-
easy to say which? Were not they beginning, one or both, to be picions of
heathen
regarded as authorities in a sense which must interfere with the teachers.
authority of the Church? Might not the porch or the academy
in which Heloise had first studied become, even for women, more
attractive than those sacred cloisters in which she had finally sought
her wisdom? Was not this the tendency of the university culture
of the 12th century? Did not Arnold show how that culture
might affect ecclesiastical order and government? Such questions
were for Popes to consider gravely. And now came an alarming The new
addition to all these perils. Not only Pagan lore was matching peril.
itself with Christian, Pagan lore was combined with Mahometan lore. Aristotle was presented surrounded with Mahometan commentaries, rendered probably as well as the Greek
text into the language of Christendom by Jews. What could be
expected from such an infusion? Must not this intercourse with
the East bring in a moral plague worse than any bodily plague
with which the hosts of the crusaders had infected Europe?

13. It is clear that the answers to these questions which the Inclination
Vatican sent forth were taking the form that was most natural and of the Popes
to anathem a-
customary. Aristotle was, what Tertullian had described him, the tize Aristotle.
parent of heresies. You could not destroy the brood if you left
the bird from which they sprang. It was idle to plead that he
had the misfortune of being a Pagan, when he was in fact doing
the work of leading baptized men into apostasy. Let censures
then go forth against him; let him be cast out of the schools—

him and all his commentators! The bolt was evidently aimed at
the right man, that is to say, at the one whom experience taught
the Papal court to dread. It had the instinct to perceive that Plato
was not then likely to do any mischief; that his day was passed;
that the stream was setting in another direction. He might be
left to enjoy the honours which Fathers of the Church had bestowed upon him. The present danger was to be guarded against.
The rival authority to the Popes was clearly the Stagyrite.

How the Mendicant Orders changed this policy.
14. It is one proof among many how much greater was the
strength of the Mendicant Orders than of him whom they exalted
as the head of Christendom, that their doctors were able not to
modify this decree, but to reverse it. The principle of these orders
was to understand the time, to sympathize with all its movements,
intellectual as well as popular, that they might direct them to the
end of which they never lost sight. The Dominicans saw clearly
that neither Aristotle nor his commentators could be put down in
the schools. It was quite as clear to them that the Church would
Motives for supporting Aristotle.
suffer grievously if they were. Was it an heretical instinct that
led men to select a guide for their footsteps in any path which they
might tread? Was it not the safest of all habits and tempers, the
most counteractive of self-will, that there should be such a guide,
provided he could be found? Or had the age been misled in
thinking that precisely such a guide might have been vouch-
safed to them in the Encyclopædist of the old world? If he had
meddled less with theology than his master, was not that a conspicuous merit? Did it not leave one field, and that the highest
of all, on which the banner of the cross might be planted, and on
which it might be seen waving above the world below? And then
his method of dealing with other subjects, how accordant was it
with the maxims which you would wish to prevail on this highest
ground! Each subject viewed as perfect in itself, carefully distinguished from every other; premises which, if they could not be
got from experience, must be given by authority, at the foundation
of all; conclusions deduced by an accurate, indisputable process
from these. Talk of Aristotle as the author of heresies! What
was wanting but the full application of the principles of Aristotle
to make heresy, so far as it could be in this evil world, impossible?

Were not the Christian Schoolmen encountered by the same dangers as the Arabian?
15. The consequences which followed from this conviction,
when adopted by men so resolute and so intelligent as the great
Dominicans of the 13th century, we shall have to trace as we proceed to notice the lives and works of *Albertus Magnus* and *Thomas
Aquinas.* But after what we have said, we must be prepared with
an answer to a question which will certainly occur to the mind of
the reader. The Christian schoolmen might hope to reconcile
Christian orthodoxy with Aristotelian physics or metaphysics, just
as the Arabian schoolmen had hoped to make the doctrine of the

Koran accord with them; but why should the success be greater
in one case than in the other? Would not the same startling
questions present themselves to the Western student as to the
Eastern? Would not he, too, have either to meet boldly, or to
evade ignominiously, the old enigma respecting the relation of the
world to God? Less acquainted with the world, less engaged in
civil transactions, than the sages of Persia or Spain, would he not
be less competent to understand the difficulties which troubled those
who looked at this inquiry from the mundane side? Less severe
in his condemnation of all mixtures of the creature with the Creator,
would he not be more unable to understand the reluctance of the
theist to confess a relation between visible things and their Author?
Supposing these commentators had forced themselves upon the
attention of the teachers in the last century, we cannot help thinking they would not have found either their theological or their
general knowledge at all adequate to the encounter of such practical enigmas. But a change, which we cannot attribute wholly
or chiefly to the Dominican order, had given the new student a
courage that did not belong to his predecessor. Merely as a doctrine, the Incarnation of our Lord had held at least as prominent
a place in the Sentences of Peter Lombard as it could occupy in
any Summa Theologiæ of the next age. But as a practical belief,
it had assumed altogether a new position and was spreading its
influence into regions that were least conscious of it. The feeling
of a human Mediator between God and Man was the ground of all
the Franciscan movement; without it, the words of the Friars
would have been dead words. Herein consisted what in the religious phraseology of a later time would have been called the
Revival of that age. The characteristic Christian conviction, that
which denoted the difference between Christendom and Islam,
had started into a new life, had made itself felt in the heart
of the nations with more might and energy than when it inspired the heroism of Leo IV. or the *Dieu le veut* of the Council
of Clermont. Therefore the philosophers of Christendom felt that
they had no cause to tremble at the difficulty which scared the
philosophers of the other faith. There was a bridge between
God and man, and therefore between God and the world, which
Avicenna and Averroes did not confess. Why then might
not the Teachers of the West boldly profit by all the wisdom
which these teachers could communicate, confident that they
could supply exactly what both they and their Greek master had
wanted?

16. The teacher of the 13th century who did most to promote the
reaction in favour of Aristotle, and who resorted most courageously
to his Arabian expositors, was Albertus Magnus. Ritter earnestly
protests against the injustice of those who have called this eminent

Marginal notes:
Why the Arabian commentators were less alarming to the 13th century than they would have been to the 12th.

The effect of a belief in the Incarnation.

Albertus Magnus.

man "the ape of Aristotle." He asserts, and we should conceive with excellent reason, that Albert understood his master as no mere imitator ever can understand the writer whom he dishonours by his mimicry; that, in fact, he contrived to arrive at a greater knowledge of his meaning through all the disadvantages of a Latin translation, than almost any modern has done with the aid of sound Greek philology. This is a very high testimony to the genius, as well as the industry of the 13th century doctor. Both, it seems to us, are abundantly attested by his fame among his contemporaries, and by his actual labours. Before we speak of these, we will tell what we know of the man himself. It has been often remarked that the physiognomy of all the Middle Age writers is, in essentials, the same, that the marked individuality which belongs to the Greek sages and even to their Roman admirers, is entirely wanting in the schoolmen. We dissent from this remark, and have taken some pains in previous chapters to show that it is at least inapplicable to the most conspicuous men in the 11th and 12th centuries. If it appears to have a better justification among the students of this time, we believe the difference is owing partly to the overwhelming amount of their books, which have left their biographers scarcely time to speak of anything else, partly to the dulness and affectation of those biographers themselves. Their desire to glorify their order and to give us portraits of heroes and saints who adorned it, leads them to conceal or varnish over the most characteristic human features of the men whom they are describing. Albert has suffered as much from this error as his contemporaries. A Dominican editor, Peter Jammy, has done his best to disguise what we are inclined to think might be the story of a very interesting life with vulgar rhetoric and reports of marvels, which, if they had happened, would not be the least worthy of record. Still there come out through his narrative distinct indications of a man who thought and did as well as wrote, of one who may have been very dear to his own disciples, may have been feared as a magician among those who judged of his knowledge by their ignorance, and may excite scarcely less astonishment among us if we compare his diligence with our indolence.

17. Albert was born in Swabia, probably in the year 1205, though there are some who place him six or seven years earlier. If the date fixed by Jammy is the true one, he was only sixteen when he joined the Dominicans. That order was still in its first youth, full of attraction for the ardent and the meditative, full of terror to parents and guardians, who saw their children yielding to an unaccountable influence and enclosed within a charmed circle. There is no reason to doubt that Albert felt the religious movement of his time; but he thought himself called, as soon as he became a member of the order, to grapple

Side notes (left margin):

Ritter. Geschichte 8. Theil, Buch 12, p. 183. Zur Beschämung mittlerer Jahrhunderte welche auf die Scholastiker mit Verachtung herabsehen, wird man gestehen müssen dass im 13 Jahrh, die Aristotelische Lehre zwar nicht ohne Vorurtheile, aber doch besser erkannt wurde, als noch in ne- uerm Jahrhundert.

The lives of the Schoolmen, how far dull or uniform.

His history.

with the problems of philosophy. The Virgin, we are told, favoured the intention, and assured him of her help, warning him at the same time, that a day would come when her power would desert him, and he would feel himself again a child. He went to Cologne, and was soon recognized as the most profound of teachers. Among those who listened to him, there was a youth, whose dull countenance led his companions to call him the Ox. Albert considered the face, and the student whose mind it expressed. "That Ox," he said, "will make his lowings heard throughout Christendom." It was Thomas of Aquino, who, from that day till the day of *Aquinas and* his death, became united to Albert in a friendship that was *Albert.* never disturbed by differences or rivalries. Albert loved Cologne, but he must of course visit Paris. There he became known, and *At Paris* thence it was proclaimed through Europe, that a Dominican had appeared who knew more of Aristotle and the subjects which Aristotle treated of, than any who had been before him. But the sage was still the member of an order. The rules of it gave him no exemption from the tasks which seemed least connected with his philosophical consecration. In 1254, he was made a Provincial, and an immense circuit was put under his superintendence. His biographer assures us, that he was a Mendicant in the strictest sense, and determined to vindicate the dignity of poverty against all opposers and all hypocrites. In the course of his inspections, he found that a lay brother had died with some unconfessed wealth ; he ordered that his body should at once be removed from the consecrated ground in which it had been laid, that his judgment even in this life might be manifest. Shortly after he was at Rome, de- *Rome.* fending the Mendicant Orders against one of their most vigorous assailants and astonishing the Cardinals with his theological insight. In 1260, he consented most reluctantly to become the *A Bishop.* Bishop of Ratisbon ; he preserved, his Dominican panegyrist assures us, the strictness of a Mendicant in private, while he fulfilled all the functions and maintained all the dignity of his new office. He managed his revenues of the see admirably, relieved it of a heavy debt, yet contrived to write a lengthened Commentary on St. Luke. After three years, he succeeded in persuading the Pope to emancipate him from these toils. He resigned his bishopric, but he was not allowed to be absent from a Council at Lyons. He was resting at Cologne on his way to Lyons, when he was overwhelmed with a sudden sorrow. He became conscious by some second-sight, that Aquinas was dying at that time, and mourned over the loss of the great light of the age. The Master retained his vigour for some years after the death of his friend. But in the midst of a lecture his memory forsook him. It was the sign that the Virgin had given him. He acknowledged

that his work was over, and waited calmly for his end. He died
at Cologne in 1280.

His power of arrangement

18. That the composer of twenty-one folios upon every subject
except the management of revenues, should have brought order
into the accounts of the Ratisbon See and should have removed
incumbrances accumulated by those whose minds were not dis-
tracted by Aristotle or Averroes, does not seem to us at all
incredible.   We should find it hard to understand how these
twenty-one folios could have been produced if their author had
not possessed the business-like habits for which the narrative gives
him credit. The mere time spent upon them may not be so astonishing; but precisely the power which such books seems to have
demanded was a power of arrangement; in which is included assuredly the skill to disentangle that which had been complicated.
Our readers must try to understand the problem which the men

The work of the age.

of the 13th century felt they had to work out. Aristotle's books
came to them not now in fragments, not a few scraps of logic or
ontology which they might speculate upon and compare with the
hints they could get about the Dialectics of Plato or of the Stoics.
A complete cycle of Logical Treatises, his Ethics, his Politics, his
Physics, his Metaphysics, all offered themselves at once to their
contemplation—not in naked vastness, but in the midst of inter-
pretations which a series of ingenious Arabian teachers of different
schools had been heaping around them.   Albertus was not to

The Univer-sal Commen-tator.

choose to which of these subjects he should devote himself.   Having dedicated himself to Philosophy, having believed that the
Queen of Heaven had accepted the dedication, he was pledged to
grapple with every subject which the master had handled ; he was
to explain what the worth of each study was in itself; what its
relation to every other.   Even then his work was not accomplished,
not perhaps half accomplished.   He was to contemplate Aristotle
from the Christian point of view, as the Arabians had contemplated
him from the Mahometan.   He must consider therefore how every
subject had been affected by the new revelation.   He must consider how far that revelation had itself given birth to a new and
distinct science.   And let it be remembered that our philosopher

Science and omne Scibile.

had expressly to inquire about *Sciences* and *the Science*.   In our
days we speak—intelligent men speak with a just contempt—of those
who profess acquaintance with *omne Scibile*.   To gather together
bits of information upon all possible subjects, is no very hard task
for a man who has the gifts of a compiler or a book-maker, and
who has been left conveniently barren of any others.   If he
undertakes by order of the publisher or the religious society that
employs him, to contemplate subjects from a Christian point of
view, he fulfils his contract and clears his conscience by appending
to the facts of nature or the events of history which he has gathered

together, some texts of Scripture or edifying reflections in a modern style. The schoolmen had no such facility. Aristotle had endea- *Aristotle and* voured to bring every subject he had treated of into an organic *Albert, or-* whole. His marvellous success in this enterprise is the secret of *ganic writers* the power which he has exerted over many generations. In this organic state his students must deal with the treasures he had bequeathed them. If Albertus had to remove any stones from the symmetrical buildings he had raised, to introduce any new stones into them, there was need of the most careful attention to the laws of this architecture, or the edifice would certainly fall to pieces. We can do the schoolmen no justice if we forget that this was the task which they had imposed upon themselves. It is not therefore fair to select passages which express their particular opinions or even which indicate their method irrespective of this consideration. We believe we shall best fulfil our duty to Albertus, without affecting a knowledge of him which we do not possess, if we endeavour to point out how a few of the cardinal doctrines of Aristotle on those subjects which we have undertaken to speak of were modified in the hands of his eminent disciple.

19. The question, what Science is and what may or may not be *Science.* called Science, seems to have occupied the mind of Albert more than it had done any of the Latins, Boethius not excepted. He may not discuss the subject with all the subtlety which the Greeks brought to bear upon it. But he seems to have felt the kind of interest in it that they did, to have felt that what could not be claimed for Science was left to the vagueness of Opinion. Instead *Albert's love* therefore of being jealous of the word, as modern divines often are, *for it* he seems to have felt it a part of his business as a Churchman no less than as a philosopher, to extend the domain of laws as widely as possible, to confine within the narrowest possible limits the realm of chance and chaos. In the beginning of his treatises on Logic, which occupy one of the largest of his folios, he inquires whether Logic is a distinct science or no? He states the objection which he seems to think was supported by the authority both of Aristotle and of Averroes, that that which is the mode of arriving at Science cannot be Science. But he disposes of the objection, affirming that there is a science of Method. There being *Definition of* one common mode of arriving at all knowledge, Logic may be *Logic.* defined the science of that mode, or the science by which one proceeds from the knowledge of the known to the knowledge of the unknown. This point being settled, it still is to be determined whether Logic can be reckoned a part of Philosophy. The reason for excluding it, which seems to have had great weight with the thinkers of that day and some with Albert himself, was that all philosophy is either physical, mathematical, or metaphysical. In *The three* other words, it is either conversant with things that are susceptible *divisions of Philosophy.*

N

of movement and which fall under the senses, with the laws and
principles of these things, or with things unchangeable and eternal.
If Logic cannot be referred to one of these divisions, what
relation has it to philosophy? The answer is, non constat that it
does not belong to either the second or the third. If it is the
process of passing from the known to the unknown, it must be
connected with the laws of the intellect even more directly than
Mathematics are. It must be therefore an organ or method which
is indispensable both to the mathematician who is investigating
the principles of moveable and sensible things and to the metaphysician who is investigating that which is immoveable and above
sense. What then, asks Albertus, is the subject of Logic? He
discusses the opinion of those who, following the etymology of the
word, affirm all language or discourse to be the subject of it.
He rejects that opinion as too vague, and concludes that reasoning
or argumentation is that with which it is strictly and exclusively
conversant.

Universals, how arrived at: what they are.

20. After these preliminaries, Albertus finds himself involved in
the great controversy of the last century. Having shown what
the syllogistic process is, he is encountered with the question,
"But you start from a universal. Where do you get it? What
is it? All your individuals are included in some comprehensive
genus. How do you arrive at the knowledge of this?" Our author
declares that the question does not properly belong to logic. That
assumes these premises. It is the function of the primary philosophy to tell us how they are obtained. He admits, however, that
the controversy has become so mixed with logic, that he must not
avail himself of this plea in practice. He addresses himself therefore courageously to the debate, though he is determined it shall

Nominalist and Realist arguments.

not interfere with the main business of his treatise. He states the
question, it seems to us, very fairly, and does justice to the reasoners on both sides. It appears to him to be between those who
assert that premises or principles lie in the naked intellect, meaning by naked intellect that which is divested of all appearances,
accidents, sensible or material admixtures, and those who maintain
that they have a substantial pre-existence and are nowise created

Dissent from Aristotle.

by the abstracting powers of the intellect. He does not dissemble
that his master, Aristotle, is in favour of the first doctrine, and
that many distinguished Arabians had defended it by plausible
arguments. His own conclusion be states to be this. Every universal is capable of a three-fold consideration,—(1.) in itself; (2.)
in the intellect; (3.) in this thing or that. When he views it
in itself, he is a realist; he contemplates it as a substance. When
he speaks of it as in the intellect, he distinguishes between the
original or archetypal intellect and the abstracting intellect. To the
former, it presents itself as it is in its own proper nature. To the

latter, it presents itself as the result of those processes to which the Nominalist ultimately refers it. Viewed in *this thing or that*, it becomes subject to the conditions of division and multiplication, which belong to the sensible world.

21. These may suffice as specimens of the way in which Albert *Physics* regarded that which had been to his predecessors the all-absorbing science. The Physics of Aristotle opened to his contemporaries an almost new world. He undertook his treatise, or rather his series of treatises upon this subject, he tells us, at the desire of the brethren of his Order, who felt that they had no satisfactory guide to a knowledge of it. He announces his determination to follow Aristotle in all *The order of* the general divisions as well as the particular titles of his works on *Sciences.* nature, introducing digressions when he thinks them necessary for the removal of any difficulties or the clearing of any points which had been overlooked. Here a similar question occurs to that in the opening of the treatises on logic, and we are again introduced to the threefold division into primary philosophy, mathematical and physical. The first, which is the metaphysical and theological region, he regards, of course, as chief in the order of dignity. But physics, he says, is first in the order of teaching; because the senses are first awakened in us and are in contact with outward things. Thence he would ascend to the mathematical or purely intellectual study, thence to the divine and absolute. Physics, therefore, had a significance in the mind of Albertus which they certainly possessed for none of his predecessors. One may understand why he obtained that reputation which has made him the hero of so many legends. His devotion to the natural caused him to be suspected of unlawful communication with the supernatural. He did, however, his best to take physical observations out of that domain in which they are the prey of the enchanter. He grapples boldly with the arguments, popularly attributed to *How Physics* Heraclitus of Ephesus, against the possibility of a science of that *can become* which is moveable and changeable. Bodies which are susceptible *scientific.* of motion, he allows are the subject of physics. Science, he allows, in itself implies the fixed and the certain. But, then, he contends that the moveable body may be contemplated in itself, that we may understand its principles and laws apart from the material accidents to which it is exposed, and then that we may discover principles regulating those very accidents. Presently, as we might expect, he finds himself obliged to distinguish between elementary and compound bodies, and so becomes involved with all those assumptions, anticipations, contradictions, which we must leave to the mercy of the modern investigator.

22. But there is one point at which the physical speculations *Life.* of Albert came into close contact with the subjects of this treatise. It is all very well to talk of bodies and moveable bodies; but the

motion of bodies implies something more than external impact.
Some of them are animated,—have *life*. The physical student,
our author says, must examine the conditions and kinds of life, or
he must abandon his task altogether. There is no subject on which
Albert seems to have entered with more earnestness than this.
To distinguish between the vegetable, the sensual, and the intellectual life, he feels is a great necessity. But he is almost equally
anxious not to separate them rudely from each other, as if there
were no relation between them. One of the thoughts which seems
to have taken greatest hold of him, is the thought of an inchoation
of the higher forms of life in the lower, so that the vegetable shall
always be the prophecy of the sensible, the sensible of the intellectual. There is, perhaps, no belief connected with the natural
world and with our own selves which has been so dear to the
devout student, who has kept his heart warm and hopeful, as this;
none of which he has had a stronger external and internal evidence; none which he has at times perceived to be susceptible of
more dangerous abuses, to be pregnant of greater phantasies and
superstitions. It is a loving link to the old schoolman of the
middle ages, to see that in his monastery he was cherishing this
genial faith, that he was preserving in his mind a sense of the harmony which there is through all creation, of a golden chain which
unites the insect to the archangel. And we may easily guess from
the knowledge we have of ourselves, how disciples of the teacher,
who had neither his reverence for God nor his conviction of the
truth of science, may have become seekers after some secret spring
of life,—may have dreamed of one when they did not find it,—
may have passed off upon the world some unworthy substitute
for it which they had invented.

23. The treatise of Albert upon the origin and nature of the
soul, and several others, not very long, which illustrate it, might,
we should imagine, be worthy of a study and exposition which we
have not time to give them. One, especially on the unity of the
intellect against Averroes, touches upon a subject in which we are
perhaps even more interested than his age was,—a subject which
we may have often occasion to speak of when we approach the
history of later schools. In what sense the intellect of each man
is distinct, in what sense there is one in all, is a question which
has tormented Greek, Arabian, and Latin thinkers alike. A Christian divine would, of course, feel that he had a deep concern in it,
and that on many points he could speak a language which the
Mahometan could not speak. It is, we think, very greatly to the
credit of Albertus, that he enters upon it with a full sense of its
importance but with perfect philosophical fairness, introducing no
arguments from any source which was not common to him with his
opponents, discussing it simply on grounds of reason. In the

Marginal notes:
Inchoative life.

His earnest studies and their per-
version.

Psychology.

course of the discussion, points arise about the connection of the *Anima* with the *Intellectus*, which bear upon the history of philosophical nomenclature as well as of philosophical thought. But we must pass to another subject.

24. The full triumph of Aristotle over the mind of the 13th century is indicated in Albert's treatise upon Ethics. In the opening of the book he assigns his reason for choosing this master in preference to all others. Socrates spoke well of morals, but Aristotle has written upon all things that can be known. Plato speaks nobly of virtue as purgative, purgatorial, and belonging to a purified soul; but he does not speak concerning all Virtue, according to genera and species. Aristotle distinguishes all qualities according to their antecedents, their consequents, their works, their properties, their effects. This is, no doubt, a very honest account of the charm which the great Grecian exercised over his Latin disciples. They were longing to have all their subjects of thought arranged and ticketed. The purgatorial effects of virtue they could discuss in their pulpits. In the schools they wanted accurate definitions. Everything must be subjected to the categories, or it wanted the test of soundness.

25. This desire to bring Ethics within the sphere of logic, involves our author in two difficulties. Aristotle tells us at the commencement of his ethics that we are not to demand mathematical accuracy in moral subjects. He himself is always clear, sharp, precise in his language, never pedantical. He is an observer and experimentalist even more in his treatment of morals than of physics; he deals with facts as a man of business. He is too much a master of logic to be embarrassed with logic. With his commentator it is otherwise. He is a subtle logician, he draws distinctions finely; he knows how to put all subjects into their proper compartments. But the faculty of handling ordinary facts, which he must have possessed, is crushed by his passion for arrangement. His pupils must have forgotten that they were speaking of the things which most nearly concerned themselves, while they were admiring how well all these things were exhibited in their relations to each other. The other difficulty more affects his consistency as a systematizer. Plato's assertion of an absolute and primary good, in virtue of which all other things are good, could not possibly be disputed by a Christian divine. Albert accordingly Platonizes through a great part of his introductory treatise. He disposes of all mere dialectical objections to the belief in the primary essential good. He distinguishes that which is highest in order, highest in comparison, highest in quantity. God himself is the highest in order. That is highest in comparison which most approaches to His nature. That is highest in quantity which most gathers up distinct forms of good into itself. He affirms that there can be no

[marginal notes:] Ethics.

Albert's failure from over love of arrangement.

Platonism.

evil in itself, no essential evil. He affirms good to be implied in
the nature of everything. But the moment we pass beyond those
preliminaries we find ourselves within the meshes of the categories. Albert returns to his allegiance. The Platonic ideas he
denounces in Aristotle's terms, sustained and illustrated by a diffuse commentary. That which is the good of man is carefully
separated from the absolute good. Happiness, with Aristotle's
definition of it, is accepted as that good. The object of the civilian is said to be altogether different from that of the ontologist.
The Platonic principle, we are told, requires that there should be
one science. How can that be when there are so many distinct
sciences, each with its own aim and its own method?

26. There is one characteristic of the Ethics which the reader
might fancy would prove a stumbling-block to a friar. The doctrine that ethics are dependent upon politics, the acknowledgment
of that as the architectonical study, because its objects are comprehensive, because the life of the citizen must be superior to the
life of the single man; this, we might suppose, would be more
popular in the 19th century than in the 13th, with a disciple of
Paley, than with a disciple of Dominic. The notion is a plausible
but an unsound one. No life is more contrasted with the hermit
life (that is to say, with the *monastic* in the strict sense of the word)
than the cœnobitic life—the life of an order. The brotherhood, by
its name and principle, is a testimony for society,—for a polity. No
doubt one all-important element of society is wanting, and that is
one to which Aristotle does special honour in his master-work. But
Albert was prepared to go along with him even here. He admits
the conjugial domestic life to be the ground-work of civil order.
He even admits man to be a conjugial domestic being. The civil
life he represents as rising above this family life. No doubt he
looked upon the ecclesiastical, what he would have called the highest type of social life, as dispensing with it. It was most happy,
however, for the Christian world at this time that the Aristotelian
polity was better understood than the Platonical. The healthy
reverence for relationships was kept alive, at least in theory; the
schools assented to that as a dogma which in practice was most
needful for the world. We have no right, however, to detain our
readers with the politics of Albertus, which are more obviously
and confessedly than his other writings dilutions of the pure
Stagyrite wine.

27. It would be inexcusable in a treatise on the history
of metaphysical thought, to pass over without notice the books
of Albertus which bear directly upon this subject. As we have
already noticed his psychology in connection with his speculations
on physics, we need scarcely say that this is not included under
the more august name of metaphysics. That confusion belongs

Marginal notes:
Aristotellan-
ism.

Politics and
Ethics inse-
parable.

Political
tendencies
of the order.

His Meta-
physics.

almost exclusively to our own time, or at least to the time since Descartes. In all the school period, metaphysics were recognized as nearly identical with Ontology, and as, therefore, being unlike in subject and in treatment to that which has so fluxional and varying a character as the life either of mere animals or of intelligent creatures. The whole first book of Albertus is concerning the *Physics.* stability of this science. All physical things, he says, are connected with matter, which is subject to motion, or mutation, or both. They cannot be conceived, therefore, apart from Time. Therefore these are much mixed with opinion, and would never arrive at the constant, confirmed, and necessary habit of science, if there were not some essential principles discovered in physics which are not dependent upon matter. The circle, the square, even and uneven, *Mathematics.* all numerical proportions, the diatessaron in music, and the like, are certain stable forms, in themselves free from motion and change; and, therefore, give rise to a study which is not mixed with opinion but contains in it the elements of a necessary science. This is disciplinary science. It wants not experience as physics do; a youth may know as much of it as a doctor. But these speculations are steps and entrances to divine speculation. The capacity of our intellect for this does not exist in virtue of its being human, but because there is in us something that is divine. This divine or metaphysical knowledge is implied in both the others. But they *The highest science.* are not the foundation of it; it is the foundation of them.

28. Theology and Ontology, according to this statement, would *Theology and Ontology.* seem to be identical; and that opinion, our readers may remember, is maintained by some of the early scholiasts upon Aristotle. Nevertheless, when Albert proceeds to more exact definitions, he rejects the two opinions, that Cause as Cause, or God as God, is the subject of the highest science, and maintains that strictly Being as Being is its only subject. He also rejects what he says is a common notion of the Latins, who fancy they have discovered a solution when they have invented a distinction, that a subject in science may be regarded in three modes, as that which is more common, that which is more certain, that which is more worthy. The more common they would call Being, the more certain, Cause, the more worthy, God. But in sciences concerning things, says Albertus, I abhor all such logical consequences, seeing that they lead to many errors. This science of Being, then, is the primary philosophy. It is a science in itself. For though all other sciences refer to Being, they refer to it analogically; this treats of it in itself. He proceeds to trace the generation of this science from the natural desire of knowledge in man, which desire is not perfected in the gratification or exercise of any sense, or in the understanding of the laws of material things, but seeks for the foundation of this knowledge and for knowledge itself. In pursuing this subject

he necessarily recurs to some of his psychological maxims.   Sense,
memory, reason, he decides, are the principles of knowledge considered in the knower.   Here we again find ourselves completely
Aristotelian. Visions of Hermes about the nexus between the soul
and God floated before us at the beginning of the treatise.   It
seemed as if we were scaling heaven, or as if heaven was coming
to meet us upon earth. But the passion for a definite science
overcomes every other. *The* Being becomes Ens or entity.   The
primary philosophy may be very stable and original; but it has
practically its circumscriptions just like every other.

Transition from Albert to Aquinas.

29. The strictly theological treatises of Albertus we shall not
touch upon.   In fact he is not at all the specimen of that tendency
of the 13th century to which we alluded when we spoke of it as
labouring to bring all subjects under the government of theology.
He was, as we have seen, formally and characteristically a philosopher.   His position as one of the order of preachers, when that
order was in its youthful vigour, sufficiently attested the predominance of divine studies over all other studies in his mind.   The
disciple of Aristotle never for a moment forgot that he was the
disciple of Dominic.   But he felt it as his function, his brethren
recognized it as his function, to assign to every branch of human
learning its proper place, to vindicate for it a distinct work,
and then to show that it could only subsist in connection with
the studies that directly relate to the being and nature of God.
He was in his way a very great organizer. Nothing was out of
place in his mind; each study fitted into that which lay next to it.

The characteristic distinction between them.

Yet he was not an organizer in the sense which his pupil and friend
Aquinas deserved that name.   No two men living in the same age,
and having continual intercourse with each other, are so unlike in
the habits and constitution of their minds; no two have left a more
different impression of themselves upon history.   Albert's name is
surrounded with a traditional haze.   Most people have a vague
notion that he was half schoolman, half magician; they scarcely
know whether he passed among his contemporaries for a servant of

Greater power of Aquinas.

God or of the evil spirit.   On the contrary, Thomas Aquinas has
abundantly fulfilled his master's prophecy of him.   The bellowings
of that bull have been heard through all countries and in all generations; there is more than a feeble echo of them in our own.   He
has governed the schools, moulded the thoughts of nearly all Roman
Catholic students, given a shape to the speculations of numbers who
have never read any of his writings and to whom his name is rather
a terror than an attraction.   Why this is so we shall endeavour to
explain as we proceed. First, it behoves us to give some account
of the Angelical Doctor himself.

30. His father and mother were both of splendid Sicilian families.   His two brothers were distinguished Generals in the army of

the Emperor Frederick ; three of his sisters were married to Counts, Life of
one became an Abbess. Some assign the birth of Thomas to the Aquinas by Echard.
year 1225, some to 1227. An uncle of his was an Abbot in the Opera, vol. L
Monastery on the Monte Casino ; there he received his first elements
of knowledge between his fifth and tenth year. In consequence of
this circumstance the Benedictines have made out a kind of claim
to the great Doctor, which is certainly unfounded. The Dominican
biographer has produced many substantial arguments against the
notion that he ever professed in the Benedictine convent, or was
intended to profess. One of great weight is derived from a
passage in his history to which we must presently advert. He
studied philosophy and letters at Naples in the year 1243 ; there
he assumed the garb of a Dominican. The brethren, fearing the A Domini-can.
influence of his mother, who was vehemently opposed to this step,
sent him privately to Rome. When she had tracked him there,
they despatched him with four companions into France. On their
way, while they were resting beside a well, soldiers sent by his
brothers in Frederick's army surprised them and carried off the
novice to his father's castle. There every influence was used to
persuade him to abjure his profession ; especially a very beautiful
woman was introduced into his room and left to try the effect of
her persuasions. Such an attempt upon the constancy of a young
man who had not yet bound himself by vows, was unrighteous
enough. But, asks the Dominican advocate, would even the sol- His perils.
diers of Frederick have dared to place such temptations in the way
of one who had already become a Monk at Monte Casino, with
the approbation of his kinsfolk ? Clearly it was in the order of
preachers that he first sought a refuge from the world. From that
order no threats and no attractions could withdraw him. His
parents saw that the struggle was fruitless. They connived at his
escape through a window. He rejoined his companions at Naples,
was embraced by the head of the order at Rome, and was sent by
him first to Paris and thence to Cologne to be under the guidance
of Albertus. According to the constitution of the Dominican
order, every one who was to profess theology must pass four years in
hearing lectures upon it. These four years were spent by Aquinas
partly in Cologne, partly in Paris.

31. It was a critical moment in the history of the Paris Univer- State of the University of Paris
sity. In the year 1229 a drunken body of students had done some Fleury, liv.
acts of great violence to the citizens ; complaint was made to the 79, § 51.
Bishop of Paris and to the Queen Blanche ; the members of the
University who had not been guilty of the outrage were violently
attacked and ill-treated by the police of the city. The Professors
suspended their lessons and demanded satisfaction. When they
were refused it, masters and scholars dispersed ; some went to
Angiers, some to Orleans, some were invited by Henry III. to

England; the great school of Europe was practically at an end.
The preachers were sure to benefit by such an occasion. When
all other chairs were vacant, they established in Paris a chair of
theology. Meantime the Pope was very vigorously urging the
restoration of the University to its old privileges. The Bishop,
the Chancellor, and the Chapter of Paris, who had found these privileges interfere with their own jurisdiction, were doing their utmost
to thwart him. A Bull dated April, 1231, reconstituted the University, established rules for the management of it, and laid down
some curious maxims which show that the Dominican influence
was beginning to be felt by the Holy See, though it had not yet
become triumphant. In 1215 the Papal Legate had positively
prohibited the Physics of Aristotle; now only those books of Physics were denounced which had not been examined and purged of
all suspicion of error. The general direction was given that the
masters and scholars of theology should not pride themselves upon
being philosophers, and should only treat in the schools of those
questions which could be decided by theological books and the
treatises of the Fathers.

Fleury,
liv. 74, § 2.

Change in
the treat-
ment of
Aristotle.

82. The restoration of the University had no direct reference
to the Dominicans. They were now firmly established in Paris.
They had acquired a name from the position they occupied which
they were to bequeath hereafter to an equally democratical, not
equally religious, order. They had become the great theological
teachers. In 1252, the body of theological doctors became jealous
of their influence, and enacted a statute ordaining that no member
of a religious order should be admitted to their society who did
not belong to a College, and that each College of the religious
should be content with a single regent Doctor and a single school.
In the following year another dispute between the civil authorities
and the University occurred. The doctors of the University
adopted their former plan of abandoning their lessons; binding
themselves by oath not to resume them till they had obtained
redress. Two of the Jacobins refused to take this oath. The
University decreed that no one should be received as master or
doctor in any faculty who had been recusant. The war was now
openly commenced. The University made a long complaint to
Innocent IV. against the pride and intrusiveness of the Mendicants.
A Bull *Et si animarum* went forth from him to restrain their influence and to support the authority of the learned body that was
opposed to them. It was the last act of Innocent IV. The whole
policy of the Court was changed in the days of his successor Alexander IV. One of his earliest acts was to revoke the last Bull.
Three months after he issued one announcing that the school of
Paris was like the tree of life in the Garden of Eden, and then
proceeded to alter the shape and growth of the said tree, the

Fleury,
liv. 64, n. 54.

The
Jacobins.

Matthew
Paris (see
the Hist.
Angl. under
the different
years) refers
often to this
quarrel, and
speaks se-
verely of the
Mendicant
Orders.

The Popes
against and
for the
Preachers.

Dominican doctors who had been suspended being restored, and the limitations which had been imposed upon their numbers removed. The doctors of Paris resisted the execution of this decree, and re- *War between the Pope and the University.* fused to receive the Jacobin brothers. The Pope's two commissioners excommunicated the University. The result was that the Paris doctors appealed to the Pope, declared that the University was dissolved, and that there was consequently no body to which his decrees applied. Alexander treated their dissolution with contempt, and desired the Chancellor of St. Genevieve not to grant the license of teaching in any faculty to those who resisted the Bull. A council which was held in Paris appointed arbiters to decide the controversy. Their decree was a mild and equitable one; but it had scarcely issued before Paris received a Brief from Alexander, denouncing as children of the devil all doctors and schools that opposed themselves to the preachers, threatening the University, and calling upon St. Louis to deal strongly with a Bishop who had attacked the Mendicants. This Bishop was the Guillaume de St. Amour, whom we have heard of already as opposing Albertus at Rome. The victory of the Dominicans there, as we have mentioned, was complete. In 1256 the book against them was formally condemned. In the same year the University submitted to the Pope, and agreed to receive into its body the brothers of the Dominican and Franciscan orders, Thomas Aquinas and Bonaventura being expressly named as representatives of each.

38. This digression has been inevitable, however much we *Influence of these disputes upon the life of Aquinas.* might wish to pass by the disputes between the University and the Orders. The effect of them was to keep Aquinas for ten years from being admitted master in the faculty of theology; it will appear presently how much the character of his books was influenced by this circumstance. He celebrated his triumph in 1257 by delivering an apology for the Mendicant orders. He had already written tracts upon Being and Essence, and upon the principles of Nature, and had been reading lectures upon the Sentences. Now he held general disputations on six *quod libeta*, i. e., upon questions of any sort that might be proposed to him. In 1258 he was primary regent, and it became his business to expound some book of Holy Scripture. In 1259 he was attending *His labours.* to the business of his order, and in conjunction with Albertus and others drew up a complete scheme of studies for the members of it. In 1260 he was at Rome, where he wrote commentaries on the Physics, Ethics, and Metaphysics of Aristotle, his Argument against the Gentiles, his Exposition of Job, his Questions on the Soul, and some other works. He undertook his Catena at the request of Pope Urban, but did not complete it till after the death of that Pope in 1264. In 1265 he formed the plan of his Summa Theologiæ. In four years, which were not, however, *The Summa*

exclusively devoted to this great work, he had completed the first
part and the first part of the second. A portion of these years was
spent in Rome, a portion in Paris. Ultimately, at the urgent request
of Charles of Anjou, he settled at Naples, positively declining the
Primacy of that city, and adhering strictly to his office as a theological doctor. He had brought his Summa to the 90th question
of the third part in the winter of 1273 ; after that a presentiment
of his end seems to have kept him from proceeding further. The
following year he was summoned to the Council of Lyons and was
about to stay for a while on his journey with one of his noble relations, when feeling that sickness had seized him, he begged that
he might be carried to a monastery of the Cistercian order, near
the castle of his niece. There he lingered for a month and died
in his forty-ninth year.

His youth.   34. The reader may be surprised to hear how much was accomplished in these forty-eight years. To us it is a greater surprise
that any body should have been strong enough to endure the
presence and the working of such an intellect as that of Aquinas for
so long a time. If we are asked why we should say this, when his
master and contemporary, Albert, lasted to old age in the fulness of
his faculties and some time after they were departed, we should
answer that the sword which was wearing out the sheath in Aquinas,
was one of an altogether different temper and edge from that
which we have been describing in the former part of this chapter.
Thomas, as we have seen, by a curious fate, was restrained from
becoming a doctor, was obliged to continue a bachelor in divinity, at
a time when these degrees imported the most real differences in the
position and work of him who attained them—when the one was
Aquinas   expected to be the lawgiver and the other the disputant. Thus our
primarily a   author was a trained arguer ; by degrees he rose to the office and
Disputant.   station of a judge ; but the old habits remained with him when
his decisions were most accepted as authorities. From first to
last he was thinking of all that could be said on both sides of the
question he was discussing ; chiefly of what might be said in
favour of the opinion which he did *not* hold, and which he was
ultimately to annihilate. Those who suppose that he was afraid of
approaching heretical or infidel opinions, can have very little
acquaintance with him. His books are a storehouse of arguments
for such opinions. The reasoner against almost any tenet of the
Catholic faith may be furnished at a short notice with almost any
kind of weapons out of the armoury of *the* great Catholic doctor.

His doubts   35. We are far from saying that all these doubts had actually
chiefly in-   tormented the inner soul of Aquinas, that he had wrestled with
tellectual.   them and overcome them there. Had this been the case, we
should think the term of his life, instead of reaching fifty years,
could not have reached thirty. Perhaps, no doubt had ever pene-

trated into the inmost sanctuary of his being; nearly all may have
dwelt in the outer court of the intellect; he may have known them
only through its forms. The name which his contemporaries gave
him, and which he has borne ever since, indicates that this was
their opinion. The "Angelical Doctor," standing in contrast with
the "Seraphic Doctor," which is the title given to the Franciscan
Bonaventura, denotes that the one was regarded as a pure Intelligence, the other as a being in whom the heart and affections were
vastly predominant. But even thought of in this way, the multitude of plausible reasons assigned by Aquinas for every opinion
which it behoved a faithful reader of the fathers in theology and
of Aristotle in philosophy to reject—against every opinion which it
behoved the same faithful reader to receive—are enough to bewilder
any man's brain, and to leave him doubtful after a while, whether
he is standing on the ground or suspended in the air, nay, whether
there is any ground to stand upon, or any air to be suspended in.

36. Perhaps, after a series of trials, the reader becomes
thoroughly convinced that the Doctor will bear him aloft through
all the perplexities which he has himself raised. He begins to
say with triumph, that the more he knows of such objections the
better, because they are sure to be effectually solved. Everything, he thinks, has been anticipated; no new arrows can pierce
him; he has been dipped in Styx; not even the part by which he
was held during the process is vulnerable. What a number of
students of theology in the schools where the Angelical Doctor
reigns must have adopted this comfortable conviction! With what
security they must have ventured into the lists with opponents!
But what an awakening has been reserved for some, who have
discovered that knowing all questions, they knew none; that one
actual experience of the world, one terrible internal temptation,
might tear the logic of the schools to pieces, and leave them feeble,
helpless, hopeless. What anguish must there be in such a revelation, yet what a blessing!

37. Some of our readers may have been more prepared for
our first statement respecting Aquinas, that he was the great
organizer of the 13th century, than for our second, that he was the
great disputant or arguer of the 13th century. They may even
find it hard to reconcile the two characters, to conceive how the
same man should have the subtlety of the objector and sceptic
and the power of reducing all things and thoughts into one perfect
comprehensive system. To understand properly this union of
powers, and how the last was trained and matured by the exercise of the first, the reader ought to examine some of the smaller
treatises of Aquinas, those in which he treats of specific questions
arising in the domain of theology or philosophy, and then to contemplate the full flowering of his intellect in the *Summa*. We

Marginal notes:
Effect of Aquinas upon his readers.

The two characteristics of Aquinas, how reconciled.

propose to give them a specimen of the earlier class of his writings, that they may enter into his method of reasoning; afterwards to show how the philosophical or properly human part of his scheme is linked to the diviner part, by giving something like a view of the course and distribution of his subject in that book upon which his glory in the schools mainly rests.

D. Thomæ
Aquinatis
Opera, vol.
14 Venetiis.
1781, pp. 5-8.

38. We cannot perhaps take a better specimen of the manner of Aquinas than from one of his questions on POWER. There are seven articles on the first question concerning the Power of God. The third of these articles is, "Whether those things which are

Arguments
to prove that
what is im-
possible to
Nature is im-
possible to
God.

impossible to Nature, are possible to God." He gives nine reasons for the negative opinion. The first is, that since God is the Mover of nature, He cannot act contrary to nature. The second is, that the first principle in all demonstration, that affirmatives and negatives are not true at the same time, applies to nature, and that God cannot cause that a negative and affirmative should be true at the same time. The third is very like the second. There are two principles subject to God, Reason, and Nature. But God cannot do that which is impossible to Reason, therefore He cannot do anything which is impossible to Nature. The fourth is, what the false and the true are to knowledge, the possible and the impossible are to work. But that which is false in nature, God cannot know, therefore what is impossible in nature God cannot work. The fifth sounds rather more subtle, perhaps more quibbling. What is proved of any one thing is understood to be proved of all similar things; as if it is demonstrated of one triangle that its three angles are equal to two right angles, it is proved concerning all. But there is an impossibility to God, to wit, that He should be able to do a thing, and not be able to do a thing, therefore, if there is some impossibility in nature which He cannot do, it would seem that He can do no impossibility. The sixth is derived from the words of Timothy, "God is faithful; He cannot deny Himself." If He could do anything against Truth He would deny Himself; He would do something against truth if he did anything that was naturally impossible. The seventh is little more than a repetition of the second. The eighth is, no artificer can work against his own art, because art is the principle of his operation. But the order of nature which makes anything naturally impossible is the consequence of the divine art. The ninth rests upon quotations from Jerome, Augustine, and Aristotle, all proving that there are certain impossibilities by accident which cannot be set aside by any power. But that is more impossible which is impossible in itself than that which is impossible by accident. Here the case for one side closes.

Arguments
on the oppo-
site side.

39. There are eight reasons on the opposite side. The first is drawn from St. Luke's words, " No word shall be impossible with

God." The second is, all power that can do this and not that, is a limited power; but God's power is unlimited. The third is, hindrances to acts by anything imply the limitation of power by that thing. The power of God is not limited by anything—not by the principle that affirmatives and negatives cannot consist, or by any other—therefore neither that principle nor any other can hinder the acts of God. The fourth is, privations do not admit of degrees. The impossible is a privation of power. If God is not deprived of power in one naturally impossible case,—e.g., the making a blind man to see, He is not deprived of it in any other like case. The fifth is, whatever resists any power resists it in virtue of some opposing principle within it; but there is no such principle opposed to the divine power. The sixth is, as blindness is opposed to vision, so virginity is opposed to bringing forth. But God could cause that one remaining a virgin should bring forth. Therefore He can cause that one being blind should see while he remains blind, and so can cause that affirmations and negations should be true at the same time. The seventh is, it is more difficult to unite substantial forms which are disparate than accidental forms. But God united into one the substantial forms that are most disparate, to wit, the human and divine, which differ as created and uncreated; much more then can He unite two accidental forms into one, so as to cause that the same thing should be white and black. The eighth argument we should have some difficulty in making intelligible to our readers; and there are other reasons for which it may be better omitted.

40. Now then, the Doctor himself appears. He has, in this instance, which is one of our motives for selecting it, to reply both to the defendant's counsel and the plaintiff's, so that his judicial character is more than commonly brought out. He begins with affirming after Aristotle that the words Possible and Impossible are used in a threefold sense. We may speak of them first in respect of some active or passive power, as when we say, it is possible for a man to walk, but impossible for him to fly. Secondly, we speak of them not in respect of any power but in respect of themselves, as when we call that impossible which is necessarily not to be, and that possible which is not impossible to be. The third sense is in respect of mathematical power, as when you speak of a line being commensurable or incommensurable, that is of having the possibility or impossibility of being measured. Passing over this last, he considers the other two kinds of possibility. It must be understood, he says, that that which is impossible in itself, is so named in virtue of an incoherency of its terms,—i.e., it affirms the co-existence of an affirmation and a negation. But this cannot be attributed to any active power, for every active power implies actuality, and actuality implies existence. Every action of an active power produces something; it has its result in that

The Solution.

The three-fold meaning of Possible and Impossible.

Why it is no detraction from Power to say it cannot transgress a Law.

which is. And though there seems to be an exception to this
rule in the case of corruption or dissolution, yet this is only
because something is generated which is incompatible with that
which was before,—*e.g.*, the existence of heat is not compatible with the existence of cold. That which is called impossible in respect of any power may arise either from some
defect of internal force, or from some accident or impediment.
Now, those things which are impossible in nature, for either of
these last reasons, God can effect. For His power, seeing it is
infinite, suffers defect in nothing. Nor is there any matter which
he cannot transmute at pleasure, for there is no resisting His power.
But that which is called on the third ground impossible, God cannot do, for the very reason that all active power is in Him and that
He is the Being of beings. When we say He is not able to do
this, we indicate not a defect in his power, but a defect inherent
in the very principle of possibility, or, as some express it, God can
do it, but it cannot be done.

The refuta-
tion.

41. These general principles are then applied to the specific
arguments on each side of the question. A few specimens may
serve as illustrations of his method. When it is said that God,
because He is the Mover of nature, cannot act against nature, it is
not meant that He cannot act otherwise than nature does, since He
frequently acts against the accustomed course of nature; but that
whatever He does in anything is not against its nature, but is its
nature inasmuch as He is the former and ordainer of nature. An
instance is taken from the tides. The water has a movement of
its own, which may be called natural to it; but surely the influence of the moon upon it is not to be called unnatural. Again, it

What is
above Nature
is not against
Nature.

is impossible for a man who is blind to see through any power of
nature; this does not imply an impossibility in itself; it implies
that second or third kind of impossibility, which has been
decided not to interfere with the divine energy. On the contrary,
the impossibilities of rational philosophy, are not impossibilities

Essential Im-
possibility.

with respect to any power, but are those essential impossibilities
which if we supposed God to transgress we should impute to Him
weakness and not power. To the objection that God does not
destroy that which is true, the answer is, He does not cause that what
was true should not have been true, but He causes that something
should be true which would otherwise not be true. In raising the
dead, He does not interfere with the fact that he who is raised was
dead. To the arguments from the constancy of God as an artificer,
the answer is, that the art of God not only extends to those things
which have been made, but to many other things. To change the
course of nature, is not to act contrary to His art, but to bring out
a new exhibition of it. To the argument on the other side, which
is drawn from the words of St. Luke, that no word is impossible
with God, it is answered that a word is not only uttered with the

mouth, but is conceived with the mind. That an affirmation and
negation should at the same time be true, cannot be conceived of
by the mind. To say that God cannot hold contraries in His
mind, is not to contradict the saying of the Angel. To the objection that is drawn from the Omnipotence of God, the answer is,
that it is no hindrance upon His free will that He cannot do that
which would imply the absence of active power. To the argument
respecting the virgin, it is answered, that virginity is not opposed
to bringing forth as blindness is opposed to sight, but is opposed to
the union of the sexes, without which nature cannot produce a
birth, but God can. The answer to the argument from the Incarna- *The Incarna-*
tion is, that the union of opposites, the Created and Uncreated *tion.*
in Christ, had respect to the two different natures that were in
Him; from whence it cannot be inferred that God would blend
together two opposites, as black and white, so that they should
become the same.

42. We have finished our quotation. The judgments of differ- *Vicissi-*
ent readers upon it will be assuredly most different. Every one of *tudes of opinions re-*
us has perhaps passed through stages in his own mind which can *specting this*
enable him to understand these differences and to be not altogether *style of writ-*
intolerant of them. The first impression probably upon a young man, *ing.*
used to the style of writing in our day,—used to find the meaning
of words taken for granted, which are here laboriously weighed
and analyzed,—is one of astonishment and confusion. He does not
know whether it is utter nonsense, as some will tell him it is, or
the most profound sense which it would be well to exchange for
much of the lore that makes us proud. In a later period, as the
importance of facts grows upon him, as he aspires after the real
and becomes disgusted with the verbal, he may be more inclined to accept the judgment of his own time, and to fall into its
contempt of the mediæval doctor. But as his experience expands
and deepens, he may discover how many verbal perplexities are
continually haunting those who are most busy about things, how
often they start unawares the questions which Aquinas started
deliberately, how they try to cut knots which he endeavoured
to untie, and do not cut them after all, but make them more embarrassing, how disagreeable their off-hand dogmatism is while
they are in the very act of censuring his painful and conscientious
dogmatism; such reflections may lead him to place the schoolman
upon even a higher pedestal than that from which he had fallen.
Again, there may be a rebellion against this reverence. He may
think over one such passage as that which we have presented to our
readers, he may consider that that extract is contained in about
two pages of a volume of 286 pages, that volume being one of the
smallest in a set of at least thirty, from which the spurious treatises
have been eliminated with tolerable care. To think of a human soul

o

being the store-house of such a collection of doubts and decisions
as that statement implies, to think of a multitude of human souls
from the 13th century downwards having all this mass of opinions
floating about them or crammed into them, is very appalling.
A cry for light and air rises out of his heart. He begins to
dwell kindly upon the legend of Caliph Omar, or to construe the
promise that Babylon the Great shall some day sink like lead in the
mighty waters, as applying to the Babel of human notions, to the
folios in which they are built up a column reaching to heaven.

Aquinas may
yet have a
work to do.

43. We hope and believe that it is not necessary to settle down
in any of these conclusions or positively to reject any of them. A
time may be coming when it will be possible to derive more good
from Aquinas than any age has owed to him, because we are free
from his trammels and have learned to walk at liberty under
higher guidance. Protestant Europe may even yet do him a
justice which cannot be done him by those who dread lest he
should make them sceptics, or who sit at his feet and receive his
words as those of one who understood all mysteries and all knowledge. Meanwhile, we will do what in us lies to give our readers
some conception of the comprehensiveness of his intellect, as we
have already attempted to give them a glimpse of its subtlety.

The Summa
Pars Prima.

44. The first part of the Summa of Aquinas is the purely
theological part. The first question is, What sacred Learning is, and
how far it extends? Within this general title are included ten
articles, or minor questions. They are these: " Whether theological
doctrine is necessary beyond other sciences, whether it is a science,
whether it is one science or more, whether it is speculative or
practical, whether it is worthier than other sciences, whether it is
wisdom, whether God is the subject of it, whether it is argu-
mentative, whether it may use metaphorical or symbolical forms
of speech, whether sacred Scripture under the same letter has
more than one sense." We merely enumerate titles; each, the
reader will understand, is treated after the same method, and with
the same fulness as those questions respecting power of which we
have given a specimen. It is very desirable to understand the
starting point of the Angelical Doctor. He begins, it will be perceived, with theology considered as a science, then he proceeds

The method
of Aquinas
wherein
Aristotelian.

to speak of God as the subject of that science. This is Aristotelianism carried to its highest point. Aquinas may become
Platonical as he proceeds; often we shall find that he does, that
he assumes God to be at once the ground and object of man's
contemplation, and builds much upon the assumption. But
beneath all this lies the conception of a science which includes Him,
and which is to determine our judgments respecting Him. It is
needful to keep this characteristic of the Teacher continually in our
mind, whilst we are studying any portion of his writings. More

perhaps than any other writer, he always recollects that the specific subject he is occupied with has to do with the general subject of his treatise. The whole is always present to him in each part. And the main cause, we shall find, of his difference from his Franciscan contemporaries lay in this, that in each department of study they were aiming successfully or unsuccessfully to keep a living object in sight, and were therefore impatient of the wonderful efforts of skill by which the Dominican brought it within what seemed to them the enclosure of a dead system.

45. We may proceed more rapidly with the other titles of this part. The second question is of God, whether He is; the third, of the Simplicity of God; the fourth, of the Perfection of God; the fifth, of Good universally; the sixth, of the Goodness of God; the seventh, of the Infinity of God; the eighth, of the Existence of God in Things; the ninth, of the Immutability of God; the tenth, of the Eternity of God; the eleventh, of the Divine Unity; the twelfth, of the Knowledge and Vision of God; the thirteenth, of the Names of God; the fourteenth, of the Knowledge which is in God Himself. Then follow three on Ideas, on Truth, on Falsehood; then eight more on the Life of God, the Will of God, the Love of God, on the Justice and Pity of God, on the Providence of God, on Predestination, on the Book of Life, on the Power of God, on the Blessedness of God. Questions concerning the Persons of the Trinity engage us till the end of the forty-third title. The forty-fourth discusses the primary cause of all Entities; the forty-fifth, Creation; the forty-sixth, the beginning of the duration of things created. The forty-seventh is on the distinction of things in common, i.e., concerning plurality as such. The forty-eighth is on the distinction of things in special, and primarily concerning evil. The forty-ninth is on the cause of evil. From the fiftieth to the sixty-fifth, all bear upon the subject of Angels. Those from the sixty-fifth to the seventy-fifth have reference to the order and works of Creation. At the seventy-fifth we enter upon a class of subjects which would seem at first not to belong to theology, but to Anthropology. In them we have discussions about man, as to the essence of his soul, about the union of the soul to the body, about things pertaining to the powers of the soul in general, about the powers of the soul in special, about the intellectual powers, about appetite, sensuality, will (*voluntas*), free-will (*liberum arbitrium*), how the soul united to the body understands the corporeal things that are beneath it, the mode and order of understanding, what the intellect of man knows in things corporeal and material, how the intellectual soul knows itself and the things that are in it, how the human soul knows those things that are above it, what is the knowledge of the soul separated from the body. Then we come, at the ninetieth question, to the production of man as far as con-

[marginal notes:] General Titles in the first Part. Pure Theology. Mixed Theology. Spiritual Nature. Human Nature.

cerns his soul, to the production of the body of the first man, to
the production of the woman, to the end of the production of the
man as expressed in the words "made in the image of God," to
the state and condition of the first man, to things which relate to
the will of the first man, to the dominion which belonged to man
in the state of innocence, to the things which concern the state
of the first man as far as the preservation of the individual,
to that which concerns the carrying on of the species; to the
condition of the race that might have been produced in the
state of innocence, to the meaning and nature of Paradise.
Then commence questions on the government of the world by
God, the effects of the divine government, the alteration of
things created by God, the offices of Angels in carrying out
the purposes of the divine government. In the course of these
questions we have a discussion respecting evil Angels, their orders,
and their assaults upon men. The five last titles in this part are
on the action of the corporeal creature, on Fate, on some secondary
influences of the action of man, on the derivation of man from man
in reference to the soul, on the propagation of men in reference to
the body.

46. There are two or three of the manifold subjects discussed
under these heads upon which we may feel desirous to learn our
author's sentiments. But we would advise the reader, first of all,
to make an effort at understanding the order in which they follow
each other. At first, it may be, this order will seem perplexed.
Do not divine and human subjects run strangely one into another?
Why should a discussion upon Ideas or upon Truth come in between discussions about the knowledge and the life of God? Why
should Angels be treated of first before man and then after him?
Why do so many psychological and physiological controversies
mix themselves with the history of the Genesis of man? Perhaps
the consideration of these apparent inconsistencies of the great
Schoolman might help us much in apprehending the difference
between his mode of thinking, and our own, as well as in tracing the course and development of his speculations. If we turn to
his fifteenth question upon Ideas, we shall at once understand why
it follows upon the very elaborate inquiries in the preceding title
respecting the knowledge of God. After stating rather more shortly
than he commonly does the reasons for thinking that there are
and that there are not ideas, he delivers his conclusions in
these terms:—" It *is* necessary to suppose ideas in the Divine
mind. What is called *Idea* in Greek, is called Form in Latin.
Wherefore by ideas are understood the forms of certain things
over and above the things themselves. Now the form of anything
existing over and above the thing itself, may be either the exemplar of that thing, or the principle of the knowledge of it in the

mind of the knower. It is necessary to assume ideas in both
senses. For in all things that are not generated by chance, the
Form is the end of the generation. But an agent does not act on
account of the form, except in so far as the similitude of it is in him.
The similitude exists *naturally* in those agents that act by nature, as man generates man, and fire fire. The similitude exists
intellectually in those agents which act by intellect. Thus the
similitude of a house pre-exists in the mind of a builder, and this
may be called the idea of the house, because the artificer *intends*
to assimilate the house to this form. Seeing, therefore, that the Ideas involve intelligence.
world is not made by chance, but is made by God acting through
intellect, it is necessary there should be in the Divine mind a Form
after the similitude of which the world has been made." Then, in
disposing of some of the objections to the existence of Ideas, he
says that "God does not understand things according to an idea
existing without Him," and therefore that Aristotle was right in Plato seen through Aristotle and de-
denouncing the opinion of Plato concerning ideas, inasmuch as he
made them self-existing, not existing in the intellect. And, nounced.
finally, he determines that the "idea in God is nothing else than
the essence of God." We have introduced this passage partly as a
justification of the method which Aquinas has adopted, and partly
as an illustration of the way in which his Aristotelian Metaphysics
blended themselves with his Christian theology, and led him to
reject the *purely* ideal philosophy which had been associated with
it by Augustine.

47. If we turn to the forty-seventh and forty-eighth questions we Distinctions.
are able to account for some of the other apparent anomalies which
we have noticed in his arrangements. After considering the Persons
of the Godhead—all that is uncreated—he goes on to Creation. The
production of creatures in *esse* leads him on to the distinction of
creatures. That distinction is threefold: first, the distinction of creatures generally; secondly, the distinction of Good and Evil; thirdly,
the distinction of the spiritual and corporeal creature. In reference
to the first subject, he has to inquire whether God is the Author of
the plurality of creatures, or whether as He is one they must not
be one so far as they proceeded from Him, and must not owe their
division to the presence of matter, or at all events to some secondary agency. He decides against this last opinion, and lays down
the doctrine that "God produced things in *esse* for the purpose of
communicating His goodness to the creatures and that it might be
represented through them. And because it cannot be adequately
represented through one creature, He produced many and diverse
creatures; so that what is wanting in one for the setting forth the
divine goodness, may be supplied from another. For the goodness
which in God is simple and uniform, is in the creatures divided
and multiform." We must not be tempted to pursue this ques-

tion by the third article wherein the modern controversy on the
plurality of worlds is entered upon, Aquinas appearing as a supporter of Dr. Whewell's hypothesis; but we must pass to what strikes
us, for people at large, as a more important subject, Good and

Evil.   Here the great point to be settled is, whether Evil is a distinct
nature, a positive existence.   Our Author decides that "one of two
opposites is known by another, as darkness by light; therefore we
can only understand what is evil by understanding what is good.
But seeing that good is what is to be desired and that every nature
desires its own being and perfection, the being and perfection of

every nature must involve goodness; therefore evil cannot signify
a certain existence or a certain form or nature.   It follows that it
can only signify a certain absence of good."   Hence is deduced
the decision of many other points, all of great interest and continually recurring in human experience, as whether evil is in good
as in its subject, whether evil corrupts the whole good to which it
attaches itself, whether evil is sufficiently divided into punishment
and fault, whether good can be ever the cause of evil, whether
there is a perfect evil in the same sense as there is a perfect good.
On all these points Aquinas has something to teach us which it
might be well worth our while to learn.   Our wish, however, is
rather that the reader may understand how all these points arise
out of the subject of distinctions in created things, and how an
investigation respecting the angelical orders as representing the
spiritual or intellectual creation and respecting man as representing
the union of the two, fairly and logically appears as another division
of the same head.   Seeing, moreover, that the nature and position
of man cannot be fully discussed without considering the mode of
God's government over him, and seeing that that government, as
Aquinas thought, was carried on through angelic agents, he was
obliged to introduce them again in their relations with our race, at
the end of this part.   Nor was it possible to ascertain in what sense
the action of man is free, without considering what is meant by
Fate, although the subject of God's predestination as bearing upon
the life of man and the principles of his being had been discussed
in some of the earlier titles.

48. It is commonly said that the second part of the *Summa*
contains the Ethics of Aquinas.   The second portion of this
second part is generally that from which the student of Aristotle is told that he may derive most help.   There is excuse for
this statement.   But any one will fail to understand the position and work of the Angelical Doctor, who tries to contemplate
the ethical questions upon which he enters, apart from the subject
which gives its title to the whole work.   To take that course with
Albertus was easy, with Aquinas it is destructive.   An attempt,
as brief as we can make it, to give some notion of the subjects

embraced in this part, will sufficiently establish our proposition. That man, in so far forth as he is man, acts with reference to some End, that there is therefore one ultimate end for all men, that this end is Blessedness, we might conclude would be the starting points of an Aristotelian Anthropologist. But then the question, what is Blessedness, carries us into a region into which Aristotle never soared. After a number of negative conclusions as to what it is not, we come at last to the decision that ultimate and perfect blessedness can only be in the vision of the Divine Essence. Then follows the inquiry, what things are required for blessedness. Whether delight is required for it, whether Vision, Comprehension, Rectitude of Will are required for it? All which points being settled in the affirmative, the question of the necessity of the Body and of the Society of friends to it, is examined and answered in the negative, it being, however, admitted that a creature endowed with a body cannot attain the full end of his being till the body is perfected.

49. The next series of questions, from the sixth to the seventeenth, refers to the Will. The distinctions of voluntary and involuntary, the circumstances of human acts in respect of the will, the motive of the will, the mode in which the will is moved, fruition, intention, election, deliberation, consent, custom, in their different bearings upon the will, finally, the acts commanded by the will, are titles which include a multitude of points with which the ethical philosopher of the old world was in some degree familiar, but which assumed a new character, importance, and complexity, in the mind of the Christian divine. Thence we proceed to the goodness and evil of human acts—these being distinguished as acts of the internal will—and to the result of these acts in virtue of their goodness and evil, a subject involving of course their merit or demerit in the sight of God. Next come the Passions of the soul in general, their distinction, their order, their relation to good and evil; love, hatred, concupiscence, joy, sorrow, the effects of both, the remedies of sorrow. These fall under the head of the passions which have to do with appetite or desire. Hope, fear, anger, are referred to another class. Thence we go on to that great subject of the Aristotelian ethics, Habits. It is thus introduced :—" After acts and passions, it behoves us to consider the principles of human acts—first, intrinsic principles, then extrinsic. An intrinsic principle is a power and a habit. Enough has been said of powers in the first part: now is the time for treating of habits. First, they are to be considered in general; secondly, in reference to virtues and vices and other habits of the like kind which are the principles of acts. There are four things to be considered in reference to habits generally,—first, their substance; secondly, their subject; thirdly, the cause of their generation, increase, and corruption; fourthly, their distinctions. In refer-

ence to the substance, four questions arise. First, whether habit
is a quality; secondly, whether it is a determinate kind of
quality; thirdly, whether it imports the direction towards an act;
fourthly, on the necessity of habit. "It would seem," thus he
begins, according to his usual method, the article on the first
of his hints, "that habit is *not* a quality. For Augustine says,
that this name, habit, is derived from the verb to have. But

having belongs not only to quality, but quite as much to quantity.
We speak of having so much money. Moreover, habit is one
category and quality another, and one is not contained under
another. Moreover, habit is a disposition; but disposition belongs
to the category of position." Of course, all these difficulties are
triumphantly settled. But that they should occur in this place,
that it should be necessary to deal with them at all in an ethical
discussion, is one example, perhaps the most striking that can be
given, of the embarrassments into which Aquinas was led by his
determination to bring the whole Aristotle, Logic, Metaphysics,
Ethics, into his *Summa Theologiæ*. We do not complain of his
design, but we cannot help thinking that it was frustrated by the
complicated machinery which he invented for the accomplishment of
it. There is, it seems to us, a very natural transition from the language of Aristotle respecting Habits, to the language of St. Paul,
concerning the putting off of the old man, and the putting on of
the new. The imagination, using language as its instrument, supplies the link. The experience of life, to which Aristotle is always
so glad to appeal, and to which, when he is speaking of habits and
energies as correlatives, he so honestly and courageously sacrifices
the formalities of logic—preferring the appearance of a circle in
reasoning to the denial of a fact—explains how the philosophical

observation falls under the Christian law. Aquinas, overlooking
this passage between the two sciences which he desired to associate
and harmonize, is forced to flounder among the predicaments, to
raise a number of difficulties (each of which cuts the throat of the
other, and yet each of which remains a difficulty, if we must seek
in *Habitus, Situs, Qualitas, Quantitas*, and their comrades, the standing points for moving the world), and then, finally, to draw a line
between habits considered as *in* us and habits considered as put
upon us, which is so sharp and deep that we lose all feeling of the

Equivoca-
tions not to
be rashly got
rid of.

relation between them. Logicians often commit a perilous violence
to words, in their efforts—honest though they are—to rid them of
their equivocations. The double meaning which the punster and
the knave play with for their respective purposes have a real inward sympathy which we should seek to bring out, not to destroy.
Had Aquinas succeeded in preserving it in the case of habits, he
would, we think, have done a greater service than he has done both
to morals and to theology.

50. From Habits, Aquinas proceeds to Virtues. Human Virtue.
Virtue is determined to be a Habit; to be an operative Habit; to
be a Habit operative of good. A definition of it is at length worked
out. Virtue is a good quality or habit of mind; upon which right
living depends; which cannot be turned to evil use; and which
God without us, works in us. The Aristotelian Energy is here
subjected to the Christian Law "He worketh in us to will and
do of his good pleasure." After what we have just said about the
treatment of Habits, we are bound to welcome such an illustration
of the link between the Ethics of the Stagyrite and of the New
Testament. But we cannot think that Aquinas has been very
felicitous in combining the two elements of which his definition
is composed; it will strike most readers as overloaded and
clumsy. Some will feel strongly that the whole force is gone out Virtue not
manliness in
Aquinas.
of the word, when its connection with *manliness* is forgotten. The
Latin of the Middle Ages might be excused for forgetting that
classical etymology. The energies of the Monk were great and
vigorous; they were not exactly the energies of the Man. From
Virtues in respect to their essences, we pass to the subject in
which virtue dwells; then to the intellectual virtues; then to the
moral virtues as distinguished from the intellectual; then to the
distinction of the moral virtues in reference to each other; then
to an article to which there is nothing corresponding in Aristotle,
the *Cardinal Virtues*. As this is one of the characteristic points in Cardinal Vir-
tues.
the School ethics, the reader may be curious to know how it is
discussed by the greatest of the Schoolmen. First, we have to
ascertain what the meaning of the epithet is. There is a perfect
and an imperfect virtue. The imperfect virtue implies only the
faculty of doing well; the perfect virtue implies a rectitude of appetite or desire. Those virtues which involve this higher idea
are called principal or cardinal. The intellectual virtue of Prudence
is included among them, because it is in a certain sense moral.
They are not the theological virtues, for those are super-human or
divine. Of the cardinal virtues there are four: Prudence, Justice,
Temperance, and Fortitude. Cicero and Gregory the Great are
the authorities for reducing all moral virtues under these as their
chiefs and directors. There are two ways of considering them
which have led to some confusion. Some suppose that they signify certain general conditions of the human mind which are found
in all virtues. In this sense each may almost be taken for
the other, rectitude and self-government being implied equally in
all; and so justice in the Aristotelian sense might include them.
But others, and in the opinion of Aquinas, with greater propriety, take these four virtues according to the subject matter of
each. Then they become of course distinct. Another division
follows upon this. Of the cardinal virtues some are political, some

are purgatorial, some belong to the purified soul, some are exemplary. This is our Doctor's explanation. The exemplar of human virtue must pre-exist in God. Virtue must therefore be considered first as it is exemplarily in God. In that sense the Divine Mind in God is called Prudence; the turning of the divine intention upon itself is called Temperance; the immutability of God is His Fortitude; the observation of the eternal law by God in His works is His Justice. As man, according to his nature, is a political animal, there must be virtues which have to do with him in this relation. But since man is intended to be perfect as his Father in Heaven is perfect, these properly human virtues must be connected with the divine or exemplary virtues. Between the Exemplary virtues and the political, there must be an intermediate class, of such as raise a man above mundane tendencies, and enable him to contemplate the *The Purga-* divine standard. These are the *purgatorial.* But there are some *torial and* who have already received the fruit of such exercises. Their Vir-*Complete* *Virtues.* tues are those of the *purified mind.* But all these are included with the term Moral, and so are distinguished from the Theological Virtues, which are Faith, Hope, Charity.

51. Whatever our readers may think of these divisions, as bearing upon practice, and as helps to the conscience, they must at least admit, that Aquinas is consistent with himself, and that no part of his book brings out more clearly than this his sense of the connection between Ethics and Theology, of their distinction, and of the subordination *Is Faith a* of the one to the other. The sixty-second question of this part, and *Virtue?* especially the third article of it, concerning the propriety of reckoning Faith among virtues, involves some of the points which were most debated between the Reformers of the 16th century, and the School Divines. But the student will not discover the grounds of that controversy, or its immense significance for the history of the world and for personal life, by poring over these passages in the great Doctor. Sometimes he will think he has detected a flaw in him, and can trace the whole pontifical doctrine of Merit in his statements. The next moment he will perceive some careful qualification in those statements, some enunciation of the ground and object of Faith, which he thinks might satisfy the most scrupulous Pro-*Schoolmen* testant. As long as scholasticism is encountered by scholasticism, *against* *Schoolmen.* the puzzle continues, and we may be driven into the position which Melanchthon seems to have occupied in his latter days, of half wondering how the dispute could have assumed such a world-wide importance, when the change of a phrase or two, perhaps the transposition of a particle, might bring about a compromise. It is when *Men against* scholasticism is brought face to face, as it was in Luther, with a *Schoolmen.* strong swimmer in his agony, with a human being wrestling for life, that we begin to understand what the war means, and why protocols and paper treaties must be always ineffectual to terminate it.

The following question on the cause of virtues, embracing the articles, whether virtue is in us by nature, whether any virtue is produced in us by the repetition of acts, whether any moral virtues are in us by infusion, whether the virtue which we acquire by repetition of acts is the same with the virtue that is infused, gives us a glimpse into another long vista of controversies; all connected with the primary one of which we have just spoken. To all, we believe, the observation we have just made is applicable. So long as we meet Aquinas on his own ground he is invincible. When you pass from him to the actual tumults of the conscience, and to the living facts of Scripture which respond to them, you are inclined to pronounce him utterly feeble.

52. We must stop a moment at the next question, which bears **The Mean.** upon the Aristotelian doctrine of the Mean. Are moral virtues, as the old philosopher affirmed, in a Mean? Aquinas states the obvious objection, that virtue is always pointing to that which is highest and ultimate. But he disposes of it, affirming that the highest excellence consists in the adherence to measure and rule: that a measure or rule implies an excess or defect, each of which it forbids: that it must, therefore, be conservative of the Mean, and that virtue must be in that mean. The following article determines that though the mean, in the case of Justice, is a mean in the thing itself (because Justice consists in assigning to each person that which is neither less nor more than what is his), yet in the moral virtues which concern the passions, the mean has reference **The absolute** to *us*, the liability of one man being to excess or defect in *this* **Mean, and** passion, of another to excess or defect in *that*. A third article **to us** brings the intellectual virtues under the same law with the moral. The end of Intellectual Virtue as such is Truth. But Truth consists in the affirmation, that that which is, is; that that which is not, is not. To affirm that to be which is not, is excess; to affirm that not to be, which is, is defect. Between them lies the mean. Nothing can be more strictly Stagyrite than this conclusion. But in the next article we are carried into another region. Theological **Theological** Virtues are determined to consist in a mean, only by accident. In **Virtues** themselves, Faith, Hope, and Charity admit of no excess, because **ferent Law.** the measure of them is the transcendent excellence of God. But considered in reference to our condition, Hope may be the mean between Despair and Presumption; Faith may be the mean between opposing heresies.

53. In one, at least, of his decisions respecting virtues, Aquinas **Relation of** has, we think, sacrificed the interests of morality and theology, not **the Virtues** to save the uniformity of his system, but at the expense of it. The doubt is started, whether virtues can exist apart from Charity. The difficulty is, that certain moral virtues must be attributed to the Heathens, and that Charity being a divine gift, cannot be

attributed to them. The only escape is in the distinction between virtues acquired by human industry, and virtues infused into us.

Aquinas is obliged to admit that the latter only possess the proper conditions of virtues. Yet, if he excludes the former, the very teacher whom he is following in his scheme of Ethics, and whose fundamental principle is, that the practice of virtues precedes the knowledge of them, must have been absolutely ignorant respecting their nature. We rejoice to expose this inconsistency, because in doing so we are gratifying no party animosity or predilection. Protestants have inherited the contradiction from the Schoolman. In many of their statements, it is far less disguised than in his. And it involves consequences to them which it does not to him. If they allow the acquisition of virtues in any sense by human industry, they relinquish the fundamental principle about which they are at issue with the Romanists. And they have no way of saving it, except either by resorting to phrases respecting Heathen virtues which identify them with vices, so shaking the foundations of all

moral order, calling good evil, and evil good ; or else by giving up the atheistical doctrine—which the creeds of the church, which every page in the Bible refutes—that the world, for four thousand years, with the exception of one little corner of it, was a Christless and a Fatherless world.

54. We must not be detained by the questions on the equality of virtues, and the duration of virtue after this life; on gifts, on beatitudes, on the fruits of the Spirit, nor even by the very important articles upon sins and vices which bring us down as far as

the ninetieth. Then we enter upon the subject of LAW. It is thus introduced :—"Next, we must treat of the exterior principles of acts. The exterior principle which inclines us to evil is the Devil. The exterior principle which moves us to good is God, who instructs us by Law, and assists us by Grace. Wherefore, we must first speak of Law, secondly of Grace. About law, it behoves us first to consider law itself in common; secondly, its portions. About law in common, there are three points to be considered. 1st, Its essence. 2d, The difference of laws. 3d, The effect of law. On the first

point (the essence of law), four questions arise. 1st, Whether the law has anything to do with reason. 2d, Its purpose. 3d, Its

cause. 4th, Its promulgation." There are three arguments which may be brought to show that law has not anything to do with reason. 1st, The apostle speaks of a law in his members; but reason has nothing to do with the members of the body. Moreover, in Reason there is nothing but power, habit, and act ; but Law is confessedly not a power, or a habit, for then it would fall under the class of intellectual virtues; not an act, for then it would be suspended when reason is suspended, as in sleep. Again, Law moves those who are under it to right action. But to move to action,

belongs to will, not to reason. Hence the foundation for the assertion of jurists, "that which has pleased the prince, has the power
of law." To all these arguments Aquinas makes answer. The
use of the phrase, *Law in the Members*, is itself a proof that there
is a dominant Law in the Reason. For since Law is a measure
and rule of human acts, you are forced to speak of it not only in
that which rules and measures, but in that which is ruled and
measured. Thus an inclination, even when it is a rebellious one,
acquires the quality and character of a Law—not essentially indeed,
but by participation, and a kind of necessary abuse. The second
point introduces a curious and not uninteresting inquiry as to what
it is in practical operations which answers to the definition proposition and syllogism in intellectual exercises. The Law which determines acts, and leads them to their issues, is this correlative.
Both a potency and habit, and an act of Reason are therefore
implied in it. The third argument is more important. The very
exercise of Will points to an end, and implies the co-operation of
Reason as the means of attaining it. The Will of the Prince, if it
has the vigour of Law, implies a Reason directing it; otherwise it
is iniquity, and not Law. The next article affirms against all
disputers, that Law is ordained for the common good, and not for
any special good. The following carries us a step farther. Seeing
that Law directs man to a common good, it is only the Reason
of the multitude, or of a prince representing the multitude, which
can make a Law. A fourth declares, that before a Law can have a
binding force, it must be promulgated and brought within the
knowledge of those who are subjected to it.

55. That propositions of this *quasi* democratical kind should be
enunciated by a Catholic Doctor will only surprise those who have
taken up their notions of the middle ages from hearsay, and have
not attended to some of the most important facts from which judgments of them must be collected. The superiority of Reason to
mere Custom or Decree, the necessity of asserting a Law of Reason
as one to which an ultimate appeal might be made, were commonplaces which were continually urged in opposition, *e.g.*, to such
Constitutions as those of Clarendon, or to the '*Nolumus leges Angli-
canas mutari*' by which our barons resisted the Canonists. And these
were not dishonest *argumenta ad hominem*, such as they may have
become in later times, when Reason is habitually pleaded against
Church authority. They were the protests which men who really
felt that there was a higher judgment seat than that of the local or
temporary prince, raised against him; they were capable of being
used—soon (as the *Divina Commedia* teaches us) they were actually
used—by the most devout Theologians, against the occupant of
the chair of St. Peter itself. That Aquinas should have anticipated Locke in asserting the dominion and the legislative authority

(marginal notes:)
Meaning of a Law in the Members.
Confutation of Absolutism.
The Common Good.
Feelings of the Middle Ages about Reason and Custom.
Aquinas a predecessor of Locke.

of a multitude or majority, and should have considered the Prince
only as its mouthpiece, may appear more strange.   It is strange—
not because Aquinas was a Dominican, but—because he was a
Philosopher.   The disposition to magnify popular suffrage was
one which he was not at all unlikely to acquire from his order ;
(the Dominicans were not only Jacobins in Paris), nay, it was one
which even Bishops sometimes encouraged before Mendicancy
began ; as we may learn from the speech of the Primate of England
at the coronation of our John.   The limits under which such an
origin of Laws can have been conceived by one who goes on to
assert an *eternal* Law, a *natural* Law which is the child of that, a
Law enacted to meet *human* necessities, and a *divine* Law by which
man is directed to supernatural ends—it is less easy to conjecture.   But we must commend these questions, which extend as
far as the 108th, and those on Grace, which conclude the book,
to the study of the reader, which they abundantly deserve ; and
proceed to the *Secunda Secunda.*

The object of Faith.   56. This part of the treatise carries us into the region of the theological virtues.   The first question treats of Faith as to its object.
The first question debated under this head is, whether the object
of Faith is primary Truth.   The point is settled by means of the
usual school distinction between the formal and the material.   If
we consider the object formally, it is primary truth, for Faith assents
to nothing except because it is revealed by God.   But materially
Faith is directed to many things besides God, which, however, do
not fall under its assent, except as having some bearing or relation
to God ; inasmuch as by certain effects of divinity, the man is
assisted in tending towards the fruition of God.   No doubt, this
statement has proved exceedingly satisfactory to a number of the
students of our Doctor.   So clear and subtle a distinction, what
may not be accomplished by the help of it ?   Everything till a man
The Formal and the Ma-   wants to believe, and begins to believe.   Then the formal and the
terial.   material are forgotten : he must have a living object, a Person who
is directly recognized, not a series of propositions which may lead
to Him eventually.   Distinctions, then, indeed, are not obliterated ;
the self-knowledge, and the divine knowledge, of women and children point to distinctions too subtle for words.   Afterwards, by
reflecting upon these, we may understand the meaning, and even
acknowledge the worth, of the logical divisions.   If we confess
that they can never help us to faith, or determine its ground, its
nature, or its end, they may assist us in observing how the
intellect confuses itself when it ventures beyond its province,
and tries to comprehend what can be only apprehended.   A
Logician by pointing out the limitations of the intellect, and
telling us when it forgets them, may help to deliver us from the
trammels and usurpations of Logic.   More commonly, he does

that work by the ambition which overleaps itself and falls on the other side.

57. We have made these remarks at the outset of the *Secunda Secundæ*, that we may not be forced to repeat them at every turn of it, and that we may, without much commentary, trace the method of it. Faith having been considered as to its interior act, which is Belief; as to its exterior act, which is Confession; as to its habit in reference to itself and to those who possess it; as to its divine cause; and finally as to its effects; we then proceed to the relation between the Intellect and Faith, to the relation of Knowledge to Faith, and to the vices that are opposed to Faith. Under this last head, we have two or three questions about which our readers may be glad to know the opinions of a 13th century doctor. The first is, whether infidels are to be compelled to faith. He considers various objections to compulsion: among others, a saying of Augustine, that a man may do other things unwillingly, but that he can only believe willingly, and that the will cannot be compelled. Still, it is written, "go out into the highways and hedges, and compel them to come in, that my house may be filled." The final conclusion is, that Jews and Gentiles who have never professed the faith are not to be compelled to believe, and that wars against them are lawful only as means of preventing them from impeding the progress of the faith. But those who have taken the faith upon them, or who still profess it, becoming heretics and apostates, are in a different condition. On such, corporal compulsion is to be exercised, that they may fulfil what they have promised, and hold fast what they have undertaken. This is true Dominican doctrine, the formal apology for the persecutions of which that order was the instrument. The argument from Augustine is soon disposed of. To vow is an act of the will, to perform the vow is an act of necessity; to accept a faith is voluntary; to hold it, if once accepted, is a thing of necessity. These sentences are worth all the more startling sentences which are sometimes culled by Protestant orators out of the schoolmen to excite the rage of Protestant mobs. The true virus of persecution is in them; the Atheism which is at the root of persecution. After the man has once believed with his will, he becomes a creature of necessity, not of God: Man is to compel him to hold fast something, *not* with his will, which God has led him to acknowledge with his will. Did Aquinas really mean this? The reply is easy. As a theologian, as a philosopher, he denies such a proposition again and again; he refutes it by unanswerable evidence. The Spirit of God he holds to be the giver and the upholder of faith in every man. So far as he was a defender of Dominican persecutions, he *did* mean this. And we, every one of us, who persecute under any pretext, however we may hate Dominicans, mean it also. The notion that

Analysis of Faith, its operations and relations.

Are Infidels to be forced into Faith?

Defence of Persecution.

What it implies.

we are to keep a man to a profession when it is no longer the
expression of that which he wills or which he is, because we have
lost all influence over his will and over himself, and because we
suppose that God has lost His influence also, this is the defence of
all Protestant as much as of all Romish attempts to punish Aposa-
tates from the true God by compelling them to serve the Spirit
of Lies.

Treatment of
the children
of infidels.

58. In the same spirit, the question of holding any communication with infidels is settled; the questions whether infidels may
have any jurisdiction over Christians, and whether the rites of
infidels are to be tolerated, in a more compromising and utilitarian
spirit; the question whether the children of Jews and of other
infidels are to be baptized against the will of their parents upon the
nobler and more Christian ground, that the custom of the Church
never sanctions any departure from natural justice, and that this is
violated if any boy is withdrawn from the care of his parents before
he has the use of his reason.   At the seventeenth question, we pass

Hope.

from Faith to Hope.   Hope is considered in itself, in its subject, in
its reference to fear, to despair, and to presumption.   Then we pass
at the twenty-third question to Charity.   Under the article which

Charity.

refers to Charity in itself we inquire whether charity is friendship,
whether it is something created in the soul, whether it is a virtue
at all, whether it is a special virtue, or the one virtue, whether
without it there can be any virtues?   Under the next article, we
consider whether Charity is in the will, its possible augmentations,
its possible diminutions, its commencement, progress, and perfection.   In reference to its object, whether God alone or our neighbour also is to be loved from charity, whether irrational creatures,
sinners, enemies, angels, dæmons, are to be loved from charity?
Then comes the debate whether there is any order in charity,
whether a greater or less is to be admitted into it?   The twenty-
seventh article brings us upon some of the questions which were
debated in the 17th century between Bossuet and Fénélon.   We
pass at the thirty-sixth to the vices opposed to charity, whence
we are led into controversies about schism, about the lawfulness of
war, about sedition, and about scandals.

Prudence.

59. At the forty-fifth question there is a transition from the
theological to the intellectual and moral virtues.   We discuss first
the gift of wisdom in its relation to charity, then the folly which
is opposed to wisdom ; thence we pass to Prudence.   Here several
topics occur in which psychology and logic are curiously inter-
mingled.   We are told that we may divide any subject integrally,
subjectively, and potentially.   *Integrally*, the wall, the roof, the
foundation, are parts of the house.   *Subjectively*, the ox and the lion
are parts of animal nature.   *Potentially*, nutrition and sensation are
parts of the soul.   In like manner the portions of any virtue may

be determined in three ways. 1st, The integral will be those parts Integral portions of Prudence. of any virtue which must concur in any perfect act of that virtue. In the case of Prudence these integral parts are eight: Memory, Intelligence, Docility, Quickness of perception, Skill in comparison, Foresight in the arrangement of means to an end, Circumspection, or the acute observation of circumstances, Caution in distinguishing counterfeits of good from the real good. 2d, The parts of Subjective virtue are its different species. In the case of Prudence, Species of Prudence in reference to its subjects. there is the prudence by which any one rules himself, and the prudence by which one rules a multitude of other men. This again admits of division according to the nature of those who are ruled. You require military prudence for an army, economical prudence for a family, directive or political prudence for a state. 3d, The potential parts of any virtue are those virtues which are directed towards some secondary or subsidiary acts necessary to its completeness. The parts of prudence contemplated in this way are denoted by Greek names—*Eubulia*, which has reference to counsel; *Synesis*, which has reference to the decision of those cases which fall under common rules; and *Gnome*, which has reference to the decision of those cases wherein it is necessary to depart from common rules. This subject, therefore, the readers will perceive, is treated by our author with even more than his wonted diligence and elaboration. There are also minute observations included within his general survey which exhibit the mind of Aquinas in a new phase. Take for instance these rules for the acquisition and Memory and the cultivation of it maintenance of a good memory. The first is, that we should call up some likenesses of the things we wish to remember, which shall not be too familiar, because those which are rarer excite our admiration more, and so the mind dwells in them more fixedly: the explanation, he judiciously adds, of the tenacity with which we recollect what we have seen in boyhood. The adhesion of the memory to sensible objects, which justifies this maxim, leads him to place the memory in the sensitive part of our nature. The second art of memory is, to dispose the things which we wish to preserve in order, so that one may immediately suggest another. The third is, to connect whatever things we wish to remember with our affections, so that we may in very deed learn them by heart. The fourth is, that we shall be frequently meditating upon them, so that they should become first habits of our own mind, and at last parts of its very nature. A more rational system of Mnemonics was perhaps never put together than this. It is unpretending and apparently common-place; yet it touches all the essential points of the subject, and gives us what no artificial, technical rules can give, hints how we may turn incidents and observations into fixed intellectual capital, not merely into a floating capital for the commerce of society.

P

60. There are a number of other remarks of much fineness and subtlety under this title; still more perhaps under that which belongs to the second head of Political Prudence. The following passage in illustration of the maxim that political government is a part of prudence, may strike some of us as very obvious; yet, how many dogmas in support of absolute government does it throw down, what a protest does it bear against some of the practices which Aquinas himself has sanctioned! "The servant is moved by a command proceeding from his master, the subject by a command proceeding from his prince. But this movement is of an altogether different kind from that which determines irrational and inanimate things. For these are acted upon solely by another. They do not act upon themselves. They have not the dominion of their own act through free choice. Therefore, the rectitude of

their government is not in any sense in them, but only in their mover. Servants, on the contrary, and any human subjects whatsoever, are so acted upon by others through precepts that they nevertheless act for themselves through free choice. Therefore, in them is required self-government; and in this, political prudence, so far as they are concerned, consists." It is of course implied in this statement—it has been directly asserted before, that the *regnativa* prudence, that which belongs to the ruler, is essentially of the same quality with the obedience which responds to it. With

equal wisdom and superior eloquence Aquinas goes on to connect that counsel which is the gift of the Holy Spirit with the prudence which he has treated as so specially human a quality. It is manifest, he says, that the rectitude of the human reason has that relation to the divine Reason which every inferior motive principle has to its superior, which last is its ultimate standard. For the eternal Reason is the supreme rule of all human rectitude. And, therefore, prudence, which imports the rectitude of reason, is helped and perfected in proportion as it is regulated and moved by the Divine Spirit. This gift and direction, and consequently the continual growth of the prudence which is the fruit of it, is to be looked for in the future world, which is the continuation and unfolding of the present.

61. Leaving this subject, we come to Right and Justice. There are four points, he says, to be considered about justice,—1st, Right, (jus); 2d, Justice itself; 3d, Injustice; 4th, Judgment. Right is affirmed to be the object of justice. Right is divided into natural right and positive right, both of which are treated by Aquinas in a somewhat utilitarian spirit. It is affirmed that there is a distinction between natural right and the right of nations, inasmuch as the one belongs to all animals, the other only to man. He distinguishes further between paternal right, and magisterial right; the right of the husband over the wife is declared to be more a

relation of equality, and less of dependence than either of the others. This recognition of the difference between family law and other law, though it may have been strengthened by Christianity, is confessed to come from Aristotle. Aquinas adopts the definition of justice, that it is the perpetual and constant will, purpose, and habit of giving to every one that which is his due. He determines that justice has always reference to a man's dealings with his neighbour that justice does not reside in the Intellect as its proper subject, but in the Will, that there is a sense in which Justice may be identified with any virtue whatever; that it is also a special virtue distinct from others; that there is a distinction between general justice and particular justice; that the special matter of the particular justice are the exterior actions of men, that it has not reference to the passions, that it is a mean between two extremes, and that it is, as Aristotle affirms, the queen of the moral virtues. The distinction of distributive and commutative justice is affirmed in the sixty-first question. There we have the treatment of various vices which are opposed to each; finally, we come, at the eightieth question, to the separate virtues which are annexed to Justice, its attendant satellites. *Object of Justice.* *Distinctions.*

62. Our readers will be surprised to hear what these annexed virtues are. They are Religion, Piety to parents, Respectfulness, Truth, Gratitude, Vindication of right, Friendship, Liberality. What relation, it may be asked, is there between these and the principal virtue to which they are referred? This, that they all imply an effort imperfectly realized, to render that which is due to another. The 15th psalm is quoted, "What shall I render unto God for all that He has given to me?" Religion is thus rendering to God, the attempt to pay a debt which never can be paid. Piety, or the rendering of duty to a parent, is the same in kind, and has a corresponding imperfection. The Reverence which is paid to worth belongs to the same class; all these three being defective from the very nature of the relation between those who render and those who receive them. The other six are defective, inasmuch as they are merely moral recompenses, and do not come up to the notion of a full legal requital. We should wish our readers carefully to consider these arrangements. They are very instructive. Much, it seems to us, of what has been most mischievous in the school morality and the school theology may be traced to them, much of what we have inherited from both. *Curious arrangement of Virtues under Justice.* *Religion.* *Piety.* *Reverence.*

63. In the questions which follow, down to the hundred and twentieth, we have discussions upon these annexed virtues, upon circumstances appertaining to them, and upon vices that are opposed to them. Then we are again reminded that all of them have been treated with an ultimate reference to justice, and the author winds up that topic by considering the precepts of the

Fortitude. decalogue as precepts of justice. Then we pass to Fortitude ; under which are considered, Martyrdom, as the highest act of fortitude, Fear as the defect of fortitude, Audacity as the vice which is the counterfeit of it. Then we are surprised by the information that *Parts of For-* Fortitude consists of four parts, Magnificence, Confidence, Patience, *titude.* and Perseverance. This strange division is justified by an allusion to our old friends the integral, the subjective, and the potential. We come to understand it rather better when Magnanimity, which is the other name for confidence, takes its place above Magnificence; so that all these qualities appear to represent different forms of internal strength, Magnanimity referring especially to honours, and having presumption, ambition, and vain-glory for its attendant vices; Munificence being occupied with outward wealth and dignities, and implying the power of sustaining them. From forti- *Temper-* tude we go on to temperance, the integral parts of which are *ance.* modesty and a sense of honour, one subjective part of which is abstinence, leading of course to questions about fasting, gluttony, sobriety, drunkenness, chastity, virginity, indulgence, continence, incontinence. Then to clemency and mildness, both of which are considered as parts of temperance, and to anger and cruelty, which are their respective opposites. The consideration of modesty, which belongs to temperance, leads us to Pride; this to the sin of the first man, consisting in pride ; then to its punishment. Aquinas winds up this subject with the general laws of temperance contained in the Scriptures.

Prophecy.   64. The last nineteen questions of this part lead us into an entirely new region. They are on Prophecy as to its essence, the cause of prophecy, the nature of the prophetical intuition, the division of prophecies, concerning raptures, concerning the different graces and gifts spoken of in Scripture, the grace of tongues, of miracles, of speech. Finally we enter on the division of life into active and contemplative, into the different offices and conditions of men generally, and then into the state of ecclesiastics, and of members of religious orders particularly. Into these and the questions discussed in the third part of the *Summa,* which are in the strict and formal sense the theological, we do not propose to enter. We have given our readers some taste of the book. We hope we may have led them to think of it and of its author respectfully and justly. The great influence which both have exerted, has made us anxious not to indulge in any hasty and superficial condemnation of them, not to pass over what seem to us the radical diseases of his system, especially when they may possibly infect our own generation.

Transition to the Francis-cans.   65. The philosophy of the 18th century is nearly comprehended in the two Mendicant orders. We have spoken enough of the

Dominicans; it remains that we should allude to two or three eminent Franciscans. First in order of time, would stand our countryman Alexander of Hales; we cannot doubt that in order of worth he must yield to Bonaventura. It is difficult to extract the particulars of his life from the florid, classical, intolerably tedious biography which is prefixed to the Roman edition of his works published in 1588. The writer, as he informs us again and again, has taken Gregory of Nazianzum for his model. He does not venture to state any fact about Bonaventura for which he cannot produce a parallel in the biography of Basil. Proceeding in so absurd a theory of his duties, it can be no surprise if he has all the faults of his prototype with very few of his excellences, and if he has contrived to diffuse an inconceivably small amount of information through an incredible amount of words. But the reader will be unwise if he allows the inanity of the panegyrist to prejudice him against the victim. Bonaventura must be judged by his own words, and by the opinions of the wisest men of his time and of subsequent times respecting him. He was regarded, and deserves to be regarded as the true spiritual heir of Francis of Assisium. The main facts of his life may be stated very briefly. His father, Johannes Fidantius (or Fidanza), and his mother Ritelia, were both of noble families, rich, and devoted, it is said, to good works. He was born in Tuscany in 1221, two years before the death of Francis. When a child, he had an illness which threatened his life; his mother, despairing of help from the physicians, fled to Francis. His prayers consoled her and restored the boy. She devoted him to the order: as soon as he was of age to understand it, he fulfilled the vow. He had none of the early struggles therefore of Aquinas, little perhaps of his intellectual robustness. He seems to have passed a remarkably pure and innocent boyhood, to have early interested himself in the sick and the poor, and to have given himself no credit for his virtues. His religious life exhibited the characteristics of his order in the highest degree. His contemplations turned much on the Passion of Christ. He had the tenderness of Francis, his fervency, his humanity, his inclination to idolatry. The Virgin, with him even more than with his master, became the main object of that idolatry. It was not an age, however, in which even the most exalted devotion was accepted as a substitute for learning, or was thought to interfere with it. Bonaventura worked hard in the study of the Fathers, framed a collection of their sentences, made two copies of the entire Scriptures with his own hand, and many times, it is added, wrote out the History of Thucydides and the Orations of Demosthenes, no doubt in a Latin version; though his biographer, who lived after the revival of letters, talks of his imbibing the juice of the Attic eloquence. At Paris he studied perhaps under Albertus Magnus, certainly under Alexander of Hales.

Bonaventura.

Life.

His childhood.

His devotion.

His learning.

Whether he frequented the lessons of a Dominican or not, it seems clear that Thomas Aquinas was his friend, and that Bonaventura paid him the honour which was due to his wisdom, and might be expected from his own humility. He pursued the usual course of study in Paris, soon became the first *His books.* teacher among the Franciscans, lectured on "the Sentences" and on the Scriptures, and declined the Archbishopric of York which Clement IV. had offered him. Having overcome this temptation or delivered himself from this responsibility, he devoted himself to literature, wrote twenty-three discourses on that favourite subject of the Fathers and the Schoolmen, tho work of the six days, expounded the four books of the Sentences, took part in the defence of the Mendicants against Gulielimus de St. Amore, and composed a Life of St. Francis. Several pleasant stories are told of his intercourse with Thomas Aquinas; one of them must have been always a favourite with the Franciscans. *Where he* The Angelical Doctor is said to have asked to see the library from *studied.* which he had derived his remarkable stores of knowledge: Bonaventura pointed to the Crucifix, and said he had learnt all that he knew there. He was appointed Minister General of his Order at a time when the greatest prudence as well as the greatest gentleness were needed to preserve it from the factions which had begun to start up within it. Questions about poverty, which rent the order in pieces afterwards, were already mooted. The strange doctrine of the Everlasting Gospel, had been circulated and was gratifying all those who were jealous of the success of the brethren. No one probably could have encountered such difficulties better than Bonaventura. His life was the best witness for the stricter principles of his master. His gentleness was the most effectual means of retaining those whom the mere rule might have alienated.

66. Two books which Bonaventura composed while he was General of the Order, will indicate by their very titles the spirit of the man who so well represented its spirit. One was the "Itine-*The Itiner-* rary of the Mind towards God," the other the "Itinerary of the *ary.* Mind towards itself." As it is from another book that we shall draw our examples of this author, we may take John Gerson's account of these. "Herein," he says, "the progress to divine knowledge is exhibited in two different methods. The first of these treatises proceeds from God as its principle, and goes down to other truths believed and held in subordination to Him. The other takes the opposite course, and ascends as by six steps of a ladder from the creatures even to the most transcendent knowledge of the Creator. And I will confess," adds Gerson, "in my folly, that for thirty years and more I have had these treatises by my side reading them often, meditating on the very words, to say nothing of the sentiments, and now at my age, with all my leisure, I

can scarcely boast that I have got the first taste of their sweets
which have always something fresh and delightful to me, as often
as I recur to them." Among Bonaventura's practical labours, we
are to reckon the influence which he exerted in putting an end to
a papal interregnum after the death of Clement IV., when he was
the means of electing Gregory X., the best prelate unquestionably
of that period, above all his efforts in the Council of Lyons to bring
about a reconciliation between the Eastern and Western churches.
It was by this Council that he was induced, we may believe with
real reluctance, to accept the dignity of a Cardinal. With far
greater satisfaction he took leave of that and of all other earthly
dignities in the year 1274, when he had reached the age of fifty-
three. His miracles, canonization, and the influence of his relics
will be found duly recorded by his biographer.

67. There is a short work of Bonaventura's concerning "the
Reduction of Arts under Theology," which exhibits, it seems to
us, very remarkably the character and the genius of the man, and
the highest tendencies of his order. Instead of plunging into the
more directly mystical and spiritual works, we believe we
shall fulfil our duty to our own subject best if we translate the
greater part of this treatise, which contains as much matter as
most long treatises that we know. The arbitrariness and absur-
dity of some of its divisions will be obvious to the reader without any suggestions of ours. But we shall be disappointed if
he does not find something in it which is not absurd but very
instructive.
De reduc-
tione Artium
ad Theolo-
giam. Opera
Romæ, 1586.
tom. 6, pp.
(1-4.)

68. "Every good and every perfect gift is coming down, saith
St. James, from the Father of lights. In this language he hints at
the origin of all illumination, and insinuates at the same time how
manifold is that light which flows freely from the fontal light.
But although all illumination becomes ours by internal cognition,
we may fairly distinguish and say that there is an *exterior* light,
to wit, the light of mechanical art ; a *lower* light, to wit, the light
of sensible cognition ; an *interior* light, to wit, the light of philosophical knowledge ; a *superior* light, to wit, the light of grace and
of the sacred Scriptures. The first illuminates in respect of artificial form, the second in respect of natural form, the third in
respect of intellectual truth, the fourth and last in respect of saving
truth. The first kind of light, having respect to those forms which
are without us, and which have been invented to supply the wants
of the body, is in a certain sense servile, and degenerates from the
true philosophical cognition. It has a sevenfold division in respect
of the seven mechanical arts which Hugo de St. Victor speaks of;
which are Manufacture of Clothes, &c. (Lanificium); the making of Instruments, especially warlike (Armatura), Agriculture,
Hunting, Navigation, the Theatrical Art, Medicine. The com-
Different
Illumina-
tions.
The seven
Mechanical
Arts.

pleteness of which division is understood thus. Seeing that every
mechanical art is either for consolation, whether that be for the
banishment of sorrow or of poverty, or else is for advantage, they
fall generally under the heads of utility or gratification, as Horace
says

Aut prodesse volunt aut delectare poetæ.

And

Omne tulit punctum qui miscuit utile dulci.

If it is for comfort and delectation, it is comprehended in the theatrical which includes every kind of entertainment, whether it be
in songs or in instruments, in fictions written or pictorial, or in
bodily gestures. If again the art has reference to utility or profit,
this may consist in the covering of the body or in the provision
of food, or in something which is ministerial to both. If it consists
Provisions of bodily cloth-ing. in the covering of the body, that is either with a soft and flexible
material or with a hard and stiff material; the first will fall under
the general head of wool-work (Lanificium), the second under the
general head of Armour, including therein whatever is fabricated
from iron or from any metal whatsoever, or from stone, or from
wood. But if it consists in something alimentary, this may be of
two kinds, because we feed upon vegetables and upon things that
have sense. All aliments of the one kind are included in agricul-
Provision of nourish-ment. ture, all of the other in hunting. Take it in another way; whatever contributes to the generation and multiplication of food, is
included under the common name of Agriculture; whatever contributes to the preparation of the food so multiplied, may be included under hunting: under which is contained whatsoever
belongs to the trade of bakers, cooks, and butchers; the denomi-
nation of these different arts being taken from that one which has
a certain excellence and superiority to the rest. That which is
ministerial either to food or clothing may be so either by supplying
a defect or by removing a hindrance; Navigation, under which is
included all merchandise as the exchange of either food or clothing, supplies defects; Medicine, consisting of the putting together
of electuaries, or potions, or unguents, or in the cure of wounds, or
in the cutting off of limbs, removes impediments. The division is
therefore satisfactory.

The Lumen Cognitionis Sensitivæ. 69. "The second light that illuminates us so that we may
apprehend natural forms, is the light of sensitive cognition, which
comes to us by the aid of corporeal light. There is a fivefold
division of this corresponding to the five senses; the completeness of which Augustine explains according to the nature of the
The Senses and their relation to each other. elements in this wise. Seeing that light serves for the distinction
of corporeal things, it either stands in its own eminency and purity,
and then it is the sense of sight; or it is mingled with the air, and
then it is hearing; or it is mingled with vapour, and then it is

smell; or it is mingled with moisture, and then it is taste; or it is mingled with terrestrial grossness, and then it is touch. For the breath hath the nature of sensible light and lives in the nerves whose nature is bright and transparent, and in these five senses is multiplied, there being in each a greater or a less degree of purity. Therefore, seeing there are five simple bodies in the world, to wit, four elements and an essence, man, in order that he may be able to perceive all corporeal forms, hath five senses corresponding to them, for there cannot be an apprehension except through some similitude and suitableness of the organ and object. There is another way of proving the completeness of the senses; but this is the one which Augustine has approved, and it seems reasonable, seeing that there is a concurrence of correspondences in the organ, the medium, and the object.

70. "The third light which illuminates and which enables us to investigate intelligible truths, is the light of philosophical cognition which is called interior, because it searches for interior and latent causes. This search it pursues by means of principles that are arrived at by learning, though they are the principles of natural truth and are naturally sown in man. This truth is threefold; it may be distinguished as *rational, natural, and moral.* For there is a truth of words, a truth of things, and a truth of manners. The rational deals with the truth of words; the natural with the truth of things; the moral with the truth of manners. Or, to state it otherwise, as we contemplate in the Supreme God an efficient cause, a formal cause, and an exemplary cause, inasmuch as there is in Him the cause by which we subsist, the reason by which we understand, the order by which we live, so the illumination of philosophy pertains either to knowing the causes of being, and then it is *Physics;* or the method of understanding, and then it is *Logic;* or the order of life, and then it is *Morals.* Or, to take it in another way still. There are three modes in which it is possible for the intelligence to be illuminated by this light of philosophical cognition. It directs the motive powers, and then it is moral; it governs the intellect itself, and then it is natural; it governs interpretation, and then it is verbal. So that man is illuminated to the truth of life, to the truth of science, and to the truth of doctrine. And seeing a man may use discourse for three purposes. 1st, That he may make known the conceptions of his own mind. 2d, That he may lead others to belief. 3d, That he may incite others to love or hatred; therefore, this discursive or rational philosophy has a threefold division, into Grammar, Logic, and Rhetoric. The first of these serves for expression, the second for teaching, the third for moving. The first respects the reason as apprehensive, the second as judicative, the third as motive. And because the reason apprehends through discourse that is congruous, judges by discourse

[marginal notes:]
Lumen Cognitionis Philosophica.

The truth which is its object - how divided.

Physics. Logic. Morals.

Grammar. Logic. Rhetoric.

that is true, moves by discourse that is ornate, hence it comes to
pass that this threefold science takes account of these three passions in reference to discourse. Again, seeing that our intellect
must have certain formal principles to direct us in judging, these
also have a threefold aspect, in relation to matter, in relation to
Division of the soul, and in relation to the Divine Wisdom. Natural Philoso-
Natural phy, therefore, is divided into physics proper, into mathematics, and
Philosophy. into metaphysics. *Physical Philosophy* is conversant with the generation and corruption of things in respect of their natural powers
and their seminal principles. *Mathematics* are conversant with
forms which are capable of being abstracted according to principles
of our intelligence (*e.g.*, with special triangles from which a law may
be abstracted that is true of all triangles). *Metaphysics* is conversant with all entities which it reduces to one primary principle,
from whence they have proceeded according to ideal principles
(as distinguished from natural and from intellectual principles).
This primary principle is God as beginning, end, and exemplar.
About these ideal principles there has been some controversy
amongst metaphysicians. *Moral Philosophy* has also a threefold
division. It concerns the governing or motive virtue in respect
of individual life, in respect of the family, in respect of a multitude,
or general society. It is therefore *monastic, economic,* and *political.*
[We have already warned the reader against the notion that the
word monastic has any special reference to the cœnobitical or conventual life, which is much more nearly akin to the political.]

The Lumen 71. "The fourth light is the light of sacred Scripture, which is
Sacræ Scrip- called superior or transcendent, because it leads us to the things
turæ. which are above our reason by first manifesting them to us. And also
because this light descends from the Father of lights, not through
induction but through inspiration. Besides the literal sense which
is single, there is a spiritual sense of Scripture which is threefold.
The allegori- 1st, The allegorical sense, which teaches what is to be believed
cal, moral and concerning divinity and concerning humanity. 2d, The moral,
anagogical wherein we are taught how to live. 3d, The anagogical, where-
view of by we learn how to adhere to God. Therefore the whole of sacred
Scripture. Scripture teaches these three things, to wit, the eternal Generation
and Incarnation of Christ, the Order of life, and the union of God and
the soul. The first respects faith, the second manners, the third
the end of both. The doctor is conversant with the first, the
preacher with the second, the contemplative student with the
third. Augustine has most to tell us about the first, Gregory the
Great about the second, Dionysius about the third ; Anselm follows
in the steps of Augustine, Bernard of Gregory, Richard de St.
Victore (not Hugo) of Dionysius.

The six Days. 72. "You may gather from the foregoing statements that though
in our primary division we spoke of the light which descends from

above as fourfold, yet that there are in fact six portions of it, to wit, the light of sacred Scripture, the light of sensitive apprehension, the light of mechanical art, the light of rational philosophy, the light of natural philosophy, and the light of moral philosophy. There are these six days in this life of ours; and they have an evening, for all this knowledge will vanish away. Therefore there succeeds to them a seventh day of rest which has not an evening, to wit, the illumination of glory. Wherefore these six illuminations may be referred to those six days of the world's creation; so that the knowledge of the sacred Scripture may respond to the first formation, the formation of light, and the others in their order. And as all these had their origin from one light, so all these kinds of knowledge are referred to the knowledge of sacred Scripture, are closed up in that, are perfected in that, and through that as a medium are directed towards the eternal illumination. Wherefore all our knowledge ought to have its ground in the knowledge of sacred Scripture, specially so far as it bears upon the understanding of that upward road (anagogia) by which our illumination is carried home to God, from whom it had its birth. Then the circle is complete; the six days are finished.

73. "Let us go on then to consider in what way the other illuminations may be reduced to this. First, let us examine that illumination which is wholly occupied with the cognition of sensible things. Wherein there are three things to consider, the medium of cognition, the exercise of the cognition, the delight or reward of the cognition. First, as to the medium of cognition, no sensible thing exercises its power except through the mediation of some likeness which goes forth from the object as the offspring from a parent; and this is necessarily its being in every sense. But this similitude does not complete itself in the act of perception till it is united with a certain organ and with the power of dwelling in that organ; and when it is united, there arises a new perception, and by that perception there is a return through the medium of the similitude into the object. And thus I understand that from that highest Mind which can be known in the interior senses of our mind, there hath eternally flowed out a Similitude, an Image, an Offspring, and that He, when the fulness of time came, was united to the mind and flesh, that is, to the man whom He had formed and who never had been before that formation, and that by Him all our minds are brought back to God if we receive that likeness of the Father by faith in the heart. If, again, we consider the exercise of the senses, we shall perceive here the right order of life. For each sense exercises itself about its proper object, avoids that which is hurtful to it, and does not intrude upon the office of any other sense. In like manner the sense of the heart lives according to order when it energizes towards that for which it is made, overcoming sloth;

[marginal notes:] The seventh day. The reduction of Sensitive Cognition. The Law of Sensible Perception, how related to the Spiritual Law. The Exercise of the Senses how related to the Exercise of Spiritual Life.

when it shuns that which is hurtful to it, overcoming concupiscence ; when it arrogates nothing which is not its own, overcoming pride. For all disorder hath its root either in sloth with respect to things that are to be done, in concupiscence in regard to things that are to be desired, or in pride with regard to things that are trans-

The delight resulting from Sensible Perception. cendent. If next we consider the delight which results from the use of the senses, herein we shall behold the union of God and the soul. For every sense seeks that object of sense which is appropriate to it with longing, finds it with delight, recurs to it without weariness; for the eye is not satiated with seeing, nor is the ear filled with hearing. In the same manner, the sense of our heart ought longingly to seek, joyfully to find, incessantly to demand again whatever is beautiful, whatever is harmonious, whatever brings to it the true perfume, whatever is sweet, whatever is softening. See how the Divine Wisdom lies wrapped and hidden in the sensitive apprehension, and how wonderful is the contemplation of the five spiritual senses in their conformity to the corporeal senses.

The reduction of the Light of Mechanical Art. 74. "Let us turn next to the light of mechanical art, the whole object of which is the production of artificial things. Consider here the starting point, the result, the benefit which follows. If we consider the starting point, we see the work going out from the artificer, an intermediate similitude existing in his mind in virtue of which the artificer thinks before he produces and then produces as *The similitude in the Artist.* he had determined. The artificer produces a work out of himself, a work as nearly assimilated as may be to the exemplar within. And if he could produce a result which would love itself and honour itself, doubtless he would do it. And if that effect could know its own author, this must be through the medium of the similitude in the mind of that author to which it corresponded. And if it had a darkened vision, so that it could not raise itself above itself, need would there be, if it was to be brought to the knowledge of its author, *Bonaventura adds nos solum creaturis hebetes rationem rationem voti- gia aed alium deorgink. We think we per- ceive his meaning, but cannot ven- ture upon a translation.* that the similitude by which it was produced, should condescend into that nature which he had first known and conceived. Understand thus how no creature has proceeded from the supreme Artificer except by the eternal Word in which He disposed all things that they might be assimilated to Him by knowledge and love. And since through sin the rational creature had the eye of contemplation darkened, most comely it was that the Eternal and Invisible should become visible, that He might bring us back to His Father. . . . . . If again we consider the effect, we shall *Conditions of a perfect work.* perceive here the order of life. For every artificer intends to produce a work that is beautiful, and useful, and stable, and it is then a clear and acceptable work when it unites these three conditions. Knowledge renders a work beautiful, the will renders it useful, *The Result* perseverance renders it stable. If we consider the benefit which results from the work, we shall discover here the union of God and the soul. For every artificer who makes any work does it either that he may be praised for it, that it may procure something for him, or that he may simply delight in it. For these three ends God made the rational soul, that it might praise Him, that it might serve Him, and that it might delight and rest in Him by virtue of that Love in which he who dwells dwells in God and God in him. See then how the illumination of mechanical art is a way to the illumination of sacred Scripture; and there is nothing in it which does not predict and foreshadow the true Wisdom. Hence it comes to pass that the Scripture so continually uses similitudes which are drawn from this art.

75. "If we turn next to the rational philosophy which is mainly occupied with discourse, we have three things to consider, the utterer of the speech, the mode of its utterance, and the hearer. If we consider the speaker, we shall see how every discourse signifies a conception of the mind; and that inward conception is the word of the mind, the offspring of the mind which is known to the conceiver. But to the intent that it may be made known to the hearer, it puts on the form of voice, and that which was a word belonging to the intelligence, with that clothing for its medium, is brought within the region of the senses and is heard without, and is taken into the listening heart, and nevertheless does not depart from the mind of the utterer. So we see in the eternal Word that the Father eternally conceived Him, as it is written, 'Before the abysses I was brought forth.' But to the end that it might be brought within the knowledge of man who has senses, it puts on the form of flesh, 'the Word was made flesh and dwelt among us,' and yet remained in the bosom of the Father. But if we consider discourse in its own nature, then we shall discover in it the order of life; for the congruity, truth, and ornament which are demanded in speech have their counterparts in the rectitude of intention, the purity of affection, and the modesty or comeliness of operation which together constitute the right order of life. Consider discourse in respect of its end or object, and we discover that a man never expresses himself except through the mediation of form, never teaches except through the mediation of a light that convinces, never moves except through the mediation of a power or virtue within. He only is the true doctor, saith Augustine, who can impress a form upon the heart of his hearer, who can pour light into it, who can give strength to it. Therefore He who teacheth the heart within hath His seat in Heaven. And so here too the truth of the union of the soul with God is latent, for that the mind should be instructed in the knowledge of God by His internal speech, it is needful that it should be united to Him who is the brightness of His glory and the form of His substance and who upholds all things by the word of His power."

(marginal notes) The Rational Philosophy. Sermunculus. The Discourse. The Method of Discourse. The Hearer.

76. [The next chapter, which is on the illumination of Natural Philosophy, we shall not attempt to translate. It would be difficult to convey an exact impression of the author's meaning to a modern reader, and very few modern readers indeed would be able to restrain a certain feeling of contempt for the physical blunders as well as for the mystical conceits of the writer, which might be more injurious to them than to him. The general course of the argument will be understood from the passages which have preceded. Here, as elsewhere, it is shown that there is a threefold way of considering the threefold division of Natural Philosophy, and that under its first aspect it involves the truth of the eternal life of the Divine Word and of His Incarnation in time; under its second the true order of life; under its third the union of the soul with God. The illumination of Moral Philosophy follows. Here again Bonaventura seems to us to repeat himself and rather to disappoint the expectation we had formed of him from his treatment of this subject at the commencement of the Essay. He follows Anselm in assuming that rectitude of will is the subject and aim of Moral Philosophy; but he investigates the idea of rectitude and right far less seriously and successfully than his guide. And he brings out that which is the conclusion of the whole matter with both, that the rectitude of God is the under-ground of the rectitude of man, far more feebly than either Anselm or Aquinas. Rectitude and Justice it is clear are not the words which were dearest to the Franciscan. If Aquinas enlarges unreasonably the ground which they cover, the seraphic wisdom would be inclined to limit it, at least as dangerously, by substituting spiritual affections and states of mind for fixed and eternal laws. Our author concludes his treatise in these words.]

77. "Thus it is manifest in what wise the multiform Wisdom of God, which is clearly delivered to us in sacred Scripture, is hidden in every kind of knowledge and in all nature. It is manifest also how all forms of knowledge minister to Theology. And therefore she assumes examples and makes use of words that belong to every part of knowledge. It is manifest also how large is the path of light and how in everything which is felt or which is known, God himself is latent. And this is the fruit of all sciences, that in all, Faith should be built up, God should be honoured, manners should be softened and harmonized, and those consolations should be imbibed which come from the union of the Bridegroom and the Bride. Which union takes place only through Charity, towards which all Holy Scripture tends and in which it terminates, which is the end consequently of that illumination which descends from above, without which all knowledge is vain, for there is no coming to the Son save through the Holy Spirit, who teaches us all truth, who is blessed for ever and ever. Amen."

78. Bonaventura is the specimen of a Franciscan at peace. The friendship which he felt for Aquinas as a man, is not qualified by any discussions with him as a philosopher. There is no reason to suppose that he was conscious of any important divergence from the general system of one who, like himself, aspired to reduce all arts and sciences under Theology. The essential Aristotelianism of the Angelical doctor, the essential Platonism of the Seraphic, discovers itself to *us* as we read and compare them ; but may have been scarcely known or confessed by either. In due time doctors were to arise who would have a very thorough consciousness of these differences, and would take pains to bring them into the fullest manifestation. The principal of these we must now introduce to our readers. We must transport them from the south to the north, from Italy to Ireland. And the change will not be merely a geographical one. The differences of climate and race were perhaps never more vividly displayed than in Bonaventura and Duns Scotus.

The Franciscan at peace.

79. The Franciscans dwell upon it as a singular providence that Duns Scotus was born in the year in which Bonaventura died. Where he was born has been, as one biographer after another informs us, a question not less interesting than where Homer was born. Seven cities, they tell us in their magnificent way, claimed the one, three countries the other. Some have referred him to a village in Northumbria near Warkworth. The countrymen of David Hume and Sir W. Hamilton, of course, think that the only proper home for a metaphysician is on the other side of the Tweed. But Ireland has been a much bolder and more resolute claimant, and treats our pretensions and those of Scotland with equal disdain. *Wadding*, the laborious biographer of the Franciscan worthies, is full of arguments geographical and philosophical on behalf of his country. The name of Scotus being confessedly indecisive, that of Duns at once fixes the doctor to an Irish village. How dearly he prized the distinction is manifested, Wadding thinks, by his paying St. Patrick the somewhat doubtful compliment of putting him in the place generally occupied by Socrates of an Ens Logicum (the John Styles or Richard Roe of Philosophy). He is more fortunate in alleging the vehemence with which Irishmen have fought not only for their own right in Duns, but for his general reputation. Wadding might, without arrogance, quote himself as an instance. Yet, for vituperative eloquence, he must yield the palm to a more recent Franciscan. Colganus or Callaghan, deals out the epithets, "liars" and "apostates," against the impugners of the fame of Scotus as well as against the wicked assertors of his English parentage, with a freedom and boldness which effectually vindicate his order from the imputation of undermining national sympathies and antipathies. Thus much, at least, as Englishmen, we may boast of ; Duns was

Duns Scotus—his birth-place.

Zeal of the Irish for him

At Oxford educated at Oxford, and at Oxford he had already displayed the learning and the faculty which became afterwards still more illustrious in Paris. He was there in the year 1304 defending various theses, and opposing some of the positions which had become generally received in the schools on the authority of Aquinas. But the year of his glory was 1307. Then he maintained in 200 distinct propositions the immaculate conception of the Virgin. An image of Mary, we are told, inclined its head in answer to a prayer for aid in pleading her cause. Paris bestowed on him the title of the Subtle Doctor, and established a festival to commemorate the victory of his opinion. That year he was sent to Cologne by the General of the Order, whether because the heretical Beghards and Beguines in that quarter had need of a corrector, or to establish the position of the Minors more firmly, or for some more recondite cause, his biographer cannot determine. It is clear, however, that he gave an example of true Mendicant obedience by at once forsaking the scene of his triumph without even taking leave of his friends. The year after, when he was not more than thirty-five years of age, he had to take a longer leave of them; report said in a strange and fearful manner. One of his detractors affirms that for some crime known only to God, he was allowed to fall into a swoon, and to be buried alive, and that he died in his efforts to break the lid of the coffin. A Franciscan admirer explains the event by affirming that he was in a rapture. More reasonable historians of the Order discredit the story in both its forms, maintaining that the special cautions which were observed by the ecclesiastics of Cologne respecting funerals, make it incredible.

The Immaculate Conception.

Traditions concerning his death.

80. The name with which the Parisians endowed Duns Scotus was, it seems to us, the happiest that could have been selected for him. And whatever we may think of the particular controversy in which he won his laurels, we believe that his subtlety was not in general used to confuse principles and to make the worse appear the better reason, but to bring out distinctions which are of real value, and which the metaphysicians of the latest periods cannot afford to overlook. Such, at least, is the inference we draw from his treatise on "the First Principle of Things," a book which appears to contain in an organic form most of the doctrines that are scattered through his other writings. An account of some of the principal questions resolved in it will, we believe, on the whole be more useful than a collection of extracts in our author's language. Not that we have found that language so entirely rugged and uncouth as it is often represented to be. Aquinas is in many ways less difficult; all who desire to have their intellectual food cooked for them will resort to him. Those who like to prepare it, and even now and then to hunt it for themselves, will find their interest in accompanying Duns.

Subtlety of Scotus.

His book on the First Principle of Things.

81. The first question discussed in the Treatise is, whether there *The Original in itself and as a Cause.* is one principle of all things simply and absolutely? Duns proposes 1st, To remove an ambiguity from the word Principle. 2d, To state different opinions on the subject. 3d, To defend the Catholic truth upon it. We must distinguish between the original in *itself* and the original in relation to other things as their cause. Not that they are different, but that it is a different process to contemplate the principle *à priori*, and to ascend to it from that which we see. Duns remarks, that the *plurality* of effects led some, as Pythagoras, *Plurality.* *Duality.* *Contrariety.* to the supposition of a *number* of different causes or principles; that the *contrariety* of effects, and again the combination of opposite effects led others, as Empedocles, to think of *two* Principles, one the principle of strife, the other of Unity or Reconciliation; that the existence of *Good* and *Evil* effects led a third class (the Mani- *The Manichean Theory* cheans) to imagine one cause of spiritual and incorruptible things, another of earthly and corruptible. To the first, our author answers, 'You cannot infer a multitude of causes from a multitude of effects. The instance of the sun teaches us that from the vigour of a single agent may proceed results the most numerous and various.' To the argument from contraries, it is answered, that in works which proceed from a human mind and will, we continually observe a perfectly harmonious result brought to pass through agencies which are in themselves warring and contradictory. To the Manichean argument it is answered, that Evil implies not efficiency, but deficiency. It is detraction from some power or virtue; as *e.g.*, lameness from the power of walking. The positive doctrine which Duns undertakes to prove in opposition to these three doctrines, is—1, That there is one efficient Principle of all things; 2, That this efficient Principle is the exemplar of all things; 3, That it is their final end.

82. The arguments in proof of a one efficient Principle, involve *Unity of Genus and Unity of Proportion.* a doctrine which metaphysically is more important than themselves. In it lies the Realism of Duns, about which we often hear much, but which is perhaps not always well understood. He starts from the assertion of Aristotle, that Genus is not Being (Ens.) The Genus Animal, as such, *excludes* its differences. It is *neither* rational nor irrational. But a Being must be one or other of these. Therefore, besides the Unity of Genus, which is a unity of *predication*, there must be a unity of *analogy* or *proportion*. In the first unity, *Negative and Positive Universality* that which is most comprehensive, is most negative. In the other, that which is most comprehensive, is most positive. I attribute health primarily to a man, I attribute it secondarily or by analogy to food, calling that healthy which contributes to health. There is a perfect unity in these two uses of the word; but it is the unity of proportion. It is the unity which has to do with being, as distinguished from my statements or affirmations about being.

Q

Ascending by this scale you do not seek in the primary Being for the last negation : you seek in it that which explains the being of all other things. Assuming this distinction, Duns goes on to argue, that if you take any two beings whatsoever, and affirm that they are primary, you must say that being is predicated of them equally, not of either in reference to the other, or of both in reference to some third. But in so doing, you take being as identical with genus, which is contrary to our hypothesis.

Platonism of Duns.

83. An earnest consideration of this statement might, we think, bring us into the very heart of the Scotian philosophy as well as remove many perplexities from our own minds. Bonaventura shows us the spiritual and theological foundation of the Franciscan Platonism ; Duns justifies it from the scholastical side. We need scarcely say how much was wanting to bring this Platonism into contact with the facts of earth ; what an absence there is in it of the purely Socratic element. Still we must accept it as a most valuable counteraction to the Encyclopedic tendencies of the Dominican; as a great vindication of the personality of Man and of God against systematic anthropology and theology. On the second point, that the one efficient Principle is the exemplar of all forms, Duns is

Form and Matter.

still Platonical. He preserves the terminology respecting Form and Matter which the Schoolmen chiefly derived from Aristotle, but that terminology acquires a new meaning in his hands. Forms, he observes, which are united to Matter, are the more perfect the more particular they are. Separate the Form from the Matter, and the case becomes reversed. Then the more universal the forms are, the more simple they are ; the more simple they are, the more they have of action and perfection. The highest form is the simplest, for it includes all others within itself. The perfect Being

The Efficient cause the end which all things aim at.

is the self-existent Whole. All other beings exist by participation of His being. The doctrine, that the efficient cause is the end which all beings are created to seek, is deduced from the effort of the soul itself. That, Duns here and elsewhere, describes as the ground of all *our* certainty. Our aspiration after an infinite Good is the witness to us that that good is, that it is the cause of our existence, that we are meant to participate in it. To speak of the Infinite as the finis or end which we are seeking, is contradictory in sound, not in fact. The τὸ ἄπειρον and the τὸ ἄπειρον might be hopeless opposites for Pythagoras and Anaximander; the Catholic Faith reconciles them.

Aristotle's difficulty.

84. The second question which Duns discusses in this treatise, whether plurality, i.e., a multitude of creatures, can proceed from a single principle, would seem to be included in the first. Nevertheless, it introduces us to some new topics, and especially to an argument with Aristotle, and with his Arabian commentator Avicenna. Aristotle, he thinks, did not feel so much difficulty in con-

necting *Plurality* with a one divine Creator, as in supposing that anything could proceed from Him which was not *eternal*, not essentially like Himself. He attributes to his Mahometan critic the doctrine, that the production of multitude presupposes an intelligence besides the one ; the Creation of all distinct things being attributed wholly to this intelligence. Duns takes these distinctions: 1st, He would have us think of the production of that which is the same in substance as taking place by *intrinsic* communication; of that which is diverse in substance by *extrinsic* communication. 2dly, He would have us observe that there is a plurality which includes and involves unity (*e.g.*, the existence of a number of men involves a humanity), and that there is a plurality which excludes unity; (*e.g.*, two souls cannot exist in the same man.) 3dly, He declares that there are contraries of which the same subject is susceptible, and that there are contraries which destroy each other. With respect to the first distinction, it is only extrinsic production which can be supposed to require *Media*. The possible media may be of three kinds, either (1.) A *Medium totaliter operans*, *i.e.*, the Intellect of Avicenna, which is in fact the Sole Creative Power standing apart from the one Principle. (2.) A *Co-operative* medium, such as the nature of the soil is in the production of a plant. (3.) An *assisting* Medium, such as is the eye to the mind in the producing of impressions. These maxims being premised, Duns ultimately affirms, " That the first Principle produces Plurality in the sense in which plurality does not exclude unity ; contraries in the sense in which contraries do not destroy each other; *immediately*, that is to say, without the necessity of either the Intelligence the Mahometan speaks of, or of the co-operation of the Nature of any existing secondary agent." Nevertheless, Duns admits, that there is a sense, or rather that there are two senses in which Avicenna's doctrine holds good. Contemplate the divine order merely as an expression of the divine purposes (*Ordo Rationum*) ; contemplate it as an expression of the ultimate results of those purposes (*Ordo Perfectionum*); and it is right to say that the Unity of God is producing Unity; that all which He does tends to Unity. But contemplate this order in reference to the Means by which these results are wrought out (*Ordo Agentium*), and then the conclusion is false. Plurality comes in, and plurality involves that fresh and ever teeming production which Aristotle knew not how to extract out of his idea of a one first cause.

85. The acknowledgment of God as the Form which is assumed in all created forms ; of Form as in its essence living, and active, the spring and source of Acts ; of a gradation of Forms ; of each higher Form as requiring less to sustain itself and its acts than the one that is subordinate to it ; of the highest as demanding no aid at all to its acts, its strength being wholly self-derived—this is the fundamental and divine part of our author's Philosophy. To con-

Intelligence of Avicenna.

Possible Media in Creation.

Conclusion.

How God's works are one.

Forms and their distinctions.

neet this with the actual things, to bring the divine Will into connection with the contingent and the Material is, with him as with
others, the great problem. In his treatment of contingencies and
their ordination, he follows in the track of Boethius; and we are
not sure that he adds much to what is said on this subject so finely
in the Consolations. Duns dwells much upon the sense in which it
may and may not be affirmed that God determined from Eternity
what should or should not be. His statements on this point could
hardly be made intelligible, unless we went at length into his opinion
Matter. respecting Time which is developed in a subsequent question. It is
more in order that we should speak now of his doctrines respecting
Matter, which are naturally suggested by the doubt whether it may
not be required as the Co-operating Medium, the co-efficient, in
Matter can- Creation. Before he develops his own theory, he addresses an *argu-*
not be eter- *mentum ad hominem* to those who assume that matter cannot have
nal. been created, that it must be assumed as necessary to the production of creatures. You hold Matter to be simply a potency, the
very antagonist of form; not partaking of being at all. It is
easier for you to suppose *anything* original than this; for by your
very hypothesis it has no strength, no element of power in itself.
It must be created, whatever is not created.

Matter in 86. Duns himself does not think so meanly of Matter as some of
what sense those do who would set it beside God and suppose it necessary to
connected
with being. his operations. Matter, according to him, is not a mere potency,
a mere negation of Being. Apart from Form, it is not quick and
vital. But Being is implied in it; it is the passive receptive
female, without which no form except the highest and most perfect
is conceivable. This he affirms again and again; it is perhaps his
Matter im- most characteristic dogma. Matter is just as much supposed in all
plied in
Spiritual ex- spiritual existences, God only excepted, as in those which we op-
istence. pose to spiritual. The Spiritual Form has its corresponding
Matter just as the Corporeal Form has that which appertains to it
and brings it into reality. The doctrine is philosophically consistent in spite of its paradoxical appearance: we do not see how
any schoolman could escape from it: yet we are not aware that
any one has affirmed it with the same breadth and courage as our
Is Matter author. With equal resolution, he faces the question whether
general or
distinct? there is a specific matter appropriated to each form, or whether
Matter is in its nature general and indeterminate. The answer is,
Matter as such is indeterminate and chaotic. But the distinct
Forms coming into contact with it give it a distinctness; Matter
united with a form becomes as separate from that which is united to
any other as the forms themselves are. Hence, says our Duns,
rising for the moment into poetry which we may believe is always
latent in him though buried for the most part under quiddities of
the understanding—"Hence, it appears that the world is a very

beautiful tree whereof the root and seed store is this primary Idea of the Universe.
matter; the moving leaves are accidents and contingencies; the
boughs and branches are all things which are liable to decay; the
flower is the rational nature; the fruit is that same in its perfection,
the angelical nature. That which alone forms this seed, and directs
its unfolding from the beginning is the Word of God, either by
immediate operation as in the case of the Heavens, the Angels, and
the rational soul, or mediately through such agents as work in
the production of whatever is subject to birth and to death. True
it is, that in the first root of this primary matter, nothing is distinct.
Then at once the root is divided into two branches, the corporeal
and the spiritual. The spiritual branch is distinguished into three
hierarchies; each of these into three orders, each order into thousands of thousands of Angels. A portion of these branches being
shaken by a blast of pride, was dried up at the beginning of the
world. The corporeal creation contains two branches, the corruptible and the incorruptible, each of which has manifold offshoots.
Thus the unity of the universe in its various elements is evolved at
last out of this indeterminate matter."

87. In many parts of this treatise we think we may trace the Duns as a Psychologist.
action of the theological tenet which procured Duns his Parisian
reputation upon his philosophy, as well as the steps by which that
philosophy might have prepared him for receiving the tenet. The
ontological and theological discussions respecting a first principle,
lead us to questions respecting the soul and body of man. No
writer has expressed himself with more reverence than Duns
for the corporeal part of man's nature. Proceeding from his
general maxim that all act and energy belong to forms, all
passivity to matter, he affirms that the intelligent soul is the true
and specific form of the body. The sensitive part, he says, has no
active energy, therefore it cannot be this form. The rational soul
considered metaphysically apart from the body, is composed of form
and matter, i. e., of an active and passive principle. But the body is Dignity of the human body.
more glorious than the mere matter (the mere receptivity), of the
soul separately considered, inasmuch as it is receptive of the whole
power of the soul, uniting both its elements. The whole man thinks
and feels; but the root and groundwork of thought and feeling is
in the intellect, and the immediate agent through which the
thought and feeling fulfil themselves is the body. The intelligent The Rela-tion of the Intellect to the Body.
soul is more truly and properly united to the human body than
any other form is to its own materia. Our Doctor therefore arrived
directly or indirectly, by one process or another, at a very high
idea of Manhood in its composite condition. Man, he maintains,
is more truly man in his original, than in his lapsed condition, in
his heavenly country than in his earthly pilgrimage. The intellect
of man, he declares, is wholly from God, not generated by the

human parent. But he bestows a quasi super-naturality on human generation, to which, though we may not attribute form, we may attribute the educing of that compound which consists of both matter and form. The soul, he affirms, is wholly in the whole body, and is present in each part. He traces the steps of knowledge, beginning at the lowest, which is the sensitive apprehension of a sensible object. This apprehension is not scientific; for science concerns the truth or substance of things, not the mere outside of them. Nevertheless, this particular sensitive apprehension he distinctly maintains to be the foundation of all science. Through the apprehension of particulars, we must rise to the knowledge of that which is universal.

88. Such a sentiment as this the reader might perhaps have listened to without great surprise from Roger Bacon, whom he has heard of as the intellectual forerunner of his great namesake. But he may be startled that it should proceed from a man like Duns—a schoolman emphatically, not an experimentalist; one of those whose dominion the scientific revolution of the 17th century is supposed to have overthrown. In what respects Roger Bacon was peculiar, how he offended the prejudices of his order, we shall have soon to explain. But we must in justice to that order say that the first maxim of experimental philosophy could never have appeared heretical to its most illustrious members. Their tendency was towards induction; the inductive minds were those which fell naturally within the circle of their influence. Duns undoubtedly knew much less of physics than Albertus Magnus; but we suspect that he had more of the characteristics which would be demanded of a physical investigator in modern times than could be found in Albert or in his illustrious friend. And we do not think that the passages in the Treatise "De Principio Rerum," which most convict him of being a Realist at all weaken the force of this assertion. Supposing he assumed the reality of those kinds or classes into which existing naturalists had distributed the subjects of their observations—we admit at once that he would have fixed a fatal limit to investigation. But as his previous assumption is that Being and Genus are not identical, he is not open to this charge. Nor can he be accused of bringing in degrees and traditions to check courageous inquiry. He is no rebel against authority; but he knows that when words are given, the force of those words requires to be ascertained. He firmly believes that a divine authority is a guide to Truth, not a dispensation from the effort of pursuing it. *Scotists* no doubt become the slaves of Scotus, as *Thomists* became the slaves of Aquinas; each repeated the dicta of a master. But the disciple of the subtle doctor must have been half conscious that he was missing his sense when he was not thinking for himself. It was far easier to be a clever

Scale of Perceptions.

Inductive tendencies of Franciscans.

Induction and Realism not necessarily hostile.

Duns not a slave of Tradition.

adept in the other school, without doing much more than commit
to memory the angelical arguments and conclusions.

89. In his thirteenth question, Art. 3, Duns enters upon the
long controversy, which will meet us again so often, whether the
apprehensions of the Intellect respecting things without are direct
like those of the senses; whether if so they are identical with the
apprehensions of the Senses; whether an image or likeness of the
thing seen is presented to the intellect, or formed by it, not the
actual thing; whether the intellect merely abstracts and knows
only by this abstracting faculty; whether the power of direct vision
can only belong to the intellect in some other state of being. The
conclusion at which our Doctor arrives is that the apprehension
of the Intellect differs in this from that of the Senses; that
whereas they *experience* the actuality of the thing under which they
are exercised, the intellect simply *knows* its actuality. The
knowledge is higher than the experience, and in fact includes it, but
each inferior faculty or capacity has something belonging to itself
which does not belong to the higher. But the Intellect loses nothing of the reality; it is not farther from the actual truth of the
thing than the Sense is; it does not substitute an abstraction of
its own for that which the eye beholds or the ear hears; it rather
enters more into the truth of the thing, into its essential reality
than the Sense does. A fruit growing on a tree, says Duns, I
attribute to the tree, the particular agent; not to the sun, the
universal agent. It is not that I deny the action of the sun in
producing that fruit. It is not that I think the tree can produce
anything without the sun. It is not that I regard the sun as less
directly productive than the tree. . Such is the relation of the Intellect to the Senses. They know nothing, realize nothing apart
from the Intellect. I ascribe to them a certain contact with the
things which I cannot ascribe to the Intellect; but that is all. The
living apprehension is *in* it only *through* them.

90. The Intellect, then, is not dependent upon any appearance
which an object makes to the senses. It gets rid of these appearances, and so arrives at the reality. But are there any *species* impressed on the Intellect itself? Does it owe to them its knowledge
of that which is universal? Duns considers at length the arguments
of those who say that the Intellect moulds Species, that they are
the effects of its abstracting power; and of those who say that
Species is only *ratione speculi*, a mirror in which the particular
object is presented to the Intellect. He treats the words Abstraction, and the like to which the supporters of the first hypothesis
resort, as terms to express processes which themselves demand an
explanation, or as dishonest subterfuges for getting rid of the
whole difficulty. Phantasies, he argues, can never supply the place
of Species. A deliverance from sensual phantasms is what the

Opera Omnia
Wadding.
vol. 3. pp.
115-116

Sensible
Species or
Likenesses.

Intellectual
apprehension
how it differs
from Sen-
sible.

Sensible ap-
prehension
more imme-
diate—and
more real
than Intel-
lectual.

Species im-
pressed on
the Intellect.

Argument
for the
reality of
Species.

Intellect desires. That deliverance becomes possible for it, if it has the power of turning itself to certain pure and real Species; not on any other condition. But to do so is possible for the Intellect even now. It must not be content to wait for this as its ultimate and heavenly perfection; for what is that perfection but the state for which God created it; that which it is to attain when it is purged from anomalies and contradictions? A Species, then, he concludes, the Intellect demands both for visible and invisible things. When the things are present, then this Species is that which prevents the Intellect from being seriously disturbed by the want of proportion in those phantasms which the Sense or the Imagination brings before it. When the object is absent, then this Species sustains and supplies the Memory. It is determined in the How the following question (the 15th), that the Mind knows itself and its Mind knows own operations, not by a Species impressed upon it (as in the case itself. of things without it), but by a Species *expressed* from it; in other words, it has an *intuitive* knowledge of its own habits.

Species and 91. We have been careful to use the word *Species* in all these Ideals. disquisitions, often as we have been tempted to substitute for it Form or Ideal; because it is a first duty in a historian not to sacrifice the strictness of language and the order of times to his own convenience or to that of his reader. That Duns Scotus meant *something like* what Plato meant, or what we might mean, by the word Idea or Ideal, when he spoke of Species, we of course believe. What the resemblance is, where the divergency begins, must be ascertained by careful reflection, which is greatly helped by the consideration of the differences of language that became necessary either from the use of Latin instead of Greek, or from the habits of the age, or from the opinions of the particular thinker. The chance of making this discovery is diminished just in proportion as the words are confounded or assumed to be identical. The Necessity of whole Nominalist controversy of the 13th century, and of that adhering which follows, becomes a hopeless riddle, if we lose hold of the strictly to Latin words. phrases which were either the catchwords of the opposite parties, or which were common to both. And this consideration is far more important in this period than it would have been in the last, since the debate is no longer about trifles, as it was in John of Salisbury's day. All the most serious feelings of the most serious men are involved in it, there is no topic of Morals or Theology with which it is not directly connected.

Time, is it 92. We must pass over several questions, not without great inonly in the terest to the modern metaphysician respecting Number, to touch Mind? upon one which he sometimes fancies is specially his own; that which is discussed in the eighteenth question of our Treatise, "Whether Time and Motion are the same in reality; whether Time is only in the Mind?" On this subject, Duns expresses himself with moderation as well as decision. Time, he affirms to be Motion *plus* a certain notion of before and after which is derived from the mind itself. To say that Time is only in the Mind, if thereby it is implied that Motion is only in the mind, is false. That belongs to things, to the world which is outside of us. But it is equally false to say that Time is in the things in any other sense than Motion is in them. Time thus, as Time, is simply from us; it is a condition of our minds. But since we should know nothing of it, since this condition of our mind could have no application or meaning if the fact of Motion were not presented to it,—we must beware of using language, which, though formally right, is materially wrong. We need scarcely tell our readers that Augustine's Confessions is the treasury of thought to which Duns and all other schoolmen resorted when their minds were exercised on this question of Time, or how many other still profounder questions respecting Eternity and the nature of God Himself were closely intertwined with it in the mind of the Bishop of Hippo and in theirs. We can only commend the passages upon this subject in the latter part of the Treatise 'De Rerum Principio,' to those who are earnestly occupied with it; still more to those who see nothing in it which can furnish them with any occupation; who fancy that they have fathomed it with their plummets; or who put it aside with the sage determination that what is unfathomable cannot concern them. To hold that opinion, seems to us like making our whole stay upon earth that live burial, that striking against the coffin lid, which the enemies of Duns Scotus imagined to be his punishment after his earthly work was over.

[marginal notes: Time, how connected with Motion. Eternity. Conclusion.]

93. When Duns Scotus came to Oxford, he must have heard strange reports respecting a brother of his own order, who was perhaps a magician, though he had written against magic, and perhaps a heretic, though he had been the friend of at least one distinguished pope. Whether the subtle Doctor may ever have conversed with the wonderful Doctor, Roger Bacon, while he was meditating at Brazennose on "the means of avoiding the infirmities of old age;" whether the youth, whom all Franciscans were to honour as the champion of orthodoxy, would have consorted with the old man whom Franciscans were told by their Superior to abhor, and whom he had cast into prison—we have no means of ascertaining. Bacon must be dearer to us than Duns can be. For he was an Englishman, not only in virtue of his birth-place, which no one disputes, but in virtue of gifts and of a character which we may boast of as specially national. Moreover, he was a martyr of science, and we should certainly be disposed to enlarge the canon which Anselm established in the case of another English divine by contending that the martyrs of science are the martyrs of God. This claim might perhaps stand good

[marginal notes: Roger Bacon. Contrast to Duns. Claims of Bacon on our reverence.]

on other grounds in the eyes of us Protestants. At all events there is so much in his position and circumstances which is deeply and vitally important to the students of Philosophy generally, that we must defy the plausible objection which might be raised against our right to speak of an investigator of Nature in a treatise on Moral and Metaphysical inquiries.

His birth.

94. Roger Bacon was born at Ilchester in the year 1214. He sprang, like Aquinas and Bonaventura, from the upper classes; he belonged to an excellent Somersetshire family. He may always have been destined to be a monk, but he appears not to have taken the Franciscan vow till he was twenty-six years of age, after he had

At Oxford and Paris.

already passed some years at Oxford as well as at Paris. The direction must have been given to his mind during those years; he must have had made many an observation, perhaps many an experiment, on the mysteries of the world about him, before he devoted himself to a society which was occupied with the mysteries of the kingdom of Heaven. By the year 1240, he may have been well able to judge in either university which of the orders was most likely to favour the bent of his genius; certainly we should say that he chose wisely, however little the events which followed may have appeared to justify the resolution. How well the special meditations of the Friar could blend with the favourite studies of

The natural and spiritual.

the Naturalist, our poet has taught us in a well-known passage which may have been suggested by the traditions (so rife among the dramatists of this period), of one who had learned his lore not in Verona, but among the fields and woods of England:—

Friar in Romeo and Juliet.

> " I must fill up this osier cage of ours,
> With baleful weeds, and precious-juiced flowers.
> The earth, that's nature's mother, is her tomb;
> What is her burying grave, that is her womb:
> And from her womb children of divers kind
> We sucking on her natural bosom find:
> Many for many virtues excellent,
> None but for some, and yet all different.
> O mickle is the powerful grace that lies
> In herbs, plants, stones, and their true qualities;
> For nought so vile that on the earth doth live,
> But to the earth some special good doth give;
> Nor aught so good, but strained from that fair use
> Revolts from true birth, stumbling on abuse:
> Virtue itself turns vice, being misapplied;
> And vice sometimes by action's dignified.
> Within the infant rind of this small flower
> Poison hath residence, and med'cine power;
> For this, being smelt, with that part cheers each part;
> Being tasted, slays all senses with the heart.
> Two such opposed foes encamp them still
> In man as well as herbs—grace and rude will;
> And where the worser is predominant,
> Full soon the canker death eats up that plant."

We have not made this extract chiefly to relieve a dull narrative with exquisite poetry. It explains more perfectly than any language we know, the processes which must have passed in a thinker who felt that he had need of external objects to sustain him against the pressure and tumult of thought; to whom these objects imparted ever fresh delight on their own account, and contained ever fresh parables concerning the regions which lie beyond the senses. Bacon, above all men, seems to have been surprised, perhaps overwhelmed, with the mysteries of nature. To dispose them under heads, as a learned Dominican would have done, could not satisfy him. There was a teeming inexhaustible life in nature and natural things, a productive power, which he must come directly into contact with; which he could not be content to learn at second-hand from Aristotle or from any one else. The Franciscan habit was favourable, as we have seen, to this kind of investigation. Bacon might persuade himself that he was only following the maxims of his order when he entered upon it. And he might have a still clearer conviction that he was obeying a call in his own soul which ought not to be resisted, and that the richest rewards of moral clearness and even perhaps of spiritual discoveries, might be looked for if he walked valiantly on in the path which had been marked out for him.

95. And valiantly indeed must a man in the 13th century have followed out his purpose, who contrived to spend £2,000 in his experiments. Such expenditure on collections may not have been without precedent, or at least without contemporary justification, in the monasteries. Albertus, with all his zeal for poverty, must have considered it legitimate. But the use of a sum of this kind might have created astonishment in any society; it may have furnished very plausible arguments to those who already regarded Bacon with hostility. What could it be for? Most astonishing processes of nature he spoke of—processes which laughed the doings of the ordinary conjuror to scorn. But he spoke not only of processes in nature. He declared and proved that, having a knowledge of these he could exercise the strangest power over nature. He seemed not to be able to measure the range of human power; he told of arts which might be tremendous to mankind if there were not the greatest care and self-restraint in the use of them. Who could tell that he had these? Was he not wandering into a new untried region, the reports of which, if they might be trusted, showed that it was full of perils to the first explorer and to those who should venture to follow in his footsteps; perhaps, to the vast majority which could not follow him at all. What if he said he hated magicians? Does not every one hate the rival whom he hopes to supersede? Might not this be a much more alarming kind of magic, than any which had yet

been practised; all the more dangerous because it assumed another name, and put on the air of a religious investigation? Shall the order sanction it? Has it not had enough of dangerous speculations already? Here might be another everlasting Gospel under the disguise of physical philosophy. Evidently Bacon was a doctor of Theology, acquainted with all its turnings and windings.

What new heresies might not be brought in from the laboratory! What a destruction of existing formulas and methods! Surely there is nothing singular in this course of thought; nothing which it is very hard for students in the reign of Victoria to conceive of; nothing which they can impute as an example of special ignorance to Oxford in the days of Henry III. And there were circumstances in the history of the Franciscans in England, just at the time which might make its members particularly anxious to avoid any new imputation; particularly jealous of those brethren who were spending money on science, though they might be departing from the maxims of the founder far less than some of the respectable.

96. Matthew Paris tells that, in the year 1249, two messengers arrived in England, armed with authority from Innocent IV., to extort what money they could from her dioceses for the use of our Lord the Pope. The King, the historian says, was deluded by their humble manner, the bulls with which they were armed, and their bland discourse, into granting them license to wander through his kingdom; under promise that they should ask gifts only for love, and should use no unlawful methods of persuasion. With this double power they proceeded to the most eminent prelates of the

land. At Lincoln they met with an unexpected rebuff. Grosseteste, the Bishop, was probably not astonished at the Papal demands. To these he was tolerably accustomed, for Innocent had been a greater plunderer of our island than all his predecessors. But the prelate was utterly confounded at the persons through whom the commands were transmitted; for they were Friars Minors, to whom he had been greatly attached and into whose order he had once desired to enter. The dress which these men had assumed was not what he had expected: they rode on horseback—their whole appearance was secular—their errand, and the amount of their claim utterly confounded him. He declared, in plain

terms, that the exaction was unheard of and dishonourable; he believed the money could not be raised. The whole kingdom, clergy and laity, were interested in the question. He could give no answer on his own responsibility. From that time the opinion of Grosseteste respecting the mendicant orders seems to have been changed. He had looked upon them as reformers; now they appeared to him agents of tyranny; money getters; wolves in sheep's clothing. His thoughts on the condition of the Church; on the crimes of its chief rulers; on the hopelessness of improvement from those who merely took a vow of poverty, appear to have deepened continually. It ended with his pronouncing Innocent to be Antichrist, and the members of the orders which connived at his covetousness implicit heretics. To numbers of the clergy, and some of the Prelates, this *monachorum corrector, Romanorum malleus et contemptor* may have recommended himself by the sanctity of his life, his genial honesty, and his thorough English sympathies. But his old Franciscan friends would surely be obliged to renounce him? One certainly did not—Roger Bacon, the seeker of truth in physics, could not desert the defender of truth in morals. He seems to have gone far with Grosseteste in his desires for clerical reformation; perhaps he may have mourned even more than his friend that Christ's mendicants should think it their chief duty to beg for the satisfaction of Papal rapacity and nepotism. How much more terrible will his magic then have appeared! What pretexts will there have been for charging him with any waste of money, when this suspicion mingled with the other! What need can there be to determine which was the chief count in the indictment? Strange sounds were heard in the laboratory; perhaps they might be explained without supposing that the friar had wicked designs against Brazennose or Oxford. Strange words have been repeated by a brother as spoken about simony, and Innocent IV., and our order, as if they might have something to do with each other. Perhaps it was only a text in the Bible, or a passage from St. Augustine that was uttered. Strange hints have been propagated about things that Nature may be doing in her recesses, and also about reforms that might take place in the Church. To be sure Aristotle spoke a little of one; St. Francis of the other. But then, what a weight of evidence lies in the accumulation of charges, each of which is nothing! Assuredly the superior did what most superiors would have done who had the same power, and only a distant responsibility to a Pope or Legate whose approbation in such a case might be fairly counted on. He forbade the reading of Bacon's writings, and apparently without the intervention of the Ecclesiastical Courts, in virtue of the dominion committed to him, cast the Friar himself into prison.

97. Such events were natural in that age; with some variations they might have happened in any. The next point we have to speak of was, it seems to us, far more remarkable. Guy Falcodi, a Cardinal Bishop, was sent as a Legate to England chiefly to settle, as far as the Church could settle, the disputes between Henry and his revolted Barons. We cannot pretend to admire his summary and yet very ineffectual methods of arranging our internal politics, either while he was the minister of Urban or when he became Clement IV. Still less can we applaud his policy

[marginal notes:] Bacon a friend of Grosseteste. — Constructive Heresy. — Punishment. — Clement IV.

respecting Italy, seeing that he adopted all the pontifical traditions
respecting the family of Frederick II., and invested Charles of
Anjou with the Kingdom of Sicily. It is all the more pleasant, as
we have these reasons for disliking him, to find how much of
worth and honour there was in him on points upon which Popes
are wont to be most deficient. A letter which he wrote to his
nephew when he was made Pope, ought to be written in golden
letters, not only in the Vatican, but in the palace of every Bishop

His freedom
from Nepot-
ism. throughout Europe. He tells him plainly that he does not wish to
see his relations much about the palace; that they are not to look
for places from him; that if his sister marries the son of some
simple gentleman, he will give her a fair dowry; if she aspires
higher because her uncle is the father of Christendom, she shall
have nothing. Such good and honest words, not being written to
be seen by the world, but in secrecy and confidence, prepare us

His support
of Bacon. for another and still nobler instance of Clement's righteousness. In
all Roger Bacon's experiments and in all his difficulties, he stood
his friend. He was evidently convinced that the Friar was a faithful
and religious man, who was doing his Master's work, if not just in
the way that the Order approved or that he understood, yet in a
way that was for the honour of God and for the good of man.
There has been much fine talking about the patronage of literature
and art by Popes who lived when literature and art were fashion-
able, and who simply glorified themselves and averted inquiries
into their scandalous promotions of nephews and sons by occasionally diverting a portion of the revenues which they had
obtained from the plunder of Europe upon sculptors and painters.
The simple and unostentatious friendship of Clement IV. for our
oppressed man of science, in an age when science was mistaken
for conjuring, will perhaps begin to be spoken of when the builder
of St. Peter's is only remembered as the hawker of indulgences.

Clement and
Leo. But Nicholas III. succeeded Clement IV. The Superior became
more ardent than ever, and his sentences were confirmed by the
head of the Church. The Franciscan was himself the next Pope.
Of course the philosopher remained in his prison. At the inter-
cession, it is said, of some English noblemen, he was set at liberty.

Bacon's
death. He returned to Oxford, and died in 1292 or 1294. His Order
had persecuted him but never quite disclaimed the honour of his

His English
fame. name; the people of England felt that he belonged to them. They
cherished traditions of the wonders which he wrought, they
believed that he had maintained the honour of his country against
the magicians of Germany. His fame lived on to the Reformation;
then it took a new spring. The dramatists of Queen Elizabeth's
time seem to have had an instinctive sense that, in seeking for the
secrets of nature he had been a witness for the freedom of man,
and that he had marked out a course into which it was the special

calling of English students to follow him. Our own conviction is, that the moral and metaphysical student is not under less obligations to him than the physical, and that he helped to teach theologians the worth of their own maxim, that the greatest rewards are for those who walk by faith not by sight. We should have liked to give our readers some specimens of his interesting little treatise against Magic; but perhaps we should be entering upon a region in which we should betray our weakness. We must leave him, therefore, and pass to one more notable Franciscan, Raymond Lully.

98. Raymond Lully has claims to be esteemed a martyr as well as Roger Bacon, a martyr of the more usual and recognized kind. Nevertheless Wadding the Biographer of his order admits him with great hesitation into the roll of his heroes. The Bollandists give him a day (the 30th of June) in the Acts of the Saints, but not without an elaborate apology. Proofs are accumulated of the reverence which was paid him from the time of his death in his own island of Majorca. A bull of Urban VIII. is produced which tacitly acknowledges that reverence as immemorial, while other illustrious children of the soil who could not plead the same prescription were deposed from their honour. This high patronage may perhaps protect Raymond not only from the imputation of being an Alchemist, which he seems to have incurred through a confusion of names, but from the dangerous admiration of Giordano Bruno, who, in later days believed himself to be a Lullist and whom Rome burnt as an Atheist. Be his reputation what it may, Raymond's life, so far as it can be extracted from the different records of it which are preserved to us (and the Jesuit editors give great help in this work), is full of an interest which does not usually belong to the biographies of schoolmen.

99. Raymond was born in 1235, at Palma, the capital of Majorca. The condition of the Balearic islands at the time of his birth must have had great effect upon his thoughts and character. They had been in the possession of the Saracens; in 1229, they were conquered by James I., king of Arragon. The father of Raymond was engaged in the battle with the Mahometans: a portion of the island was bestowed on him for his services; the boy grew up in the midst of wealth and luxury. He had some considerable office to which the name of Seneschal is given by his biographers, about the nature of which the Jesuit editor indulges in a learned disquisition. At all events it is clear that Raymond lived in the heart of an aristocratical, if not a courtly circle, and that he plunged more deeply into the vices of such a circle than most of his companions. His libertinism seems to have been very vehement and reckless; one biographer speaks of it as arrested by a frightful discovery made to him by a lady of whom he was insanely fond;

(margin notes:) Raymond Lully. — Acta Sanctorum, Dies 30 Junii III. p. 629. — Majorca. — His early years.

others tell of a vision of the cross which was five times presented to his eyes and to his mind. Both stories may in substance be true. A character like his would require some outward event to stop him in his career. Such an event would have been powerless **His Conversion.** if it had not been attended by a sense of the love which caused the Son of God to become a sacrifice. A profound impression followed that the convert had a call to become the converter of others. It was most natural in his age and country that he should think first of the Saracens.

His projects.   100. Raymond belonged to what may be called a literary period. But the habits of his youth had estranged him from literature; he had less than the ordinary knowledge of grammar. His first thought was to write a book against Mahometanism; his second was that he had the slenderest possible apparatus for such an undertaking and that his ignorance of Arabic put a hopeless barrier between him and the objects of his interest. Raymond wept and prayed. At last he became filled with the design of going to the Pope and all the princes of Christendom, that he might persuade them to found monasteries in which the Eastern languages should be studied and from which well trained missionaries should go forth. Strongly as he was possessed with these thoughts, he was still, says his biographer, far too much imbued with his secular tastes and habits, till he heard a sermon on the festival of St. Francis. That at once determined him to leave all that he had, to join the order, and to walk as nearly as he could in the steps of the founder. He visited various holy shrines to seek strength for his purpose, then he desired to go to Paris that he might commence **Studies Arabic.** his studies in earnest. He was persuaded, however, rather to re **The Slave.** turn to his own home, where he bought a Saracen slave and commenced the study of Arabic under his direction. A story is told of them which bears internal evidence of truth, and which appears to us very instructive. The slave once was heard to blaspheme the name of Christ. The crime was reported to his pupil. He struck the man on the face. The Saracen meditated vengeance, and seized an opportunity of stabbing Raymond. Though severely wounded, he was able to throw the infidel down and snatch the weapon; servants presently came to the rescue and bound him. Then Raymond's mind was greatly exercised. Should he let a man loose who was sure to complete his crime; should he punish a man who had taught him what he cared most to know? He retired to the hills for meditation and devotion, but gained no light; on his return, he found that the slave had strangled himself in prison; which discovery, we are told, gave him great relief and much occasion for thanksgiving!

The Vision.   101. But he had soon a greater cause for gratitude. He had ascended a hill not far from his house for quiet contemplation.

After he had stayed there a week, it came to pass on a certain day as he was looking up to Heaven, that his mind became illuminated respecting the form and nature of the book which he was to write against the Mahometans. This illumination had not reference to the argument or the style of a single treatise. It was *His Art.* the discovery to him of an universal art of acquisition, demonstration, confutation; an art which expanded more and more in his mind, till the defence and illustration of it became the end of his life, though never to the neglect or forgetfulness of the other earlier object. In one sense, the whole art was to be ministerial to the special work of convincing the Saracens; in another sense, it was to cover the whole field of knowledge; to supersede the inadequate methods of previous schoolmen. The vision and blessing of *How Ray-* a mysterious Shepherd on the mountains having strengthened the *mond taught* purpose of Raymond, he was able to meet the king of Majorca *in Majorca.* who had heard of his zeal and desired to see him; to endure an examination from a brother of the order of the Minors respecting his art; to publish his method of demonstration and to lecture upon the same—making it manifest, says his biographer (who we suspect, did not very well understand Lully or himself) "how the primary form and the primary matter constitute an elementary chaos, and how the five Universals and the ten Predicaments descend out of this chaos and are contained in the same, according to Catholic Theological truth." Raymond might afford the same excuse for a Poem on the "Loves of the Predicaments," which Darwin did for one "on the Loves of the Triangles;" but he never quite talked the nonsense which is imputed to him here.

102. With some difficulty Raymond succeeded in persuading *The King* the king of Majorca to found and endow a Society of fifteen *and the Pope* Franciscan Friars who were to be trained in Arabic and fitted for Saracen warfare. Why might he not hope that the Pope and the Cardinals should be willing to institute similar monasteries throughout the world? He went to Rome full of this expectation. Honorius IV. was dead; every one was occupied about his successor; that was not precisely the moment in which he could hope for suc- *Quæ quidem* cess. Unhappily the moment never came. Again and again the *supplicatio* biographer presents to us the indefatigable Lully beseeching the *Papæ quam-* Vatican for help; again and again we are told that certain *Cardinalibus* impediments in the Papal Palace obliged him to return without *modicum* accomplishing the least part of his purpose. He tried Rome; he *Lulli ab* tried Avignon; he besieged Celestine V.; he tormented Bonifacio *corvo Scrip-* VIII.; he hunted Clement V. to Lyons: the story is the same in *ta c. 3 Acta* every case. He profited nothing; Popes and Cardinals cared about *map. p. 681.* none of these things. Meantime he was working in other ways. He went to Paris, read in the University there his book upon the Ars Generalis, produced another book on the art for the discovery

B

of Truth, "having," says the narrator, "on account of the weakness of the human intellect which he had experienced in Paris, reduced his sixteen figures into twelve." We shall hear more of these figures presently; perhaps our experience of the weakness of the human intellect in London may tempt us to reduce them still farther. The use of them he determined to put to an immediate test by sailing from Genoa to Africa, that he might manifest to the Saracens, according to the art given him by God, the Incarnation of the Son of God and the Trinity of divine Persons in a blessed and perfect Unity. Great confidence seems to have been in the brother's own mind, great expectation among the Genoese. All his books and goods were on board. A sudden panic overtook him. He could not encounter the probable risk of death; he remained on the shore. His cowardice and the scandal he had brought on his cause filled him with horror, he was attacked with violent illness, heard of another galley which was going to Tunis, roused himself, and ill as he was, went on board. His friends seized him and carried him home; he escaped from their hands entered half dead into a third ship; and speedily recovered.

His revulsion of feeling.

103. When Raymond had arrived at Tunis, he gathered about him, we are told, the more learned Mahometans. He informed them that he understood all the doctrines which were held sacred among Christians and that he was very anxious to know what they had to say for their faith, to the end that he might embrace it if he found it better than his own. The Dervises accepted the challenge and defended vigorously their Monotheism. Raymond, adopting their premiss, maintained that every wise man should hold that faith which attributes to the eternal God in whom all wise men believe, the greatest goodness, power, glory, and perfection, and all these in the greatest equality and harmony. Then he went on to point out to them that they were in fact only acknowledging two active principles in God, Will and Wisdom; that Goodness and Greatness were, in their faith, indolent qualities, which might exist in the Divine Being but of which there was no exercise. That the ground of this defect was, that they did not acknowledge any internal intrinsic communication, such as that between the Father and the Son, which Christians believed; and that the idea of Divinity, that which expresses the fullness of the Divine perfection and shows how that perfection can be manifested and can be operative, is the idea of a Trinity of Persons, the Father the Son and the Holy Spirit in one most simple nature and essence. Proceeding from this ground, he went on to announce that a certain art had been revealed to him, a poor Christian hermit, whereby he could demonstrate to them these truths by the most evident reasons if they would confer with him about them for a few days with a quiet mind. "For it will appear to you," he

Raymond among the Saracens.

Subject and method of his discourse.

The Divine art.

said, "if it pleaseth you to listen, most rationally by this same art, that in the Incarnation of the Son of God, by the union of the Creator and the creature in the one person of Christ, the primary and highest cause is in most intimate and rational accordance with its effect. This harmony of cause and effect moreover shines forth in the Passion of Christ the same Son of God which He fitly sustained in the humanity He had assumed of His own voluntary and most pitiful condescension to redeem us sinners from sin and the corruption of our first parents and to bring us back to the state of glory and divine fruition which was the final object of the blessed God in the Creation of us men."

104. Without this discourse, which must, we conceive, have been on the whole faithfully reported by the anonymous biographer, it would be difficult for our readers to perceive the connection between the Art of Raymond of which we must speak presently, and the practical object of his life. The result which the biographer speaks of is at least internally probable; and is not so discreditable to the Saracens that we need suppose it to be invented. One of his auditors, it is said, perceiving the intention of Raymond, earnestly besought the king that he would give orders that the man who was endeavouring to subvert the nation of the Saracens and the law of Mahomet should lose his head. But another prudent and scientific counsellor represented that, though Raymond was a Christian advocate, he was, nevertheless, evidently a man of goodness as well as of sagacity; and that it would be a virtuous act in any Saracen to propagate his own lore among Christians, as this Christian was propagating his among the Mahometans. The king, it is said, was so far swayed by these arguments, that he changed the sentence of death, against Raymond, into one of banishment; with the addition that he should be stoned if he were found any longer in that country. There seems to have been a great conflict in the mind of the missionary whether he ought not to stay in spite of this edict, for the sake of those whose minds seemed inclining to embrace his doctrine. But ultimately, finding that he could do nothing for the service of Christ there, he availed himself of a ship which was bound for Naples. Thenceforth all his time was spent in fruitless missions to popes and kings respecting his college, in the incessant writing of books, and in journeys into the land of the infidels. Once he appears to have spent a considerable time in a Saracen prison, and to have resisted promises of wives, honour, a house and money, if he would embrace the Mahometan faith. Once he succeeded at Pisa in establishing a military order to accomplish, by material arms, what he was endeavouring to accomplish with spiritual. Finally (as two of his biographers tell us, Bovillus and Nicolaus de Pax), when he had become an old man,—old in body but still strong and growing

How the Mahometans behave.

His sentence.

every day stronger in mind,—he passed over once more from Majorca to Tunis for the purpose of preaching the Gospel. Where, when he had come, being straightway recognized by the inhabitants, a concourse of people cast him out of the city, stoned him, and buried him under the stones. The following night it pleased God, that certain merchants of Majorca, as they entered the port of Tunis, perceived afar off an immense pyramid of light, proceeding from the heap of stones under which the body was lying. Wondering at the novelty of the appearance, they turned in without delay, removed the stones, discovered the body, recognized their fellow-citizen, brought his remains to Majorca, and placed them in a ground on which many illustrious miracles were afterwards wrought. If we gave the whole list of his works, as it is given in one of the sketches of his life, our readers would think any enumeration of marvels at his tomb very superfluous. We shall only speak of two of them, one called the Ars Brevis, a compendium of the Ars Generalis, which is the foundation and key to all Arts,—the other a tract on the Principles of Philosophy, which was addressed to Philip the Fair against the Averroists.

His Martyrdom.

105. The Lullian Art may seem to those who look at it carelessly, a kind of *Memoria technica*, or a logical short-hand. They will find nine letters of the alphabet, each of which stands for certain principles, subjects of thought, forms of the understanding. They will meet with a number of figures, circles, and triangles, which may seem to them more or less useful, more or less clumsy, expedients for suggesting certain distinctions to the mind, or for preserving them in the recollection. But they will wonder how an earnest and devout man, such as Raymond certainly was, can have supposed that these were special communications from above during his watches on the Majorcan hill, or can have mingled them, almost identified them, with the great Catholic doctrines, of which he felt that it was his calling to bear witness in Tunis. That he overrated the grandness and value of the discovery, we make no doubt; that he was in the peril, in which we all are, of confounding methods which he had found serviceable with the ends which those methods were to attain, seems to us also unquestionable. Whatever stones any of us being consciously free from these sins may think fit to cast at him, may wound his fame, as much as the stones which the Africans cast at him wounded his body. But we are not inclined to call him either presumptuous or foolish for tracing any light which made the passages of his own mind clearer, to a divine source, and we cannot blame him for thinking that there is a link, however often we may fail in tracing it, between the deepest, most universal principles, and those forms which we discover either in our own minds or in the natural world. All philosophers in ancient times suspected that there must be such a connection; they thought that

The Art not a new Art of Memory.

The Art, and what the Art was to do.

The Forms of Thought, and the realities to which they correspond.

it was the very business of philosophy to find out what the connection was. If the brave Lully was one of those who stumbled in the search, we may at least honour the experiment more than we denounce the failure, and may perhaps believe that no experiment seriously conceived and faithfully followed up, does fail. It must leave seeds behind when it dies, which bear much fruit.

106. Lully wishes us to learn his alphabet by heart before we proceed with the rest of his grammar. It seems a reasonable request, and yet it is one which we find it hard to comply with. Why *B* should signify Goodness, Difference, Whether or no, God, Justice, Avarice—awakens questions which somewhat interfere with the process of learning by heart. Before we arrive at *K* we discover that there is a consistency in his scheme,—that each letter does the same kind of office as its predecessor,—and that there must be some reason for what strikes us at first as a mere wilful classification. But we do not feel that we know much of the reason till we have paid some attention to his figures, his rules, and his definitions; and have seen what part the alphabet plays in expounding the purpose of each of them.

107. The first figure is called the figure of Absolute Predicates. It is a circle, of which the centre is *A*. About it revolve nine principles, — Goodness, Magnitude, Duration, Power, Wisdom, Will, Virtue, Truth, Glory. These we are told are subjects, each of which may be converted into a predicate of the other; goodness is great, greatness is good, &c. The second figure is the figure of Predicates denoting Relation. It consists of three triangles. The first triangle has the three angles of Difference, Agreement, Contrariety. The second triangle has for its three angles, Beginning, Middle, and End. The third has for its three angles, the Greater, the Equal, the Less, or as Raymond says, Majority, Equality, Minority. When we descend farther into the properties of these figures, we find that there may be a difference, agreement, or contrariety between two objects of sense, as between a stone and a tree; between an object of the intellect and an object of sense, as between soul and body; between two objects of the intellect, as between God and an Angel. We find that beginning includes the efficient, formal, material, and final cause; that there is a mean between the subject and the predicate, as between man and animal; a mean of *mensuration* between the agent and that which is acted upon (thus love is the medium between the lover and that which is loved); and a medium of *extremities*, as a line between its two points. We find that there are three ends, the end of *privation*, the end of *termination*, the end of *perfection*. We find that Majority, Equality, and Minority may have place between substance and substance, between substance and accident, between accident and accident. This second figure, *T*, is subordinate to the first

Ars Brevis. Opera, Argent. 1617. pp. 1-42.

The Alphabet.

The Figures.

Absolute Predicates.

Predicates of Relation.

Combination
of the First
and Second
Figures.
figure, *A*. By the union of them science is acquired. The third
figure introduces us to their combination. It consists of thirty-six
chambers or compartments. The letters which have already been
defined distinctly are united, BC, BD, BE; then CB, CD, CE, and
so on; expressing in their combination a vast number of predi-
cations which are to serve as the next step in our logical education.
The fourth figure introduces us into a wider exercise of the
intellect. Three circles are revolving within each other: in tracing
The fourth
Figure.
their revolutions, we learn the interdependence of all those principles which have been previously brought out, upon each other;
our study has become more intricate, but also more harmonious
and more available for practice.

Definitions.
108. Then follow a set of definitions not very numerous, in reference to the nine principles of A. Among them stands conspicuous
the doctrine that Good is Being, Evil not Being, which most of
the schoolmen, whether Dominicans or Franciscans, assumed almost
as a starting point of philosophy. Next we have the ten possible
Questions.
questions, Whether a thing is? What it is? Whence it is? Why
it is? How great it is? Of what kind it is? When it is?
Where it is? How it is, and With what it is? After this we
discuss the mode of working out the third figure, and the mode of
multiplying or spreading into different applications the fourth.
Next we come to the nine subjects of which anything can be predicated; God, Angels, Heaven, Man, the imaginative principle, the
sensitive principle, the negative, the elementary, the instrumental.
Our former inquiries have given us so much aid in clearing up
the whole method of reasoning, that we can now proceed to the
investigation of each of these subjects, and may understand how they
are related to each other, and how the higher is implied in the
lower.

Subjects.
109. We cannot go at large into these subjects, but we may
glean a sentence here and there which will illustrate the mind, if
Man.
not the art, of Lully. *Man* is more general than any other
Heaven.
created being. He is the greater part of the world. *Heaven*, we
are told, is the first invisible substance. Its motion is its end and
rest. It has natural goodness, magnitude, and duration. The
The Imagi-
nation.
Imaginative faculty abstracts species from those things which
are perceived by the particular senses. It has the power of
magnifying (*e.g.*, of creating a golden mountain), and of mini-
fying (*e.g.*, of conceiving a point without parts or magnitude).
It has an instinct of its own, just as a kid has an instinct
to avoid a wolf. The principles of Vegetative life are more
condensed than the principles of Sensitive life; and the principles
of Sensation than those of Imagination. What Elementation is we
shall learn better from another Treatise. There is no part of the
Ars Brevis in which we feel so utterly at a loss as this. Why

these nine subjects should be considered satisfactory and exhaustive we are unable to pronounce. Occasionally we fancy we have a glimpse of their order and interdependence, but we lose it again. We dare not assume how far Heaven, according to Lully, was sensible or spiritual, or both or neither; we only presume, from its "natural goodness," that it must have something to do with personal being, or with moral objects; but we are not the least sure. We would willingly allow the author to be at a loss on this question, as so many have been, and to make it the business of his philosophy to search it out. But we are afraid the Universal Art will tolerate no such allowances. If all things can be demonstrated there is no breathing room for discussion. Questions which Lully's Method excites.

110. The 100 intellectual formulas which Lully devises for the purpose of connecting these subjects with the intellect, and the various questions which he propounds in reference to them, give us a great feeling of the vivacity of his mind, and of its power of sustaining itself against a weight of system by which most minds would have been crushed. In his conclusion he declares that his Art has three friends: to wit, Subtlety of Intellect, Reason, and Good Intention. Without these, no one, he affirms, can learn it. With respect to the first, we may be permitted to doubt whether Lully possessed it in anything like the same degree as some men of his time; certainly he could stand no comparison with Duns Scotus. With Reason, if by that is understood a pertinacious desire to find a reason for everything, or to make one, he was most liberally endowed. If it implies a capacity of looking into principles and ends, we should hesitate before we applied it to him;— he was too often entangled in the machinery of his art to be in a condition of competency for seeing clearly that which is independent of all art. But good intention he had a right to claim in a high, almost in a supreme, measure. And this great gift glorified his intellect; glorified even what would else have been mere technical refinement. He might have been a better philosopher if he had not always been seeking for middle terms with which to confound the Saracens. But, on the other hand, his eagerness to convert them made him feel that nothing was good, except as it contributed to the elucidation and discovery of fixed and eternal verities. It made him impatient of the thought that anything could ever be true for faith, which was not true for reason. At first we may be startled to hear a maxim on which the stamp of heresy is often affixed, connected with a man of even supercilious orthodoxy. But these contradictions are not rare in the Middle Ages, or in any ages. The opinion that what may be quite true under one name is quite false under another was intolerable to Raymond. He found it prevalent in the University of Paris. The Averroists, he complains, had gained Lully's three Friends. His good intention. Faith and Reason.

Paris.
The Aver-
rotists.
a complete ascendency over Catholic doctors. None thought it
was any harm to hold a doctrine which had been imported from
the Mahometan schools, provided he could pass it as an intellectual
opinion, and could keep his faith for other uses. There might,
we suppose, be much good practice and even sincere belief amongst
those who used this language. But a man who had been all his
life exercised in finding an intellectual weapon for propagating
the faith, was not likely to regard them with much toleration; and
it is without surprise that we hear him meditating the entire overthrow of such compromisers. He always designed to fight Mahometanism on Christian ground as well as in its native dominions;
here he had a field prepared for the purpose.

Duodecim
Principia
Philosophiae
quae et La-
mentatio et
expostulatio
Philosophiae
contra Aver-
roistas dici
possunt
Opera Ray-
mundi,
Argent.
1617, pp. 112-
147.
111. He was aroused to the combat by a very august personage.
He had strayed, it appears, out of the city of Paris with two companions, who perhaps were never much attached to that locality,
Contrition and Satisfaction. Raymond and these ladies were
mourning together over the degeneracy of the world, under a certain
tree in a very delicious meadow, when they found that they were not
alone in their grief. Listening to the songs of the birds, and apparently deriving some consolation from them, as well as from the
shadow of the tree and the sight of a beautiful fountain hard by,
stood Philosophy with twelve attendants. She was complaining
piteously of the Averroists who had spread cruel reports about her
which had divided her from Theology, whose handmaid she had
always believed herself to be. She does not speak merely for herself. She can appeal to her twelve principles, whether this is not
Her Com-
panions.
the light in which they always regarded her. Eleven of these, to
wit, Form, Matter, Generation, Corruption, Elementation, Vegetation, Sense, Imagination, Will, and Memory instantly express their
assent. *Intellect* remains silent. On being directly appealed to,
he declares that he is wholly perplexed and perverted. Paris
is his dear and proper home. There his light ought to shine
with especial brightness. But it is so dimmed with the errors
of philosophy, that all power—even the power of breathing,
has forsaken him. He and his mistress seem entirely agreed
about the only feasible remedy. Our readers may be at a loss
Philip the
Fair.
to guess it. Their help lies in the most Christian King, Philip
the Fair! To this king, Intellect would resort as his defender, for
all Parisians talk of the Intellect; to him Philosophy would go,
because she has heard of his great zeal, and faith, and charity. But
who shall carry her petition to the throne? other religious and
literary men have failed her; will Raymond undertake the cause?

The
speeches.
112. That our advocate may be furnished with his brief, the
twelve Principles come before him and deliver their testimony in
turn. The doctrine which all aim to express and illustrate is,
that there is one Goodness, Greatness, Eternity, Power, Wisdom,

Will, Virtue, Truth, Glory, Perfection, Justice, and Piety, presup- *Their general object.*
posed in all their functions and exercises; of which they cannot
be the authors and producers; to which they, and Philosophy,
their mistress, alike do homage; on which she bestows her golden
crown, though each of them may have a silver crown. Having
this general purpose, it behoves each of the twelve to show how
each is related to the other, and to her. We must, we fear,
commit various blunders of sex in speaking of these personages.
Raymond describes them generally as ladies, but when he comes
to Intellect, he is naturally puzzled. *Our* puzzle begins sooner.
Form should be feminine, and yet there is a very masculine tone *The discourse of Form.*
about the speech. In the course of it, she or he says: "I am the
likeness of God, Matter is the *unlikeness*. It follows that I am
more good, great, durable, intelligible, loveable, true, perfect and
glorious than Matter; therefore I can act more upon Matter, than
Matter can suffer from me. That *more* dwells in me potentially;
it cannot be brought into act by reason of the incapacity for it in
Matter." This language may sound disparaging. But when
Matter takes up the argument, she sufficiently justifies her own *Of Matter.*
dignity and position without claiming what has been denied her.
"I," she says, "am *passively* good, great; powerful, virtuous. I am
the potency of iron to become a sword; of Grammar, in one who
is not a Grammarian. . . . . . God can act by my nature
or above my nature, that his own great power, and infinite
virtue, and infinite liberty may be made known." *Generation* follows *Of Generation.*
at great length, and with much learning, claiming a high function in
vegetable natures, animal natures, and finally in moral virtues.
"Justice is a habit (saith Generation), implied in the just doing of
the just man, and it is brought by me, first into potency, secondly
into act." The like is affirmed of Prudence, Fortitude, Temperance,
Hope, Charity. *Corruption* announces herself boldly and eloquently *Of Corruption.*
as the contradictory of generation, and traces her influence in all
the subjects treated of by the previous speaker. *Elementation* de- *Of Elementation.*
clares herself to be a natural virtue proceeding from elementary forms
as well substantial as accidental. She is constituted of the four
substantial elements, Earth, Air, Fire, and Water, together with
the four qualities, Warmth, Cold, Moisture, Dryness. *Vegetation* *Of Vegetation.*
speaks of herself as that in virtue of which any plant grows and
brings forth. "I have," she says, "an instinct in me whereby
each particular rose in a rosary acquires its own special figure, leafage,
colour, odour. These come from me as much as the figure, leafage, and colour of painted roses proceed from the intellect of the
painter." *Sensation* then explains with much subtlety *her* function; *Of Sensation.*
how it cannot be understood alone in the things seen, heard, tasted,
or alone in the sense of hearing, seeing, tasting; how the organ of sense
implies a sense to use it; how a common sense is implied in each

particular sense; how all its senses imply that which is above themselves. *Imagination* shows how she is connected with Sense, how
she too is not subject to Sense, how she abstracts from Sense.
Motion declares himself to be that virtue by which latent heat
passes into actual warmth, by which smoke ascends, water descends,
&c. *Intellect* observes, in the course of his able apology, "It is my
condition to be busy in collecting species, in distinguishing, harmon-
izing, opposing. By accident, therefore, I may be strongly positive.
I may demand belief. There is a time when I am occupied with
opinions, and doubts, and am restless. My toil may issue in a
true or a false conclusion. If it is true, I am at peace; if it is
false, ignorance becomes a habit with me." *Intellect* observes
further, "In two methods I produce science; the first method is
by Sense and Imagination, from inferior things, as in the liberal,
mechanical, and moral arts; the other is altogether different—
through God, and through separate substances (substances unmixed
with accidents). Both inferior and superior science I create by
applying tests of possibility and impossibility. But these tests I
can use more loftily and securely in reference to the superior
than to the inferior. I know that God with His goodness and
greatness *must* do well and greatly. I know that He cannot do ill.
I confess that God is a higher object than I can take in. His
goodness and greatness are intelligible by themselves. Even intrinsic and extrinsic actions are more intelligible in that way than by
my exercises, seeing that He is a superior power, I an inferior.
But with the inferior science, which comes into existence through
the Sense and Imagination, it is not so. For seeing I am spiritual,
I am more disposed and prepared to understand the superior than
that the Sense and Imagination which partake of corporeity
should be sufficient for me." WILL speaks next. There is a fra-
ternal bond between Intellect and Will. They demand the same
object; neither can be satisfied without the other. Will produces
love, as Intellect produces science by the Sense and Imagination,
when dealing with lower things, participant of body: in another
method, when seeking fellowship with the Divine Will and Reason.
Will is subject to the same kind of peril as the Intellect. It may
embrace an evil object, and become evil; it may rest in a good object
and be satisfied. Moral goodness in man, is the choice of good by the
Will; moral evil is the choice of evil by the Will. Will declares
itself to be higher and more spiritual than Sense and Imagination;
to be at once optative and imperative, inasmuch as it bids the Intellect and Memory desire that which they desire. *Memory* says it
belongs to her by nature to recollect; by accident to forget. She is
in a direct relation to Intellect and Will; they work together;
their union is the evidence that the soul is immortal. She takes
the species that are given to her by the Intellect and Will. How

Side notes:
Of Imagina-
tion.
Of Motion.
Of Intellect.
Science of
that which is
above, and of
that which is
below the In-
tellect.
Of Will.
Of Memory.

essentially goodness is implied in her nature and being appears from this,—If the Intellect and Will bid her recall the name of a man, she is often at a loss; but if she can recover some good deed done by the man, something which takes hold of the heart, then the probability is very great that she shall be able to do their bidding, and to find the title which had been lost. The conclusion of Raymond's book is not one in which nothing is concluded. We are assured that he and philosophy, and her twelve Principles actually obtained an audience of the king; that the king, because he was humble, true, and devout, received what they spoke benignantly, and was evidently much moved. He left Raymond and the ladies confident that he would do some useful work. *Conclusion.*

113. Raymond may well terminate a sketch of Middle Age Philosophy which Boethius commenced. The same lady who visited the Roman statesman in his cell met the Spanish devotee as he was musing in his meadow. She came to the first as a guide and judge; to the other, as a mourner and a petitioner for help. She was cheering the one against the injuries of kings; the other she was conjuring to ask the aid of a king for her protection. The first she pointed to the letter on her vest, which told her of a higher Teacher to which she could lead him, and of which as yet he was ignorant. To the latter she complained that her ministries to that higher Teacher had been interrupted and that they had been changed into rivals. The comparison is curious, and suggests many thoughts of what has been passing in the busy interval between the 5th century and the 14th. Other portions of Raymond's work and life lead to the same reflection. The struggle of Christian and Saracen has been *the* struggle of the Middle Ages. From the hour when Mahomet returned from his exile, a monarch and a conqueror, to the hour in which Louis IX. breathed out his noble soul on the African coast, it had been a battle for life and death, with actual swords and spears. The best and holiest men, recluses who lived only for the unseen world, like Bernard of Clairvaux—righteous Kings who cared for the well-being of their subjects, and would not willingly spill their blood, like St. Louis,—yet felt that wars for the Sepulchre were the bonds of Christian faith and fellowship; the securities against the indifference which would cause all moral energies to rust. That day was past. The Divine sentence had gone forth against the bravest of all these enterprises, undertaken by the best and most single-minded of all the champions that had worn the Cross. The clergy and the people of the 13th century who, in a former age, would have cried with all their hearts, "God wills it," had begun, in audible murmurs, loud sometimes as well as deep, to declare that the religious wars had become a pretext to Popes for irreligious and dishonest extortion. And now came forth our Lully, *Boethius and Raymond.* *Relation of Philosophy to Theology.* *Christians and Mahometans.* *The new warfare*

to avouch that a divine art, taught him in the hills, and monasteries, for learning Arabic, and, what is more than both, a bold proclamation by a man of that which he believes and for which he is ready to die, will conquer the Saracens better than the hosts of the West. It is a great change—the sign that other changes have taken place—or are at hand.

The Pope and the King.

114. One of them which has been hinted at, we might be less prepared for. How comes Philip the Fair, the overthrower and enemy of Popes, to be the champion whom Raymond and Philosophy seek in their deep distress? Of old, religious men fled from those whom they called civil Tyrants, to the Spiritual Rulers. By the one they expected that all thoughts concerning the invisible would be scorned; the others were the natural protectors of intellectual force as opposed to material, especially when that intellectual force, as in Raymond's treatise, renders such willing and eager homage

Louis IX., and Philip the Fair.

to Faith. Philip certainly was no paragon of monarchs; in nearly every respect he was the very reverse of that predecessor, who was canonized, and deserved to be canonized. Philosophy was not happy in her choice of a patron. But experience had taught her votaries that, whatever was earnest and strong, might *possibly* find sympathy from those who were doing the work of the world, but could expect only rebuffs, indifference, or positive obstructions from the chair which some held to be the chair of St. Peter, and by some of Simon Magus. Raymond did not turn to Philip till he had tried the Popes.

The Divina Commedia.

Dante's treatment of Popes and their enemies.

Of the Mendicant Orders.

115. There was another far grander spirit than Raymond's which was passing at the same time through a very similar crisis. Dante Alighieri was changed from a Guelph into a Ghibelline. Dante Alighieri, the most earnest Theologian of his time, found the persecuted Manfred in Purgatory, and some Popes in one of the hopeless circles of the world below. Yet no one more thoroughly honoured the founders of the Mendicant Orders. The Dominican Aquinas in the Paradiso, celebrates the praises of St. Francis. He himself proved his claim to be the Angelic Doctor by untying, there as here, the most complicated knots of the intellect. But the poet who listened with delight to these solutions is the poet of Florence and of Italy; the transcendental Metaphysician never for an instant forgets the sorrows of the actual world in which

His patriotism and love.

he is living; the student sustains the patriot. Drenched in the school lore, it is still the vulgar eloquence—the speech of the people that is dear to him. Virgil is his Master, because Virgil was a Mantuan, and sang of Italy. And neither Theology, Politics, nor the study of ancient Song, crushes the life of the individual man. Fervent human love was the commencement to the poet of a new life. Through the little child of nine years old he rises to the contemplation of the Divine charity, which governs all things in heaven, and subdues earth to itself.

116. Wise men of our own day have said that Dante embodies Reasons for choosing his time to mak a an epoch. the spirit of the Mediæval time, and is a prophet of the time which followed. We testify our assent to that remark by accepting his poem, coeval as it is with the great judgment of the Papacy under Indications of it. Boniface, with the practical termination of the religious wars, and with the rise of a native literature, not only in the south but the north—as a better epoch from which to commence the new age of European thought, than the German Reformation of the 16th century. That we do not think less of that mighty event than those do who suppose that it winds up the scholastic period, we trust we shall be able to show hereafter. But its real importance for philosophy as well as humanity we think is The North and the South imperfectly appreciated, when it is looked upon as a new starting point in the history of either. There is a danger also lest our northern and Teutonic sympathies, which ought to be very strong, which cannot be too strong if they do not lead us to forget that God is the King of the whole earth, may make us unmindful of the grand place which Italy has occupied, and we trust is one day again to occupy, in the annals of mankind. We have no disposition to set Thomas of Aquino above Albert the Suabian, The natural and the universal or Roger Bacon of Ilchester; still less have we any disposition to exalt the 14th century above the 16th. But the Florentine poet may be taken as a hopeful augury that better things are in reserve for the 19th century than for either;—that in place of the false universalism which he felt inwardly to be an incubus upon his country and upon mankind—a true universal society— such as he longed for on earth, and had the vision of in heaven,— may yet include England, Germany, and Italy within its circle.

GLASGOW : PRINTED BY BELL AND BAIN.

16, BEDFORD STREET, COVENT GARDEN, LONDON
January, 1870.

*MACMILLAN & Co.'s GENERAL CATALOGUE
of Works in the Departments of History,
Biography, Travels, Poetry, and Belles
Lettres. With some short Account or
Critical Notice concerning each Book.*

SECTION I.

HISTORY, BIOGRAPHY, and TRAVELS.

Baker (Sir Samuel W.).—THE NILE TRIBUTARIES OF
ABYSSINIA, and the Sword Hunters of the Hamran Arabs.
By SIR SAMUEL W. BAKER, M.A., F.R.G.S. With Portraits,
Maps, and Illustrations. Third Edition, 8vo. 21*s.*

*Sir Samuel Baker here describes twelve months' exploration, during
which he examined the rivers that are tributary to the Nile from Abyssinia,
including the Atbara, Settite, Royan, Salaam, Angrab, Rahad, Dinder,
and the Blue Nile. The interest attached to these portions of Africa differs
entirely from that of the White Nile regions, as the whole of Upper Egypt
and Abyssinia is capable of development, and is inhabited by races having
some degree of civilisation; while Central Africa is peopled by a race o
savages, whose future is more problematical.*

THE ALBERT N'YANZA Great Basin of the Nile, and Exploration of the Nile Sources. New and cheaper Edition, with
Portraits, Maps, and Illustrations. Two vols. crown 8vo. 16*s.*

"*Bruce won the source of the Blue Nile; Speke and Grant won the
Victoria source of the great White Nile; and I have been permitted to
succeed in completing the Nile Sources by the discovery of the great
reservoir of the equatorial waters, the Albert N'yanza, from which the
river issues as the entire White Nile.*"—PREFACE.

NEW AND CHEAP EDITION OF THE ALBERT N'YANZA.
I vol. crown 8vo. With Maps and Illustrations. 7*s.* 6*d.*

A

Baker (Sir Samuel W.) *(continued)*—

CAST UP BY THE SEA; or, The Adventures of NED GREY.
By SIR SAMUEL W. BAKER, M.A., F.R.G.S. Second Edition.
Crown 8vo. cloth gilt, 7s. 6d.

" *A story of adventure by sea and land in the good old style. It appears
to us to be the best book of the kind since ' Masterman Ready,' and it runs
that established favourite very close.*"—PALL MALL GAZETTE.

" *No book written for boys has for a long time created so much interest,
or been so successful. Every parent ought to provide his boy with a copy.*"
DAILY TELEGRAPH.

Barker (Lady).—STATION LIFE IN NEW ZEALAND.
By LADY BARKER. Crown 8vo. 7s. 6d.

" *These letters are the exact account of a lady's experience of the brighter
and less practical side of colonisation. They record the expeditions, adventures, and emergencies diversifying the daily life of the wife of a New
Zealand sheep-farmer; and, as each was written while the novelty and
excitement of the scenes it describes were fresh upon her, they may succeed
in giving here in England an adequate impression of the delight and freedom of an existence so far removed from our own highly-wrought civilization.*"—PREFACE.

Baxter (R. Dudley, M.A.).—THE TAXATION OF THE
UNITED KINGDOM. By R. DUDLEY BAXTER, M.A. 8vo.
cloth, 4s. 6d.

*The First Part of this work, originally read before the Statistical
Society of London, deals with the Amount of Taxation; the Second Part,
which now constitutes the main portion of the work, is almost entirely new,
and embraces the important questions of Rating, of the relative Taxation
of Land, Personalty, and Industry, and of the direct effect of Taxes upon
Prices. The author trusts that the body of facts here collected may be of
permanent value as a record of the past progress and present condition of
the population of the United Kingdom, independently of the transitory
circumstances of its present Taxation.*

Baxter (R. Dudley, M.A.) *(continued)*—

NATIONAL INCOME. With Coloured Diagrams. 8vo. *3s. 6d.*

PART I.—*Classification of the Population, Upper, Middle, and Labour Classes.* II.—*Income of the United Kingdom.*

"*A painstaking and certainly most interesting inquiry.*"—PALL MALL GAZETTE.

Bernard.—FOUR LECTURES ON SUBJECTS CONNECTED WITH DIPLOMACY. By MOUNTAGUE BERNARD, M.A., Chichele Professor of International Law and Diplomacy, Oxford. 8vo. *9s.*

Four Lectures, dealing with (1) *The Congress of Westphalia;* (2) *Systems of Policy;* (3) *Diplomacy, Past and Present;* (4) *The Obligations of Treaties.*

Blake.—THE LIFE OF WILLIAM BLAKE, THE ARTIST. By ALEXANDER GILCHRIST. With numerous Illustrations from Blake's designs, and Fac-similes of his studies of the "Book of Job." Two vols. medium 8vo. *32s.*

These volumes contain a Life of Blake; Selections from his Writings, including Poems; Letters; Annotated Catalogue of Pictures and Drawings; List, with occasional notes, of Blake's Engravings and Writings. There are appended Engraved Designs by Blake: (1) *The Book of Job, twenty-one photo-lithographs from the originals;* (2) *Songs of Innocence and Experience, sixteen of the original Plates.*

Bright (John, M.P.).—SPEECHES ON QUESTIONS OF PUBLIC POLICY. By JOHN BRIGHT, M.P. Edited by Professor THOROLD ROGERS. Two Vols. 8vo. *25s.* Second Edition, with Portrait.

"*I have divided the Speeches contained in these volumes into groups. The materials for selection are so abundant, that I have been constrained to omit many a speech which is worthy of careful perusal. I have naturally given prominence to those subjects with which Mr. Bright has been especially identified, as, for example, India, America, Ireland, and Parliamentary Reform. But nearly every topic of great public interest on which Mr. Bright has spoken is represented in these volumes."*

EDITOR'S PREFACE.

AUTHOR'S POPULAR EDITION. Extra fcap. 8vo. cloth. Second Edition. 3*s.* 6*d.*

Bryce.—THE HOLY ROMAN EMPIRE. By JAMES BRYCE, B.C.L., Fellow of Oriel College, Oxford. [*Reprinting.*

CAMBRIDGE CHARACTERISTICS. *See* MULLINGER.

CHATTERTON : A Biographical Study. BY DANIEL WILSON, LL.D., Professor of History and English in University College, Toronto. Crown 8vo. 6*s.* 6*d.*

The Author here regards Chatterton as a Poet, not as a mere " resetter and defacer of stolen literary treasures." Reviewed in this light, he has found much in the old materials capable of being turned to new account ; and to these materials research in various directions has enabled him to make some additions.

Clay.—THE PRISON CHAPLAIN. A Memoir of the Rev. JOHN CLAY, B.D., late Chaplain of the Preston Gaol. With Selections from his Reports and Correspondence, and a Sketch of Prison Discipline in England. By his Son, the Rev. W. L. CLAY, M.A. 8vo. 15*s.*

" Few books have appeared of late years better entitled to an attentive perusal. . . . It presents a complete narrative of all that has been done and attempted by various philanthropists for the amelioration of the condition and the improvement of the morals of the criminal classes in the British dominions."—LONDON REVIEW.

Cooper.—ATHENÆ CANTABRIGIENSES. By CHARLES HENRY COOPER, F.S.A., and THOMPSON COOPER, F.S.A. Vol. I. 8vo., 1500—85, 18s. Vol. II., 1586—1609, 18s.

This elaborate work, which is dedicated by permission to Lord Macaulay, contains lives of the eminent men sent forth by Cambridge, after the fashion of Anthony à Wood, in his famous "Athenæ Oxonienses."

Dilke.—GREATER BRITAIN. A Record of Travel in English-speaking Countries during 1866-7. (America, Australia, India.) By Sir CHARLES WENTWORTH DILKE, M.P. Fourth and Cheap Edition. Crown 8vo. 6s.

" Mr. Dilke has written a book which is probably as well worth reading as any book of the same aims and character that ever was written. Its merits are that it is written in a lively and agreeable style, that it implies a great deal of physical pluck, that no page of it fails to show an acute and highly intelligent observer, that it stimulates the imagination as well as the judgment of the reader, and that it is on perhaps the most interesting subject that can attract an Englishman who cares about his country."
SATURDAY REVIEW.

Dürer (Albrecht).—HISTORY OF THE LIFE OF ALBRECHT DÜRER, of Nürnberg. With a Translation of his Letters and Journal, and some account of his works. By Mrs. CHARLES HEATON. Royal 8vo. bevelled boards, extra gilt. 31s. 6d.

This work contains about Thirty Illustrations, ten of which are productions by the Autotype (carbon) process, and are printed in permanent tints by Messrs. Cundall and Fleming, under license from the Autotype Company, Limited ; the rest are Photographs and Woodcuts.

EARLY EGYPTIAN HISTORY FOR THE YOUNG. See "JUVENILE SECTION."

Elliott.—LIFE OF HENRY VENN ELLIOTT, of Brighton. By JOSIAH BATEMAN, M.A., Author of "Life of Daniel Wilson, Bishop of Calcutta," &c. With Portrait, engraved by JEENS. Crown 8vo. 8s. 6d. Second Edition, with Appendix.

"*A very charming piece of religious biography; no one can read it without both pleasure and profit.*"—BRITISH QUARTERLY REVIEW.

Forbes.—LIFE OF PROFESSOR EDWARD FORBES, F.R.S. By GEORGE WILSON, M.D., F.R.S.E., and ARCHIBALD GEIKIE, F.R.S. 8vo. with Portrait, 14s.

"*From the first page to the last the book claims careful reading, as being a full but not overcrowded rehearsal of a most instructive life, and the true picture of a mind that was rare in strength and beauty.*"—EXAMINER.

Freeman.—HISTORY OF FEDERAL GOVERNMENT, from the Foundation of the Achaian League to the Disruption of the United States. By EDWARD A. FREEMAN, M.A. Vol. I. General Introduction. History of the Greek Federations. 8vo. 21s.

"*The task Mr. Freeman has undertaken is one of great magnitude and importance. It is also a task of an almost entirely novel character. No other work professing to give the history of a political principle occurs to us, except the slight contributions to the history of representative government that is contained in a course of M. Guizot's lectures .... The history of the development of a principle is at least as important as the history of a dynasty, or of a race.*' - SATURDAY REVIEW.

OLD ENGLISH HISTORY FOR CHILDREN. By EDWARD A. FREEMAN, M.A., late Fellow of Trinity College, Oxford. With *Five Coloured Maps.* Extra fcap. 8vo., half-bound. 6s.

"*Its object is to show that clear, accurate, and scientific views of history, or indeed of any subject, may be easily given to children from the very first... I have, I hope, shown that it is perfectly easy to teach children, from* *the very first, to distinguish true history alike from legend and from wilful invention, and also to understand the nature of historical authorities, and to weigh one statement against another. . . . . I have throughout striven to connect the history of England with the general history of civilised Europe, and I have especially tried to make the book serve as an incentive to a more accurate study of historical geography."—*PREFACE.

French (George Russell).—SHAKSPEAREANA GENEALOGICA. 8vo. cloth extra, 15s. Uniform with the "Cambridge Shakespeare."

Part I.—Identification of the dramatis personæ in the historical plays, from King John to King Henry VIII.; Notes on Characters in Macbeth and Hamlet; Persons and Places belonging to Warwickshire alluded to. Part II.—The Shakspeare and Arden families and their connexions, with Tables of descent. The present is the first attempt to give a detailed description, in consecutive order, of each of the dramatis personæ in Shakspeare's immortal chronicle-histories, and some of the characters have been, it is believed, herein identified for the first time. A clue is furnished which, followed up with ordinary diligence, may enable any one, with a taste for the pursuit, to trace a distinguished Shakspearean worthy to his lineal representative in the present day.

Galileo.—THE PRIVATE LIFE OF GALILEO. Compiled principally from his Correspondence and that of his eldest daughter, Sister Maria Celeste, Nun in the Franciscan Convent of S. Matthew in Arcetri. With Portrait. Crown 8vo. 7s. 6d.

It has been the endeavour of the compiler to place before the reader a plain, ungarbled statement of facts; and as a means to this end, to allow Galileo, his friends, and his judges to speak for themselves as far as possible.

Gladstone (Right. Hon. W. E., M.P.).—JUVENTUS MUNDI. The Gods and Men of the Heroic Age. Crown 8vo. cloth extra. With Map. 10s. 6d. Second Edition.

This new work of Mr. Gladstone deals especially with the historic element in Homer, expounding that element and furnishing by its aid a full account of the Homeric men and the Homeric religion. It starts, after the introductory chapter, with a discussion of the several races then existing in Hellas, including the influence of the Phœnicians and Egyptians. It contains chapters on the Olympian system, with its several deities; on the Ethics and the Polity of the Heroic age; on the geography of Homer; on the characters of the Poems; presenting, in fine, a view of primitive life and primitive society as found in the poems of Homer.

"GLOBE" ATLAS OF EUROPE. Uniform in size with Macmillan's Globe Series, containing 45 Coloured Maps, on a uniform scale and projection; with Plans of London and Paris, and a copious Index. Strongly bound in half-morocco, with flexible back, 9s.

This Atlas includes all the countries of Europe in a series of 48 Maps, drawn on the same scale, with an Alphabetical Index to the situation of more than ten thousand places, and the relation of the various maps and countries to each other is defined in a general Key-map. All the maps being on a uniform scale facilitates the comparison of extent and distance, and conveys a just impression of the relative magnitude of different countries. The size suffices to show the provincial divisions, the railways and main roads, the principal rivers and mountain ranges. "This atlas," writes the British Quarterly, "will be an invaluable boon for the school, the desk, or the traveller's portmanteau."

Guizot.—(Author of "JOHN HALIFAX, GENTLEMAN.")—M. DE BARANTE, A Memoir, Biographical and Autobiographical. By M. GUIZOT. Translated by the Author of "JOHN HALIFAX, GENTLEMAN." Crown 8vo. 6s. 6d.

" *The highest purposes of both history and biography are answered by a memoir so lifelike, so faithful, and so philosophical.*"
                                    BRITISH QUARTERLY REVIEW.

HISTORICAL SELECTIONS. Readings from the best Authorities on English and European History. Selected and arranged by E. M. SEWELL and C. M. YONGE. Crown 8vo. 6s.

When young children have acquired the outlines of history from abridgments and catechisms, and it becomes desirable to give a more enlarged view of the subject, in order to render it really useful and interesting, a difficulty often arises as to the choice of books. Two courses are open, either to take a general and consequently dry history of facts, such as Russell's Modern Europe, or to choose some work treating of a particular period or subject, such as the works of Macaulay and Froude. The former course usually renders history uninteresting; the latter is unsatisfactory, because it is not sufficiently comprehensive. To remedy this difficulty, selections, continuous and chronological, have in the present volume been taken from the larger works of Freeman, Milman, Palgrave, and others, which may serve as distinct landmarks of historical reading. "We know of scarcely anything," says the Guardian, *of this volume, "which is so likely to raise to a higher level the average standard of English education."*

Hole.—A GENEALOGICAL STEMMA OF THE KINGS OF ENGLAND AND FRANCE. By the Rev. C. HOLE, M.A., Trinity College, Cambridge. On Sheet, 1s.

The different families are printed in distinguishing colours, thus facilitating reference.

A BRIEF BIOGRAPHICAL DICTIONARY. Compiled and Arranged by the Rev. CHARLES HOLE, M.A. Second Edition. 18mo. neatly and strongly bound in cloth, 4s. 6d.

One of the most comprehensive and accurate Biographical Dictionaries in the world, containing more than 18,000 persons of all countries, with dates of birth and death, and what they were distinguished for. Extreme care has been bestowed on the verification of the dates ; and thus numerous errors, current in previous works, have been corrected. Its size adapts it for the desk, portmanteau, or pocket.

"An invaluable addition to our manuals of reference, and, from its moderate price, cannot fail to become as popular as it is useful."—TIMES.

Hozier.—THE SEVEN WEEKS' WAR ; Its Antecedents and
its Incidents. By. H. M. Hozier. With Maps and Plans. Two
vols. 8vo. 28s.

*This work is based upon letters reprinted by permission from "The
Times." For the most part it is a product of a personal eye-witness of some
of the most interesting incidents of a war which, for rapidity and decisive
results, may claim an almost unrivalled position in history.*

THE BRITISH EXPEDITION TO ABYSSINIA. Compiled from
Authentic Documents. By CAPTAIN HENRY M. HOZIER, late
Assistant Military Secretary to Lord Napier of Magdala. 8vo. 9s.

*" Several accounts of the British Expedition have been published. . . . .
They have, however, been written by those who have not had access to those
authentic documents, which cannot be collected directly after the termination
of a campaign. . . . . The endeavour of the author of this sketch has been to
present to readers a succinct and impartial account of an enterprise which
has rarely been equalled in the annals of war."* —PREFACE.

Irving.—THE ANNALS OF OUR TIME. A Diurnal of Events,
Social and Political, which have happened in or had relation to
the Kingdom of Great Britain, from the Accession of Queen
Victoria to the Opening of the present Parliament. By JOSEPH
IRVING. 8vo. half-bound. 18s.

*" We have before us a trusty and ready guide to the events of the past
thirty years, available equally for the statesman, the politician, the public
writer, and the general reader. If Mr. Irving's object has been to bring
before the reader all the most noteworthy occurrences which have happened
since the beginning of Her Majesty's reign, he may justly claim the credit
of having done so most briefly, succinctly, and simply, and in such a
manner, too, as to furnish him with the details necessary in each case to
comprehend the event of which he is in search in an intelligent manner.
Reflection will serve to show the great value of such a work as this to the
journalist and statesman, and indeed to every one who feels an interest in
the progress of the age ; and we may add that its value is considerably increased by the addition of that most important of all appendices, an
accurate and instructive index."* —TIMES.

Kingsley (Canon).—ON THE ANCIEN REGIME as it Existed on the Continent before the FRENCH REVOLUTION. Three Lectures delivered at the Royal Institution. By the Rev. C. KINGSLEY, M.A., formerly Professor of Modern History in the University of Cambridge. Crown 8vo. 6s.

These three lectures discuss severally (1) *Caste,* (2) *Centralization,* (3) *The Explosive Forces by which the Revolution was superinduced. The Preface deals at some length with certain political questions of the present day.*

THE ROMAN AND THE TEUTON. A Series of Lectures delivered before the University of Cambridge. By Rev. C. KINGSLEY, M.A. 8vo. 12s.

CONTENTS :—*Inaugural Lecture ; The Forest Children ; The Dying Empire ; The Human Deluge ; The Gothic Civilizer ; Dietrich's End ; The Nemesis of the Goths ; Paulus Diaconus ; The Clergy and the Heathen : The Monk a Civilizer ; The Lombard Laws ; The Popes and the Lombards ; The Strategy of Providence.*

Kingsley (Henry, F.R.G.S.).—TALES OF OLD TRAVEL. Re-narrated by HENRY KINGSLEY, F.R.G.S. With *Eight Illustrations* by HUARD. Crown 8vo. 6s.

CONTENTS :—*Marco Polo ; The Shipwreck of Pelsart ; The Wonderful Adventures of Andrew Battel ; The Wanderings of a Capuchin ; Peter Carder ; The Preservation of the "Terra Nova ;" Spitzbergen ; D'Ermenonville's Acclimatisation Adventure ; The Old Slave Trade ; Miles Philips ; The Sufferings of Robert Everard ; John Fox ; Alvaro Nunez ; The Foundation of an Empire.*

Latham.—BLACK AND WHITE : A Journal of a Three Months' Tour in the United States. By HENRY LATHAM, M.A., Barrister-at-Law. 8vo. 10s. 6d.

" *The spirit in which Mr. Latham has written about our brethren in America is commendable in high degree.*"—ATHENÆUM.

Law.—THE ALPS OF HANNIBAL. By WILLIAM JOHN LAW, M.A., formerly Student of Christ Church, Oxford. Two vols. 8vo. 21*s.*

"*No one can read the work and not acquire a conviction that, in addition to a thorough grasp of a particular topic, its writer has at command a large store of reading and thought upon many cognate points of ancient history and geography.*"—QUARTERLY REVIEW.

Liverpool.—THE LIFE AND ADMINISTRATION OF ROBERT BANKS, SECOND EARL OF LIVERPOOL, K.G. Compiled from Original Family Documents by CHARLES DUKE YONGE, Regius Professor of History and English Literature in Queen's College, Belfast; and Author of "The History of the British Navy," "The History of France under the Bourbons," etc. Three vols. 8vo. 42*s.*

Since the time of Lord Burleigh no one, except the second Pitt, ever enjoyed so long a tenure of power; with the same exception, no one ever held office at so critical a time. . . . Lord Liverpool is the very last minister who has been able fully to carry out his own political views; who has been so strong that in matters of general policy the Opposition could extort no concessions from him which were not sanctioned by his own deliberate judgment. The present work is founded almost entirely on the correspondence left behind him by Lord Liverpool, and now in the possession of Colonel and Lady Catherine Harcourt.

"*Full of information and instruction.*"—FORTNIGHTLY REVIEW.

Maclear.—*See Section,* "ECCLESIASTICAL HISTORY."

Macmillan (Rev. Hugh).—HOLIDAYS ON HIGH LANDS; or, Rambles and Incidents in search of Alpine Plants. By the Rev. HUGH MACMILLAN, Author of "Bible Teachings in Nature," etc. Crown 8vo. cloth. 6*s.*

"*Botanical knowledge is blended with a love of nature, a pious enthusiasm, and a rich felicity of diction not to be met with in any works of kindred character, if we except those of Hugh Miller.*"—DAILY TELEGRAPH.

Macmillan (Rev. Hugh), *(continued)*—

FOOT-NOTES FROM THE PAGE OF NATURE. With numerous Illustrations. Fcap. 8vo. 5*s.*

"*Those who have derived pleasure and profit from the study of flowers and ferns—subjects, it is pleasing to find, now everywhere popular—by descending lower into the arcana of the vegetable kingdom, will find a still more interesting and delightful field of research in the objects brought under review in the following pages.*"—PREFACE.

BIBLE TEACHINGS IN NATURE. Fourth Edition. Fcap 8vo. 6*s.* – *See also* "SCIENTIFIC SECTION."

Martin (Frederick).—THE STATESMAN'S YEAR-BOOK : A Statistical and Historical Account of the States of the Civilised World. Manual for Politician and Merchants for the year 1870. BY FREDERICK MARTIN. *Seventh Annual Publication.* Crown 8vo. 10*s.* 6*d.*

The new issue has been entirely re-written, revised, and corrected, on the basis of official reports received direct from the heads of the leading Governments of the World, in reply to letters sent to them by the Editor.

"*Everybody who knows this work is aware that it is a book that is indispensable to writers, financiers, politicians, statesmen, and all who are directly or indirectly interested in the political, social, industrial, commercial, and financial condition of their fellow-creatures at home and abroad. Mr. Martin deserves warm commendation for the care he takes in making ' The Statesman's Year Book' complete and correct.*"

STANDARD.

Martineau.—BIOGRAPHICAL SKETCHES, 1852—1868. By HARRIET MARTINEAU. Third Edition, with New Preface. Crown 8vo. 8*s.* 6*d.*

*A Collection of Memoirs under these several sections :—(1) Royal, (2) Politicians, (3) Professional, (4) Scientific, (5) Social, (6) Literary. These Memoirs appeared originally in the columns of the "*Daily News.*"*

Masson (Professor).—ESSAYS, BIOGRAPHICAL AND CRITICAL. *See Section headed* "POETRY AND BELLES LETTRES."

LIFE OF JOHN MILTON. Narrated In connexion with the Political, Ecclesiastical, and Literary History of his Time. By DAVID MASSON, M.A., LL.D., Professor of Rhetoric at Edinburgh. Vol. I. with Portraits. 8vo. 18s. Vol. II. in the Press.

It is intended to exhibit Milton's life in its connexions with all the more notable phenomena of the period of British history in which it was cast— its state politics, its ecclesiastical variations, its literature and speculative thought. Commencing in 1608, the Life of Milton proceeds through the last sixteen years of the reign of James I., includes the whole of the reign of Charles I. and the subsequent years of the Commonwealth and the Protectorate, and then, passing the Restoration, extends itself to 1674, or through fourteen years of the new state of things under Charles II. The first volume deals with the life of Milton as extending from 1608 to 1640, which was the period of his education and of his minor poems.

Morison.—THE LIFE AND TIMES OF SAINT BERNARD, Abbot of Clairvaux. By JAMES COTTER MORISON, M.A. New Edition, revised. Crown 8vo. 7s. 6d.

"*One of the best contributions in our literature towards a vivid, intelligent, and worthy knowledge of European interests and thoughts and feelings during the twelfth century. A delightful and instructive volume, and one of the best products of the modern historic spirit.*"

PALL MALL GAZETTE.

Morley (John).—EDMUND BURKE, a Historical Study. By JOHN MORLEY, B.A. Oxon. Crown 8vo. 7s. 6d.

"*The style is terse and incisive, and brilliant with epigram and point. It contains pithy aphoristic sentences which Burke himself would not have disowned. But these are not its best features: its sustained power of reasoning, its wide sweep of observation and reflection, its elevated ethical and social tone, stamp it as a work of high excellence, and as such we cordially recommend it to our readers.*"—SATURDAY REVIEW.

Mullinger.—CAMBRIDGE CHARACTERISTICS IN THE SEVENTEENTH CENTURY. By J. B. MULLINGER, B.A. Crown 8vo. 4s. 6d.

" *It is a very entertaining and readable book.*"—SATURDAY REVIEW.

" *The chapters on the Cartesian Philosophy and the Cambridge Platonists are admirable.*"—ATHENÆUM.

Palgrave.—HISTORY OF NORMANDY AND OF ENG-LAND. By Sir FRANCIS PALGRAVE, Deputy Keeper of Her Majesty's Public Records. Completing the History to the Death of William Rufus. Four vols. 8vo. £4 4s.

Volume I. General Relations of Mediæval Europe—The Carlovingian Empire—The Danish Expeditions in the Gauls—And the Establishment of Rollo. Volume II. The Three First Dukes of Normandy; Rollo, Guillaume Longue-Épée, and Richard Sans-Peur—The Carlovingian line supplanted by the Capets. Volume III. Richard Sans-Peur—Richard Le-Bon—Richard III.—Robert Le Diable—William the Conqueror. Volume IV. William Rufus—Accession of Henry Beauclerc.

Palgrave (W. G.).—A NARRATIVE OF A YEAR'S JOURNEY THROUGH CENTRAL AND EASTERN ARABIA, 1862-3. By WILLIAM GIFFORD PALGRAVE, late of the Eighth Regiment Bombay N.I. Fifth and cheaper Edition. With Maps, Plans, and Portrait of Author, engraved on steel by Jeens. Crown 8vo. 6s.

" *Considering the extent of our previous ignorance, the amount of his achievements, and the importance of his contributions to our knowledge, we cannot say less of him than was once said of a far greater discoverer. Mr. Palgrave has indeed given a new world to Europe.*"—PALL MALL GAZETTE.

Parkes (Henry).—AUSTRALIAN VIEWS OF ENGLAND.
By HENRY PARKES. Crown 8vo. cloth.   3s. 6d.

" The following letters were written during a residence in England, in the years 1861 and 1862, and were published in the Sydney Morning Herald *on the arrival of the monthly mails . . . . On re-perusal, these letters appear to contain views of English life and impressions of English notabilities which, as the views and impressions of an Englishman on his return to his native country after an absence of twenty years, may not be without interest to the English reader. The writer had opportunities of mixing with different classes of the British people, and of hearing opinions on passing events from opposite standpoints of observation."*—AUTHOR'S PREFACE.

Prichard.—THE ADMINISTRATION OF INDIA. From
1859 to 1868. The First Ten Years of Administration under the Crown.   By ILTUDUS THOMAS PRICHARD, Barrister-at-Law. Two vols. Demy 8vo. With Map. 21s.

In these volumes the author has aimed to supply a full, impartial, and independent account of British India between 1859 and 1868—which is in many respects the most important epoch in the history of that country which the present century has seen.

Ralegh.—THE LIFE OF SIR WALTER RALEGH, based
upon Contemporary Documents. By EDWARD EDWARDS. Together with Ralegh's Letters, now first collected. With Portrait. Two vols. 8vo.   32s.

" Mr. Edwards has certainly written the Life of Ralegh from fuller information than any previous biographer. He is intelligent, industrious, sympathetic : and the world has in his two volumes larger means afforded it of knowing Ralegh than it ever possessed before. The new letters and the newly-edited old letters are in themselves a boon."—PALL MALL GAZETTE.

Robinson (Crabb).—DIARY, REMINISCENCES, AND CORRESPONDENCE OF CRABB ROBINSON. Selected and Edited by Dr. SADLER. With Portrait. Second Edition. Three vols. 8vo. cloth. 36s.

Mr. Crabb Robinson's Diary extends over the greater part of three-quarters of a century. It contains personal reminiscences of some of the most distinguished characters of that period, including Goethe, Wieland, De Quincey, Wordsworth (with whom Mr. Crabb Robinson was on terms of great intimacy), Madame de Staël, Lafayette, Coleridge, Lamb, Milman, &c. &c.: and includes a vast variety of subjects, political, literary, ecclesiastical, and miscellaneous.

Rogers (James E. Thorold).—HISTORICAL GLEANINGS : A Series of Sketches. Montague, Walpole, Adam Smith, Cobbett. By Rev. J. E. T. ROGERS. Crown 8vo. 4s. 6d.

Professor Rogers's object in the following sketches is to present a set of historical facts, grouped round a principal figure. The essays are in the form of lectures.

Smith (Professor Goldwin).—THREE ENGLISH STATESMEN : PYM, CROMWELL, PITT. A Course of Lectures on the Political History of England. By GOLDWIN SMITH, M.A. Extra fcap. 8vo. New and Cheaper Edition. 5s.

"A work which neither historian nor politician can safely afford to neglect."—SATURDAY REVIEW.

Tacitus.—THE HISTORY OF TACITUS, translated into English. By A. J. CHURCH, M.A. and W. J. BRODRIBB, M.A. With a Map and Notes. 8vo. 10s. 6d.

The translators have endeavoured to adhere as closely to the original as was thought consistent with a proper observance of English idiom. At the same time it has been their aim to reproduce the precise expressions of the author. This work is characterised by the Spectator *as "a scholarly and faithful translation."*

B

THE AGRICOLA AND GERMANIA. Translated into English by
A. J. CHURCH, M.A. and W. J. BRODRIBB, M.A. With Maps
and Notes. Extra fcap. 8vo. 2s. 6d.

*The translators have sought to produce such a version as may satisfy
scholars who demand a faithful rendering of the original, and English
readers who are offended by the baldness and frigidity which commonly
disfigure translations. The treatises are accompanied by introductions,
notes, maps, and a chronological summary. The Athenæum says of
this work that it is " a version at once readable and exact, which may be
perused with pleasure by all, and consulted with advantage by the classical
student."*

Taylor (Rev. Isaac).—WORDS AND PLACES; or
Etymological Illustrations of History, Etymology, and Geography.
By the Rev. ISAAC TAYLOR. Second Edition. Crown 8vo.
12s. 6d.

*" Mr. Taylor has produced a really useful book, and one which stands
alone in our language."*—SATURDAY REVIEW.

Trench (Archbishop).—GUSTAVUS ADOLPHUS : Social
Aspects of the Thirty Years' War. By R. CHENEVIX TRENCH,
D.D., Archbishop of Dublin. Fcap. 8vo. 2s. 6d.

*" Clear and lucid in style, these lectures will be a treasure to many to
whom the subject is unfamiliar."*—DUBLIN EVENING MAIL.

Trench (Mrs. R.).—Edited by ARCHBISHOP TRENCH. Remains
of the late MRS. RICHARD TRENCH. Being Selections from
her Journals, Letters, and other Papers. New and Cheaper Issue,
with Portrait, 8vo. 6s.

*Contains notices and anecdotes illustrating the social life of the period
—extending over a quarter of a century (1799—1827). It includes also
poems and other miscellaneous pieces by Mrs. Trench.*

Trench (Capt. F., F.R.G.S.).—THE RUSSO-INDIAN QUESTION, Historically, Strategically, and Politically considered. By Capt. TRENCH, F.R.G.S. With a Sketch of Central Asiatic Politics and Map of Central Asia. Crown 8vo. 7s. 6d.

" *The Russo-Indian, or Central Asian question has for several obvious reasons been attracting much public attention in England, in Russia, and also on the Continent, within the last year or two. . . . I have thought that the present volume, giving a short sketch of the history of this question from its earliest origin, and condensing much of the most recent and interesting information on the subject, and on its collateral phases, might perhaps be acceptable to those who take an interest in it.*"—AUTHOR'S PREFACE.

Trevelyan (G.O., M.P.).—CAWNPORE. Illustrated with Plan. By G. O. TREVELYAN, M.P., Author of "The Competition Wallah." Second Edition. Crown 8vo. 6s.

" *In this book we are not spared one fact of the sad story ; but our feelings are not harrowed by the recital of imaginary outrages. It is good for us at home that we have one who tells his tale so well as does Mr. Trevelyan.*"—PALL MALL GAZETTE.

THE COMPETITION WALLAH. New Edition. Crown 8vo. 6s.

" *The earlier letters are especially interesting for their racy descriptions of European life in India. . . . . Those that follow are of more serious import, seeking to tell the truth about the Hindoo character and English influences, good and bad, upon it, as well as to suggest some better course of treatment than that hitherto adopted.*"—EXAMINER.

Vaughan (late Rev. Dr. Robert, of the British Quarterly).—MEMOIR OF ROBERT A. VAUGHAN. Author of "Hours with the Mystics." By ROBERT VAUGHAN, D.D. Second Edition, revised and enlarged. Extra fcap. 8vo. 5s.

" *It deserves a place on the same shelf with Stanley's ' Life of Arnold,' and Carlyle's ' Stirling.' Dr. Vaughan has performed his painful but not all unpleasing task with exquisite good taste and feeling.*"—NONCONFORMIST.

Wagner.—MEMOIR OF THE REV. GEORGE WAGNER, M.A., late Incumbent of St. Stephen's Church, Brighton. By the Rev. J. N. SIMPKINSON, M.A. Third and cheaper Edition, corrected and abridged. 5*s.*

"*A more edifying biography we have rarely met with.*"
　　　　　　　　　　　　　　　LITERARY CHURCHMAN.

Wallace.—THE MALAY ARCHIPELAGO : the Land of the Orang Utan and the Bird of Paradise. A Narrative of Travels with Studies of Man and Nature. By ALFRED RUSSEL WALLACE. With Maps and Illustrations. Second Edition. Two vols. crown 8vo. 24*s.*

"*A carefully and deliberately composed narrative. . . . We advise our readers to do as we have done, read his book through.*"—TIMES.

Ward (Professor).—THE HOUSE OF AUSTRIA IN THE THIRTY YEARS' WAR. Two Lectures, with Notes and Illustrations. By ADOLPHUS W. WARD, M.A., Professor of History in Owens College, Manchester. Extra fcap. 8vo. 2*s.* 6*d.*

"*Very compact and instructive.*"—FORTNIGHTLY REVIEW.

Warren.—AN ESSAY ON GREEK FEDERAL COINAGE. By the Hon. J. LEICESTER WARREN, M.A. 8vo. 2*s.* 6*d.*

"*The present essay is an attempt to illustrate Mr. Freeman's Federal Government by evidence deduced from the coinage of the times and countries therein treated of.*"—PREFACE.

Wilson.—A MEMOIR OF GEORGE WILSON, M.D., F.R.S.E., Regius Professor of Technology in the University of Edinburgh. By his SISTER. New Edition. Crown 8vo. 6*s.*
"*An exquisite and touching portrait of a rare and beautiful spirit.*"
　　　　　　　　　　　　　　　GUARDIAN.

Wilson (Daniel, LL.D.).—PREHISTORIC ANNALS
OF SCOTLAND. By DANIEL WILSON, LL.D., Professor of
History and English Literature in University College, Toronto.
New Edition, with numerous Illustrations.   Two vols. demy
8vo.   36*s.*

*This elaborate and learned work is divided into four Parts.   Part I.
deals with* The Primeval or Stone Period : *Aboriginal Traces, Sepulchral
Memorials, Dwellings, and Catacombs, Temples, Weapons, &c. &c.;
Part II.,* The Bronze Period : *The Metallurgic Transition, Primitive
Bronze, Personal Ornaments, Religion, Arts, and Domestic Habits, with
other topics ; Part III.,* The Iron Period : *The Introduction of Iron, The
Roman Invasion, Strongholds, &c. &c.; Part IV.,* The Christian Period:
*Historical Data, the Norrie's Law Relics, Primitive and Mediæval
Ecclesiology, Ecclesiastical and Miscellaneous Antiquities.   The work is
furnished with an elaborate Index.*

PREHISTORIC MAN.   New Edition, revised and partly re-written,
with numerous Illustrations.   One vol. 8vo.   21*s.*

*This work, which carries out the principle of the preceding one, but with
a wider scope, aims to " view Man, as far as possible, unaffected by those
modifying influences which accompany the development of nations and the
maturity of a true historic period, in order thereby to ascertain the sources
from whence such development and maturity proceed."   It contains, for
example, chapters on the Primeval Transition ; Speech ; Metals ; the
Mound-Builders ; Primitive Architecture; the American Type; the Red
Blood of the West, &c. &c.*

SECTION II.

POETRY AND BELLES LETTRES.

Allingham.—LAURENCE BLOOMFIELD IN IRELAND; or, the New Landlord. By WILLIAM ALLINGHAM. New and cheaper Issue, with a Preface. Fcap. 8vo. cloth, 4s. 6d.

In the new Preface, the state of Ireland, with special reference to the Church measure, is discussed.

" It is vital with the national character. . . . It has something of Pope's point and Goldsmith's simplicity, touched to a more modern issue."— ATHENÆUM.

Arnold (Matthew).—POEMS. By MATTHEW ARNOLD. Two vols. Extra fcap. 8vo. cloth. 12s. Also sold separately at 6s. each.

Volume I. contains Narrative and Elegiac Poems; Volume II. Dramatic and Lyric Poems. The two volumes comprehend the First and Second Series of the Poems, and the New Poems.

NEW POEMS. Extra fcap. 8vo. 6s. 6a.

In this volume will be found " Empedocles on Etna;" " Thyrsis " (written in commemoration of the late Professor Clough); " Epilogue to Lessing's Laocoön;" " Heine's Grave;" " Obermann once more." All these poems are also included in the Edition (two vols.) above-mentioned.

Arnold (Matthew), *(continued)*—

ESSAYS IN CRITICISM. New Edition, with Additions. Extra fcap. 8vo. 6s.

CONTENTS :—*Preface ; The Function of Criticism at the present time ; The Literary Influence of Academies ; Maurice de Guerin ; Eugenie de Guerin ; Heinrich Heine ; Pagan and Mediæval Religious Sentiment ; Joubert ; Spinoza and the Bible ; Marcus Aurelius.*

ASPROMONTE, AND OTHER POEMS. Fcap. 8vo. cloth extra. 4s. 6d.

CONTENTS :—*Poems for Italy ; Dramatic Lyrics ; Miscellaneous.*

Barnes (Rev. W.).—POEMS OF RURAL LIFE IN COMMON ENGLISH. By the REV. W. BARNES, Author of "Poems of Rural Life in the Dorset Dialect." Fcap. 8vo. 6s.

"*In a high degree pleasant and novel. The book is by no means one which the lovers of descriptive poetry can afford to lose.*"—ATHENÆUM.

Bell.—ROMANCES AND MINOR POEMS. By HENRY GLASSFORD BELL. Fcap. 8vo. 6s.

"*Full of life and genius.*"—COURT CIRCULAR.

Besant.—STUDIES IN EARLY FRENCH POETRY. By WALTER BESANT, M.A. Crown. 8vo. 8s. 6d.

A sort of impression rests on most minds that French literature begins with the "siècle de Louis Quatorze ;" any previous literature being for the most part unknown or ignored. Few know anything of the enormous literary activity that began in the thirteenth century, was carried on by Rutebeuf, Marie de France, Gaston de Foix, Thibault de Champagne, and Lorris ; was fostered by Charles of Orleans, by Margaret of Valois, by Francis the First ; that grew a crowd of versifiers to France, enriched, strengthened, developed, and fixed the French language, and prepared the way for Corneille and for Racine. The present work aims to afford nformation and direction touching the early efforts of France in poetical literature.

"*In one moderately sized volume he has contrived to introduce us to the very best, if not to all of the early French poets.*"—ATHENÆUM.

Bradshaw.—AN ATTEMPT TO ASCERTAIN THE STATE OF CHAUCER'S WORKS, AS THEY WERE LEFT AT HIS DEATH. With some Notes of their Subsequent History. By HENRY BRADSHAW, of King's College, and the University Library, Cambridge. [*In the Press.*

Brimley.—ESSAYS BY THE LATE GEORGE BRIMLEY. M.A. Edited by the Rev. W. G. CLARK, M.A. With Portrait. Cheaper Edition. Fcap. 8vo. 3*s.* 6*d.*

Essays on literary topics, such as Tennyson's "Poems," Carlyle's "Life of Stirling," "Bleak House," &c., reprinted from Fraser, the Spectator, and like periodicals.

Broome.—THE STRANGER OF SERIPHOS. A Dramatic Poem. By FREDERICK NAPIER BROOME. Fcap. 8vo. 5*s.*

Founded on the Greek legend of Danae and Perseus.

Clough (Arthur Hugh).—THE POEMS AND PROSE REMAINS OF ARTHUR HUGH CLOUGH. With a Selection from his Letters and a Memoir. Edited by his Wife. With Portrait. Two vols. crown 8vo. 21*s.* Or Poems separately, as below.

The late Professor Clough is well known as a graceful, tender poet, and as the scholarly translator of Plutarch. The letters possess high interest, not biographical only, but literary—discussing, as they do, the most important questions of the time, always in a genial spirit. The "Remains" include papers on "Retrenchment at Oxford;" on Professor F. W. Newman's book "The Soul;" on Wordsworth; on the Formation of Classical English; on some Modern Poems (Matthew Arnold and the late Alexander Smith), &c. &c.

Clough (Arthur Hugh), *(continued)*—

THE POEMS OF ARTHUR HUGH CLOUGH, sometime Fellow
of Oriel College, Oxford. With a Memoir by F. T. PALGRAVE.
Second Edition. Fcap. 8vo. 6*s.*

"*From the higher mind of cultivated, all-questioning, but still conservative England, in this our puzzled generation, we do not know of any
utterance in literature so characteristic as the poems of Arthur Hugh
Clough.*"—FRASER'S MAGAZINE.

Dante.—DANTE'S COMEDY, THE HELL. Translated by
W. M. ROSSETTI. Fcap. 8vo. cloth. 5*s.*

"*The aim of this translation of Dante may be summed up in one word
—Literality. . . . To follow Dante sentence for sentence, line for line,
word for word—neither more nor less—has been my strenuous endeavour.*"
—AUTHOR'S PREFACE.

De Vere.—THE INFANT BRIDAL, and other Poems. By
AUBREY DE VERE. Fcap. 8vo. 7*s. 6d.*

"*Mr. De Vere has taken his place among the poets of the day. Pure
and tender feeling, and that polished restraint of style which is called
classical, are the charms of the volume.*"—SPECTATOR.

Doyle (Sir F. H.).—Works by Sir FRANCIS HASTINGS DOYLE,
Professor of Poetry in the University of Oxford :—

THE RETURN OF THE GUARDS, AND OTHER POEMS.
Fcap. 8vo. 7*s.*

"*Good wine needs no bush, nor good verse a preface; and Sir Francis
Doyle's verses run bright and clear, and smack of a classic vintage. . . .
His chief characteristic, as it is his greatest charm, is the simple manliness
which gives force to all he writes. It is a characteristic in these days rare
enough.*"—EXAMINER.

Doyle (Sir F. H.), (*continued*)—

LECTURES ON POETRY, delivered before the University of Oxford in 1868. Extra crown 8vo. 3*s.* 6*d.*

THREE LECTURES :—(1) *Inaugural* ; (2) *Provincial Poetry* ; (3) *Dr. Newman's " Dream of Gerontius."*
" *Full of thoughtful discrimination and fine insight : the lecture on 'Provincial Poetry' seems to us singularly true, eloquent, and instructive."*
                                        SPECTATOR.

Evans.—BROTHER FABIAN'S MANUSCRIPT, AND OTHER POEMS. By SEBASTIAN EVANS. Fcap. 8vo. cloth. 6*s.*
" *In this volume we have full assurance that he has ' the vision and the faculty divine.' . . . Clever and full of kindly humour."*—GLOBE.

Furnivall.—LE MORTE D'ARTHUR. Edited from the *Harleian* M.S. 2252, in the British Museum. By F. J. FURNIVALL, M.A. With Essay by the late HERBERT COLERIDGE. Fcap. 8vo. 7*s.* 6*d.*

Looking to the interest shown by so many thousands in Mr. Tennyson's Arthurian poems, the editor and publishers have thought that the old version would possess considerable interest. It is a reprint of the celebrated Harleian copy ; and is accompanied by index and glossary.

Garnett.—IDYLLS AND EPIGRAMS. Chiefly from the Greek Anthology. By RICHARD GARNETT. Fcap. 8vo. 2*s.* 6*d.*
" *A charming little book. For English readers, Mr. Garnett's transla-lations will open a new world of thought."*—WESTMINSTER REVIEW.

GUESSES AT TRUTH. By TWO BROTHERS. With Vignette, Title, and Frontispiece. New Edition, with Memoir. Fcap. 8vo. 6*s.*
" *The following year was memorable for the commencement of the ' Guesses at Truth.' He and his Oxford brother, living as they did in constant and free interchange of thought on questions of philosophy and*

*literature and art; delighting, each of them, in the epigrammatic terseness which is the charm of the ' Pensées' of Pascal, and the ' Caractères' of La Bruyère—agreed to utter themselves in this form, and the book appeared, anonymously, in two volumes, in 1827."—*Memoir.*

Hamerton.—A PAINTER'S CAMP.   By Philip Gilbert Hamerton.   Second Edition, revised.   Extra fcap. 8vo.   6s.

Book I. *In England;* Book II. *In Scotland;* Book III. *In France. This is the story of an Artist's encampments and adventures. The headings of a few chapters may serve to convey a notion of the character of the book: A Walk on the Lancashire Moors; the Author his own Housekeeper and Cook; Tents and Boats for the Highlands; The Author encamps on an uninhabited Island; A Lake Voyage; A Gipsy Journey to Glen Coe; Concerning Moonlight and Old Castles; A little French City; A Farm in the Autunois, &c. &c.*

" *His pages sparkle with happy turns of expression, not a few well-told anecdotes, and many observations which are the fruit of attentive study and wise reflection on the complicated phenomena of human life, as well as of unconscious nature."*—Westminster Review.

ETCHING AND ETCHERS.   A Treatise Critical and Practical. By P. G. Hamerton.   With Original Plates by Rembrandt, Callot, Dujardin, Paul Potter, &c.   Royal 8vo.   Half morocco.   31s. 6d.

" *It is a work of which author, printer, and publisher may alike feel proud. It is a work, too, of which none but a genuine artist could by possibility have been the author."*—Saturday Review.

Helps.—REALMAH.   By Arthur Helps.   Cheap Edition. Crown 8vo.   6s.

Of this work, by the Author of " Friends in Council," the Saturday Review *says: " Underneath the form (that of dialogue) is so much shrewdness, fancy, and above all, so much wise kindliness, that we should think all the better of a man or woman who likes the book."*

Herschel.—THE ILIAD OF HOMER. Translated into English
Hexameters. By Sir JOHN HERSCHEL, Bart. 8vo. 18s.

*A version of the Iliad in English Hexameters. The question of Homeric
translation is fully discussed in the Preface.*

" *It is admirable, not only for many intrinsic merits, but as a great
man's tribute to Genius.*"—ILLUSTRATED LONDON NEWS.

HIATUS : the Void in Modern Education. Its Cause and Antidote.
By OUTIS. 8vo. 8s. 6d.

*The main object of this Essay is to point out how the emotional element
which underlies the Fine Arts is disregarded and undeveloped at this time
so far as (despite a pretence at filling it up) to constitute an Educational
Hiatus.*

HYMNI ECCLESIÆ. *See* "THEOLOGICAL SECTION."

Kennedy.—LEGENDARY FICTIONS OF THE IRISH
CELTS. Collected and Narrated by PATRICK KENNEDY. Crown
8vo. 7s. 6d.

"*A very admirable popular selection of the Irish fairy stories and legends,
in which those who are familiar with Mr. Croker's, and other selections
of the same kind, will find much that is fresh, and full of the peculiar
vivacity and humour, and sometimes even of the ideal beauty, of the true
Celtic Legend.*"—SPECTATOR.

Kingsley (Canon).—*See also* "HISTORIC SECTION," "WORKS
OF FICTION," *and* "PHILOSOPHY;" *also* "JUVENILE BOOKS,"
and "THEOLOGY."

THE SAINTS' TRAGEDY : or, The True Story of Elizabeth of
Hungary. By the Rev. CHARLES KINGSLEY. With a Preface by
the Rev. F. D. MAURICE. Third Edition. Fcap. 8vo. 5s.

ANDROMEDA, AND OTHER POEMS. Third Edition. Fcap.
8vo. 5s.

Kingsley (Canon), *(continued)*—

PHAETHON; or, Loose Thoughts for Loose Thinkers. Third Edition. Crown 8vo. 2s.

Kingsley (Henry).—*See* "WORKS OF FICTION."

Lowell.—UNDER THE WILLOWS, AND OTHER POEMS. By JAMES RUSSELL LOWELL. Fcap. 8vo. 6s.

"Under the Willows *is one of the most admirable bits of idyllic work, short as it is, or perhaps because it is short, that have been done in our generation.*"—SATURDAY REVIEW.

Masson (Professor).—ESSAYS, BIOGRAPHICAL AND CRITICAL. Chiefly on the British Poets. By DAVID MASSON, L.L.D., Professor of Rhetoric in the University of Edinburgh. 8vo. 12s. 6d.

"*Distinguished by a remarkable power of analysis, a clear statement of the actual facts on which speculation is based, and an appropriate beauty of Language. These essays should be popular with serious men.*"
                                                                ATHENÆUM.

BRITISH NOVELISTS AND THEIR STYLES. Being a Critical Sketch of the History of British Prose Fiction. Crown 8vo. 7s. 6d.

"*Valuable for its lucid analysis of fundamental principles, its breadth of view, and sustained animation of style.*"—SPECTATOR.

MRS. JERNINGHAM'S JOURNAL. Extra fcap. 8vo. 3s. 6d. A Poem of the boudoir or domestic class, purporting to be the journal of a newly-married lady.

"*One quality in the piece, sufficient of itself to claim a moment's attention, is that it is unique—original, indeed, is not too strong a word—in the manner of its conception and execution.*"—PALL MALL GAZETTE.

Mistral (F.).—MIRELLE: a Pastoral Epic of Provence. Translated by H. Crichton. Extra fcap. 8vo. 6s.

"*This is a capital translation of the elegant and richly-coloured pastoral epic poem of M. Mistral which, in 1859, he dedicated in enthusiastic terms to Lamartine. . . . . . It would be hard to overpraise the sweetness and pleasing freshness of this charming epic.*"—ATHENÆUM.

Myers (Ernest).—THE PURITANS. By ERNEST MYERS. Extra fcap. 8vo. cloth. 2s. 6d.

"*It is not too much to call it a really grand poem, stately and dignified, and showing not only a high poetic mind, but also great power over poetic expression.*"—LITERARY CHURCHMAN.

Myers (F. W. H.)—ST. PAUL. A Poem. By F. W. H. MYERS. Second Edition. Extra fcap. 8vo. 2s. 6d.

"*It breathes throughout the spirit of St. Paul, and with a singular stately melody of verse.*"—FORTNIGHTLY REVIEW.

Nettleship.— ESSAYS ON ROBERT BROWNING'S POETRY. By JOHN T. NETTLESHIP. Extra fcap. 8vo. 6s. 6d.

Noel.—BEATRICE, AND OTHER POEMS. By the Hon. RODEN NOEL. Fcap. 8vo. 6s.

"*Beatrice is in many respects a noble poem; it displays a splendour of landscape painting, a strong definite precision of highly-coloured description, which has not often been surpassed.*"—PALL MALL GAZETTE.

Norton.—THE LADY OF LA GARAYE. By the HON. MRS. NORTON. With Vignette and Frontispiece. Sixth Edition. Fcap. 8vo. 4s. 6d.

"*There is no lack of vigour, no faltering of power, plenty of passion, much bright description, much musical verse. . . . Full of thoughts well-expressed, and may be classed among her best works.*"—TIMES.

Orwell.—THE BISHOP'S WALK AND THE BISHOP'S TIMES. Poems on the days of Archbishop Leighton and the Scottish Covenant. By ORWELL. Fcap. 8vo. 5s.

"*Pure taste and faultless precision of language, the fruits of deep thought, insight into human nature, and lively sympathy.*"—NONCONFORMIST.

Palgrave (Francis T.).—ESSAYS ON ART. By FRANCIS TURNER PALGRAVE, M.A., late Fellow of Exeter College, Oxford. Extra fcap. 8vo. 6s.

Mulready—Dyce—Holman Hunt—Herbert—Poetry, Prose, and Sensationalism in Art—Sculpture in England—The Albert Cross, &c.

SHAKESPEARE'S SONNETS AND SONGS. Edited by F. T. PALGRAVE. Gem Edition. With Vignette Title by JEENS. 3s. 6d.

"*For minute elegance no volume could possibly exed the 'Gem Edition.'*"—SCOTSMAN.

Patmore.—Works by COVENTRY PATMORE :—

THE ANGEL IN THE HOUSE.

BOOK I. *The Betrothal*; BOOK II. *The Espousals*; BOOK III. *Faithful for Ever. With Tamerton Church Tower. Two vols. fcap. 8vo. 12s.

*** *A New and Cheap Edition in one vol. 18mo., beautifully printed on toned paper, price 2s. 6d.*

THE VICTORIES OF LOVE. Fcap. 8vo. 4s. 6d.

The intrinsic merit of his poem will secure it a permanent place in literature. . . . Mr. Patmore has fully earned a place in the catalogue of poets by the finished idealisation of domestic life."—SATURDAY REVIEW.

Rossetti.—Works by CHRISTINA ROSSETTI :—

GOBLIN MARKET, AND OTHER POEMS. With two Designs by D. G. ROSSETTI. Second Edition. Fcap. 8vo. 5s.

"She handles her little marvel with that rare poetic discrimination which neither exhausts it of its simple wonders by pushing symbolism too far, nor keeps those wonders in the merely fabulous and capricious stage. In fact she has produced a true children's poem, which is far more delightful to the mature than to children, though it would be delightful to all."—SPECTATOR.

THE PRINCE'S PROGRESS, AND OTHER POEMS. With two Designs by D. G. ROSSETTI. Fcap. 8vo. 6s.

" Miss Rossetti's poems are of the kind which recalls Shelley's definition of Poetry as the record of the best and happiest moments of the best and happiest minds. . . . They are like the piping of a bird on the spray in the sunshine, or the quaint singing with which a child amuses itself when it forgets that anybody is listening."—SATURDAY REVIEW.

Rossetti (W. M.).—DANTE'S HELL. *See* " DANTE."

FINE ART, chiefly Contemporary. By WILLIAM M. ROSSETTI. Crown 8vo. 10s. 6d.

This volume consists of Criticism on Contemporary Art, reprinted from Fraser, The Saturday Review, The Pall Mall Gazette, and other publications.

Roby.—STORY OF A HOUSEHOLD, AND OTHER POEMS. By MARY K. ROBY. Fcap. 8vo. 5s.

Shairp (Principal).—KILMAHOE, a Highland Pastoral, with other Poems. By JOHN CAMPBELL SHAIRP. Fcap. 8vo. 5s.

" Kilmahoe is a Highland Pastoral, redolent of the warm soft air of the Western Lochs and Moors, sketched out with remarkable grace and picturesqueness."—SATURDAY REVIEW.

Smith.—Works by ALEXANDER SMITH :—

A LIFE DRAMA, AND OTHER POEMS. Fcap. 8vo. 2s. 6d.

CITY POEMS. Fcap. 8vo. 5s.

EDWIN OF DEIRA. Second Edition. Fcap. 8vo. 5s.

"*A poem which is marked by the strength, sustained sweetness, and compact texture of real life.*"—NORTH BRITISH REVIEW.

Smith.—POEMS. By CATHERINE BARNARD SMITH. Fcap. 8vo. 5s.

"*Wealthy in feeling, meaning, finish, and grace ; not without passion, which is suppressed, but the keener for that.*"—ATHENÆUM.

Smith (Rev. Walter).—HYMNS OF CHRIST AND THE CHRISTIAN LIFE. By the Rev. WALTER C. SMITH, M.A. Fcap. 8vo. 6s.

"*These are among the sweetest sacred poems we have read for a long time. With no profuse imagery, expressing a range of feeling and expression by no means uncommon, they are true and elevated, and their pathos is profound and simple.*"—NONCONFORMIST.

Stratford de Redcliffe (Viscount).—SHADOWS OF THE PAST, in Verse. By VISCOUNT STRATFORD DE RED-CLIFFE. Crown 8vo. 10s. 6d.

"*The vigorous words of one who has acted vigorously. They combine the fervour of politician and poet.*"—GUARDIAN.

Trench.—Works by R. CHENEVIX TRENCH, D.D., Archbishop of Dublin. See also Sections "PHILOSOPHY," "THEOLOGY," &c.

POEMS. Collected and arranged anew. Fcap. 8vo. 7s. 6d.

ELEGIAC POEMS. Third Edition. Fcap. 8vo. 2s. 6d.

Trench (Archbishop), (*continued*)—

CALDERON'S LIFE'S A DREAM: The Great Theatre of the
World. With an Essay on his Life and Genius. Fcap. 8vo.
4s. 6d.

HOUSEHOLD BOOK OF ENGLISH POETRY. Selected and
arranged, with Notes, by R. C. TRENCH, D.D., Archbishop of
Dublin. Extra fcap. 8vo. 5s. 6d.

*This volume is called a "Household Book," by this name implying that
it is a book for all—that there is nothing in it to prevent it from being
confidently placed in the hands of every member of the household. Specimens of all classes of poetry are given, including selections from living
authors. The Editor has aimed to produce a book "which the emigrant,
finding room for little not absolutely necessary, might yet find room for
in his trunk, and the traveller in his knapsack, and that on some narrow
shelves where there are few books this might be one."*

*"The Archbishop has conferred in this delightful volume an important
gift on the whole English-speaking population of the world."*—PALL
MALL GAZETTE.

SACRED LATIN POETRY, Chiefly Lyrical. Selected and arranged
for Use. Second Edition, Corrected and Improved. Fcap. 8vo.
7s.

*"The aim of the present volume is to offer to members of our English
Church a collection of the best sacred Latin poetry, such as they shall be
able entirely and heartily to accept and approve—a collection, that is, in which
they shall not be evermore liable to be offended, and to have the current of
their sympathies checked, by coming upon that which, however beautiful as
poetry, out of higher respects they must reject and condemn—in which, too,
they shall not fear that snares are being laid for them, to entangle them
unawares in admiration for ought which is inconsistent with their faith
and fealty to their own spiritual mother."*—PREFACE.

Turner.—SONNETS. By the Rev. CHARLES TENNYSON TURNER. Dedicated to his brother, the Poet Laureate. Fcap. 8vo. 4*s.* 6*d.*

"*The Sonnets are dedicated to Mr. Tennyson by his brother, and have, independently of their merits, an interest of association. They both love to write in simple expressive Saxon; both love to touch their imagery in epithets rather than in formal similes; both have a delicate perception of rythmical movement, and thus Mr. Turner has occasional lines which, for phrase and music, might be ascribed to his brother. . . He knows the haunts of the wild rose, the shady nooks where light quivers through the leaves, the ruralities, in short, of the land of imagination.*"—ATHENÆUM.

SMALL TABLEAUX. Fcap. 8vo. 4*s.* 6*d.*

"*These brief poems have not only a peculiar kind of interest for the student of English poetry, but are intrinsically delightful, and will reward a careful and frequent perusal. Full of naïveté, piety, love, and knowledge of natural objects, and each expressing a single and generally a simple subject by means of minute and original pictorial touches, these sonnets have a place of their own.*"—PALL MALL GAZETTE.

Vittoria Colonna.—LIFE AND POEMS. By Mrs. HENRY ROSCOE. Crown 8vo. 9*s.*

The life of Vittoria Colonna, the celebrated Marchesa di Pescara, has received but cursory notice from any English writer, though in every history of Italy her name is mentioned with great honour among the poets of the sixteenth century. "In three hundred and fifty years," says her biographer Visconti, "there has been no other Italian lady who can be compared to her."

"*It is written with good taste, with quick and intelligent sympathy, occasionally with a real freshness and charm of style.*"—PALL MALL GAZETTE.

Webster.—Works by AUGUSTA WEBSTER :—

DRAMATIC STUDIES. Extra fcap. 8vo. 5*s.*

"*A volume as strongly marked by perfect taste as by poetic power.*"
NONCONFORMIST.

PROMETHEUS BOUND OF ÆSCHYLUS. Literally translated
into English Verse. Extra fcap. 8vo. 3*s.* 6*d.*

" *Clearness and simplicity combined with literary skill.*"—ATHENÆUM.

MEDEA OF EURIPIDES. Literally translated into English Verse.
Extra fcap. 8vo. 3*s.* 6*d.*

"*Mrs. Webster's translation surpasses our utmost expectations. It is a
photograph of the original without any of that harshness which so often
accompanies a photograph.*"—WESTMINSTER REVIEW.

A WOMAN SOLD, AND OTHER POEMS. Crown 8vo. 7*s.* 6*d.*

" *Mrs. Webster has shown us that she is able to draw admirably from
the life; that she can observe with subtlety, and render her observations
with delicacy; that she can impersonate complex conceptions, and venture
into which few living writers can follow her.*"—GUARDIAN.

Woolner.—MY BEAUTIFUL LADY. By THOMAS WOOLNER.
With a Vignette by ARTHUR HUGHES. *Third Edition.* Fcap.
8vo. 5*s.*

" *It is clearly the product of no idle hour, but a highly-conceived and
faithfully-executed task, self-imposed, and prompted by that inward yearn-
ing to utter great thoughts, and a wealth of passionate feeling which is
poetic genius. No man can read this poem without being struck by the
fitness and finish of the workmanship, so to speak, as well as by the chas-
tened and unpretending loftiness of thought which pervades the whole.*"
GLOBE.

WORDS FROM THE POETS. Selected by the Editor of " Rays of
Sunlight." With a Vignette and Frontispiece. 18mo. Extra
cloth gilt. 2*s.* 6*d. Cheaper Edition,* 18mo. limp., 1*s.*

GLOBE EDITIONS.

UNDER the title GLOBE EDITIONS, the Publishers are issuing a uniform Series of Standard English Authors, carefully edited, clearly and elegantly printed on toned paper, strongly bound, and at a small cost. The names of the Editors whom they have been fortunate enough to secure constitute an indisputable guarantee as to the character of the Series. The greatest care has been taken to ensure accuracy of text; adequate notes, elucidating historical, literary, and philological points, have been supplied; and, to the older Authors, glossaries are appended. The series is especially adapted to Students of our national Literature; while the small price places good editions of certain books, hitherto popularly inaccessible, within the reach of all.

Shakespeare.—THE COMPLETE WORKS OF WILLIAM SHAKESPEARE. Edited by W. G. CLARK and W. ALDIS WRIGHT. Ninety-first Thousand. Globe 8vo. 3s. 6d.

" A marvel of beauty, cheapness, and compactness. The whole works—plays, poems, and sonnets—are contained in one small volume: yet the page is perfectly clear and readable. . . . For the busy man, above all for the working Student, the Globe Edition is the best of all existing Shakespeare books."—ATHENÆUM.

Morte D'Arthur.—SIR THOMAS MALORY'S BOOK OF
KING ARTHUR AND OF HIS NOBLE KNIGHTS OF
THE ROUND TABLE. The Edition of CAXTON, revised for
Modern Use. With an Introduction by SIR EDWARD STRACHEY,
Bart. Globe 8vo. 3s. 6d. Third Edition.

"*It is with the most perfect confidence that we recommend this edition of
the old romance to every class of readers.*"—PALL MALL GAZETTE.

Scott.—THE POETICAL WORKS OF SIR WALTER
SCOTT. With Biographical Essay, by F. T. PALGRAVE.
Globe 8vo. 3s. 6d. New Edition.

"*As a popular edition it leaves nothing to be desired. The want of
such an one has long been felt, combining real excellence with cheapness.*"
SPECTATOR.

Burns.—THE POETICAL WORKS AND LETTERS OF
ROBERT BURNS. Edited, with Life, by ALEXANDER SMITH.
Globe 8vo. 3s. 6d. Second Edition.

"*The works of the bard have never been offered in such a complete form
in a single volume.*"—GLASGOW DAILY HERALD.
"*Admirable in all respects.*"—SPECTATOR.

Robinson Crusoe.—THE ADVENTURES OF ROBINSON
CRUSOE. By DEFOE. Edited, from the Original Edition, by
J. W. CLARK, M.A., Fellow of Trinity College, Cambridge.
With Introduction by HENRY KINGSLEY. Globe 8vo. 3s. 6d.

"*The Globe Edition of Robinson Crusoe is a book to have and to keep.
It is printed after the original editions, with the quaint old spelling, and
is published in admirable style as regards type, paper, and binding. A
well-written and genial biographical introduction, by Mr. Henry Kingsley,
is likewise an attractive feature of this edition.*"—MORNING STAR.

Goldsmith.—GOLDSMITH'S MISCELLANEOUS WORKS. With Biographical Essay by Professor MASSON. Globe 8vo. 3s. 6d.

This edition includes the whole of Goldsmith's Miscellaneous Works— the Vicar of Wakefield, Plays, Poems, &c. Of the memoir the SCOTSMAN *newspaper writes: " Such an admirable compendium of the facts of Goldsmith's life, and so careful and minute a delineation of the mixed traits of his peculiar character, as to be a very model of a literary biography."*

Pope.—THE POETICAL WORKS OF ALEXANDER POPE. Edited, with Memoir and Notes, by Professor WARD. Globe 8vo. 3s. 6d.

" The book is handsome and handy. . . . The notes are many, and the matter of them is rich in interest."—ATHENÆUM.

Spenser. — THE COMPLETE WORKS OF EDMUND SPENSER. Edited from the Original Editions and Manuscripts, by R. MORRIS, Member of the Council of the Philological Society. With a Memoir by J. W. HALES, M.A., late Fellow of Christ's College, Cambridge, Member of the Council of the Philological Society. Globe 8vo. 3s. 6d.

" A complete and clearly printed edition of the whole works of Spenser, carefully collated with the originals, with copious glossary, worthy—and higher praise it needs not—of the beautiful Globe Series. The work is edited with all the care so noble a poet deserves."—DAILY NEWS.

. Other Standard Works are in the Press.

. The Volumes of this Series may also be had in a variety of morocco and calf bindings at very moderate Prices.

GOLDEN TREASURY SERIES.

Uniformly printed in 18mo., with Vignette Titles by SIR NOEL PATON, T. WOOLNER, W. HOLMAN HUNT, J. E. MILLAIS, ARTHUR HUGHES, &c. Engraved on Steel by JEENS. Bound in extra cloth, 4s. 6d. each volume. Also kept in morocco.

" *Messrs. Macmillan have, in their Golden Treasury Series especially, provided editions of standard works, volumes of selected poetry, and original compositions, which entitle this series to be called classical. Nothing can be better than the literary execution, nothing more elegant than the material workmanship.*"—BRITISH QUARTERLY REVIEW.

THE GOLDEN TREASURY OF THE BEST SONGS AND LYRICAL POEMS IN THE ENGLISH LANGUAGE. Selected and arranged, with Notes, by FRANCIS TURNER PALGRAVE.

" *This delightful little volume, the Golden Treasury, which contains many of the best original lyrical pieces and songs in our language, grouped with rare and skill, so as to illustrate each other like the pictures in a well-arranged gallery.*"—QUARTERLY REVIEW.

THE CHILDREN'S GARLAND FROM THE BEST POETS. Selected and arranged by COVENTRY PATMORE.

" *It includes specimens of all the great masters in the art of poetry, selected with the matured judgment of a man concentrated on obtaining insight into the feelings and tastes of childhood, and desirous to awaken its finest impulses, to cultivate its keenest sensibilities.*"—MORNING POST.

THE BOOK OF PRAISE. From the Best English Hymn Writers. Selected and arranged by SIR ROUNDELL PALMER. *A New and Enlarged Edition.*

"*All previous compilations of this kind must undeniably for the present give place to the Book of Praise. . . . The selection has been made throughout with sound judgment and critical taste. The pains involved in this compilation must have been immense, embracing, as it does, every writer of note in this special province of English literature, and ranging over the most widely divergent tracts of religious thought.*"—SATURDAY REVIEW.

THE FAIRY BOOK ; the Best Popular Fairy Stories. Selected and rendered anew by the Author of "JOHN HALIFAX, GENTLEMAN:"

"*A delightful selection, in a delightful external form ; full of the physical splendour and vast opulence of proper fairy tales.*"—SPECTATOR.

THE BALLAD BOOK. A Selection of the Choicest British Ballads. Edited by WILLIAM ALLINGHAM.

"*His taste as a judge of old poetry will be found, by all acquainted with the various readings of old English ballads, true enough to justify his undertaking so critical a task.*"—SATURDAY REVIEW.

THE JEST BOOK. The Choicest Anecdotes and Sayings. Selected and arranged by MARK LEMON.

"*The fullest and best jest book that has yet appeared.*"—SATURDAY REVIEW.

BACON'S ESSAYS AND COLOURS OF GOOD AND EVIL. With Notes and Glossarial Index. By W. ALDIS WRIGHT, M.A.

"*The beautiful little edition of Bacon's Essays, now before us, does credit to the taste and scholarship of Mr. Aldis Wright. . . . It puts the reader in possession of all the essential literary facts and chronology necessary for reading the Essays in connexion with Bacon's life and times.*"—SPECTATOR.

"*By far the most complete as well as the most elegant edition we possess.*"—WESTMINSTER REVIEW.

D

THE PILGRIM'S PROGRESS from this World to that which is to
come. By JOHN BUNYAN.

   " *A beautiful and scholarly reprint.*"—SPECTATOR.

THE SUNDAY BOOK OF POETRY FOR THE YOUNG.
Selected and arranged by C. F. ALEXANDER.

   " *A beautiful and scholarly reprint.*"—SPECTATOR.

A BOOK OF GOLDEN DEEDS of all Times and all Countries.
Gathered and narrated anew. By the Author of " THE HEIR OF
REDCLYFFE."

   " . . . *To the young, for whom it is especially intended, as a most interesting
collection of thrilling tales well told ; and to their elders, as a useful hand-
book of reference, and a pleasant one to take up when their wish is to while
away a weary half-hour. We have seen no prettier gift-book for a long
time.*"—ATHENÆUM.

THE POETICAL WORKS OF ROBERT BURNS. Edited, with
Biographical Memoir, Notes, and Glossary, by ALEXANDER
SMITH. Two Vols.

   " *Beyond all question this is the most beautiful edition of Burns
'et out.*"—EDINBURGH DAILY REVIEW.

THE ADVENTURES OF ROBINSON CRUSOE. Edited from
the Original Edition by J. W. CLARK, M.A., Fellow of Trinity
College, Cambridge.

   " *Mutilated and modified editions of this English classic are so much
the rule, that a cheap and pretty copy of it, rigidly exact to the original,
will be a prize to many book-buyers.*"—EXAMINER.

THE REPUBLIC OF PLATO. TRANSLATED into ENGLISH, with
Notes by J. Ll. DAVIES; M.A. and D. J. VAUGHAN, M.A.

   " *A dainty and cheap little edition.*"—EXAMINER.

H,

THE SONG BOOK. Words and Tunes from the best Poets and
Musicians. Selected and arranged by JOHN HULLAH, Professor
of Vocal Music in King's College, London.

"*A choice collection of the sterling songs of England, Scotland, and
Ireland, with the music of each prefixed to the words. How much true
wholesome pleasure, such a book can diffuse, and will diffuse, we trust,
through many thousand families.*"—EXAMINER.

LA LYRE FRANCAISE. Selected and arranged, with Notes, by
GUSTAVE MASSON, French Master in Harrow School.

A selection of the best French songs and lyrical pieces.

TOM BROWN'S SCHOOL DAYS. By an OLD BOY.

"*A perfect gem of a book. The best and most healthy book about boys
for boys that ever was written.*"—ILLUSTRATED TIMES.

A BOOK OF WORTHIES. Gathered from the Old Histories and
written anew by the Author of "THE HEIR OF REDCLYFFE."
With Vignette.

"*An admirable edition to an admirable series.*"
                                        WESTMINSTER REVIEW.